The Letters We Couldn't Read

A Story of Love, Faith, and the Light that Stayed

Ricky Kiser

SUMMIT & SHORE PUBLISHING

Published by Summit & Shore Publishing Kingsport, Tennessee

ISBN 979-8-9933274-3-3 (eBook)

ISBN 979-8-9933274-4-0 (Paperback)

First Edition, 2026

Cover design by R. M. Kiser (art elements created with ArtSpace)

This is a work of fiction inspired by real events

Names, characters, places, and identifying details have been changed

or fictionalized for privacy. While the emotional truth of the story is

real, the narrative has been fictionalized. Any resemblance to actual

persons, living or deceased, or to actual events is used fictitiously and

with respect.

Printed in the United States of America

For Jennifer—
my wife, my always,
and the love that did not end.

Author's Note

This book is a work of fiction inspired by real events. While the story draws from lived experience, names, places, timelines, and identifying details have been changed or imagined for privacy.

The emotional truth at the heart of this story is real. The letters that appear throughout the book are part of the narrative itself—a way of holding memory, love, and grief in a form that can be returned to.

I am Ricky Kiser, and I wrote this story with care and respect for the lives that shaped it, and for the love that made it worth telling.

What we remember

still speaks.

Prologue

Snow fell so quietly you could hear it land. Each flake touched the earth with the sound of breath. Caleb Harper stood with his hands deep in his coat pockets, fingers curled around an unopened envelope that had already molded to his palm. The paper was soft at the edges from being handled too often. He kept telling himself waiting was mercy, that the heart knew its own timing. But the truth was simpler—he was afraid of what would start once he broke the seal.

The sky over Blountville Cemetery looked like gray cloth stretched across a lamp. Light still existed behind it; you just couldn't see it. The hill held a hush that winter knew how to keep. Stones along the ridge wore small white caps like sleep. From the church on the rise, one bell gave a slow note, then stopped—as if sound itself had paused to listen.

Beside him, Connor shifted and kicked at the glazed path. Steam rose from his breath. He'd grown taller this year—shoulders squaring, voice lower—but grief could still find the child in his face. When he looked at the headstone, the corners of his eyes folded the same way they had when he was five and trying not to cry in church.

They had been standing there long enough for the snow beneath their boots to melt and refreeze. Between them the granite gleamed, too new, too clean: *Lauren Grace Harper*. The snow clung to each carved letter as if trying to fill what was missing.

Caleb cleared his throat and found nothing inside it but air. He brushed the drift from her name.

"She'd fuss at us for standing out here," he said quietly.

"Yeah." Connor's voice came out in a puff of white. "She'd say you're gonna lose a finger."

A faint smile moved across Caleb's mouth. "Then she'd offer me her mittens, anyway."

"And kept none for herself," Connor said, half laughing, half breaking.

They let the silence fall back. Somewhere behind them, a crow hopped onto a branch, shaking down a lace of snow. A red ribbon left over from Christmas trembled on a shepherd's hook. The world had narrowed to the few feet between them and the two white envelopes that felt heavier than stone.

The one in Caleb's hand was addressed in her looping script—letters tilting upward like hope. *To my love, for the days that feel longest.* A small blot marked the tail of the y, a place where the pen had paused. He traced it through his glove, foolish and forgiven in the same motion.

Connor's envelope was tied with a navy ribbon, flat, not a bow, as if she trusted the reader to finish what she'd begun. He kept gripping the lower corner until the paper gave. Then he moved his hand to the middle, gentling it like a sleeping bird.

"You don't have to open it," Caleb said—not as a rule but as a release.

"I know." Connor stared at the stone. "I just—if I open it, I can't unread it."

Caleb nodded. "That's true."

"What if once I hear her words, the sound of her isn't in my head anymore? Like they get swapped out."

"She's not a song that disappears when you play another one," Caleb said. "You can keep both."

Connor didn't answer. He lifted his chin, facing the hill like someone watching the sea.

Wind came up and pressed against them, rattling the envelopes. Caleb turned his body to shield his son's letter. Memory struck without warning—the echo of a phone call in a tiled room, a boy's voice cracking through static: *Dad, Mom is dead. Please do not give me up.*

Then the scolding of a stranger's voice, the breathless *yes*, the click.

The bell on the hill tolled once more. He breathed through the scrape in his chest.

Snow gathered in the small gap where stone met soil, as if the world were making a soft place for grief to rest. Caleb crouched and set a bouquet of white roses at the base. The stems were wrapped in a damp paper towel, the grocery clerk's rubber band already brittle from the cold. He'd tried to find the kind she liked—simple, not showy. The rubber band snapped, and the stems slid apart; he rewrapped them clumsily with his gloves on.

"We brought what we could," he murmured. He didn't know whether he was speaking to her, to God, or to the air that still smelled faintly of iron and pine. "I know they're grocery store roses. You'd tell me that's fine."

Connor kneeled beside him and set down a smooth heart-shaped stone, rubbing it once before letting go. His breath fogged the letter and drifted away.

"Dad?" the boy asked, voice so soft the wind bent toward it. "Does it make me awful that I want to read it and don't want to read it at the same time?"

"It makes you human," Caleb said.

"I keep thinking she's going to tell me I'm wrong about something," Connor said. "Like I've been doing everything wrong since she left."

Caleb had thought that too—that the letter might contain a map proving every step since had been a degree off. "If she does," he said, "it'll be the kind of wrong you can forgive yourself for. She was good at that."

Wind pressed at them again and eased. The hush returned. A train far off let out a long exhale that rolled over the valley. Time slowed to the rhythm of that sound.

A thin brightness slipped behind the bell tower—no sun yet, but lighter than gray. Sometimes light made grief harder. Clouds kept pain in one color; light made you see.

"Do you ever smell her?" Connor asked suddenly.

Caleb blinked. "Smell her?"

"The way she always smelled like clean towels and cocoa powder," the boy said, embarrassed. "Sometimes I smell it, and there's nothing there."

"I smell it," Caleb said. He didn't mention the mornings he stood with his face in her robe on the back of the door because the house wouldn't start without it. "It comes and goes."

Connor nodded. "Do you think she knew we'd find the box?"

"Under the bed?" Caleb smiled faintly. "She knew. She hid birthday gifts there for twenty years."

He saw her bending at the waist, hair falling forward, sliding something into that narrow space, grinning at him over her shoulder like he'd already spoiled the surprise. The memory landed gently, like snow on a branch that doesn't break.

"She didn't tell us," Connor said. "About the letters."

"She didn't," Caleb said. Saying it aloud made the fact real and tender at once. "Sometimes love builds a room inside the house and locks it until the day you need what's there."

The boy frowned. "I don't know what that means."

"It means she trusted the timing," Caleb said.

Connor fell quiet. The envelopes stayed closed.

They stayed long enough for the first flurries to turn the gravel path white. A car came and went, its tires sighing over snow. A couple passed on the lower loop and kept a respectful distance, the woman's hand tucked into the man's elbow.

Caleb's gloves were too thin. The tips of his fingers had gone past stinging into dull. He flexed them and felt the envelope move with the motion, a living thing before it is read, a part of the body after.

"Do you remember the joke she used to tell about the sunrise?" he asked, trying to find a sound that wasn't sorrow.

Connor shook his head.

"When we sat on the porch too early, she would say, 'Well, boys, we made it to the edge of the night.'" "Keep your hands inside the ride."

A small laugh escaped Connor. "That was so dumb."

"So dumb," Caleb said. "And she said it every time."

"And she made cocoa."

"And forgot her own mug in the microwave," Caleb added. For a moment, all three of them were there again. Then they weren't.

The bell gave another low tone, soft as breath. It moved through Caleb's chest and settled behind his ribs like a steady hand. He didn't make a speech; words didn't belong on a hill like this. He only nodded once—the same small gesture he and Lauren had used in the hallway when words were unnecessary.

"Dad?" Connor said. "If I read it and it hurts worse, will you make me stop?"

"No," Caleb said. "But I'll sit with you until it changes shape. And if you don't read it, I'll sit with you then too."

Connor nodded. He slid his envelope into his jacket pocket and pressed his hand over it like that could keep the contents safe. "I can't do it here."

"Needing to wait isn't the same as not being brave," Caleb said.

"I hate that you're right."

"Me too," Caleb answered, and both let the smallest smile live and die on their mouths.

A wind scraped across the ridge and lifted a veil of snow from the stone. The letters of her name filled with white and then cleared again. The world didn't offer a sign; it offered weather, and sometimes weather was enough.

"I keep hearing it," Connor whispered. "What I said on the phone."

Caleb knew. "Me too."

"*Please do not give me up,*" the boy said aloud, the words carrying like a confession. He blinked hard. "I wish I could take that back."

"You were afraid," Caleb said.

"I made it about me."

"You were a son losing his mother," Caleb said quietly. "You were inside a storm and asking not to be thrown out of it." He swallowed. "I know that prayer."

Connor pressed his lips together. "Does God get mad when we say the wrong thing?"

Caleb thought of the verse still pinned on the refrigerator back home, the one that had outlasted a thousand grocery lists: *The Lord is nigh unto them that are of a broken heart.* "I don't think He counts seconds the way we do," he said.

"I wish He'd answer like a person," the boy said.

"Sometimes He does," Caleb said.

"Through her?"

He looked at the stone. A flake settled on the bevel of *Harper* and disappeared. "Through her," he said.

They stood there until the cold found their ears again. Connor brushed his eyes with his sleeve and took a long, full breath.

"Can we come back tomorrow?" he asked.

"We can come back as many times as the road will let us," Caleb said.

Connor laid his hand flat against the top of the stone, just above the name, and left it there. When he lifted it, a print of warmth showed for a second before the chill reclaimed it.

"Not yet," he said.

"Not yet," Connor echoed, relieved to have words that could hold them both.

They bent and brushed the roses once more, not for the flowers but for what the gesture meant: *We came. We stayed. We'll be back.* The stone said nothing and said enough.

The cold tightened the skin below Caleb's ear until he felt his pulse there. He closed his eyes and let the world be counted by that rhythm. When he opened them, the horizon had lifted a shade. It meant that the Earth was still turning. Sometimes that was miracle enough.

He touched the corner of the envelope to the carved date, then slipped it into his pocket. He didn't need an oath. He had an ordinary man's stubbornness and a love that hadn't learned past tense, and those were enough.

"Ready?" he asked.

"No," Connor said. "But I'll walk."

They stepped back from the stone in half-bows, the living do around the dead. Snow was falling in long threads now, the kind that fill a field before you realize there's a field to fill. Their footprints made dark mouths behind them; soon the next drift would close them like a blessing.

At the gate, they both turned. The roses were nearly hidden, the stone fading into white on white. The bell stayed silent but seemed to listen.

"Stay close," Caleb whispered, not sure whether he meant God, Lauren, or the part of himself that would try to outrun remembering. The wind gathered the words and folded them away, the way a careful hand puts letters back in a box and sets the lid without hurry.

They stood one breath longer—the kind you take when you step into cold water and it takes you back—then turned and walked. They did not open their letters, not on this hill, not on this day.

As they crossed the flattened snow near the fence, the day held; it did not break. Their boots rose and fell in a rhythm that felt like prayer.

"Dad?" Connor said at the gate. His breath made a small cloud that didn't leave.

"Yeah?"

"When we do read them," he asked, "and it hurts the worst it's ever hurt—what do I do with it?"

Caleb didn't reach for a tidy answer. He looked at the letters in their pockets, the stone with its new name, the sky that kept its gray. "You bring it where love can hear it," he said. "And let it echo until it's not only pain anymore."

Connor tested the words with a small nod. "Where love can hear it."

They pushed the gate. The hinge sighed. Snow squeaked beneath their feet, that winter-squeal that sounds like something alive. Connor lifted his face into the falling white until flakes melted on his lashes. When he looked back at the hill, his mouth shaped the kind of boy who has seen a storm and knows there's a boat.

They didn't say goodbye. Goodbye was the wrong tense. They didn't say *see you soon* either, because this wasn't a visit. It was a place where one kind of time stopped so another could begin.

"Not yet," Connor said once more, not to the letters but to leaving.

"Not yet," Caleb echoed.

They turned toward the hill—the white, the stone, the roses, the silent bell—and stood until the cold claimed their breath. Then they walked, their footprints already fading behind them. Within the hour the field would look untouched, but something invisible had shifted: the way a father and son carried unopened letters no longer felt like loss.

Caleb touched the edge of the envelope in his pocket and felt a warmth rise through his hand. He didn't speak her name. He didn't have to. His heart answered it anyway.

CHAPTER ONE

The Call That Changed Everything

The hum of GracePoint Theater carried through the old wooden seats — that faint mingling of dust, velvet, and stage paint. Caleb sat in the third row of the small auditorium, a folded program on his lap, waiting while the director—a man with a strong voice and kind eyes—handed out parts for the Easter production.

"You'll find your names highlighted," the director said, passing another sheaf of pages down the aisle. The air smelled faintly of cocoa and cold brick.

Caleb rubbed his hands together for warmth. January light slanted through the high windows, pale and thin. Beneath the floor, the old radiator ticked and breathed in uneven sighs.

He shifted in the seat, the wood giving a tired groan. From somewhere behind the curtain came the soft tap of someone adjusting lights, the distant rattle of a prop table. Sawdust and the starch of pressed costumes threaded the air.

Lauren had texted him that morning—*Remember to smile when you read the angel lines; you always get too serious.*

He'd laughed at the message, thumb hovering over a reply, but instead he'd called her on his way to the theater.

"How're you feeling?" he'd asked, easing the truck to a stop beneath the flickering streetlight.

"Still a little tired," she'd said, her voice soft but light. "I'll rest a bit while you're at practice."

"All right," he'd told her. "I love you."

"I love you too. Don't overdo it."

He smiled then, tucking the sound of her voice into memory without realizing that was what he was doing.

Now, sitting under that same flickering bulb, he almost typed it again: *You'd roll your eyes at this scene, LOL.* The thought stayed tucked behind his teeth, small and warm, like breath on glass.

His phone vibrated once in his coat pocket. He let it pass.

A minute later, it buzzed again.

He slipped his hand into his pocket, glanced down, and saw his father's name. Twice. Missed calls.

He frowned and, instead of calling back, slid the phone out enough to type a message to Lauren. *Hey, can you call Dad and tell him I'll get back to him after practice? We're just starting at the theater.*

He tucked the phone away again.

Onstage, the director paced through the blocking for the resurrection scene. "No pretending," he said. "We tell this story as if we've never heard it before. We let the silence do its work."

Caleb thought of how Lauren loved this place—how it held people without asking anything of them.

Caleb nodded absently, watching a shadow drift across the curtains. His heartbeat had picked up without reason. He exhaled slowly, the way he did before home visits, counting to four and back again.

The phone vibrated once more.

This time it was Connor.

Caleb answered quickly, slipping out of the row and walking up the side aisle toward the back doors. "Hey, bud."

"Dad?"

The voice was thin, frayed at the edges.

"Yeah, I'm here. What's going on?"

"Mom—she's passed out. I can't wake her up."

The sound of his own breath filled his ears. "Okay. Okay, just—just hold on. I'm coming home right now. Call 911."

He didn't remember hanging up. He stood for a second in the dim lobby, the director's voice still carrying from the stage like a far radio.

His legs shook. He headed down the hall to the restroom, moving like a man underwater.

Inside, fluorescent light turned the tile too bright. He splashed water on his face, tried to breathe, tried to think. The phone buzzed again.

Connor.

He answered with wet hands. "Connor, I'm—"

"Dad..." the boy's voice broke. "Mom's dead. Please don't give me up."

Caleb stopped breathing.

The echo of those words filled the tiled room like something with weight. *Mom's dead. Please don't give me up.*

Then another voice came on the line, older, firm but shaking. "Sir—this is one of the paramedics. I'm sorry, but your wife has passed. We're doing everything we can, but she's gone." A muffled aside, not unkind, drifted near the phone: "Hey, son—let your dad get here before you say it like that again, okay?"

He stared at the floor drain, water still ticking from the faucet. "Are you sure?" he heard himself say.

"Yes, sir," the paramedic said softly. "I'm sure."

Faint movement on the other end—directions given, the click of a medical bag, a door swinging. The line went silent.

A voice from the hall called his name—one of his castmates. He didn't answer.

He lowered the phone. The screen's light washed his face in a pale square. In the mirror he looked unfamiliar—gray around the mouth, eyes wide and far away.

He stepped into the lobby. His friend spotted him, concern gathering fast. "Caleb? You all right?"

He shook his head. "I have to go. Lauren is gone."

"Do you want me to drive you?" someone else asked.

He almost said yes. His voice came out flat. "No. I'll be okay."

He wasn't.

He pushed through the double doors into the cold. Wind knifed across the parking lot. His keys slipped twice before the truck unlocked. The world tilted, distances losing their edges.

He sank into the driver's seat. The leather creaked, releasing a faint trace of Lauren's vanilla hand cream from where she'd last ridden shotgun. The scent punched through his ribs. He gripped the wheel until his knuckles blanched and stared at the marquee through the windshield—*GracePoint Theater Presents: "Easter Morn"*—red bulbs swimming in the glass like distant fireflies.

A pale moth thudded softly against the overhead light, paper wings shivering above the dash. Alive! Stubbornly alive. His throat tightened.

Through the rearview mirror, the theater doors swung open. Cast members spilled into the cold, laughter bright behind glass. A woman waved—Mary Ellen, playing Magdalene. Her smile faltered when he didn't wave back.

He turned the key. The engine caught, vibrations traveling up through the seat. His phone lay face-up on the passenger side, screen dark. He pictured it ringing again, pictured Connor's voice fracturing further. *Please don't give me up.*

Wind pressed against the truck. A loose shutter clattered against brick, sharp as a hammer on tin. For a second, Caleb couldn't remember which way to turn the wheel to get home. Left? Right? The road ahead blurred, asphalt bleeding into early twilight.

A horn barked behind him. He jerked forward, tires crunching gravel as he pulled out too fast. The steering wheel trembled in his hands. At the stop sign, he rolled through, mind snagging on the paramedic's words—*she's gone*—each syllable a splinter.

Streetlights began to wake, one by one—the Piggly Wiggly, the shuttered feed store, the small park where Lauren used to push Connor on the swings. Familiar things under gauze. His jaw ached from clenching.

At the red light near Grace Hill Church, he glanced at the passenger seat. Lauren's knitting bag sat there, half-finished scarf in cobalt yarn pooling soft as water. He reached over, fingers brushing the loose edge where her needles had last pressed. Vanilla and wool filled the cab—her scent layered with unfinished purpose. The yarn caught against his calluses. He tucked the strand back into the bag and closed his fist, as if he could keep anything from unraveling.

Snow filled the air. He pressed the accelerator until wind threaded through the truck's seams loud enough to drown his first broken sob.

The truck's engine roared louder than he'd ever noticed, a metallic heartbeat trembling through the steering column. Caleb's knuckles ached where they gripped the wheel—white bone pressed against reddened skin. Each breath scraped his throat raw, winter air, and diesel fumes tangling in his lungs.

He kept waiting for the world to right itself. For the sun to break through the flat gray sky. For Connor's voice on the phone to reshape itself into something survivable. But the road kept unraveling, asphalt blurring into slush beneath tires that felt suddenly too thin, too fragile.

A small wooden cross swung from the rearview mirror—Lauren's, hung there after her last hospital stay. The pendant caught the pale light with each curve, throwing small flashes across the dash. His thumb found the smooth edge without meaning to. *Our Father, full of grace*, the rhythm of the road syncopated by potholes.

Halfway down Route 394, the smell hit him—vanilla air freshener undercut with bleach. Lauren's cleaning spray. She'd scrubbed the truck's floor mats yesterday, humming that Shania Twain song through the open window. He turned his face toward the passenger seat as if she might still be there, hair wind-tossed, eyes glinting with that mix of teasing and love.

Empty seat. Empty coat hook where her cardigan should've been.

The phone buzzed again in the cupholder. He didn't look. Couldn't. The vibration crawled up his forearm like a live wire.

Snow gathered in the ditches, dirty white clumps clinging to barbed-wire fences. Caleb's boot hovered over the brake as he passed the Andersons' hayfield—muscle memory from a hundred summer evenings when deer would dart across the road. Now only stillness. Only the faint fog of his own breath catching the glass.

Three miles out, his vision blurred. He blinked hard, lashes scraping dry air. The truck drifted left. A rumble strip growled beneath the tires, shaking the frame until his teeth rattled. When he righted the wheel, his hand had drifted to the cross again, thumb pressing hard enough to leave a groove.

Fields gave way to clustered pines. Their shadows stretched across the road like reaching hands. Caleb's collar stuck damp against his neck. He cracked the window just enough to let the wind slice his cheek.

Sirens wailed in the distance.

No. Not sirens. Wind through power lines. He'd heard that phantom wail before—every time the fear got too close.

The final hill rose before him, asphalt steepening where the road cut through rock. Caleb's foot pressed harder. The hood tilted skyward before leveling.

Red-and-blue lights strobed through bare maples. Two cruisers parked askew at the foot of the driveway, light bars painting the snow in shifting color. An ambulance idled behind them, rear doors yawning open.

Caleb's foot slipped off the gas. The truck rolled forward, momentum carrying him toward the flickering tableau. His tongue found the roof of his mouth, dry and thick. Somewhere beneath the engine's growl, a thin whine—his own breath locked in his throat.

The farmhouse emerged in pulses of color. Tires skidded on black ice—a half-second loss of control that threw his shoulder against the door. Gravel spat beneath the tires as he fishtailed into the drive. His father's silhouette appeared in the headlights, face carved by shadow into something ancient.

Cold air rushed in when Caleb shoved the door open, stinging his lungs. His boots hit frozen mud where Lauren's marigolds would bloom come April. The ambulance's rear doors caught the light, doubling the chaos.

Connor stood on the porch steps, jacket gaping open to show the Superman shirt he'd worn three days straight. The boy's chin trembled—not from January's bite, but from the kind of cold no coat could touch. Caleb's legs moved on instinct, each step compressing snow into the shape of absence.

Their collision knocked the air out of both. Connor's fingers dug between Caleb's shoulders like anchor points. He smelled of sweat and strawberry shampoo—Lauren's favorite. Caleb's throat closed around the truth: this embrace was already a memory.

Behind them, a stretcher hinge squeaked. Caleb pressed his palm to the back of Connor's head, feeling the pulse at his son's temple sync with the hammering in his own neck. Snow swirled around them, flakes suspended midair like sparks frozen in place.

Voices drifted from the kitchen. "...found her at sixteen-thirty... no response to stimuli..." The words blurred into sound beneath the creak of branches. Caleb focused on the cross pendant pressed between them—Lauren's birthday gift last year, its edges biting faintly through his flannel.

Connor's breath hitched. Caleb whispered into his hair, "I've got you," though he wasn't sure who he meant it for.

His father hovered near the steps. "Son—"

Caleb shook his head once. Sharp. The older man stepped back, his girlfriend tugging at his sleeve, both retreating toward the patrol cars.

The porch light burned steadily above them. Snow gathered in Connor's hood, tiny stars clinging to his lashes. Caleb brushed them away with his thumb, the gesture breaking him open. The ambulance engine hummed low, a background heartbeat.

A siren down the road rose and then died away. Wind moved through the trees, slow and hollow. Caleb tightened his hold until their breaths aligned—two uneven rhythms finding the same fragile measure.

He closed his eyes and tried to form words that could reach God through the ache in his chest, but there weren't any—only the ache itself.

They stayed like that until the last of the lights dimmed, until snow began again in small, weightless flakes that vanished against his coat.

Snow thickened in the air, soft as breath. Connor's hand stayed fisted in his coat sleeve, their joined shadow swaying across the porch boards. The ambulance engine cut off at last, leaving a ringing kind of silence—the kind that makes you think maybe Heaven's leaning close. Caleb's eyes burned from the cold, but he kept them open, memorizing the porch light haloing his boy's face.

The door behind them stood half-closed, the warm air fading, and he thought of Lauren's voice saying, *Keep the light on if I'm running late.* He would. Forever, if he had to.

The porch light flickered once, its glow soft against the snow. He stayed where he was, the cold wrapping around them both like an unfinished prayer.

CHAPTER TWO

The Letters and the Box

———— ♥ ————

The house smelled faintly of lavender detergent and something else—roses, maybe. He couldn't tell if it was memory or something the walls had kept for her, but the scent lingered near the curtains in the front room where she kept a short glass vase filled with artificial blooms because the real ones "just couldn't last long enough." She liked the pretend ones anyway, said it was mercy to the real flowers to let them keep the wind.

Connor hovered behind him, hands buried in his jacket pockets. His sneakers scuffed once before he whispered, "It still smells like her."

Caleb nodded. "Yeah." The word scraped.

He reached for the switch, but the bulb above the table was already on—a timer she'd set months ago. Every evening at six, it lit without asking. He couldn't bear to change it.

The house looked smaller, quieter. Every chair seemed to keep her shape. A cardigan hung on the peg, sleeve turned inside out like she'd planned to fix it later. By the recliner where she'd slept sitting up those last nights, a folded blanket waited, cocoa stain browned into the knit. On the side table: a stack of mail bound with a rubber band, a cheap pen with teeth marks, and her cocoa mug, rim faintly stained from the last night she used it.

"Can I feed the cats?" Connor asked, already edging toward the kitchen.

"Yeah. They'll be waiting."

From under the table came a soft trill—Maverick first, the black one she'd called her good-luck charm. Willow followed, her gray fur stirring like smoke, and Elvis padded close behind, yellow coat catching the light. The three of them circled Connor's legs in loose figure eights, tails high and hopeful.

"Hey, you guys," he said, voice softening. "I'm back."

He rummaged through the cabinet and came up with the last two cans. "Papaw said he'd bring more."

Caleb cleared his throat. "He's on his way." He could already hear the ghost of the truck, muffler rattling near the drive.

He set his keys in the bowl. The clink rang the way it always had. Little sounds were louder now, as if grief gave them permission. He stood and let the house breathe—the soft rattle of the vent, the tick of the clock, the faint country station pressed thin by static. Ordinary kept going. He felt both relieved and betrayed by that.

He picked up the folded blanket, put it down, straightened a frame without looking at the faces inside it. The top piece of mail was a sympathy card with lilies. Beneath it, a grocery flyer promising paper towels, chicken breasts, cocoa.

"Bowls are clean," Connor said, too bright, like he had to say something useful so he wouldn't say the other thing. Willow rubbed his shin while Elvis and Maverick hovered near the dish. "Yeah, yeah. Drama queen."

Caleb watched his hands open the can, the way he tipped the spoon so the gelatin ring slid into the dish. For years that sound had announced evening. He was grateful for it now—a thing that asked nothing but presence.

Frost gathered on the window in feathery lines, as if the cold had written in cursive. Outside, the rosebush she babied stood brittle but alive. In summer she clipped blossoms and floated them in bowls. He closed his eyes and tried to remember the tilt of her wrist when she snipped, the way she inhaled as if the scent could carry Scripture behind her ribs.

The driveway answered tires. Papaw's truck rattled like it always had.

He was Caleb's father, but somewhere along the years of raising Connor, "Papaw" had replaced every other name. It fit him, and it stuck—even for Caleb.

Caleb let out a breath he hadn't known he was holding.

Papaw knocked once and walked in, cap low, hands full—a grocery sack of cans and a gallon of milk hugged to his side, another bag smelling of fried chicken from the market.

"Didn't figure either of you wanted to cook," he said. "Smells the same."

Connor took the bags and grinned faintly. "You know me too well."

Papaw winked. "Your mama used to say that was your love language—chicken strips." He set the milk down. "Got the right cocoa too. The brand she liked."

"Janice helped me pick it out," he added, meaning his girlfriend, the way someone names help without needing to explain it.

Connor's smile faltered. Papaw touched his shoulder, then busied himself stacking cans label-out, corners square.

Caleb stood by the recliner, watching dust drift through the pale evening. "Thanks for picking that up."

"House feels heavy, doesn't it?" Papaw said. He didn't mean the kind you could weigh.

"Yeah." Caleb's voice came small. "Like it's waiting on something."

"Maybe it's waiting on nothing," Papaw said gently. "Sometimes nothing's the only honest thing we got." He nodded toward the cats. "You feed the cats, Con?"

"Already done." Connor scratched under Willow's chin until she tilted her head just so. She turned her head to show the best spot. He laughed, a real sound, then pressed his forehead to her fur.

They ate at the counter because the table felt too formal for grief. The chicken tasted like it always did—hot salt, pepper, crunch—and like something missing. Papaw talked about the weather changing, a truck for sale on Bloomingdale Pike, how the fella wanted too much for rust. He gave the air small stories so it wouldn't have to hold the big one.

Afterward he washed the plates though Caleb said he'd get them, then stood in the doorway with his coat over one shoulder. "I'll check on you boys in the morning," he said. "You call if the night gets loud."

Caleb almost asked him to stay. The word please sat on the back of his tongue like a coin. But Connor was watching, and something in his face said we can try this.

"Thank you," Caleb said instead.

Papaw tipped his cap to the room—the cats, the blanket, the timer light—and stepped into the cold.

Connor gathered empty boxes because it felt wrong to leave them. When the counters were clear, they lingered, waiting for instructions.

"I'm gonna check my charger," Connor said. "My phone's dead."

Caleb nodded and stayed while Connor disappeared down the hall. He heard drawers sliding, a muffled thud, the frustrated sigh teenage lungs specialized in. He didn't move. He listened to the sound of being a father in a house that had become a museum of the week before everything changed.

"Dad?" The voice came smaller. "Can you... come here?"

His feet felt heavy but faithful. They carried him to the bedroom he hadn't entered since before the funeral. The door stood half-closed. He eased it open. The air inside was still. A stripe of moonlight lay across the bedspread they'd bought when the one she wanted went on sale—soft blue, tiny stitched roses. Her robe hung from the chair, belt looped neat.

Connor kneeled where the bed skirt lifted, hand halfway under as if reaching into a creek. He tugged a small chest free. The wood glowed a deep red; corners softened by time or gentle hands. Brass latch, simple hook clasp. No lock.

"It was all the way back," Connor said, almost proud, almost ashamed. "I was looking for the charger and it... bumped my knuckles."

Caleb crouched beside him. His knees complained, an old familiar pain. He set his palm on the lid. Cedar rose—rich, sweet, sharp. The scent hit so suddenly his eyes watered. "Smells like when she lined the drawers," he said. "Remember? Said it kept out moths and made shirts behave."

"I used to think she was hiding candy," Connor said, smiling. "Like secret cinnamon."

Caleb almost laughed. They stared at the box, a patient thing between them. Under his thumb, the grain felt heart-like.

"Should we, um—" Connor didn't finish. Open hung there.

Caleb looked at his boy—the freckles that showed up this summer; the piece of Lauren in the way he waited and wanted at once. He looked at the bed—her pillow still hollowed, the nightstand with the book she'd left mid-sentence and the cocoa mug cooling beside it, like she might come back for both.

He lifted a hand, asking for mercy. "I will. Just... not tonight."

Connor's jaw tightened. He nodded. "Okay." He traced the edge of the lid, then drew his hand back like he'd touched something holy.

"There's... an envelope," he said, pointing where the clasp met the curve.

Caleb saw it—cream paper, Lauren's handwriting curling across the front: For Both of You — When You're Ready. The ink held the soft sheen of a pen coaxed to life. He touched the letters. It was the closest he'd felt to her hand in days.

Something in him cracked, small but deep. He took his hand away and flattened it on his thigh until the shaking tamed.

Beneath the stack, something heavier and unmarked rested against the cedar—there, then purposefully ignored.

They carried the box—together, without speaking—down the hall as if it were a sleeping child. The cats trailed because cats always do when rooms change. Connor set the chest on the coffee table with a care that would have made his mother proud. Caleb slid the envelope free and set it on top. He didn't turn it over. He let it be simple.

He glanced toward the window. The roses beyond were shadow and thorn and the memory of red. Yet under the fan's slow whisper and the furnace's sigh, the air carried that faint sweetness again. Roses, real as breath.

Neither of them reached for the clasp.

Later, after Connor showered and went to his room, and the cats folded themselves into warm punctuation at the end of the couch, Caleb stayed in the recliner with the blanket over his lap. The house hummed its nighttime rhythm—the clock's patient tick, the vent's soft rattle, the small expansion pops of old metal accepting heat. The envelope lay beside the box, its face tipped toward him like an invitation that refused to hurry.

He thought of how she must have written it—maybe in the evenings while he worked, or when Connor was asleep. Maybe in those quiet mornings when she sat by the window with her cocoa and talked to God as if He were right across from her. She would cup the mug in both hands and listen more than speak, and when she did, it was like she told Someone who already knew but liked to hear it anyway.

He pictured her choosing the paper. She would've fussed—held two envelopes to the light and asked which one looked kinder. He could almost hear her teasing herself: Roses again? Of course roses again. Don't roll your eyes, Caleb. He smiled without meaning to. The smile hurt and helped at once.

Cedar mingled with roses, faint but unmistakable, as if the wood had trapped every bouquet he ever brought her and let them loose now in the quiet. It filled the room enough that he almost spoke aloud. "Lauren?" The name had to climb over gravel to get out.

He rubbed his face, embarrassed even though no one could hear. "If you can hear me…" He stopped. He wasn't sure what came after that. If you can hear me, tell me how. Tell me when. Tell me how to be somebody's father when the one who taught me the soft parts is gone.

Moonlight pooled on the floor, silvering the edge of the box. The envelope's corner caught the glow. His chest ached—not sharp, just heavy—the way grief settles when it stops being new and starts being air.

Down the hall, Connor shifted in bed, a restless sound. Caleb listened, head tilted toward it, heart already halfway down the hall. He stayed. When the boy was younger, he used to stand outside his door at night and say the same simple thing: "Help me, Lord." No bargains. Just that.

He said it now, voice low enough not to trouble the cats. "Help me know when we're ready." The words felt like setting a small stone on an altar no one else could see.

He meant we. He could try to be brave alone; he couldn't be brave for both of them without learning a new way to breathe.

The vent sighed to a stop. The quiet that followed wasn't empty. It was the kind that makes you think maybe Heaven leans close to listen. Neither spoke. They sat with fingers wrapped around warm mugs, knees nearly touching, the cedar box between them like another living thing at the table. Words didn't have a job in that minute. Presence did.

Caleb set his cup down and reached—not for the clasp—but for Connor's wrist. He didn't grip. He just touched and left his hand there. Connor didn't move away. He pressed back, not much, just enough to say Here.

Time slowed to the size of breath. Somewhere a screen door sighed and settled. Wind brushed the eaves and went quiet. The timer light over the table burned matte and constant, as if it had been keeping vigil all along. On the side table, a sympathy card lay open to a verse neither read. Across the room, the blanket's cocoa stain marked its small, stubborn half-moon.

They stayed. Light gathered on the floorboards. The envelope waited without insistence. The box waited without threat. Maybe she knew that when she slid the paper under the latch and wrote the word ready. Maybe God did, letting dawn come the way it always had—slow, certain, never in a hurry.

He didn't open the box. He didn't have to. He only had to be here. He could do that. They could.

Outside, beyond the roses, a neighbor's wind chime answered a small breeze with a trembling song. Inside, the clock kept patient time. The cats sighed in their sleep. In the quiet, love kept happening—the kind that doesn't make headlines, the kind that stays.

CHAPTER THREE

When We First Met

The house was quiet enough to hear the heater cycle off. Outside, a thin fog lay across the yard, the kind that blurred edges until everything looked half-remembered. Connor sat at the kitchen table with the cedar box between them, the lid already open. The faint scent of cedar and paper rose into the still air.

Caleb reached inside, fingertips brushing the stack of envelopes lined neatly against the velvet. One, near the top, caught the morning light. Her handwriting curved across it, careful and steady—*When We First Met.*

Connor tilted his head, reading it aloud. "You think it's, like... the first one she wrote?"

"Maybe." Caleb's voice came soft, still rough from the cocoa he hadn't finished. He half-smiled. "Or maybe she just wanted to tell it again."

He passed the letter across the table. Connor hesitated before sliding a finger under the flap. The sound of paper giving way filled the room, small and fragile. Inside was the first page, folded twice, edges yellowed from time. He handed it back to his dad.

"You should read it," he said. "She wrote it for you."

Caleb nodded, though his throat tightened too much for words. He opened the letter slowly, the paper soft like fabric where her hand had pressed it smooth.

My love,

You once told me that we met because God was bored and needed entertainment. I told you He probably just got creative with timing. Either way, we found each other, and that's the only part that matters.

It started with that newspaper ad. I can still see it in the corner of the page, tucked between "Used Cars" and "Yard Sales." My friends dared me to write it. I was twenty-one, bored, and thought it would make them laugh. "Looking for someone who can make conversation, not just noise," I wrote. I didn't expect an answer. Then yours came—three sentences, all nerves, and sincerity. You said you worked in the office at the plant—what everybody in Kingsport just called "the plant"—and that you liked driving the back roads just to think, and that you'd never done anything like this before.

I think I knew, even then, that you meant every word.

Caleb smiled faintly. He could still picture the classified ad—black ink, his own words squeezed between furniture listings. He'd almost torn it out three times before sending it. Lauren used to joke that God must have grabbed the envelope midair and made sure it landed on her desk.

He read on.

You asked for a letter instead of a phone call first. You said you liked seeing a person's heart before you heard their voice. I thought that was the sweetest thing I'd ever read. I wrote back the same night, and by the end of that week, we had a rhythm—your letter on Monday, mine on Thursday. I kept them all, you know. Every single one. Mom and I would sit on the couch and read them, and she'd giggle like a teenager while I tried not to hide my smile. You were so shy on paper. So honest.

Connor looked up. "You used to write letters to each other? Like, actual letters?"

Caleb nodded, eyes still on the page. "Every one of them by hand. No phones, no email. Just pens and hope."

Connor leaned back, absorbing that. "Guess that's why she liked writing so much."

"She said writing slows you down enough to mean it," Caleb murmured.

Lauren's voice came alive again on the page.

You wrote about everything—the sound of the machines at work, the cat that kept stealing your socks, the old gospel songs your mom hummed when she cooked. You asked what my favorite color was, what I thought heaven looked like, what I wanted out of life. You said you didn't have much to offer except your heart, and I remember thinking, That's already everything.

Then came the first phone call. I told you to call at seven. You did—right on the dot. You sounded nervous, polite, like someone afraid of scaring happiness away. But an hour later, you were laughing. By midnight, you were telling stories. By two a.m., you were singing off-key. And by sunrise, we were both sitting in our cars outside the plant, half-awake, watching the same dawn and knowing we'd never really be strangers again.

Caleb's chest tightened. "That night," he said softly, more to himself than to Connor. "We talked twelve hours straight."

Connor's eyes widened. "Twelve hours?"

"Till we had to clock in." He smiled. "My boss thought I was hungover. I was. Just not from anything in a bottle."

The boy laughed—a quick, warm sound that filled the kitchen. Caleb folded the top of the letter slightly, tracing the familiar loop of her handwriting.

"She wrote like she talked," he said. "Like the words were smiling."

Lauren's letter continued.

You told me once that I made you believe in timing again. That maybe every wrong turn had been leading here. I didn't know what to say then, but I do now. I think grace looks a lot like you standing in the break room that morning, hair a mess, eyes barely open, and still smiling like you'd found something worth losing sleep for.

We started messaging through the computers at work after that—back when you had to wait for the screen to blink before the words appeared. You'd send things like, "cocoa's cold but thinking of you keeps me awake," and I'd roll my eyes so hard Mom could hear it from home. Still, I'd save every message before logging off. I guess I wanted proof that something good was happening.

You didn't know it then, but I'd already told Nanny about you. She said, "That boy's got an old soul," and I said, "So does his truck."

Caleb laughed under his breath. "She loved to tease," he said. "She got that from her grandmother."

"Is that the same Nanny from the picnic story?" Connor asked.

"The same one," Caleb said. "Fireworks and biscuits and everything."

Connor nodded, grinning faintly. "Guess she was right about you."

Caleb looked down at the letter again. "She was right about both of us."

Lauren's handwriting grew a little smaller toward the bottom of the page.

When I think of that summer, I don't remember what we wore or what we said half the time. I just remember laughter. The kind that didn't need to end. You were quiet, but your eyes gave you away. Every time you looked at me, it felt like you were trying to memorize the moment before it was gone. You said once that if you could bottle time, you'd keep every minute we spent together. I think, in a way, you did.

Caleb stopped reading. His hand lingered on the paper, palm warm against the faded ink.

Connor leaned forward. "What's it say?"

Caleb took a breath. "Just... that she remembered."

He looked up at the ceiling as if the air itself might still hold her voice. The heater kicked on again, a low hum filling the space between them.

Caleb lifted the next page, careful with the crease. The paper held a faint scent of whatever lotion she'd used back then—something floral and light. He glanced at Connor, who sat forward with his elbows on the table like he was listening for a sound that might not come again.

He read.

We decided to meet at Duck Island at Warriors' Path. Public. Safe. I told Mom, and she pretended not to worry while worrying, anyway. I got there early and parked where I could see the footbridge. You were already there, though you didn't know I was watching. You stood by your car mirror, combing your hair like you were about to meet the Queen of England. You smoothed the same spot three times, stepped back, checked again, and then laughed at yourself. That's when I knew you were nervous and kind in the same breath.

I stayed in the car another minute, just to be sure I could walk without my knees giving out. When I finally opened the door and crossed the lot, I remember the way the gravel sounded under my shoes. You turned at the noise. I thought your eyes were going to break my heart, the way they lit up and then tried not to.

You said, "Hi," like the word might float away if you breathed too hard. I said, "Hi," back because it seemed fair.

Then you reached into your pocket and pulled out a folded piece of paper. You opened it and there he was—baby Mickey Mouse, cut out with the careful hands of a man who wanted to make me laugh. "In case your grandmother thinks I'm slipping you a Mickey," you said. I snorted right there on the walkway, and the sound broke the moment in all the right ways.

Caleb paused, remembering the angle of the afternoon light on the water, the way the ripples caught pieces of sky and handed them back.

Connor grinned. "You brought a paper Mickey?"

"I did," Caleb said, warmth moving through his face. "Her grandmother warned her I might 'slip her a Mickey.' I figured I'd beat the joke to the punch."

"Mom loved that kind of thing," Connor said. "Silly but smart."

"She did," Caleb said softly. "It made her laugh every single time we talked about it."

He lifted the page again.

We walked the loop around the little island. Families were feeding ducks from the bridge, and a boy in a red jacket kept trying to see how far he could lean without falling. I asked about your job at the plant; you asked about mine. We discovered we'd been working under the same roof for months and had somehow missed each other in the hallways of ordinary days. It felt like God had been hiding us in plain sight until we were ready.

I liked the way you listened. You didn't rush to fill the quiet. You looked at me like words mattered. When you finally told me you'd memorized the route to my mailbox from the last letter you mailed, I pretended to be scandalized and you went red, and then we both laughed.

We ended up at a gas station afterward because neither one of us wanted the day to end. You bought soft drinks and a pack of crackers, and we sat in your car with the windows fogging just a little. You told me your favorite color was blue "because it looks like forgiveness," and I told you mine was purple because it feels like peace. Then we both admitted we loved teal—the place where forgiveness and peace almost touch. We argued gently about which shade of sky meant rain and which meant mercy. I still think I was right.

Connor made a small sound—half chuckle, half ache. "You two would pick teal."

"It became a thing," Caleb said, smiling. "You'll see."

You were careful about the first touch. Your hand brushed mine when you passed the bottle back, and you waited. I remember thinking, If he asks to hold my hand, I'm going to say yes and then call Nanny and tell her I met a good man. You didn't ask with words, which felt braver. You just turned your palm up between us like an invitation. I put my hand in it and the world calmed down in a way I didn't know it could.

When you drove me back to my car, we sat there listening to the thrum of other lives—doors slamming, a radio in the distance, somebody laughing near the pump. You said, "I don't want to mess this up," and I said, "Then let's not." It seemed simple at the time. Maybe simple was the point.

You walked me to my car door. We both pretended to look for something in the sky that wasn't there. And then you did it—you leaned in. Our noses bumped. We both laughed into the almost, and somehow the laughter made room for the kiss. It wasn't perfect. It didn't have to be. It felt like finding a room in a house I'd always lived in and never opened.

You said, "I'll call you when I get home so you know I made it," which made no sense because I was the one driving farther. But I understood the meaning underneath. You were already careful with my heart. I drove away with my cheeks hurting from smiling. When I got home, I put the paper Mickey on my dresser where I'd see it every morning until we married. It kept making me laugh. It still does wherever it is now.

Caleb's eyes stung. He set the page down a second and breathed, counting the beats the way he'd learned to do when the ache rose too fast.

Connor watched him, quiet. "It's good," he said. "It feels like I'm there."

Caleb nodded and turned to the last sheet.

If I could go back to that first day, I wouldn't change a single thing—not the nervous comb, not the gravel, not the way our noses collided like they were trying to be introduced first. I'd leave all the imperfections exactly where they were.

You told me once you wished you could bottle time. I think you did, in a way. You poured it into letters and paper and the spaces between laughter. You taught me that love is not grand speeches but small faithful things—the way you looked for me in a crowd, the way you made sure I got to my car, the way you left notes folded into places I'd find them on hard days. You showed me how God sneaks into ordinary hours and makes them holy.

So this is me, bottling it back for you. In case there are days when memory feels like fog and you can't find the footbridge or the sound of gravel under your feet, here is the path: a paper Mickey in your pocket, my hand finding yours, and both of us laughing before the kiss.

I love you. I loved you then, exactly as you were, and I love you now, exactly as you are.

— Lauren

The last line seemed to hang in the kitchen like steam after a kettle. Caleb folded the letter the way she would have, careful at the corners, then slid it back into the envelope.

Connor stared at the cedar box, eyes bright. "So... that's how it started."

"That's how it started," Caleb said.

"Did you know that day?" Connor asked. "Like—know know?"

Caleb looked past the window to where the yard blurred into a gray morning. "I knew I didn't want to go a day without telling her something," he said. "And that felt close enough to knowing for the first day."

They sat with the quiet a moment, not empty, not heavy—just full. The heater clicked on, and a little ribbon of warm air moved the edge of a grocery list by the phone. Connor reached out and straightened it without thinking, a gesture so small and familiar that Caleb's chest tightened again.

"Can I see the Mickey?" Connor asked suddenly.

Caleb blinked. "The what?"

"The paper Mickey," Connor said, half-smiling. "You kept everything. Don't act like you didn't."

Caleb laughed, a soft sound. "If it's anywhere, it's upstairs in the top drawer of the old dresser with the loose handle."

Connor stood like a boy on a mission. "I'll check."

He took two steps and then stopped. "Dad?"

"Yeah?"

"Thanks for reading it out loud."

Caleb nodded. "Thanks for listening."

Connor disappeared down the hall, footfalls light, and Caleb stayed where he was, palm resting on the envelope. Outside, the fog had started to lift; the fence posts came back into focus one by one.

He slid the letter into the cedar box and closed the lid. The faint scent of wood and paper lingered in the air, warm and clean.

"Thank You," he whispered, not to the room.

From upstairs came the sound of a drawer gliding open, then Connor's voice, thin with surprise and something like delight. "Found it!"

Caleb let out a breath he hadn't realized he was holding. He stood, joints protesting a little, and headed for the stairs.

As he reached the first step, he touched the banister the way he always did—out of habit, out of gratitude, out of the quiet understanding that some things, once found, should be held with both hands.

CHAPTER FOUR

Grasping at Straws

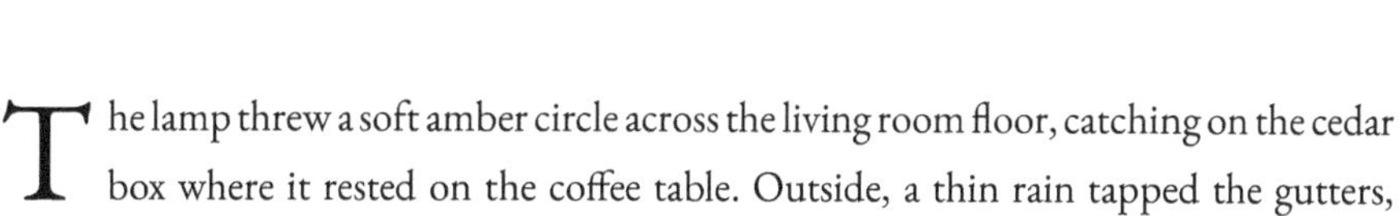

The lamp threw a soft amber circle across the living room floor, catching on the cedar box where it rested on the coffee table. Outside, a thin rain tapped the gutters, steady as a clock nobody needed to wind. Connor sat cross-legged on the rug, sleeves pulled over his hands, watching the light find the brass latch.

"You sure about this one?" he asked.

Caleb nodded, though the motion felt like a tremor. "If we wait till it doesn't hurt," he said, "we might never read it."

Connor reached for the envelope, then paused halfway, letting his dad take it instead. The paper crackled, warm from the lamp's heat. Lauren's handwriting curved across the front—*Sharing the Hard Truth.* The scent of cedar lifted as Caleb slid a finger under the flap.

He cleared his throat. "All right," he whispered, more to himself than to Connor, and began to read.

You told me once you'd rather lose a hand than lie to me, and that's how I knew something heavy was coming.

It was late—mid-evening, the color between gold and ash. You sat at the edge of the couch with your elbows on your knees, eyes fixed on the floor like it had answers. My mother's TV murmured in the other room, a laugh track too bright for the moment. You said you needed to tell me the truth before we built anything that mattered.

I remember the cocoa cooling between us. You kept turning the mug, so the handle faced the same direction every time, as if symmetry could save you.

You started slow, words rubbing together like stones trying to make fire. You told me about the years between eight and thirteen—the silence you'd kept since then, the one confession to your sister that never got believed, the way guilt soaked through you until even the house fire felt like punishment. You told me you'd carried it alone because you thought it changed who you were.

Your hands shook so hard you gripped them together. I wanted to stop you, to tell you that you'd done enough by breathing, but I let you finish because truth deserves its whole sentence.

When you looked up, there wasn't shame in your face—only fear that I'd step back.

I didn't.

I moved closer until our knees touched. You said you didn't know if you could ever be close to anyone again, not really, because you weren't sure what closeness meant anymore. You stared at your hands like they were evidence.

That was the first time I ever touched your face.

I said the words before I even thought them: "It didn't change you. It hurt you. There's a difference."

You nodded once, but I could tell the sentence hadn't landed yet. So I said it again, slower, the way you talk to a frightened animal: "It hurt you. It did not change you."

Something in the air went still then. Even the TV laugh track faded into static. I swear the whole world paused just to listen.

You cried, quiet and unashamed. I kept my hand on your cheek until the shaking eased.

You told me you'd never told anyone else, not your parents, not a soul since your sister. I could hear the boy you'd been hiding inside the man you'd become, waiting for someone to tell him it wasn't his fault. So I did. I said the words you'd needed since you were eight: "You were the one who was hurt, Caleb. Not the one who did wrong."

You didn't answer right away. You just breathed, long and broken, like the first exhale after almost drowning.

I didn't pray out loud that night, but I did pray. I told God thank You for trusting me with something so fragile. I asked Him to help me hold it the way He would—without flinching.

I wasn't raised in church, you know that. But I've always believed God shows up when truth does.

When we finally spoke again, the clock said midnight. You looked younger somehow, like laying the words down had peeled back the years. I told you I loved you. You said you didn't deserve that yet. I said that's what grace is for.

We never talked about it again in detail, and I think that's right. Some truths don't need retelling; they just need living. But every time you've looked at me since, I've seen that night sitting quietly behind your eyes, and I've loved you for your courage all over again.

—Lauren

Caleb's voice thinned near the end and went quiet on Lauren's name. He kept the page lifted an inch above the table like he was afraid setting it down might break something. The room didn't rush in after the reading; it settled. The lamp hummed so softly he wondered if he was imagining it. Outside, rain ticked against the gutter and slowed.

Connor didn't speak at first. He watched his dad's hands—how they hovered, then eased the letter back into its envelope the way you tuck in a child. The boy's breath came steady, a careful choice.

"Dad?" he said finally.

"Yeah, bud."

"She knew something... heavy." Connor's eyes stayed on the cedar grain. "I don't have to know it. I just—can you tell me if you're okay?"

Caleb looked down at his fingers. They weren't shaking. That felt new. "I'm okay," he said. He swallowed. "I wasn't, for a long time. But she helped me be."

Connor nodded, slow. "I could feel that. In the letter."

They sat with that a moment. The heater clicked and sighed like it had been holding its breath. Willow stretched along the back of the couch and blinked at them as if to say, Keep going.

"I told your mom something back then," Caleb said, his voice getting gentle at the edges. "Something that made me think I didn't deserve... a lot of things. She didn't step back. She moved closer." He tapped the envelope once, small. "That's who she was."

Connor's mouth pulled tight and then softened. "Yeah." He cleared his throat. "She moved closer to everybody."

Caleb let his eyes find the window. Rain traced lines down the glass; the streetlight outside turned each drop to a silver thread. "I want you to know this," he said, still looking at the rain. "There is nothing you could ever bring me that would make me step back."

Connor's head came up. "You mean—"

"I mean nothing," Caleb said. He turned back to him. "That night, with your mom, I learned love can carry what truth breaks open. If you ever need me to carry something, I will."

Connor's hand tightened around his mug. He didn't drink. He nodded like a promise to himself and set the cup down, careful not to clink. "Okay," he whispered. "Me too."

They let the quiet have the table again.

"Do you want to ask anything?" Caleb said. "You don't have to."

Connor opened his mouth, then closed it. He glanced at the envelope. "Did it make you different?"

Caleb held his breath for a second and then let it out. "It hurt me," he said. "But it didn't change who I am. Your mom told me that. I believe her."

Connor nodded, relief loosening something in his shoulders he hadn't realized was tight. "Then that's enough."

Caleb smiled—small, honest. "Yeah."

He slid the envelope back onto the cedar lid and set his palm over it. The wood was warm from the lamp. He could still smell the faint sweet of Lauren's lotion in memory, layered over cedar and cocoa. He'd have sworn the room carried a trace of roses too, even with the window shut.

"Want more cocoa?" Connor asked, too bright and then catching himself. "Or... I can warm these."

Caleb lifted his cup and tilted it toward his son the way they used to do on winter afternoons. "Top me off," he said. "Not because I need it. Just because."

Connor stood, grateful for the motion. In the kitchen he moved like he remembered being watched by a gentle teacher: pan on, milk low, patient heat. He tapped the tin lid twice, the way Lauren had taught him. Steam furled into the light and softened the corners of the room. When he brought the mugs back, the table felt different.

Caleb took one and let the warmth sit in his hands. "Thank you."

Connor shrugged, but the corner of his mouth lifted. "She'd say it needs three little marshmallows." He opened the bag and counted them into his dad's cup like it mattered, then into his own.

Caleb laughed under his breath. It was a quiet, grateful sound. "She would."

They sipped. The letter lay between them, face down, edges square with the lid. After a minute, Connor spoke again. "It's weird," he said. "Feels like it should make me sadder. But I don't know." He searched for the word. "It makes me feel... steadier? Like she knew how to hold us even now."

"She did," Caleb said.

Connor rubbed the heel of his hand across his eye, quick, pretending it was a scratch. "Do you think she knew we'd read this together?"

"I think she wrote it that way," Caleb said. He looked at the handwriting again, at the loops he could trace with his eyes closed. "I think she trusted the timing more than we did."

Rain ticked a little harder, then eased like a thought finishing. The lamp's glow made the brass latch a small star.

"Do you want to... put it with the others?" Connor asked.

He shook his head. "Let's let it sit here with us awhile. Some things deserve a seat at the table."

Connor smiled without showing teeth. "Okay."

Willow dropped to the cushion and arranged herself with the ceremony of a queen. Maverick paced once along the window, pawed at a raindrop he couldn't catch, and gave up, tail high. Elvis hopped to the rug and flopped as if this had taken planning.

"Do you remember," Connor said after a while, "when she told me—after that fight with the kid at school—that telling the truth feels like taking a splinter out? Hurts different, but then you can heal?"

Caleb's eyes warmed. "I remember." He lifted the cup and let the steam fog his glasses for a second before taking a sip. "She practiced what she preached."

They fell quiet again. The house answered with small domestic sounds: the tick of cooling metal somewhere in the vent, the thread-soft rasp of pages settling inside the family Bible on the shelf, the far off drip in the sink that meant a washer needed attention. The ordinary worked beside the holy and neither apologized for itself.

After a time, Connor leaned forward, elbows on knees. "Dad?"

"Yeah."

"Do you think we should... write her back? Not with answers," he added quickly. "Just... I don't know. So she can see we heard her."

Caleb looked at the envelope. He thought of all the years Lauren had tucked notes into lunches, scratched love you on grocery lists, taped scriptures to mirrors. He thought of how Emily Dickinson wrote that "this World is not Conclusion," and how Lauren would have laughed at him quoting poetry at the table. He nodded slowly. "I think that's a good idea," he said. "Letters for the letters."

Connor swallowed, as if the choice had weight and the weight was welcome. "Okay."

Caleb reached for the pen on the side table—the one with the bite marks she and Connor shared—and set it beside the envelope like a candle before a hymn. "Not tonight," he said, more to the room than to his son. "But soon."

Connor gathered their empty plates from earlier and carried them to the sink. When he came back, he didn't sit where he'd been; he slid onto the couch nearer his dad, leaving the cedar box between them but closing the space just the same. "Can we read another one?" he asked, even as his shoulders asked for rest.

"Tomorrow," Caleb said, gentle. "This one needs to breathe."

Connor nodded. He leaned his temple against the cushion's seam and let his eyes half-close. "I get that," he murmured. "Breathing is work."

Caleb set his cup down and turned the envelope so Lauren's name faced the lamp. He flattened his palm over the paper again. A prayer rose without words, the kind that tucks itself into breath. Thank You.

He didn't feel thunder. He didn't look for signs. But a small thing happened: the rain eased to a fine whisper, and somewhere down the hall a draft lifted the corner of a curtain and set it back down like a hand on a shoulder. The air felt tended.

"Dad?"

"Hmm?"

"Do you think God was really there? That night?"

Caleb stared at the letter. When he answered, his voice had that soft surety his son recognized from other sacred places—hospital rooms, late drives, the porch the night the lights finally went dark. "I don't think He left," he said.

Connor let that settle. "Okay."

They didn't move to put the letter away. They didn't need to. The keeping felt better out in the open.

Minutes passed in kind company. The heater paused. The house shifted its weight and grew still. Caleb watched Connor breathe, slow and even, and thought about the boy he had been and the man across from him and the bridge between them made of her words.

He picked up the pen and set it back down. "When you're ready," he said, out loud and not to anyone, or maybe to both of them.

Connor's eyes opened again at the sound of his father's voice. "I'm getting there," he said.

"I am too," Caleb replied.

They sat like that until the lamp began to draw shadows long across the floorboards. Then Caleb reached for the envelope and slid it into the stack already read. He didn't tuck it at the bottom. He placed it at the top, easy to find. The cedar box, faithful as ever, waited for the lid. He didn't close it yet.

"Come on," he said softly, standing. "Let's rinse these cups."

In the kitchen, water ran warm over ceramic; steam traced the air with a friendly curl. Connor bumped his dad's shoulder with his own, casual and shy, and Caleb bumped him back the same way. They dried the mugs and set them mouth-down like two small bells waiting for morning.

Back in the living room, Caleb rested his fingertips on the box lid. He glanced toward the window where the rain had thinned to a mist. A neighbor's wind chime gave one quiet note and then kept its peace.

"Thank You for letting her write it," he said, almost without sound.

He lowered the lid.

He didn't latch it.

Later, after Connor had gone to his room and the cats had decided which lap belonged to which cushion, Caleb sat alone with the lamp off. The house held its own small glow from the streetlight sifting through blinds. He could make out the shape of the box on the table by the way it refused the dark.

He leaned back and let his head rest against the cushion. He thought of the man in his twenties, fingers knotted, trying to name a pain that had stolen years and not his name. He thought of the woman who put a hand to his face and returned the name to him without conditions. He breathed in and out and called that memory mercy.

Across the room, the family Bible lay where it always did. He didn't open it. He remembered what it said all the same. He wasn't sure if the verse had found him or if Lauren had left it around the house so many times his bones remembered, but it was there, present as the chair under him, as the cup ring drying on the coaster she'd cross-stitched.

"Help me love like that," he whispered into the room. No flourish. No bargain. Just the petition of a man who knew what saved him.

From down the hall, a floorboard gave a friendly creak as the house resettled. Connor coughed once and turned over.

Caleb stood and clicked the lamp with two fingers. The brass knob made a tiny sound like a pin struck against glass. The room surrendered to the softer dark. He didn't feel alone in it.

At the doorway he looked back at the coffee table. The envelope sat at a slight angle on top of the box where he'd left it—a small flag on a hill they'd begun to climb together. He pictured tomorrow's cocoa, tomorrow's light, the steady work of reading and being read by what she'd written.

"Goodnight," he said, to the room and to the woman who kept filling it. "We'll read more when it's time."

He stepped into the hall. The curtain lifted and fell once, like a breath. The rain had almost stopped. The air smelled faintly of cedar, and—if he let himself believe it—roses.

He closed the door to his room halfway and left the gap the size of a promise.

The house listened, and then it rested.

CHAPTER FIVE

The Ring and the Blessing

♥

The cocoa had skinned over, little islands sliding when Connor tipped his mug. The house smelled faintly of dish soap and cedar—the box on the table holding the quiet.. Evening leaned against the windows. In the lamplight, her handwriting curved across the next envelope: *The Ring and The Blessing.*

Connor didn't grab it. He tucked his sleeves into his fists and watched the brass latch catch the light. "You ever wish you could've watched yourself?" he asked. "Like, stepped outside and seen your face when you did something brave?"

Caleb huffed a small laugh. "Sometimes I'm grateful I didn't."

Connor nodded at the envelope. "We doing it?"

"We're doing it."

He slid a finger under the flap. The paper gave with that dry little sigh Lauren loved—*the sound of something letting itself be known,* she used to say. The faint scent of her lotion rose a second and was gone. Caleb rested the first page on the table between them so Connor could see the curve of her letters.

He could feel his son lean closer—not to the words yet, but to the place the words might take them.

It was June, love—hot enough the mall doors were a blessing. Your Aunt Betty came with him because courage is easier in pairs. I imagine her bracelets were singing the whole way from the car. He pretended he knew what he was doing. He never has liked buying things that try to measure how much a heart holds.

The jewelry store was bright as a confession. The lady's name was Marla, and she wore that patient face people keep when they handle beginnings. He pressed his palm to the glass and said he didn't want anything that would snag a sweater, which is still the kindest thing anyone has ever said about my future cardigans.

He chose the ring that didn't hoard the light. That's how I've always thought of him since: low and sure, not loud, giving the light back.

I didn't know he'd called the radio. I didn't know he'd asked a stranger to hold the moment so his voice wouldn't shake through it. I only knew I was sitting in your grandparents' den with my feet tucked under me pretending to care about some tidy little TV couple while the air grew thick like a storm was waiting for its cue.

Then the DJ cleared his throat and made a space where our lives could fit. Then your daddy's voice came through the speaker like a bird that finally found the open window. He said my name once, and I said "yes" twice, before the chorus could show off. Some things don't need all the lyrics. God already knows the tune.

Afterward we didn't talk much. Some joy is better in the quiet. He slipped the ring on my finger while the radio glowed that soft orange, and the room decided to be still for a minute. We didn't force it. We just sat in the pew of the couch and let gratitude wash our faces from the inside.

Caleb paused. Connor's eyes stayed on the page, but his hand drifted out until his knuckles touched the cedar box. He didn't pull away when Caleb's thumb brushed them.

"What did the ring look like?" Connor asked without looking up.

"Like it meant to last," Caleb said. "Low setting. Gold band. It didn't grab the light. It gave it back."

"That sounds like Mom."

"It does."

Caleb read on.

A week later we came through the garage into your grandparents' den—the way we always did when the day was too warm to start over. I went in first, and as I walked past the small set of steps that rose to the foyer, I thought I saw someone standing there. The light caught the rail just right, and for a blink it looked like a man waiting kindly for us to notice him. I didn't say anything. I just kept walking.

Your daddy came in right behind me. Later I learned he'd seen it too—a figure on the foyer landing, still and certain, like someone guarding the door. Neither of us spoke. We just went on into the den and sat down.

After a few minutes, I looked toward the coffee table where a framed picture sat—a photo of his grandfather. I pointed at it and asked, "Who is that?" He said, "That's my granddaddy." I told him quietly, "I just saw him standing on the foyer."

He went still for a second, then said, "I did too."

We both knew then it hadn't been the light playing tricks. He was there—whole this time, standing tall without the crutches he'd needed all his life. The air in that room settled. There wasn't any glow or sound, just a deep, good peace. We didn't tell anyone. We didn't have to. It felt like a blessing meant only for the two of us.

A few days later, it happened again.

You were at your parents' house alone that afternoon. You'd grabbed a bucket and sponge, planning to wash your car before the sun dropped behind the hill. Ordinary chore, ordinary day. You walked down the hallway toward the front door... and froze.

He was there.

Not a shadow. Not a flicker. Just a man at the far end of the hall, standing steady and sure—your grandfather, whole again, without the crutches he'd needed his whole life. The same quiet presence as before. The same peace. Only closer this time. Watching over you like he was waiting for you to see him.

You said the bucket thumped your knee when you stopped. Your heart jumped hard enough you could taste metal. And before you could decide whether to breathe or run, your body chose for you. You turned, unlocked nothing, opened nothing—you just bolted. You were in the car before your mind caught up with your hands.

You drove to Blountville like you had somewhere urgent to be. Maybe you did. Maybe Heaven wanted a witness.

When you pulled into my parents' driveway, you were pale around the edges, the way people get when they see something true too close. I came onto the porch before you knocked—I could feel something had followed you that wasn't fear, just weight.

We sat on the concrete step and you told me what you saw. Every detail. Every second. You kept saying, "I don't know why I ran," and I told you maybe it wasn't running—maybe it was being called home to tell the story to somebody who would believe you.

And I did believe you. Every word.

I didn't think it was a haunting, and neither did you, once your breath settled. It felt like protection. Like a grandfather finally standing tall enough to guard the hallway of your life. First on the landing. Then here. Two small visitations carrying one quiet blessing: Don't be afraid. You're being watched over.

You nodded, slow and real. "I just want to make him proud," you said. And I told you—you already were.

We let the den breathe. The house knew how.

Connor's mouth worked around a thought. "So you both... like actually saw him?"

"We did."

"And nobody freaked out."

"It didn't feel like a thing to fear," Caleb said. "It felt like someone making sure we'd found the right road."

Connor nodded very slowly, as if agreeing with a person he couldn't see. "I like that he didn't need the crutches."

"So did I," Caleb said, and had to swallow once.

The heater clicked. Somewhere in the ductwork, metal relaxed. Connor reached for the page and turned it himself.

When I think about it now, sitting where I am—fewer breaths left than I had hoped, more love than I know what to do with—I see how ordinary things braided themselves to hold us: a mall that smelled like pretzels, a radio with a bulb behind its face, a landing that learned how to be a threshold twice. He doesn't always use stained glass. Sometimes He uses glass counters and take-a-number dispensers and the way a saleslady says "Are you sure?" like a blessing she's been waiting to give.

I kept looking at the ring that week. Not because it was large. Because it was faithful. It didn't try to be more than it was. It didn't need to. Somewhere around the time your grandfather stood whole on that landing, I decided that's what we were promising—not fireworks (even though we got those too) but faithfulness that gave the light back.

—L.

They let the letter rest on the table a moment. The lamp hummed. A car passed outside, tire-whisper on wet pavement.

Connor said, "I didn't know the ring part felt like church."

Caleb's mouth bent. "It did for me."

"Did you know she'd say yes?"

"I hoped more than I knew." He let the truth in. "I asked God to hold my voice steady. He used the radio."

Connor smiled sideways. "That tracks."

Caleb tapped the paper. "You want to hear the part you'll like best?"

"There's a part better than Papaw being whole?"

Caleb cleared his throat and found Lauren's next page.

You'll want to know what he looked like when he asked for the ring, Connor. Your Aunt Betty says he looked like a man trying to talk a thunderstorm into waiting until after the wedding. He wore the shirt he thought made him look older. He wiped his fingerprints off the glass like that would keep him from leaving any on my life. When Marla asked, "This one?" he said "That one," but his mouth said a prayer first, the short kind, because God already knew what he meant.

Betty made him eat a pretzel so he wouldn't faint. He burned his tongue on the first bite and chewed bravely, anyway. That's how he's loved me all these years—burned once in a while, but brave about it.

If you're reading this, my darling boy, you already know he kept his promise. If he's reading with you, tell him I still think he looked handsome in the glow of that little radio light. Tell him I forgave him for practicing saying my name in the hallway mirror, because I watched him do it and loved him even more for being nervous about forever.

Connor's eyebrows rose. "You practiced?"

"I did," Caleb said, sheepish. "In the bathroom, too."

"That's terrible."

"It worked."

They grinned at each other like people who'd found the same trail in the woods from different directions.

"Keep going," Connor said. His voice had softened around the edges.

Caleb did.

We drove to Bristol for the Fourth not long after. Nanny put potato salad in every bowl that wasn't nailed down and kissed your daddy's head and called him a show off. She only said that to people she meant to bless. The sky did what skies do when they are sure of themselves. Fireworks did their part. I could feel the ring cool against my finger when the breeze came up from the field. I thought, This is what God's smile sounds like when it crackles.

Somewhere around midnight, the neighborhood got quiet again. The kind of quiet that doesn't ask for a reason. Your daddy and I didn't talk then either. We were learning to be more than words.

I'm telling you all this because I need you both to know what we're standing on. Memory isn't just a place we visit to hurt. It's the floor God built under our feet so we can cross the rooms we don't understand yet.

If you're reading this together, hold each other's hands for me a second. The left one will do. Feel where the ring used to sit. That space is still holy.

Caleb stopped because his eyes needed a minute. Connor didn't look away, which was its own kind of holding. He reached his hand across, palm up. Caleb set his left hand in it. Connor's thumb found the pale band of skin a ring had made and had long since surrendered.

They sat like that until the knot in Caleb's chest loosened enough to let the next breath all the way down.

"Do you want the rest?" he asked.

"I do," Connor said, and caught his own pun a half-second later. "Okay, that was not on purpose."

"It was pretty good," Caleb admitted.

Connor gestured for him to keep reading.

I know you two have your own language—silences that say more than other people's speeches. Keep it. Guard it. When grief tries to teach you a new grammar, don't let it erase the old one. Remember how the radio held his words that night when he couldn't trust his voice? That's what love does when you can't do it alone—it holds the part you're dropping until you can pick it up again.

Sometimes the blessing looks like a man on a landing without his crutches. Sometimes it looks like a son who stays at the table until his father can finish a sentence. Either way, it's the same Giver.

I'm not far. You know that, but it helps to write it down. I'm the hum behind your song. I'm the light that finds the glass and comes back kinder. When you stand at any landing, check your shoulders. If they feel easy, you're being blessed again.

—L.

Caleb folded the last page and pressed the fold like he could iron her voice flat enough to keep, then unfolded it because he couldn't bear to crease what carried her.

Connor's gaze had gone somewhere softer. The corners of his mouth hadn't found a smile, but they had given up the fight against it.

"So... the blessing wasn't just for you two," he said at last. "It's... still happening."

Caleb nodded. "That's how it feels to me."

"And the ring—"

"—was never the point," Caleb finished. "It was the promise. The point was what it did with the light."

They were quiet. Not empty - quiet. The useful kind.

Connor tipped his head toward the den. "Can we... turn on the radio? Not loud."

"We can."

They carried the letter with them like a small, good fire from room to room. In the den, the old stereo lit up—amber again, or maybe their eyes made it that way. Caleb spun the dial until a song found itself. Not their song—close cousin. The melody threaded through the house and into the hallway, found the places where air gathers and made a home there.

They didn't speak for a while. Connor leaned back and put his feet on the ottoman the way Lauren scolded and then forgave a thousand times. Caleb let the chair take his weight and didn't try to sit up straighter than his bones wanted.

He thought of the landing at his parents' house. For a second—the small, honest kind—he felt the cool of a presence pass through and set itself down. Nothing to be proven. Nothing to hoard.

Connor said, barely above the music, "Dad?"

"Yeah."

"I think... I think I'm ready to hear more. Like... not just the happy parts."

Caleb looked at him the way you look at a sunrise you didn't order but got, anyway. "Me too."

They let the song finish its work. When the last note went where music goes when it's finished being sound, they left the radio on. It talked soft to the corners. The cedar box on the table in the other room kept its shape. Nothing was forced. Nothing was rushed. The blessing looked like two people who weren't alone in a room, and the ring—where it had been and where it would be again—gave the light back.

CHAPTER SIX

The Wrong Name

The kitchen had settled into that hour between supper and dark, when the window showed more of the room than the yard. The timer lamp in the front room flicked on with its little click, and the light laid a soft square against the wall. The cedar box sat between them on the table, lid propped open, velvet catching the lamplight like a shallow pool.

Connor drummed his fingers once, then tucked his hands under his thighs. "Which one is it tonight?"

Caleb sifted the envelopes with two fingers, careful as if they were sleeping birds. The unmarked envelope showed itself briefly at the bottom. He skimmed past it and lifted a slimmer one whose edges had softened with handling. Lauren's handwriting curved across the front: The Wrong Name.

He swallowed. "This one."

Connor's mouth pulled tight, a quick nod he didn't mean to show. "You messed up?"

Caleb breathed out something like a laugh and not quite. "I did."

They sat with it for a moment—the word did thudding like a knuckle on wood. Connor glanced at the unmarked envelope and then away, like his eyes had burned on something bright. Caleb slid a finger under the flap of the chosen letter, and the paper gave with a quiet sigh. The scent of cedar and old ink rose up, clean and a little sweet.

"Do you want me to—" Connor started.

"I'll read," Caleb said, voice low. "But I want you here for it."

Connor nodded again, steadier this time. Outside, a car went by, tires whispering on damp pavement. Caleb unfolded the first page and let Lauren's voice come back to meet them.

The couch in your parents' den sloped just enough to make us lean toward each other. Your mama had set out a bowl of candy like she always did, even when it wasn't a holiday, and you ignored it like you always did, even when you wanted some.

I remember the way the afternoon was giving up its last piece of gold through the small window above the TV. I remember your knee brushing mine when you turned, and how the cushion dipped and we tipped together like two people who'd been learning the same dance without knowing.

And then you said it —

— not my name.

It wasn't loud. It wasn't cruel. It just slipped out, worn smooth from whoever you'd been before me. We both heard it land. Fresh air will slam a door if you don't catch it. That's how it sounded inside me. Not anger at first—just the door.

You knew the second you said it. Your mouth stayed open around the wrong syllables like you wanted to pull them back by the tail. You reached for my hand and said, "Lauren, I—" and it didn't matter what came next because I felt the old ghost of comparison I swore I'd never feed.

I didn't plan it. I slid the ring from my finger like you slide a strand of hair from your face, easy and practiced, and I put it in your palm. The metal felt warm from my skin. Your hand didn't close at first. It just waited, surprised.

You said my name then. Right this time. You said it like a prayer you were trying to catch in both hands. I stood. You stood. Your dad's footsteps crossed upstairs, steady as a metronome, and I thought: people breathe and floors creak and love is still learning our names.

I didn't slam the door when I left. I just put my hand on the knob and turned. The hinges turned easy.

Caleb paused. He could hear Connor swallow, that small click like someone testing a key in a lock.

"How long?" Connor asked, voice pitched quieter than the room.

"Keep reading," Caleb said.

He looked back to the page.

It took me the whole drive home to cry. Not right away—my body held it like a cup you carry full so it won't spill. When it did, it wasn't even about the name. It was about every story a wrong name makes you tell yourself. I'm not enough. I am a placeholder. I am the intermission before he goes back to his old show.

I knew better in my bones, but bones remember old falls, and I was still learning that loving you meant telling my bones the truth.

I put my hand to my finger that night three times out of habit and touched air. The skin there felt like a note cut off mid-song. I slept badly. I woke up early. I went to work and nobody knew, because grief doesn't announce itself at time clocks.

I didn't call you for nineteen days.

Connor looked up quickly. "Nineteen?"

Caleb nodded once.

"What did you do?" Connor asked. No challenge in it—just curiosity with edges of worry, like he wanted to find himself somewhere safe in the answer.

Caleb let himself feel that summer again: the heat that made shirts tack between the shoulders, the sound of a box fan chopping the air in his old room, the ring cool and heavy in his pocket.

He read on.

On the second day, you came by my work with a paper bag you didn't make me open. My supervisor told me later you'd stood too long beside the soda machine like you couldn't remember how to leave.

On the fifth, your mama called me "sweet girl" in the grocery store and asked were strawberries as high at my house as they were at hers. She never said my name. She didn't need to. She squeezed my elbow in the cereal aisle and it meant, "He is a good boy, even when he forgets."

On the seventh, you left a note on my windshield that said only: "I'm sorry. Not for the word. For what the word did in you." It was the first time I could breathe without feeling the shape of the ring around a finger that wasn't there.

On the eleventh, I went for a walk and saw a paper Mickey Mouse in a neighbor's window and had to sit down on the curb. You used that silly cutout to make me laugh the first day we met, and I started to believe again that your heart might be learning my name the way you'd taught me to trust my own.

On the fifteenth, I stood in my kitchen and said out loud, "Lord, I do not know what to do with this ache. If it's mercy, let it teach me. And if it's pride, let it go." The floor was cool

under my feet. The fridge clicked and sighed. Somewhere in the neighborhood a screen door
snapped and settled. The world kept going because it always does, and He was there.

On the nineteenth, I told you to meet me at the park by the duck pond at six.

Caleb glanced over the paper at Connor. "Warriors Path," he said softly.

"I know," Connor said. "Duck Island." His mouth tugged toward a smile they both felt.

Caleb read.

You got there early. I could tell you'd tried to be perfect, which always made me want to tease
you. Your hair was combed like you were hoping for an interview with grace. You had the
ring in your hand, thumb rubbing the band as if you could polish away what we'd learned.

We walked. Neither of us sat on the bench right away. Ducks made their small noises,
fussy as old men. The water had that thin skin of evening on it, and the sky carried the color
between blue and ash that happens right before the lights come on in houses.

You said, "Lauren," and stopped. I waited. You started again. "I can't ask you to believe
me just because I'm hurting. I want to say it was a slip, but the truth is I had a life before
you and sometimes the grooves in a person take a while to re-carve. That's not an excuse. I
don't want a life where your face ever has to share space with a ghost."

You looked at the ring like it was heavier than it had any right to be. "I carried this every
day because I needed to carry the wait," you said, and I heard the word the way you meant
it—W-A-I-T—and I think that's when my heart started to put the furniture back.

"I hurt you," you said. "Not just your pride. I hurt your quiet. I'm sorry."

It was the way you said quiet. You didn't grab for forgiveness like a prize you'd earned by showing up. You set your apology down like a cup of water and stepped back.

I told you I needed time. You nodded. And then I surprised myself and held out my hand for the ring. Not to put it on. Just to feel it again. You didn't flinch when I didn't slide it onto my finger. You didn't rush the moment or perform your pain. You let the space be what it was.

I put the ring in your palm first and turned your hand over so it fell into mine. I wanted to feel the weight move between us. "I don't care about the name," I said, and we both knew I did. "I care about not watching you learn me."

You said, "I am learning you. I want to learn you until my last day."

So I took a breath—the kind you have to go down into to find—and I slipped the ring back where it had belonged all along.

We sat on the bench after that. We didn't talk much. A boy rode past on a dirt-skinned bicycle with playing cards clipped to the spokes. It sounded like applause that didn't know where to go, so it went everywhere.

We watched the fountain throw up its greenish spray, the way that poor water always wanted to be the ocean. I remember thinking about waves and vows and how both of them keep coming as long as you do.

Caleb lowered the page. The room had gone a shade darker; the timer lamp pushed a warm square farther across the floor, inching toward their feet.

Connor's eyes were wet and stubborn about it. "You really carried it every day?"

Caleb reached into his pocket on instinct—as if it might be there even now—and touched the nothing that had replaced it. "Every day," he said. "I didn't deserve a shortcut."

Connor nodded, breathing through his nose the way he did when he was trying not to let something become a whole thing. "I... get it," he said after a moment. "Like when I mess up and want Mom's—" He stopped himself, throat working. "When I wanted Mom to just say it was okay right then, but sometimes the only real okay is the kind you wait for."

Caleb didn't reach for him. He let the space be theirs. "Yeah."

"Keep going," Connor said, tapping the edge of the letter like it could pull them forward.

After you walked me to my car, you asked if I wanted to go get soft drinks like we did that first day when we were too full of newness to go home. I said yes because sometimes grace is a bottle cap turning.

The gas station lights were the color that makes skin look tired, but you looked like the same boy who'd brought me crackers and watched the windows fog while we told each other about the kinds of skies that meant rain. You asked if I wanted grape or orange, and I said "purple feels like peace" just to make you smile at an old joke. You did. You always did.

We didn't bring up the name again. Not as a test. Not even as a story. We carried it the way you carry a healed place on your body—you remember the break when the weather changes, and you ask God to keep making it strong.

On the drive home, I put my fingers to the ring and felt it cool under the car's AC. I whispered, "Thank You," into the quiet and meant it.

The next morning, Nanny called to ask what color hydrangeas I liked, and I told her you'd say blue because it looks like forgiveness. She laughed the laugh that made me feel eight and held. "Maybe plant both," she said. "So you remember peace too."

Baby, if you are reading this years from now, I want you to know: I didn't forgive you because you suffered. I forgave you because love is promise more than performance, and because God held us in that waiting and kept the wrong story from becoming our truth. I forgave you because your apology didn't try to build a ladder out of excuses. You just opened your hands.

We were always going to be learning each other's names. That's not a failure. That's marriage practicing eternity.

— Your Lauren

Caleb let the page lower until it touched the table. For a moment, he kept his hand there, grounding himself to wood and paper and the lamp-square's warmth touching his knuckles. The house made one of those old sounds—wood settling somewhere in the hallway—and the silence folded itself back around them, gentle as a shawl.

Connor sniffed and didn't pretend otherwise. "Nineteen days," he said again, softer. "I don't think I've waited nineteen minutes for anything without losing my mind."

"You waited for her," Caleb said. He didn't mean to say it out loud. But once it was in the air, neither of them tried to take it back. "Since January."

Connor's shoulders rose and fell. He lifted his hands, then put them down again like he'd decided to keep words simple. "I'm still waiting," he said. "Just... different."

They let that be true without fixing it.

Connor reached forward and traced the edge of the letter's last page. "I like how she said it," he murmured. "About not asking forgiveness because you suffered. That's... I mean, that's right."

Caleb nodded. "She had a way of saying the thing without stabbing."

"I don't know if I could have given it back," Connor said, meaning the ring, meaning the nineteen days, meaning any number of losses he didn't name.

"She didn't give up," Caleb said. "She gave God room."

They sat a while. Somewhere outside, rain began in a finer thread, pattering on the gutter elbows and the thin leaves that hung over the porch. The air in the kitchen felt a degree cooler, and the lamp kept its small promise against the dim.

"Dad?"

"Mm?"

"I'm not asking you to, like, be perfect or anything." Connor's mouth twitched—humor trying on its shoes. "But if you ever call me by another kid's name, I'm keeping your truck keys for nineteen days."

Caleb huffed a laugh. It startled a little warmth up his throat. "Deal," he said. "Though if you keep my keys, nobody gets anywhere."

"That's kind of the point," Connor said, and smiled for real.

Caleb gathered the letter pages, smoothing the creases as if that could keep them from aging one more second. He slid them back into the envelope and set it on the table, not quite ready to return it to the box. Connor watched him do it—watched the way his hands were careful with what they loved—and didn't make a joke about it, which was its own kind of reverence.

"Do you think she ever... like, messed up with names?" Connor asked.

"She called me angel once when I was being anything but," Caleb said. "Does that count?"

Connor's smile tilted. "Mom had a lot of faith."

"She did," Caleb said. The words came out soft. "And she taught me most of mine. Sometimes without talking."

He touched the stack of envelopes in the cedar box, and the unmarked one showed itself again at the bottom—the large shape a different color from the rest, as if time had pressed it heavier. He didn't reach for it. He only let his eyes rest there long enough to feel both the ache and the pull.

"Another night," he said, and Connor nodded.

Caleb closed the box with the same care he used to open it. The latch settled with a small click. He carried the envelope they'd just read to the shelf by the window where the finished letters now rested, a line of soft-edged white against the darker wood. The lamp's glow laid itself over them.

When he came back to the table, Connor was holding the cocoa tin askew, considering whether the evening needed the ritual.

"Two mugs?" Connor asked.

"Two," Caleb said.

They worked around each other without instruction—one reaching for the kettle, the other for the chipped blue mugs she'd loved. The faint sweetness of cocoa dust lifted when Connor tapped the spoon; the kettle began its small complaint and then its stronger song. Steam fogged the window for a moment, blurring the reflection of the room into something gentler: two figures at a table, a square of light, a box that kept giving.

Connor handed him a mug. "To names," he said.

"To learning them right," Caleb said.

They sipped. The heat settled into their chests, not fixing anything and fixing something, anyway. Outside, the rain steadied. Inside, the house held.

After a while, Connor set his mug down and said, "Hey, Dad?"

"Yeah?"

"I'm proud of you," he said, eyes on the lamplight, as if he didn't trust himself to look directly at the person he meant. "For carrying the wait."

Caleb blinked once, twice, the way a man does when a light surprises him in a dark hallway. "Me too," he said, and knew Connor would hear what he meant: proud of you, for waiting too.

They didn't go hunting for a lesson to hang on the night. They let it be what it was—a letter placed back in its envelope, a ring remembered, a small mercy poured into two chipped mugs. Somewhere near the porch, water overflowed the lip of a gutter and fell in a bright thread, and the sound was simple, ongoing, enough.

CHAPTER SEVEN

The Camping Letter

The house held that just-after-supper quiet, the kind that made footsteps sound softer. A lamp glowed in the corner. The cedar box rested on the coffee table.

"You sure?" Connor asked from the doorway, hoodie half-zipped.

Caleb set the dish towel aside. "We don't have to."

"I want to," Connor said. "Just... maybe not a heavy one."

Caleb turned through the envelopes until one curved neatly forward. *The Camping Letter.* The paper smelled faintly of cedar and something older, like air that had remembered fall once and didn't want to let go.

Outside, rain began somewhere between a whisper and a thought. He sat, thumb tracing the ink.

"Pick it," Connor said.

"All right." Caleb took a breath that felt like it had corners and slid the envelope free.

The rain had slowed to a soft patter against the living room windows, the kind that whispered instead of fell. The lamp threw a low amber circle across the table. Connor sat cross-legged on the rug, steam from his mug curling toward the light.

Caleb smoothed the page and began to read.

You were gone only two nights, but the quiet at my parents' house stretched too far. Even the clock seemed to tick slower knowing there wasn't any way for the phone to ring.

You'd said the campground didn't have phones, and you were right. I still kept glancing at ours like I could pray it into ringing. The September air slipped through the trailer windows, cool and sweet, and the crickets outside sounded lonelier than usual. I sat on the couch under Nanny's crocheted throw and tried not to count the hours.

I wanted you to have your fun with Aunt Betty and Uncle Ed—fishing, the fire, the stars—but mercy, it was hard knowing the silence wasn't going to break. That was the part I didn't tell you when you got home. I wanted your memories to be joy, not my waiting.

Douglas Tailwater Campground. The overlook above the dam shined like hammered metal under a thin sun. The water stretched out in a broad sheet held still by concrete and will; below, the French Broad slipped away cold and quick, the tailwater shouldering past stone like it had somewhere to be.

Aunt Betty's chili simmered in a dented pot, steam rising in small white knots that came apart in the breeze. "Stir that, honey," she said, handing over the wooden spoon like a scepter. "If you scorch it, I'll say it was Ed's fault."

Uncle Ed was set up with his short-wave, fingers tapping the dial until a gospel station came clean through the static. A man's voice declared something about grace, then faded, then returned, almost like the river itself—there and then not, but always moving.

Caleb did what he was supposed to do. He stirred. He laughed in the right places. He held the flashlight for Uncle Ed while he tied a new line. But his mind ran ahead of him, back along the highway, through Sevierville and Kodak, through shadows of billboards and the ghost-glow of gas station lights, all the way to a single-wide trailer where a box fan sometimes rattled in the window and a girl he loved pressed her thumb into a fold of a blanket when she was trying not to worry.

He felt the ache of distance like an extra layer of clothing he couldn't take off. Every time he thought he'd gotten used to it, some small thing tugged at him—the way sap sweetened the air, the way the short-wave preacher said *home* and drew it out like a promise.

Evening sagged into night. They ate out of paper bowls balanced on their knees, saltines going soft from steam. Aunt Betty told the story about the time she'd burned biscuits and tried to pass them off as "country crackers." Uncle Ed pretended to cry. The river talked and talked, low and steady, a language made of breath.

When the fire went to coals and the tent zippers sang their soft song, Caleb waited a minute more. Then he eased out to the car. The cold found the gap between collar and neck. He sat in the passenger seat so the steering wheel wouldn't crowd his notebook and clicked on the flashlight, angling it against his knee. A weak cone of light opened over the paper.

The dash clock hummed that small electricity hum older cars make, steady as a heartbeat. Crickets stitched the dark. A single owl questioned the night and was answered by the river.

He wrote.

He told her how Aunt Betty laughed with her whole shoulders and how Uncle Ed talked to the radio like it could hear him. He told her the tailwater wasn't like ocean waves; it didn't throw itself down at the same place again and again to make a point—it kept on. He wrote her name and then wrote it again, because he liked the shape of it in his hand. He reminded her of the gas station after their first date, the windows fogging just a little, the blue forgiveness sky, and said he could still feel the warmth of her cheek under his hand if he closed his eyes. He wrote that the stars looked so close from that gravel pull-off that he felt like he could reach a finger up and smudge them. He said he tried to talk himself into enjoying the moment for what it was and not for what it wasn't, but the moment kept answering, *She isn't here.*

When his words ran out, he held them like a cup he didn't want to spill. He whispered, *God, keep her,* and then, *And keep me from hurrying my life so fast I miss what You're giving.* The prayer surprised him—it carried more patience than he felt.

He signed it: *Yours until the stars quit.* He kissed the corner because sometimes love needs a foolish signpost to know which way to go. Then he folded the pages and sat without moving, watching his breath show up and fade on the glass.

Your Aunt Betty told me later you were hopeless the whole weekend, Lauren wrote. She said she tried to make you fish, and you held the pole like a borrowed umbrella. Said you kept staring toward the road like it owed you a shortcut. She laughed telling me you drove home like you were chasing daylight. I believed her. I could feel the hurry in your handwriting before I even opened the envelope.

I read it on the old couch in our single-wide, window cracked to the night air, the box fan quiet so I wouldn't miss Daddy calling from the back room. The paper smelled like smoke and sap. I traced the groove where your pen pressed hardest and thought, "Love can travel without a phone."

I used to think love was loud—big songs and fireworks and some boy telling you something dramatic in a parking lot—but your letter taught me the holy kind of quiet. The kind where God sits with you and the clock ticks and you learn that waiting is also love.

I wanted to call you so bad it ached, and there wasn't a thing to dial. I remember folding my hands and feeling silly for it, like prayer was a phone with no cord, and then I felt that peace I get when I quit trying to manage what belongs to the Lord. He was there. I don't know how else to say it.

Caleb lifted his eyes from the page. The lamp hummed softly, and the rain tapped the window like a careful hand.

"You really sped all the way home?" Connor asked, voice angled halfway between a grin and a dare.

Caleb half-smiled. "Your Aunt Betty told on me, huh?"

"Sounds like her," Connor said, then paused, the smile thinning. "I didn't know her. I just know what you said."

"She'd have kept me honest," Caleb said. "You'd have liked her."

"I think I would have." Connor glanced toward the window. "Did you get pulled over?"

"Twice almost." Caleb's eyes warmed. "Mercy covered me."

"Mom would've said the same thing." Connor's mouth tugged. "She would've teased you and then prayed for the officer."

"She would've." The ache in Caleb's chest softened around the edges. "She prayed over everything."

"Keep going," Connor said. "Please."

Caleb nodded and returned to the letter.

I prayed after I read it, the letter went on. *I thanked God for a man who'd rather hurry home than learn how to have fun without me. Then I asked Him to teach us patience. We were young and wanted forever by Friday, but He knew the pace our hearts could stand.*

I kept the letter tucked in my Bible between Psalm 121 and 23. On nights when the quiet stretched too wide, I'd slide that page out and let the paper remind me: love returns. Love keeps. Love waits without sulking.

Do you remember the overlook above the dam? You wrote me that there was a bench with scratched initials and a gum wrapper that wouldn't blow away. I took my Bible up there a week later with the letter inside it and sat on a different bench and told God thank You again.

Later, when the cooler was packed, and the tent folded the wrong way twice and then the right way, they all piled into his car—Aunt Betty riding shotgun, Uncle Ed settling into the back seat with his hat tipped over his eyes. The car still smelled like smoke and hand lotion and last night's chili. Betty patted the dash. "Let's see if this old thing can outrun your heart," she said, laughing.

Caleb drove with both hands on the wheel and his heart leaning forward. Highway to highway, county to town, the needle climbed a little higher than it should have. Aunt Betty kept her eyes on the road ahead, still smiling. "You're driving like a man chasing daylight," she said. "Just don't get us pulled over."

"I'll try," he answered.

"Liar," she said, but there was no bite in it. "I know what hurry looks like when it's love."

Uncle Ed snored softly in the back, the brim of his hat dipping with every bump. Betty shook her head. "That man could sleep through Revelation," she said, and both of them laughed.

They wound through the hills, the French Broad slipping in and out of view beside them. Sunlight broke through the clouds in moving patches, lighting up the wet fields like pages being turned. By the time they reached town, the air had cooled and the scent of the river had followed them the whole way.

Caleb turned into the gravel drive a touch too fast, the pebbles whispering under the tires. He didn't honk. He didn't have to. The screen door opened like it had been waiting.

Aunt Betty was out first, straightening her blouse and waving as Lauren stepped onto the porch. Betty pulled her into a hug before anyone could say a word. "He was impossible," she told her, laughing. "Couldn't enjoy himself a lick."

Lauren smiled the kind of smile that rises slow and sure. "I know," she said, and when her eyes met Caleb's, nothing else needed saying.

I know you're going to argue with me about this someday, Lauren wrote, *but I think God has favorite sounds. I think He likes wood settling and children laughing and pages turning and the way footsteps sound when somebody you love is coming down the hall.*

Distance told me something true that weekend. It told me you weren't practicing how to be without me. You were practicing how to wait. There's a difference.

You wrote "Yours until the stars quit," and I believed you. To be safe, I'm writing it here where it can live as long as cedar does.

Yours until the stars quit,

Lauren

Caleb let the last words settle. The room didn't rush him. The rain thinned until it was almost just the air remembering how. In the lamp glow, the envelope's crease looked deeper than some of the others, a small valley time had pressed into it.

"She kept it in her Bible?" Connor asked.

"Mm-hmm. Between Psalm 121 and 23," Caleb said. "She said depending on the day, one of them knew what to do with her heart."

"Lift my eyes, or walk the valley," Connor said.

"Yeah."

Connor drew his sleeve over his fingers and set his mug down on the rug with the carefulness of someone setting down a thought. "I like Aunt Betty," he said after a moment.

Caleb's smile was soft. "Me too."

"I mean... I like that she laughed at you and blessed you at the same time."

"That was her way." He paused. "She died before you were born."

"I know." Connor's voice didn't wobble. "I still feel like I kind of know her."

"That means I told the stories right," Caleb said.

"Yeah." Connor considered the open box. "Sometimes when we read these, it hurts, and sometimes it... it helps the hurt find a place to sit down."

Caleb brushed a thumb over the envelope's edge. "That's what she was good at."

"Letting hurt sit down?"

"Giving it a chair and a blanket and a prayer," Caleb said.

Connor nodded. "Sounds like Mom."

"It does."

The unmarked envelope waited at the bottom the way it always did. The light found it but didn't insist. Caleb let his gaze rest there a second and then lifted it away.

"You think God smiled when you hurried home?" Connor asked.

Caleb looked toward the rain-polished window. "I hope so," he said. "He knows what it means to want to be with the ones you love."

"Then He probably smiled a lot," Connor said.

"Maybe He's smiling now," Caleb said.

They sat without fixing the cocoa. The heater clicked and breathed, warm air moving through the vents like a promise kept.

Caleb closed the envelope and slid it back into its place. His palm lingered on the cedar lid. "Thank You," he whispered.

Connor shifted closer until his shoulder touched the couch cushion against Caleb's knee. Caleb straightened the part in his hair the way muscle memory sometimes carries love when words don't know how.

They stayed like that a while longer. Outside, the mist lifted from the streetlight, and the dark looked rinsed. Somewhere above the clouds, the patient stars kept their place—*not quitting at all.*

CHAPTER EIGHT

Before the Bells

The evening had folded in soft around the house. A thin band of leftover daylight clung to the horizon outside the kitchen window, but inside everything felt settled and warm. The timer lamp on the counter threw a warm coin of light across the table, bright enough to make the cedar box shine and dim enough to let the rest of the room rest.

Connor padded in from the hallway in sock feet, hair still damp from a shower, the smell of cocoa faint in the air from earlier.

"You too wired to sleep yet?" he asked, leaning a shoulder against the doorframe.

Caleb closed the cabinet he'd been pretending to straighten. "Probably."

Connor's gaze dropped to the cedar box. "We could... do another letter. If you're up for it."

Caleb let his hand rest on the lid, palm curved over the worn grain. "Yeah," he said quietly. "I think I am."

Connor came to the table but didn't sit right away. He lingered behind the chair opposite Caleb, fingers drumming once like he was testing the air. "Feels like there's a chapter missing between camping and the actual wedding."

"There is," Caleb said. "She wrote it."

He eased into Lauren's old chair—the one that remembered bills and grocery lists and little notes folded beside lunchbox cookies. The wood gave a familiar creak under his weight. Connor sank into his seat across from him, folding one leg up under himself the way he did when he was trying to look relaxed and ready at the same time.

Caleb lifted the lid. Cedar breathed up, warm and faintly sweet, like old closets and hope. The envelopes shifted softly against each other. He thumbed through until her handwriting rose to meet him—tidy loops, steady lines.

Before the Bells.

He smiled without meaning to. "Of course she named it that."

Connor's mouth tugged at one corner. "Feels like a movie title."

"It kind of was," Caleb said. "At least to us."

He slid his thumb beneath the flap. The paper made that small, clean sound that always felt like opening a little door. The house seemed to lean in.

My love,

If I close my eyes, that whole morning is still there—like it's been waiting behind my eyelids for you to remember it with me. It didn't feel cinematic then. It felt like trying to get through a list and asking God to catch what I dropped.

I woke up before my alarm. The light in my old bedroom was gray and quiet. I heard my mother in the kitchen, cabinet doors, the soft clink of plates. Somewhere down the hall a radio murmured a country song, and the pipes groaned when somebody turned on the shower. I stared at the ceiling with my hands on my stomach like I could hold the butterflies still.

"This is the last morning I'll wake up in this room as just me," I thought. And right behind it came, "Thank You," because underneath the nerves was something very simple—you were on the other side of that day, and I wanted to get there.

Across town, you were in the barbershop chair. The shop smelled like talc and aftershave and clipper oil. A jar of blue combs sat on the counter like it had never been moved. The barber saw your suit and asked, "What's the occasion?"

"Getting married," you said. "Today?" he asked, and when you nodded he slapped the towel over your shoulders like he'd just joined the story. He asked if you were nervous. You told him, "A little," which I know meant "a lot." He trimmed the back of your neck carefully, as if he understood how much you wanted to look like the best version of yourself when I saw you at the end of the aisle. In the mirror your eyes gave you away—running through vows while he talked about being married thirty years and how the trick was to keep talking and not forget to listen. You said you'd try. You did more than try. You lived it.

By then I was at the beauty shop. It smelled like hairspray and hot metal and too much perfume. The dryer over my head sounded like rain on a tin roof. Women filled the air with talk—shoes that pinched, cousins who were late, whether the preacher would go on forever. My stylist, Marlene, pinned another curl and promised my hair would "behave for Jesus," and I laughed even though my throat felt tight.

She asked if I was scared. I told her I wasn't scared to marry you, just scared of tripping over the runner or my veil doing something dramatic at the wrong time. She said, "If he loves you, he'll love you with a crooked veil too." I tucked that away. Above the chatter and the dryer hum, I kept praying small prayers. "Keep us steady." "Get him there safe." "Help me walk without tripping over my own excitement."

Your parents came for you just before noon. Your dad drove—he always did on big days. Your mom rode beside him, hands wrapped around her pocketbook like she was keeping herself from flying apart. You sat in the back seat in your suit, knees nearly brushing the front because you'd outgrown her memory. She turned around twice to straighten your tie even though it was already straight. Your dad teased her — "He's not going to his first school dance, hon"—but his voice was proud. The car smelled like fabric softener and her breath mints.

On the way through town, storefronts slid by—the florist, the little diner with the wobbly sign, the gas station where the flags flapped lazy in almost-summer air. None of you really registered Covered Bridge Days. Maybe you'd seen a flyer. Maybe someone had mentioned "something at the bridge." But nobody was thinking about roads closing. You told me later the streets were surprisingly clear. It felt like an answer to a prayer you hadn't fully formed—no long red lights, no stalled cars, no wrong turns. Just your dad's hands steady on the wheel and the turn signal ticking toward the chapel.

I was outside the Magic Moments Wedding Chapel when your car rounded the corner. The building was simple—peach trim, white rails, teal ribbons tied to the railings, ends flicking in the breeze. It looked smaller than the brochure and bigger than anything I'd ever dreamed, all at once. My bouquet felt solid and right in my hands—white roses with just enough green to look like they'd lived somewhere before they met us.

I saw your car ease toward the curb. Through the windshield I saw you—fresh haircut, suit jacket not quite sure how to sit on your shoulders, your face caught between boy and man. My heart went wild. Tradition whispered that you shouldn't see me in my dress yet. My nerves shouted amen. I didn't want you to see me until I was walking toward you for real. I held my breath. Without hearing a word from me, you leaned forward and told your dad to drive around the block.

He didn't ask why. He just turned, giving me thirty seconds of mercy. I rushed inside in a blur of fabric and heartbeat. By the time you came back around, I was tucked behind the door, out of sight but closer than either of us realized.

Inside, the chapel smelled like carnations and furniture polish. The sanctuary was small and bright. Sun lay in soft blocks across the aisle runner. Peach bows marked the pews; teal glass beads lined the window sills, catching the light like tiny promises. The air felt like it had been waiting all morning.

The reception room behind the sanctuary was everything I love about small-town weddings—nothing matching perfectly, everything fitting anyway. A folding table wore a lace cloth that had seen more than one celebration. Peach streamers looped overhead. Your mom was lining up punch cups, your aunt was rearranging the mints ("They look better in a spiral"), my mom was smoothing the cloth like she could iron worry out of it, and one of my cousins kept sneaking glances at the cake.

Your mom had planned to bake our cake herself. Her cakes had been at every big moment. But her grandmother was in the hospital, and some days love can't be in two places. So she bought a beautiful tiered cake and rented the fountain you'd always said you wanted underneath. It felt like a compromise. It turned out to be a sermon.

She poured water into the base, added teal food coloring until it looked like a tiny pond, and plugged it in. For a breath, nothing. Then the pump sputtered awake. For about three seconds it was perfect—water bubbling gently, glowing under the cake plate.

Then it spat.

A bright arc of teal shot across the space between the fountain and your mother as if it had decided to paint. It hit the front of her dress first, then flecked the tablecloth and the wall. The room froze. Sugar and dye and that sharp, fizzy smell of panic rushed the air. Your aunt gasped. My aunt whispered, "Oh no, oh no." I just held my bouquet like it might throw me a lifeline.

You stepped into the doorway like you'd heard an alarm. Your eyes went wide for half a second, then softened the way they always do when you decide not to let something win. "It's okay," you said. "It's okay. We're fine." Someone shoved a towel into your hands. Someone else found club soda. Your mom blinked hard and made that tiny sound she made when she was trying not to cry.

You kneeled beside her and started blotting the teal splotches. "Mom, it's okay. I promise. It's just a dress. We're all here. That's what matters." Every new gasp in the room met the same answer: "We're okay." You kept saying it until it sounded less like you were trying to convince yourself and more like something that had already been decided.

The club soda did its work. The teal loosened its grip on fabric and lace, fading from disaster to almost gone. Someone used a hair dryer to warm the damp spots. Your mom stood there while three women fussed over her, and then she laughed. Shaky at first, then real. The unplugged fountain sat there looking harmless, like it hadn't just tried to baptize the whole reception.

I watched you and thought, This is what he does. He walks into messes and doesn't pretend they aren't messes, but he keeps his voice soft until everybody remembers how to breathe.

When the crisis was over and the fountain had been tested again—with someone hovering near the plug—you went straight for the cassette deck. I leaned against the doorframe and watched you test the music. Play. Stop. Rewind. Play. You checked the volume. You straightened the tapes. You weren't chasing perfection. You were offering care. There's a difference. I loved you for knowing it without knowing you knew it.

Guests began to arrive—uncles in stiff suits, cousins in shoes they regretted, kids tugging at collars and asking when they could eat. The sanctuary filled with the shuffle of people, the low hum of voices, the creak of pews. The air-conditioning kicked on and off, sending little currents down the aisle and making the ribbons dance.

Your dad found you near the front and laid his hand on your shoulder. Your shoulders dropped just enough for me to see it, the way they do when "just me" turns into "us." That's what fathers are supposed to do. It's what you've done for our boys more times than you realize.

Then someone asked, "Where's the preacher?"

The question slipped through the room like a draft. Heads turned toward the door. Your sister went outside to check the lot and came back with that look that meant she didn't have an answer yet. You started pacing a short path near the front. I heard scraps of whispers. "He'll be here." "They always cut it close." "We can't start without him."

You pulled your old flip phone from your pocket and stepped into the hallway to call. I couldn't hear his words, but I saw them in the lines of your back. "Hey, just checking where you are," you said. "Covered Bridge Days? Okay. We're here. Just get here when you can. We'll wait." Your voice stayed gentle, but I knew your heart was pounding.

When you came back, you told everyone the truth—he was stuck in traffic because of the celebration at the covered bridge, roads blocked, detours everywhere. You smiled that smile you use when you're trying to be the calm you wish someone could hand back to you. "He's coming," you said. "He's just caught up for a bit."

For about ten minutes, we lived in that in between place. The sanctuary sat full of family and friends under peach bows and teal beads, most of them unaware how close we were to not having a minister at all. Our parents stood near the door. Your aunt straightened the stack of programs again. The flower girl practiced tiny steps with her basket because she could feel something important in the air and didn't know what to do with her hands.

Then somebody said, "He's here," and the whole building seemed to exhale. The minister came in with his collar a little crooked and his cheeks flushed from hurrying. "Traffic was terrible," he said. "They've got the whole town rerouted. I thought I was going to have to hitch a ride on a parade float. But the Lord cleared a lane right at the end."

You laughed—not because it was clever, but because it was true. God hadn't just cleared the way for him. He'd done it earlier too—before anyone knew the roads would change, before the stain had time to settle. He'd been quietly making room where there shouldn't have been any.

After that, everything tucked itself in. People took their seats. The minister straightened his collar and opened his little black book. Our mothers gave each other that look women share when they've survived the warm-up. The flower girl checked her petals. The room settled around the idea that this was really happening now.

I went to stand behind the closed sanctuary door, bouquet in both hands, heart beating its own uneven rhythm. For the first time all day, I was truly alone. The sounds on the other side went soft and blurry, like the world had moved one room over. It was just me and God and the knowledge that when the music started, everything would tilt toward forever.

I thought about you in that barber chair, telling a stranger you were getting married. I thought about you checking the tapes, the way you always double-check what matters. I thought of Duck Island and a paper Mickey, phone calls that ran from dusk to dawn, your voice over the radio asking if I would be your wife. I thought of Nanny's blessing on the Fourth of July when fireworks wrote "amen" across the sky. I thought of teal water fading from a dress like a stain that didn't get the last word, and your voice in the hallway saying, "We'll wait."

I breathed in and prayed one last line—not a list, not a speech. Just: "Please stand in the spaces we can't fill."

The cassette deck clicked. The tape began to move. The opening chords wobbled just a bit, human, and imperfect, and somehow that felt right. We weren't walking into a flawless scene. We were walking into a real one. Ours.

It was time.

—Lauren

Caleb let the last words settle in the quiet. The kitchen felt different—not bigger or smaller, just fuller, like the room had been holding its breath and finally let it go.

Connor sat forward, forearms on the table, fingers laced. "She really remembered all that?" he asked softly.

"Every bit of it," Caleb said. "Probably more than she wrote."

Connor huffed a small breath. "I kind of love that she was more worried about tripping over the runner than about marrying you."

"That sounds like her." Caleb smiled. "She never doubted us. Just her own feet."

Outside, headlights slid past and were gone. Somewhere down the hall, warm air moved through the vents as the house settled.

"The part with Grandma… and the fountain," Connor said. "I can see it. Her trying not to cry. You telling her it was okay."

Caleb swallowed around the ache that rose, slow and familiar. "I was terrified it would ruin the day for her," he admitted. "For your mom, too. I wanted everything perfect."

He tapped the letter lightly. "She's right, though. It wasn't about perfect. It was about showing up when it wasn't."

"And you called the preacher." Connor looked up. "I never heard that part. Just the joke about him being late because of the parade."

"Yeah." Caleb let out a breath. "There's a world where he turns around. Where we don't get married that day. But that's not the world we got." A small smile tugged at his mouth. "God made a way—then made another."

Connor stared at the box, then back at his dad. "Do you ever... read these and get mad?" he asked quietly. "Like... why did God clear lanes back then and not... later?"

The question hung between them, honest and heavy.

Caleb didn't look away. "Sometimes," he said. "I've had that thought more than once." His fingers rested on the envelope's edge. "But I also read this and feel... grateful. He didn't have to give us any of it. The fountain. The parade. The vows. You boys. The years. None of that was owed. It was all gift." He paused. "Doesn't make losing her hurt less. But it makes the love feel bigger than what the hurt can erase."

Connor nodded slowly, eyes bright. "She really was funny," he said, clearing his throat. "I like how she tells it. Even the disasters sound like stories, not... reasons to give up."

"That was her," Caleb said. "She could find grace in a broken fountain."

He folded the letter along its old crease with careful hands and slipped it back into its envelope, laying it on top of the small stack of read ones.

The unmarked, heavier envelope at the bottom of the box caught a thin sliver of light and gave nothing back. Connor's hand drifted toward it and stopped, like he'd touched heat.

"Not yet," he murmured.

"Not yet," Caleb echoed. "We've still got some steps before that one."

He closed the cedar lid. The hinge gave that soft wooden sigh he'd come to think of as the box's quiet amen.

"Cocoa?" he asked.

Connor rubbed his hand over his face and nodded. "Yeah. I could drink another."

They moved around the kitchen in an easy, wordless choreography. Caleb set the pot on the burner and poured milk while Connor lined two mugs on the counter. The whisk rasped against the side as cocoa dissolved, steam rising in soft curls that caught the lamplight.

"Peach and teal," Connor said suddenly, half-smiling. "Kind of a weird combo."

Caleb chuckled. "Yeah. I thought so at first, too."

"But it worked?"

"It did," Caleb said. "Because she chose it. Once she picked something, it just... fit." He shrugged. "Same with me. I wasn't exactly the obvious choice either."

Connor's smile deepened. "I don't know. Sounds like you did pretty good for a barbershop groom."

Caleb slid a mug toward him. "I did better than I deserved," he said. "In a lot of ways."

They carried their cocoa back to the table and sat where they'd been before. For a little while they just drank and listened—to the vents, to a distant car at the intersection, to the small sounds a house makes when it's done with its day.

Caleb glanced toward the cedar box, then up at the window where their reflections hovered faint and double—him and his son, past, and future, grief and something gentler growing around it.

"Thank You," he said quietly.

He didn't say it to the box or the letters. He said it toward the space where memory and presence blur, where he still believed God was big enough to hold both the day of the teal fountain and this quiet night in the kitchen.

Connor didn't ask who he meant. He just nodded once, as if he'd heard it too.

Later, when the mugs were rinsed, and the lamp switched off, the kitchen slipped back into shadow. The outline of the cedar box was just visible on the table, a dark, patient shape against the faint glow from the hallway.

The house held what it could.

The Wedding That Almost Wasn't

The house had gone back to its usual sounds—the soft tick of the hallway clock, the occasional sigh of the heater—but Caleb could still feel last night pressed into the walls.

The cedar box waited on the table where he'd left it, its outline just visible in the late afternoon light that slipped through the kitchen blinds. Outside, the sky was sliding toward evening again, a pale wash of color fading behind the bare trees.

Connor came in from the hallway, socks whispering against the floor. His hair was damp from a shower, a faint trace of soap clinging to the surrounding air. He glanced at the box, then at his dad, then away again.

"You thinking about another one?" he asked.

Caleb had been. He nodded. "If you are."

Connor shrugged, the motion smaller than usual. "I mean... we kind of stopped right before the big part."

"The big part," Caleb echoed. "Yeah. We did."

They stood there for a breath, neither moving toward the box nor leaving the room. The house felt like it was listening.

"You want cocoa first?" Caleb asked.

Connor's mouth tugged up just a little. "You just want an excuse to stall."

"Possibly," Caleb said. "You still want some?"

"Yeah," Connor admitted. "I do."

They moved around each other in familiar patterns—Caleb reaching for the pot and the cocoa mix, Connor getting milk from the fridge and setting two mugs on the counter. The whisk made a soft scraping sound as Caleb stirred. Steam curled up in slow ribbons, catching the light from the small lamp on the counter.

"Was she always that detailed?" Connor asked, leaning on his elbows while the milk warmed. "Like... remembering every little thing?"

"Your mom?" Caleb smiled faintly. "She could tell you what color shirt you were wearing on your first day of second grade. And who was standing beside you."

"Seriously?"

"Seriously," he said. "She remembered everything she loved."

Connor went quiet at that, eyes drifting back toward the cedar box.

When the cocoa was ready, they carried their mugs to the table and sat. The wood felt cool under Caleb's forearms. He set his cup down and let his hand rest beside the box, fingers barely touching the edge.

"Do you want to pick it?" he asked.

Connor's gaze flicked to his. There was a flash of fifteen-year-old defiance there—you're the one who should be deciding—but it softened almost immediately. "We both know which one it is," he said. "We might as well stop pretending it's a surprise."

Caleb exhaled slowly. "Yeah."

He lifted the lid. The familiar cedar scent rose up, warm and faintly sweet, and underneath it something older, like the inside of a drawer that hadn't been opened in years. The stack of envelopes lay neatly where they'd left them, titles in Lauren's handwriting slanting gently across each one.

His fingers hovered, tracing the words without quite touching.

The Call That Changed Everything.

The Letters and the Box.

When We First Met.

Others they'd already read, each now with its own weight.

Near the middle, an envelope waited with a title that still made his chest feel too small.

The Wedding That Almost Wasn't.

Connor's eyes fixed on it. "That one," he said quietly.

Caleb eased it free. The heavier, unmarked envelope at the bottom of the box shifted just enough to catch the lamplight, its edge glinting like the rim of a sealed secret. Connor noticed. His jaw tightened.

"Later," he said.

"Later," Caleb agreed.

He set the unmarked envelope flat again, then closed the lid and slid the box to one side, so only the wedding letter remained between them. The paper had yellowed just slightly at the edges, time brushing its fingers across the fibers.

"You sure?" Caleb asked.

"Yeah." Connor's voice had that brittle steadiness to it, the one that meant he'd already decided and was just waiting for the rest of him to catch up. "I... I want to know how she tells it."

Caleb nodded. "Okay."

He opened the envelope with careful hands and unfolded the pages. Lauren's handwriting ran in its familiar slope, neat but slightly more hurried in places, as if emotion had tugged at the pen.

He cleared his throat once, more to loosen the tightness in his chest than to get her words out, and began to read.

Dear Caleb,

I've already told you how the tape wobbled and how I almost tripped over the runner. I told you about standing behind that sanctuary door, just me and God and the knowing that everything was about to tilt. I told you how I prayed: "Please stand in the spaces we can't fill."

This is what happened when the door opened.

They didn't swing wide and dramatic—not like in the movies. The coordinator just eased one side open, gentle and practical, and suddenly I could see a slice of aisle and the end of your shoe.

The music was a tiny bit too loud. The air in the hallway felt at least five degrees hotter than the rest of the church. I remember thinking that if I started sweating through my dress, I was going to haunt somebody.

"Ready?" the coordinator whispered.

No, I thought. Yes, I thought. I don't know, I don't know, I don't know.

But I nodded anyway, because you were on the other end of that aisle and we both knew God had cleared more than one lane to get us there.

When I stepped forward, the sanctuary light felt different from the hallway—softer, cooler, like the room had been holding its breath. People turned toward me, a sea of faces, some blurred by nerves and some sharp as photographs. I saw your mom first—eyes shining, hands already halfway up to her mouth. I saw my mother, too, her posture straight as a ruler, jaw set like she was determined not to cry, no matter what anyone expected of her. I saw empty spots where other people had sworn they'd sit. I felt those gaps like missing puzzle pieces, even with all the chairs that were full.

And then I saw you.

That was the part that stilled everything. You in that tux you thought looked wrong on you. (It didn't.) You standing there with this expression that was half terror, half awe, and somehow absolutely certain all at once. You looked like you'd just been handed the whole world and were still trying to figure out the right way to hold it.

My knees stopped wobbling.

I walked down the aisle, one careful step at a time, bouquet trembling just enough to make the ribbon shake. The tape crackled once as it moved to the next measure. Somewhere behind me, a shoe squeaked on the tile. The flowers in my hands smelled like every wedding cliché, and I loved them for it. They made me feel like I belonged in the story we were stepping into.

You smiled at me in that way you do when you're trying not to cry. Your mouth lifts, but your eyes do the heavy lifting. I thought: That's the face I want to see for the rest of my life. However long that is.

When I reached you, you took my hand and didn't let go. Your fingers were a little cold. Mine were too. They warmed up together.

The minister started talking. I know he did, because people laughed at the right places and nodded at the right places. I heard words like "covenant" and "promise" and "in sickness and in health," and they wrapped themselves around us like a quilt your Nanny might have sewn—stitched with a thousand small, faithful pieces. But if you asked me to quote him exactly, I couldn't. My brain had decided to record you instead.

You kept rubbing your thumb over my knuckles, small circles like you were memorizing my skin. Every time my eyes tried to dart to the side—to count who was there and who was missing—they came back to you.

Then came the roses.

We hadn't practiced that part. We'd talked about it, sure. We'd picked out the flowers and told each other how meaningful it would be to honor our mothers, to say thank you for bringing us this far. I think in my head I'd pictured it as this easy, tearful, Hallmark-commercial moment. Roses, hugs, everyone dabbing their eyes in the soft lighting.

Reality had other plans.

They handed us two roses each, pale pink with a blush at the edges. Mine shook just enough to make the petals whisper. We stepped down from the altar together—your shoulder brushing mine, both of us breathing a little too fast—and turned toward the front pews.

We split in the aisle. You veered toward your mom; I turned toward my mother.

Your mom's face opened the second she saw you. There's no other word for it. It was like someone had taken all the curtains in that room and thrown them wide. Her hands were already reaching out before you even got there. When you held the rose out to her, her fingers closed around it gently, like it was something holy. She pulled you into a hug that looked like it had been waiting your whole life to land. I heard her whisper, "I'm so proud of you," even over the music.

I could almost feel the warmth of it from across the room.

Then I looked at my mother.

She was composed. She is always composed. Her spine straight, shoulders back, chin lifted just so. When I stepped in front of her, rose in hand, her eyes flicked down to it and back up to my face. There was a small tightness around her mouth that I knew meant she was trying not to show too much of anything.

I held the rose out. She took it, but her fingers brushed mine only briefly. Her grip was precise, careful, like she was afraid of bruising the petals—or of someone seeing her soften.

When I leaned in to hug her, her arms came up, but only just. There was space between our bodies. Her shoulders stayed rigid. Her hands patted my back in two exact motions, the way you might pat a child who's fallen and needs to be told they're fine.

You know how sometimes a hug feels like a door opening? This one felt like knocking on a door that stays mostly shut.

I pulled back with my smile in the right place, because that's what we do. But there was a small ache under my ribs that I couldn't name yet.

Then we switched.

You went to her with your second rose. I went to your mom with mine.

Watching you hand a rose to my mother made my stomach knot. You were trying so hard to honor her, to love who I loved, even when she didn't always make it easy. You held that rose out just as gently as you had with your own mom. She took it. Her lips pressed into something like a smile, but it didn't reach her eyes. The hug she gave you was even stiffer than mine. Your hands stayed awkwardly at your sides, like you weren't sure where you were allowed to put them.

I wanted, very suddenly, to shield you. From that coolness. From that distance.

And then I turned to your mom.

She took the rose like it was the most natural thing in the world, eyes shining, fingers soft against mine. Before I could say anything, she wrapped me in a hug that was full and certain and completely without performance. No calculation. No measuring. Just arms around me, solid and warm, like a second home I hadn't known I'd been missing.

"Thank you for loving him," she whispered in my ear. "We're so glad you're ours."

I believed her. It went all the way in.

If the ceremony was a vow written aloud, that moment with our mothers felt like another vow written quietly under it—one of them saying, I will keep trying to control how you live this, and one of them saying, I will stand beside you whenever you ask. I didn't understand all of that yet. But Heaven did. I think God tucked it away in the margins for us to find later.

We went back to the altar with our hands a little steadier. The rest of the ceremony moved in pieces, like beads on a string.

Your voice shaking when you promised to love me "as long as we both shall live."

My throat tightening when I tried to repeat the same words back.

The tiny click of the ring as it slid over my knuckle.

The way your eyelashes flickered when I slid yours into place, like you were blinking back a whole lost childhood that had told you that you didn't deserve this.

Somewhere in the second row, someone sniffled. Somewhere behind them, someone laughed softly when your ring got stuck for half a second and you made that little face you make when you're trying not to panic.

And all the while, in the back of my mind, I could feel the empty chairs. The uncle who had demanded an invitation and never showed. The ones who later told people they'd been there and that you'd worn jeans and a t-shirt, as if rewriting the story would cost them nothing. It stung, in the way absence always does. But when I looked at you—at the earnest, shaking way you held my hands—it didn't feel like the missing people got the last word, either.

The minister lifted his hands. His voice sounded clearer in that moment, as if someone had turned the world's volume down everywhere else.

"By the authority given to me," he said, "I now pronounce you husband and wife."

The words hit like a bell.

I felt them in my bones, in my breath, in every bruise the past had ever left on you. It was like God stamped something over all the pages behind us: Mine. Mine. Mine.

"You may kiss the bride."

You leaned in, careful and reverent, your hands hovering at my waist like you were still asking for permission even now. I answered by closing the distance. Our first kiss as husband and wife wasn't some dramatic dip or cinematic swoop. It was simple and warm and a little shaky, a soft press of mouths that tasted like all-nighters and gas station crackers and forgiveness and the exact color of sky we argued about that first night.

When we pulled back, our foreheads rested together, and you whispered, "We made it."

I whispered back, "We did."

The room exhaled around us—applause, laughter, a rustle of fabric, your mom's unashamed crying, my mother's quiet, restrained clapping. Somewhere outside, the muffled sound of the rubber duck festival drifted in—a loudspeaker calling numbers, children shouting near the covered bridge where plastic ducks crowded a man-made river. Roads closed. Fountains stained. People missed their cues and their invitations. But we were there. You and me and God and the vows we'd just spoken.

We walked back up the aisle with rice in our hair and too many cameras pointed at us. You kept my hand in yours the whole time, like you were afraid someone might try to argue with what had just been declared.

They didn't get a vote.

Later, after the pictures and the reception and the awkwardness and the laughter and the way your mom and aunt packed plates because we never sat long enough to eat, I sat down to write this, wanting you to know how I saw it. How I saw you. How I saw us, right there in the middle of a day that was never perfect but somehow still holy.

God must've smiled that day—He let us forget perfection long enough to remember love. May He keep smiling on us when the roads close, when the ducks crowd the river, when the fountain stains and the seats are empty, and when all the chairs are full and we don't know what to do with such goodness. May He be the air the door lets in every time we turn toward each other.

Your wife (I love writing that),

Lauren

Caleb read the last lines slower, like he was afraid they might slip away if he moved too fast. When his voice fell silent, the kitchen felt as full as the little chapel must have—air thick with something that wasn't quite sorrow and wasn't quite joy, but some third thing that held both without dropping either.

Connor had gone very still.

He stared at the table, jaw set, eyes bright in a way that told on him even when he blinked. His hands were clasped in front of him, thumbs pressed together hard enough to blanch the skin.

"She really... she really wrote about Grandma like that," he said finally, voice quiet.

Caleb nodded. "She did."

"The hug thing." Connor swallowed. "With her. And with Nana."

"Yeah."

"I mean, I knew." He shrugged one shoulder, a small, helpless motion. "I always kind of felt it. How different they were. But hearing Mom say it... it's like... it makes it more real. Not just in my head."

Caleb let his fingers rest on the edge of the letter, not quite folding it yet. "She wanted you to know how it felt. Not to hurt anybody. Just... so the story was honest."

Connor nodded once. "Nana really said that? About being glad Mom loved you? And being glad she was theirs?"

"She did," Caleb said. His throat pulled tight around the memory. "And she meant every word."

Connor blinked hard and looked away toward the window. Outside, a car passed, headlights dragging a brief strip of light across the wall. The heat clicked on again, air whispering softly through the vent.

"And Grandma," Connor said, "would've been more like... 'you should've done this' or 'why didn't you do that'?"

Caleb hesitated, then decided he owed his son the same honesty Lauren had. "She... loved your mom the way she knew how," he said slowly. "But a lot of the time, yeah. It came out as control more than comfort. Advice even when no one asked for it. Expectations without much room to breathe."

Connor's mouth tipped down. "That tracks."

"The roses just... showed it early," Caleb added. "In a way we didn't fully understand yet."

They sat with that for a moment. Neither rushed to fill the silence. It had weight, but not the crushing kind. More like a blanket laid gently over something tender.

"What about the uncle?" Connor asked, blinking back to the page. "The one who told people you wore jeans?"

Caleb huffed out a small, humorless laugh. "Yeah. That was a whole thing."

"He really wasn't there?"

"Nope." Caleb shook his head. "Never saw him. But later he told one of my uncles in Florida he'd been at the wedding, said I got married in jeans and a t-shirt. Your mom found that hilarious. She said it proved some people would rather rewrite the story than admit they didn't show up."

Connor snorted softly. "She's not wrong."

"She usually wasn't," Caleb said.

For a moment, a half-smile tugged at Connor's mouth. Then it slipped, replaced by something more fragile.

"You and Mom," he said slowly, "you really believed... God was in it. Back then."

"We did," Caleb answered. "We saw Him all over it. In the timing. In the near-misses. In the people who did show up, even when others didn't. In the way your mom felt like home the first time she stepped into my mama's arms."

"Do you still?" Connor asked. "Believe He was in it?"

Caleb thought about the chapel's soft light, the rose exchange, the cheap cassette tape wobbling into the right song at the right time. He thought about Lauren's handwriting on the page in front of him. He thought about the years that followed—the wreck, the fire, the hospital rooms, the way love had stubbornly kept showing up, anyway.

"Yeah," he said quietly. "I do."

Connor pressed his lips together. "Even with how it ended?"

"It didn't end," Caleb said, surprising himself with how quickly the words came. "Not really. Not if what we believed together is true. It changed. It... shifted rooms. But this?" He tapped the letter gently. "This is still part of it. You reading this with me is still part of it. She's not here, but somehow she's still... in the spaces between us."

Connor's eyes shone again. He looked away, wiping at his cheek with the heel of his hand like maybe it was just an itch. "That sounds like something she'd write."

"It's probably stolen from her, yeah," Caleb said softly.

They both laughed once, a thin, shared sound that eased some of the tightness in the air.

Caleb folded the letter along its crease, fingers smoothing the paper with a reverence that felt a little like prayer. He slid it back into its envelope and laid it on top of the others they'd already read.

The unmarked envelope at the bottom of the box sat completely still. It didn't glow or hum or insist. It just waited, heavier than the rest.

Connor's gaze flicked to it again, then quickly away.

"We're not there yet," Caleb said.

"I know." Connor took a breath. "I don't... I don't want to skip this stuff. Like... the beginning. The wedding. The good parts." His voice wobbled once. "Feels like if we jump to the end, I'll miss who she was when everything wasn't... falling apart."

Caleb's chest ached, but there was a strange kind of relief in it. "That's exactly why we're doing it this way," he said. "One piece at a time. So we don't lose her to just one part of the story."

Connor nodded. "Okay."

Caleb closed the box gently. The soft wooden sigh of the hinge sounded again—less like an ending this time and more like a pause.

"Want to go sit in the living room?" he asked. "Let the house cool off from all this holy ground talk?"

Connor half-smiled. "Yeah. Maybe put something stupid on the TV."

"Stupid I can handle," Caleb said.

They carried their empty mugs to the sink, the clink of ceramic mingling with the ordinary noises of the evening. As they walked past the table, Caleb glanced back once at the box, at the letters, at the space they'd opened up and the space they were still afraid to touch.

"Thank You," he breathed again, almost under his breath.

He didn't specify for what—the wedding, the years, the chance to read it all aloud with his son. All of it ran together, anyway.

Connor didn't ask. He just bumped his shoulder lightly against his dad's as they stepped into the dim glow of the living room, and for now, that was answer enough.

The house remembered. And tonight, it felt like it was remembering with them.

CHAPTER TEN

The Road to Cosby

The evening air through the cracked kitchen window felt softer than it had in months—cool, but not cold, carrying that early spring smell of damp earth and something waking up. A few frogs had started their nightly chorus down near the drainage ditch by the road, their uneven chirping filling the quiet like a reminder that seasons really do change, even when it feels like nothing else does.

Connor stood at the counter, tapping the edge of his root beer bottle against his palm in a restless rhythm that matched the frogs outside. His hair was still damp from a shower, sticking up in places he hadn't bothered to tame. Caleb poured the last of the sweet tea into his own glass, the ice melting fast enough to clink softly.

"You good tonight?" Caleb asked.

Connor shrugged—less defensive than uncertain. "Yeah. Just... thinking, I guess."

"Thinking's allowed."

Connor huffed a small laugh and drifted toward the table where the cedar box rested.

Tonight it didn't feel heavy. Winter had made it seem like something solemn, like the room leaned toward grief whenever they opened it. But in the gentler spring light, the box looked almost calm—warm grain glowing under the lamp, the metal clasp catching a thin stripe of light from the window.

Connor brushed his thumb along the lid. "It doesn't feel as... scary as it did before," he said quietly.

"No," Caleb answered. "It doesn't."

"Still feels like a lot, though."

"It is a lot."

Caleb pulled out his chair and sat. When he lifted the lid, the cedar scent drifted up—soft, clean, a little sweet. The opened letters they'd already read sat on the small bookshelf nearby, edges a little loosened from use. Inside the box, the remaining envelopes waited in their careful stack, corners faintly softened from being handled.

Connor leaned in. "Which one's next?"

Caleb looked through the stack until his fingers found it—an envelope tucked near the top, its title simple and steady.

The Road to Cosby.

"This is the honeymoon one, right?" Connor asked.

"Yeah," Caleb said. "The drive after the wedding."

Connor's foot tapped lightly against the chair rung—his tell when he was bracing for something. "Let's do it."

"You sure?"

"Yeah," Connor said, quieter this time. "I kind of want to know what happened after... all that. What it felt like."

Something in Caleb warmed at that—the wanting to understand the love that had shaped his life.

"All right."

He slid the letter free, the paper making a faint, familiar crackle as it opened. Connor settled into his chair, bottle resting between both hands.

Caleb took a slow breath and began to read.

I didn't know the world could feel so full and so light at the same time.

We were still standing on the chapel stage when the photographer told us to hold still for "just a few more," but I could feel it in my bones—we were already on the other side of everything. The vows, the nerves, the teal fountain disaster... all of it behind us. You kept squeezing my hand like you were making sure I was real.

Somewhere in the middle of those last pictures, Daddy slipped something into your hand. I saw the way your eyebrows jumped, just a little. He must have said something funny, because your mouth twitched like you were trying not to laugh. I knew that look. Daddy never could resist a joke when he was emotional.

Later the photographer showed us the proof sheets, and there it was: Daddy handing you a folded bill, you looking stunned, me half-hiding behind my bouquet. Fifty dollars. That picture made me laugh every single year. I still hear you saying, "Your fifty's due again," and the way Daddy would roll his eyes like you were the biggest burden he'd ever taken on—even though he adored you.

Part of me wonders if he ever knew how grateful I was for that moment. He cried so many times that day. Sometimes a joke is the only way a father can say, "I trust you."

After the pictures, people began to gather near the front pews, and the air changed into something softer. Your mom hugged you first—full arms, full heart, nothing held back. Then she hugged me, warm and real, like she'd already claimed me. I don't think she knew how much I needed that. I'd always felt like a guest in the world, but she held me like a daughter.

My mother came next, all poise and careful posture. Her hugs were always polite—performed more than felt—but she tried. I'll give her that. She held my arms and said she was happy for me, and I knew she meant it in her own way, even if she never knew how to loosen her shoulders.

Your aunt cried and laughed at the same time, pressing both our hands like she was sending us out with a blessing tucked between our palms. My aunt followed, teary and fluttering, smoothing my hair like she used to when I was little.

Daddy hugged me last. I felt his breath tremble, and then he stepped back and wiped his eyes with the heel of his hand, pretending he was done crying for the day. He wasn't.

Somewhere behind us, your niece had wandered toward the little upright piano near the front pews, still in her flower girl dress. She began pressing single keys with one finger, each note bright and sweet and just slightly out of place. People smiled, whispering soft laughs. You squeezed my hand again. It was such a small moment, but it felt like a blessing—joy showing up right in the middle of all the formality.

We changed in that little side room—me slipping out of my dress, you out of your tux—and suddenly we looked like ourselves again. Jeans, t-shirts, sneakers. Husband and wife, not bride and groom.

"Much better," you said, and it was.

When we opened the chapel doors, the world exploded.

Birdseed flew in every direction, raining down on us like a tiny storm. People cheered, clapped, shouted our names. Kids dumped handfuls right over our heads. There was no running from it—we just laughed and let ourselves get covered.

I remember brushing seed out of my hair, only to find more. You kept picking it off your shirt and muttering, "It's everywhere," and I couldn't stop laughing.

And then we saw the car.

Oh my goodness. Condoms. Everywhere. Hanging from the antenna, tied to the mirrors, wrapped around the gearshift, taped to the dash. Someone had gone overboard in the most ridiculous, affectionate way possible. I bent over laughing, and you put your hands on your knees like you needed to steady yourself.

"Everywhere we touched," I said, "there was one."

You just nodded like a man who had accepted defeat.

People were doubled over. My cousins were proud of themselves, wiping tears from laughing so hard as we tried to get into the car without touching anything. They hadn't just taped things on—they'd opened every single condom and stretched them over the mirrors, the gearshift, the door handles, and even the blinker switch. Someone shouted, "Y'all have fun now!" and I thought you might actually dissolve into the pavement from embarrassment. I laughed until my ribs hurt.

We made it a couple of miles down the road before hunger reminded us we hadn't eaten anything but a bite of cake. You pulled into the burger place, and the girl at the drive-thru window didn't even try to hide her grin. The car was covered in condoms, "Just Married" written across the window, birdseed still clinging to my hair.

"Congratulations," she said, and I hid my face in my hands while you tried to act like this was perfectly normal.

We ate in the parking lot, laughing every time someone walked by and did a double-take. The fries were way too salty for me, but somehow still perfect because I was eating them with you. That was the moment I remember thinking, If this is marriage, I'm going to like it.

Gatlinburg was glowing by the time we got there—storefront lights catching the windshield, people strolling with that relaxed, vacation pace. We stopped at the grocery store to get breakfast for the cabin.

As we drove across the lot, a teenage boy pushing a line of buggies stopped dead in his tracks when he saw our car. He just stared, shook his head slowly like an old man saying, "Well, you've done it now," and then started laughing.

I grabbed your arm. "He didn't even say anything!"

"He didn't have to," you said.

Inside we grabbed eggs, bacon, cereal, milk, snacks, and a few things we didn't need but pretended we did. Every few steps you brushed more birdseed off my shirt, and every time you did, more fell out.

I think that's when it hit me we were really married—walking through a grocery store in Gatlinburg with birdseed in our hair and people smiling at us like we were something bright they hadn't expected to see.

Then came the moment that nearly killed me.

We pulled out of the parking lot with the windows down because it was warm, and the radio jumped to life with a loud, unmistakable beat:

Whoomp! There it is!

You started singing immediately—loud, joyful, like the steering wheel was part of the percussion. I was busy watching you have the time of your life.

And just as you yelled the chorus—

"Whoomp! There it is!"

—a woman with a very large backside leaned out of a van window.

At the exact same second.

She jerked around, eyes wide, her face twisting like you had personally insulted her existence.

You froze.

She froze.

I died.

I laughed so hard I slid down in my seat and hit my head on the glove compartment.

"I was singing the song!" you said, horrified.

"She thinks you meant her!" I wheezed, crying real tears.

She kept staring like she was going to chase us down, and you sped up just a little, purely for survival.

I thought I might stop breathing from laughing so hard.

The farther we drove, the quieter things became. The road stretched out, the town lights falling away behind us. The mountains rose like dark shapes against a softer sky, and the air through the cracked windows cooled as we climbed higher.

We didn't talk much—not because we had nothing to say, but because peace had a way of filling the spaces all on its own. Birdseed still fell out of our clothes every time one of us shifted, tapping softly against the floorboards.

Your hand found mine on the console.

That was enough.

When the cabin finally came into view—gold porch light glowing, wood dark against the trees—it felt like stepping into the first page of the rest of our lives. The gravel crunched under the tires, and the woods leaned in close, like the mountains were promising to hold us for the night.

I stepped out of the car, brushed the last bit of birdseed off my shirt, and whispered, "Thank You."

You echoed it a second later.

Not to each other.

To God, I think.

Or maybe to the moment. Or maybe to every thread of grace that had brought us there.

Maybe all of it.

It was the sweetest road I've ever traveled.

Caleb folded the letter slowly, pressing the crease the way he always did, then slid it into the growing stack of read letters on the bookshelf. The kitchen was quiet except for the faint chorus of frogs outside and the soft clink of Connor setting his empty root beer bottle down.

Connor rubbed the back of his neck, eyes a little glassy from laughing earlier. "I didn't know you all... laughed that much," he said.

Caleb smiled. "We did."

"It sounds like..." Connor searched for the word. "Like you were happy."

"We were."

Connor nodded, absorbing it. "It's good to know."

Caleb reached for his sweet tea, the ice long melted. "You okay?"

"Yeah." Connor exhaled. "I like hearing this stuff. It helps. Makes her feel... closer."

"It does that," Caleb said gently.

He closed the cedar box, letting the clasp fall into place with a soft click. No heaviness tonight. No winter weight. Just memory and warmth settling into the room.

"Come on," Caleb said, standing. "Let's call it a night."

They left the kitchen lights off behind them, walking toward the living room where the spring air moved softly through the cracked window—cool, gentle, and full of something that felt one step shy of hope.

CHAPTER ELEVEN

Cosby (Honeymoon Part I)

The frogs had started early for March, their voices rising from the hollow the way steam lifts from warm ground after rain. Connor paused in the kitchen doorway, listening. The sound wrapped around the house, a soft, steady chorus under the faint clink of mugs on the table.

Caleb stood at the counter, pouring cocoa into two chipped cups. The overhead light threw a warm pool of light over the table, where the cedar box sat like a third place setting—familiar now, not as frightening as it had been at the beginning. On the shelf behind the table, the letters they'd already opened lay in a loose stack, edges softened from being read and re-folded.

"Come on in," Caleb said, glancing up. "Feels like a good night for one."

Connor tugged his hoodie sleeves down over his hands and crossed the room. The cracked kitchen window let in a thin thread of air that smelled like damp earth and cold creek water. Spring wasn't all the way here yet, but it was close enough to taste.

He slid into his usual chair and wrapped his fingers around the warm mug. "The wedding stuff was... a lot," he said. "The drive one helped, but I think I'm ready for something easier tonight."

"I don't want to quit," Connor added quickly, eyes flicking up to meet his dad's. "I just want something easy. Even if there's some sad in it. Just... nothing too heavy."

Caleb's mouth tugged into a small smile. "We've got those too."

Connor reached for the cedar box and eased the latch open. The faint scent of cedar rose up, familiar now in a way that made his chest tighten and relax at the same time. Inside, only the unread envelopes remained—Lauren's looping handwriting on each one—and at the bottom, the thick, unmarked envelope resting like a quiet stone.

He didn't touch that one. He never did. But he looked at it for a heartbeat longer before shifting his attention back to the letters above it.

His fingers brushed lightly across the envelopes inside the box, reading the unread labels under his breath. When his hand hesitated—as if reaching on instinct for something familiar—he glanced toward the shelf where *The Road to Cosby* and *The Wedding That Almost Wasn't* sat in their soft, re-folded stack.

"Those we've already done," he murmured, almost to himself.

He looked back into the box, moved past the remaining envelopes, and paused at one labeled simply *Cosby*.

He traced the word with his thumb. "What about this one?" he asked. "I mean, we've done the road. This feels like... the next part."

Caleb's chest warmed. "Yeah," he said softly. "That's the cabin. Honeymoon. Before Cherokees and hospitals and everything else."

"Lighter?" Connor asked.

Caleb considered. "There's grief in it," he said honestly. "But there's a lot of joy too. More joy than anything."

Connor nodded slowly. "I can handle that."

He slipped the *Cosby* envelope out and handed it across the table. Then he leaned forward, elbows on the wood, chin balanced on his folded hands the way he had as a kid when he wanted a story at bedtime.

Outside, the frogs pushed their song a little louder. A soft breeze slipped through the cracked window, stirring the edge of the curtain. The house seemed to settle into the moment with them.

Caleb unfolded the pages carefully. Lauren's handwriting curved across the paper, steady and sure. He swallowed, then began to read.

My love,

Do you remember the drive to Cosby that afternoon? June sunlight spread across the mountains, everything washed in that deep, hazy green they only get when spring has finally tipped into summer. The air was warm but not smothering, just soft and clean, so we rolled the windows down and let the wind tangle our hair and carry in the smell of wildflowers and sun-warmed pine.

I watched you drive with one hand on the wheel and the other reaching for mine whenever you forgot to be shy about it. We were barely a day into being husband and wife, our rings still feeling strange and right on our hands. You had that focus you get when you're soaking everything in—quiet, steady, like you're trying to memorize the road and the sky and the way my hand fits in yours all at once.

I remember thinking, "So this is what the beginning of us looks like."

When we pulled up to the cabin, I think we both stopped breathing for a second. It wasn't big, but it was beautiful in a way I wasn't prepared for—A-frame roofline, weathered planks, a little porch with a soft amber light already glowing like someone had turned it on just for us. The world felt loud right up until that moment, and then all at once it didn't.

Inside, everything opened into one big room. A small kitchen tucked along one wall, a cozy living area on the other, a stone fireplace bridging the space between. And there, tucked against the back wall like it had wandered into the wrong part of the house and decided to stay, was the hot tub. In the living room. I'd never seen anything like it.

The loft above us held the bed. The stairs creaked when we climbed them that first time, and from up there we could see it all in one glance: the fireplace ready for a match, the little couch, the tiny kitchen table by the window, the top edge of the hot tub gleaming in the late afternoon light. It felt like stepping into our own little world—a place that belonged to nobody but us for a handful of days.

Then we opened the back door.

The porch was barely big enough for the two of us to stand side by side, but it didn't need to be. A narrow mountain stream ran just a few feet beyond the railing, water slipping over rocks and fallen branches with a sound that wrapped around the cabin like a lullaby. You walked out there first, and I followed, and the two of us just stood for a minute, listening to the water and the crickets and the faint hum of the mountains breathing around us.

You slipped your arm around my shoulders and pulled me in close. "Listen," you whispered, even though I already was. "You hear that?"

"Yeah," I said. "It sounds like peace."

I didn't know, standing there with your chin resting on my hair and the stream singing below us, how much I'd come back to that sound later, in harder seasons. But I think God did. I think He was already saving it for us.

We didn't rush that first evening. We carried our bags in, unpacked slowly, laughed at how the hot tub kept steaming up the living room windows every time we tested it. You fiddled with the fireplace like you wanted to prove you could get it going without help, and I pretended not to watch you kneeling there, determined and gentle and mine.

Then you took me to the steakhouse you'd been talking about for weeks.

I still didn't really understand what you meant when you said they cut and cooked the steak "right at the table." I pictured maybe a little burner or a fancy cart. I did not picture a waiter walking out holding a platter of raw steak like a sacred offering. I think my eyes nearly fell out of my head. You tried so hard not to laugh—but your shoulders shook, and your mouth twisted the way it always does when you're not supposed to be amused and absolutely are.

He cut the steak right there next to us, inches from my elbow, with so much care it felt like we were the only table in the world. Then he disappeared and returned with it sizzling and perfect. When I took the first bite, I understood why you'd wanted to bring me there. It really was one of the best steaks we ever had. But if I'm honest, what made it perfect wasn't just the food. It was the way you watched me—like my reaction meant more to you than your own plate.

We drove back through Gatlinburg with the windows rolled down, June air warm against our faces. The town lights blurred by, soft and gold, and somewhere between the stoplights and the little shops, you found a radio station playing a song you knew. You sang under your breath, not loud, just enough that I could hear you. I looked over at you in that dashboard glow and thought, "I am so grateful I get to spend the rest of my life listening to this voice sing along to songs on back roads."

We got back to the cabin feeling like real newlyweds, and that's where we made one of our more questionable decisions.

We wanted to be "fancy." Neither of us drank, not really, but honeymoons in movies always seemed to come with champagne. So we bought a bottle, the kind we knew nothing about, and brought it back to the cabin like we were about to star in our own commercial.

We changed into our bathing suits, turned down the lights, climbed into the hot tub in the middle of the living room, and tried to act like we knew what we were doing. Steam fogged the windows, the jets hummed, and you poured us each a glass with more reverence than that champagne deserved.

"To us," you said, raising your glass.

"To us," I echoed, and we clinked the rims together like we'd seen in the movies.

We took a sip at the exact same moment.

My love, we did not swallow it.

You jerked forward and spit yours over the edge of the tub like your life depended on getting it out. I did the same. For a second, there was only choking and coughing and the sound of bubbles roaring while we both tried to scrub the taste off our tongues with the backs of our hands.

Then we looked at each other—and we broke.

We laughed so hard the water sloshed up the sides. You grabbed the bottle like it had offended you personally and set it on the floor, shaking your head. "Never again," you wheezed. My sides hurt from laughing. We climbed out, wrapped ourselves in towels, and tossed the rest of that bottle before it could assault anybody else.

That night we fell asleep in the loft with the windows cracked just enough to hear the stream and the crickets outside. Your arm around me felt like the most natural thing in the world. Somewhere in the dark, before sleep pulled me under, I whispered, "Thank You," into the quiet—thank You for you, for that cabin, for that terrible champagne, for laughter that felt like blessing.

The next morning, the phone rang.

It was earlier than we wanted to be awake. The light coming in through the loft window was still soft and pale. You answered with that thick, just-woken voice, and I knew by the way you said "Hey, Mama" that something was wrong.

Your great grandmother had passed in the night.

I watched the news hit you. It started in your eyes—they went distant and wet all at once. Your shoulders folded inward, like you were trying to make yourself smaller, like maybe you could step out of what was happening if you took up less space. You kept saying, "We shouldn't be here. We should go home. I should be with them." You paced that tiny kitchen, the phone dangling in your hand.

I heard your mama's voice through the plastic and distance, steady and sad. She told you your great grandmother would've wanted you to finish your honeymoon. That you were exactly where you were supposed to be. That your being there didn't mean you loved your family any less.

You listened, but you didn't quite believe it yet. Guilt and grief tangled together in your chest, and you didn't know where one ended and the other began. When you finally hung up, you stayed there with your hands braced on the counter, head bowed, shoulders trembling in that way you tried to hide from me.

I walked up behind you and laid my hands flat against your back. "Hey," I whispered. "Look at me."

You turned slowly. Your eyes were shining, and your jaw was tight, and you looked like you were waiting for me to tell you what a terrible person you were for smiling in a cabin when someone you loved had just gone home to Jesus.

"It's okay to stay," I told you. "It doesn't mean you love them any less. It just means you're honoring what they wanted for you."

You searched my face for a long moment, like you were checking to see if I meant it. And when you finally believed that I did, something in you loosened. We sat down at that tiny table and bowed our heads together, and you prayed—halting and simple and honest. You thanked God for your great grandmother's life. You asked Him to be with your family. You asked Him to help you be present where you were.

That was the first time I remember us really praying together as husband and wife. Not just meal-time prayers. Not just church prayers. Real-life, messy-heart, "we don't know what to do but we'll hold on to You" prayers. It set a tone I am still grateful for.

The days after that became gentle on purpose. We seemed to move slower, talk softer. We grilled hamburgers and hot dogs on the little grill outside one evening, standing shoulder to shoulder while the smoke curled up into the trees. You flipped the burgers with way too much focus, and I teased you about treating them like gourmet steaks. We ate on the porch, paper plates balanced on our knees, the stream singing backup and crickets tuning their instruments all around us.

Another day we drove through the mountains just because we could. Windows down, hands laced on the console between us, you pointing out ridgelines and clouds and every patch of sunlight that looked like it was doing something special. We drove over to Cades Cove and took the loop slow, watching for deer and bears and whatever else might show itself. Long stretches of road passed in comfortable silence. We didn't need to fill every space with words; the mountains talked enough for all of us.

At the little store near the campground, you bought us vanilla soft-serve cones—the kind that twist up too tall for their own good. You knew it was one of my favorites. We stood outside while it melted down the sides faster than we could keep up, laughing as we tried not to lose chunks of it to gravity. A couple of kids ran past us, sticky and loud, and I remember thinking how beautiful it would be someday if we had our own little ones dragging us through spots like that.

We spent another afternoon in Gatlinburg, wandering hand in hand past windows full of souvenirs we didn't need. We went to Christus Gardens, that walk-through story of the life of Christ. The rooms were dim and reverent, scenes from His life laid out quietly around us. They had artifacts from Bethlehem, pieces of stone and pottery and history, and I watched your face go soft as you took it all in. We didn't say much, but when we stepped back out into the bright day, you squeezed my hand and said, "Feels like God just walked the halls with us."

Later—because we were young and stubborn and you didn't want fear having the last say—we went through that haunted house maze. You told me about the one from your childhood, how it had shaken you so badly you carried the memory for years. I saw the tightness in your shoulders as we stepped into the dark. I felt your hand grip mine like it was the only solid thing in the whole place. So I held on and talked you through the twists and wrong turns and jump scares, reminding you, "I'm right here. I'm not letting go."

By the time we stepped back out into the sunlight, you were laughing in that breathless way you get when you've pushed through something that once owned you. I'll never forget the look in your eyes—part triumph, part relief, part little boy who realized the monster under the bed didn't get to win this time.

And then, because we still hadn't had enough adventure, we accidentally stole a ride on the Space Needle.

We walked in honestly thinking we were doing everything right. We looked for a ticket booth outside and couldn't find one. We didn't see any signs. So when the elevator doors opened, we stepped inside like that was exactly what we were supposed to do.

Halfway up, you gave me this sideways look that said, "Did we miss something?" I shrugged because I genuinely didn't know.

At the top, we enjoyed the view like two people who believed they had followed every instruction the world had given them.

It wasn't until we rode back down and stepped off the elevator that we finally noticed the sign explaining the ticket process—clear as day, sitting off to the side where we somehow never saw it. The moment our feet hit the sidewalk, the truth hit us too, and we burst out laughing. You doubled over, and I clung to your arm, both of us realizing we had just unknowingly taken the world's most innocent free ride.

We laughed all the way back to the cabin. Laughed when we grilled again, laughed when we climbed into that ridiculous living room hot tub, laughed when crickets and frogs and the stream tried to outsing each other in the dark.

Looking back now, I see how kind God was to give us those days—the steakhouse and champagne disaster, the stream, and the hot dogs, the soft-serve at Cades Cove, Christus Gardens, the haunted maze where you let me hold your fear, the Space Needle that forgot to charge us. None of it was grand by the world's standards. But it was holy in its own way.

Those days were a soft beginning. A gentle place to rest our hearts at the start of this long road. When the years ahead turned hard—and they did—it helped to know we had once stood on a tiny porch above a mountain stream, fingers laced, hearts quiet, surrounded by a peace we didn't yet know we would need.

Thank you for those days. For driving and laughing and praying and trusting. For letting mountains and streams and simple food and shared fear and shared faith knit us together.

Always yours,

Lauren

Caleb let the last words hang between them before he folded the pages along their old creases. The kitchen felt different now—full but not heavy, like the room had drawn a long breath with them and was exhaling slowly.

Connor hadn't moved since he started reading. He sat with his forearms on the table, hands clasped loosely, eyes fixed on some point just beyond the wood grain. His face wasn't tight like it sometimes got. It was softer, almost younger.

"So you two," he said quietly, "were like... real people."

Caleb's mouth twitched. "I hope so."

"I mean..." Connor let out a little breath that could've been a laugh. "It's weird. I know you're my parents. I know you are both people. But hearing all that—Christus Gardens, the haunted house, innocent Space Needle heist, hot dogs on paper plates—it just... it makes you feel more like..."

"Like more than just Mom and Dad?" Caleb offered.

"Yeah." Connor nodded. "Like a couple. Like two dorks in love out in the mountains."

Caleb huffed a soft laugh. "We were definitely that."

Connor's gaze slid toward the window. Outside, the frogs kept at their chorus, joined now by the faint scrape of bare branches stirring against each other. The air that came through the crack in the window smelled like rain-soaked dirt and something new trying to wake up.

"She really loved all that, didn't she?" he asked. "The mountains. The drives. Little museums. Ice cream."

"She did," Caleb said. "Soft-serve especially. Any excuse."

Connor smiled faintly. "I didn't know about Cades Cove," he said. "Or Christus Gardens. Or you being scared of haunted houses."

"You weren't supposed to know that last one," Caleb said, and Connor snorted.

"Too late."

They fell quiet for a moment. Caleb reached out and rested his hand on the cedar box. Inside, the remaining unread letters waited. On the shelf, the opened ones sat like a short row of white spines, Lauren's handwriting hidden inside every fold.

Connor's eyes flicked briefly to the unmarked envelope at the bottom of the box before he closed the lid gently. He didn't flinch from it this time. He just acknowledged it and let it be.

"I like this one," he said after a moment. "Cosby. It's... it's not that the others are bad. They're just... hard. This one feels... I don't know. Safe, I guess."

"It was," Caleb said. "For both of us."

"I like knowing you had that," Connor said. "Before the car wreck. Before the fire. Before hospitals and... all of it." His fingers tapped a little rhythm on the table. "And I like knowing God was there too. Not just when everything was falling apart."

"He was always there," Caleb said. "We just saw Him more clearly some days than others."

Connor nodded, thinking. "It makes everything else feel less... random," he said finally. "Like He wasn't just showing up for the bad parts. He was laughing with you too."

The words landed between them with a simple kind of truth that made Caleb's throat tighten. He reached across the table, palm up. Connor looked at it, then at him, and slid his hand into his dad's. His grip was solid, warm.

Outside, the frogs shifted their song a little, like some unseen conductor had given them a cue. The breeze at the window cooled, then warmed again, carrying the faintest hint of mud and budding grass.

"Thank you for reading these with me," Caleb said.

"Thank you for keeping them," Connor replied. "And for not... I don't know. For not trying to rush this."

Caleb squeezed his hand once more before letting go. "We'll take them one at a time," he said. "Same as we've been doing. The letters. The memories. The grief. The good stuff. All of it."

Connor pushed his chair back and stood, stretching until his back popped. "I'm good with that," he said. He hesitated, then leaned down and pressed his hand briefly to the lid of the cedar box. "Night, Mom," he murmured, so soft Caleb barely heard it.

Then he straightened. "Good night, Dad."

"Good night, son."

Connor padded down the hallway toward his room. The house settled around the absence of his footsteps, back into its evening rhythm. Caleb stayed at the table a little longer, fingers resting on the edge of the box.

He could still hear the stream from that cabin if he tried—the rush over rocks, the crickets, the low hum of Lauren's laughter in the dark. For the first time in a long time, the memory didn't feel like a door he couldn't open. It felt like a place he'd visited with his son and come back from together.

Outside, the frogs sang on. The early spring air slipped in through the window, cool and smelling faintly of new things pushing up through the soil. Caleb closed his eyes for a moment and let the gentleness of it wash over him.

Laughter, he realized, did its own kind of healing.

Lauren said someday they'd come back with stories to tell, and Caleb believed her without realizing how much belief costs.

CHAPTER TWELVE

Cherokee (Honeymoon Part II)

The heater clicked in that stubborn late winter rhythm again, the one that kept promising warmth but only delivering it in small, uneven breaths. Caleb sat on the couch, elbows braced on his knees, the cedar box resting beside him. Snow feathered quietly against the windows, not in thick sheets—just a soft brush of flakes drifting sideways in thin white strokes.

The house always felt different on days like this—like the walls had pulled in closer to listen.

Connor padded in from the hallway, hoodie sleeves half covering his hands, socks mismatched again. He didn't make eye contact at first. Instead, he lowered himself onto the couch beside his father in that tentative way he always did when he wasn't sure if sitting close was allowed.

Caleb nudged the blanket toward him. "Cold?"

Connor shrugged, then pulled the blanket over his lap, anyway. "Just... comfy."

Caleb smiled softly. It wasn't much, but it was honest.

On the coffee table, the cedar box waited. Caleb could feel its presence even without touching it—the way it seemed to hold breath and memory and everything he'd never gotten the chance to say. The cedar scent drifted faintly in the warm air, mixing with the cinnamon candle Lauren used to love.

Connor's eyes flicked toward the box for half a second. "We said we'd do another today."

"We did," Caleb said. "But we don't have to. If you're worn out, we can stop."

"I'm not worn out." Connor tugged the blanket higher. "I just… don't know what it's gonna be about this time."

"That's okay," Caleb said. "Neither do I."

He lifted the lid slowly. The envelopes rustled, the faint cedar rising as the letters shifted. Only the unread ones remained now, lined neatly at the front—Lauren's handwriting looping across each in blue ink. Beneath them all, still and patient, the large unmarked envelope rested like a stone in deep water.

Not today, he told himself.

Not yet.

He reached for the next labeled envelope.

"Cherokee," he read aloud.

Lauren's handwriting curved across the front in that looping script she used on grocery lists and birthday cards and notes taped to his steering wheel.

Connor watched quietly as Caleb held the envelope toward him.

"You want to open it?" Caleb asked.

Connor hesitated. His fingers flexed inside his sleeves. Then he nodded and reached out. He held the envelope tenderly, opening it slow so nothing tore. He unfolded the pages, but didn't try to read them. Instead, he passed them over, eyes bright, face carefully still.

"Go ahead," he murmured.

Caleb took the pages, smoothing the first one against his knee. The heater clicked again. Snow slid down the window in thin, melting ribbons.

He began reading.

My love,

By the time we left Cosby and drove toward Cherokee for the second half of our honeymoon, something in both of us had settled. Not everything—not after the phone call about your great grandmother—but enough that the air felt different. You moved quieter that morning, almost like you were listening for something bigger than either of us. Maybe you were.

The drive wasn't long, but the mountains looked different that day. Mist still clung to the lower ridges, but the sky above was turning that clear blue you always loved. You kept pointing things out—the sunlight through the pines, the curve of the road bending around the hillside, the little houses tucked into the trees. I remember thinking, If peace could sit in someone's hands, it would look like the way you held that steering wheel.

Cherokee greeted us like a place that didn't need to hurry. The air felt cleaner somehow. People walked slow. Even the river beside the road moved with a kind of patience. I stepped out of the car and felt something loosen in my chest. And when I looked at you, I saw the same thing in your eyes.

Our motel wasn't fancy. A simple room, a simple bedspread, a small window facing a stand of trees. But the moment you dropped our bags and wrapped your arms around me from behind, it felt like the whole world shrank down to the space between your shoulder and mine. You whispered, "We made it," like we'd climbed a mountain instead of driven an hour. But I knew what you meant.

That evening we went to see Unto These Hills, the outdoor drama about the Trail of Tears. I don't think either of us expected it to hit as hard as it did. We'd always admired the Cherokee people—their resilience, their history—but sitting under the darkening sky, watching that story unfold with real faces and real voices... it settled into me like a stone and a prayer at the same time.

I still remember the moment it shifted for you. A young Cherokee mother held her child while soldiers pushed families from their homes. She didn't scream. She didn't fight. She just looked over the crowd with this quiet, breaking pain. And your hand found mine and tightened—not out of fear, but reverence. Respect. Grief for something that happened long before we were born. That was when I realized how deeply you felt things. How gently you held the world, even the parts that hurt.

We barely spoke afterward. Some moments deserve silence. When you finally did speak, your voice was soft. "I didn't know it was like that," you said. And I remember thinking, This man doesn't turn away from hard truths. He holds them with kindness.

The next day we went to the Oconaluftee Indian Village. You listened to every guide like their words were precious. You asked careful questions. You stopped to watch every demonstration—pottery, carving, weaving. I watched you lean forward as a young woman shaped a clay bowl, your eyes tracing every movement. When she finished, you said, "It's amazing how much of a person ends up in the things they make." She smiled like you'd given her a gift.

Being there wasn't like sightseeing. It felt like being allowed to step, for a moment, into a story that didn't belong to us. And we treated it that way—with respect, with gratitude. I think that's why that day stayed with me. We were learning together. Listening together. Growing together.

That night, you stepped outside the motel room for a minute. When you came back in, you told me the mountains looked like they were holding their breath. I didn't understand until I looked out the window. The night had settled over the ridge like a blanket—soft, steady, full. And I felt it too. A stillness that didn't feel empty. A stillness that felt like God saying, Here. Remember this.

I have, my love. I still do.

Thank you for taking me to Cherokee. Thank you for letting that place become part of the story God was writing in us.

Your wife,

Lauren

Caleb let the last lines fall into the quiet between them. For a long moment, neither he nor Connor spoke. The room felt wrapped in something soft—almost like the hush Lauren had described by the ridge all those years ago. Snow brushed lightly against the window, melting in thin trails.

Connor sniffed once, quick and embarrassed. He wiped his cheek with his sleeve and kept his gaze fixed on the blanket.

"I didn't cry," he muttered.

Caleb tilted his head. "Okay."

"I didn't," Connor insisted, though his voice wavered. "Something just... got in my eye."

"Must've been the snow," Caleb said lightly.

Connor huffed a shaky laugh.

Caleb folded the letter gently. He set it aside on the table, keeping his hand there a moment longer than needed.

"She really loved you, didn't she?" Connor asked.

"With everything she had."

"And you loved her like that back?"

"Every day."

Connor nodded slowly, absorbing it like truth settling into place.

"I didn't know she liked... all that stuff," he murmured. "The stories. The history. Walking slow and listening to rivers."

Caleb smiled faintly. "She loved anything that made her feel close to people. Their past. Their families. Their traditions. She wanted to make sure nothing got lost."

Connor swallowed. "Maybe that's why she wrote these. So she wouldn't get lost."

"Maybe," Caleb said. "Or maybe she wanted us to remember where we came from."

Connor stared at the cedar box. "Did she ever talk to me about Cherokee? When I was little?"

"She did," Caleb said gently. "A lot. She used to show you pictures from our honeymoon album—there's one of me standing by the river looking like a lost tourist. She laughed every time."

Connor blinked. "She... showed me pictures?"

"All the time. You were nine. She wanted you to feel like you were part of everything we lived before you came along."

Connor's voice dipped. "I wish I remembered her that way. Happy. Laughing. Not sick."

"I know," Caleb said quietly.

"I mostly remember the hospital stuff," Connor whispered. "Machines. Her being tired. Her breathing funny. I don't want that to be all I've got."

"That's why we're doing this," Caleb said. "So you can see more of who she was."

"But they don't feel like my memories," Connor said. "They feel like I'm borrowing yours."

"Sometimes that's what family is," Caleb said softly. "We hold each other's memories until they settle into our own."

Connor was quiet for a moment.

"Do you really think she felt God there? In Cherokee?"

"I do," Caleb said without hesitation. "Not because the place was magical. Because we finally slowed down enough to notice Him."

Connor's eyes drifted. "I don't know what that feels like."

"You will," Caleb said. "In your own time."

Another quiet stretch passed.

"Do you think she meant it," Connor asked, "when she said that week stitched something into your marriage?"

"I think she meant every word."

Connor's breath trembled. "Then why does it feel like she got... taken from us?"

Caleb let the question settle. "I don't know why she died when she did," he said softly. "But her death doesn't erase her life. Or what God built in this family. Or the love she gave you."

Connor's voice thinned. "What did He give us?"

"Love that lasts," Caleb said. "The kind you don't lose, even when you lose someone's body."

Connor didn't move for a long moment. Then he shifted his blanket-wrapped hand and rested it lightly against Caleb's fingers.

Not grabbing.

Not clinging.

Just touching.

Caleb breathed out slowly, like something unclenched inside him.

"You ready to put it away?" he asked.

Connor nodded.

Caleb stood and placed the Cherokee letter on the small shelf near the TV, where the others now rested. Only the unread letters remained in the cedar box, the unmarked envelope waiting at the bottom like a held breath.

"Not yet," Connor whispered.

"No," Caleb agreed. "Not yet."

They settled back on the couch. The house creaked as the temperature dipped. Snow brushed the windows again. The heater clicked once, then sighed warm air into the room.

Connor leaned gently into his father—hesitant at first, then fully. Caleb wrapped an arm around his shoulders.

For the first time since the funeral, Connor didn't flinch.

"Dad?" he murmured.

"Yeah?"

"Can we... do another one tomorrow?"

Caleb kissed the top of his son's head, just like Lauren used to. "Yeah, buddy. We can."

Quiet filled the room—deep, warm, and close.

The kind Cherokee had given them once.

The kind that felt like God was near.

CHAPTER THIRTEEN

The Crack in the Foundation

By late afternoon the rain had settled into a soft, steady fall, the kind that blurred the yard into gray shapes and made the house feel smaller around the edges. The kitchen light was on even though it wasn't quite dark yet, a warm circle over the table where Caleb and Connor sat with the cedar box between them.

Connor rested his hands on either side of the box but didn't open it. The faint scent of cedar still slipped out around the lid, familiar now in a way that made his chest feel tight.

"We can stop for today," Caleb said quietly. "Nobody's grading us on how fast we go."

Connor shook his head, eyes still on the box. "You said there was one about when things almost broke," he said. "Between you and Mom."

Caleb's gaze dropped to the lid too. "Yeah," he said. "There is."

"I want to know that one," Connor said. "If we're doing this... I don't just want the easy ones."

Something in Caleb's face softened. "Okay," he said. "We'll do that one."

He lifted the lid. The smell of cedar and paper rose a little stronger, like the past exhaling. Inside, the remaining envelopes sat in quiet rows, each one still sealed, each one still waiting. The letters they'd already read—The Camping Letter, Before the Bells, The

Wedding That Almost Wasn't—rested on the small shelf behind them now, lined up in the order they'd opened them. Caleb reached toward the untouched envelopes in the box and stopped on one near the middle.

The ink on this envelope was a touch more faded. Across the front, in her neat script:

The Crack in the Foundation

Caleb's thumb lingered on the edge of it.

"That a bad sign?" Connor asked, trying to sound lighter than he felt.

"It's a hard one," Caleb admitted. "But important. It's about the first time our marriage really shook."

"You still made it," Connor said quietly. "I'm here."

Caleb gave a small, crooked smile. "Yeah," he said. "You are."

He slid the envelope out, closed the lid halfway, and set the letter on the table.

"Same as always," he said. "I read. You listen. We talk as much or as little as you want."

Connor nodded. "Okay."

Caleb opened the envelope and unfolded the pages. The paper felt thinner at the creases where Lauren's hand had smoothed it years ago.

He took a breath and began to read.

Caleb, my love,

Some letters are written out of joy. Some out of gratitude. This one is written because silence has become too heavy to carry by myself. I have carried shame for this season for a long time. I don't want you to carry it alone anymore either. If you are reading this, I hope enough years have passed that we can look back at this as something we survived together, even though it almost broke us.

You already know the year. The year after Jeff was killed.

I still can't soften that word. "Killed." People say "passed away" or "gone home to be with the Lord," and I believe Heaven is real, but none of those words match what happened. One phone call ripped him out of our lives. Nothing about it felt gentle or finished. It felt like the floor gave way and never came back.

I remember the call more than the words—just a ringing in my ears and the feeling of everything sliding sideways. Later, when we were at my parents' house, it was my dad who broke. He sat down hard at the kitchen table like someone had taken the floor out from under him, his hands shaking as he said Jeff's name over and over like he was trying to bring him back. You were there beside him, trying to steady him, trying to steady me, trying to hold together what none of us could fix. I remember the funeral—flowers I couldn't smell, songs I couldn't sing, hands on my shoulders that felt like too much and not enough at the same time. And then the house emptied, and you and I were left with the kind of silence that sinks into the walls.

You sat with me through all of it. On the couch. On the edge of the bed. In the parking lot when I couldn't make myself go into the store. You brought me food I barely tasted. You listened when I cried and when I stared at the same spot on the wall for an hour. You kept asking, "How can I help?" and I kept saying, "You can't," because I didn't believe anyone could touch that kind of hurt.

Slowly, grief stopped being something I had and started being something that had us. It sat between us at the table. It lay down between us at night. It stood in the doorway every time you reached for me. Somewhere in there, I stopped seeing you clearly through it. Every word sounded wrong. Every silence felt like you'd given up, even when you hadn't.

That's how the crack started.

I began to pull away. At first it was little things: turning my face when you kissed my cheek, saying I was too tired when you reached for my hand. Then it grew. I picked fights over nothing—how you loaded the dishwasher, how you folded towels, how long you'd been gone even when you were home on time. I told myself I was mad at you, but really I was mad at death and at God and at the whole unfair world. You were closest, so you caught the shrapnel.

You tried to stay steady. You gave me space when I asked and stayed close when the space scared me. You suggested counseling. I said I was fine. I thought if I admitted how bad it was, I'd shatter for good.

Then came the day I walked out without telling you where I was really going.

The house felt too small. Every room held a ghost—Jeff's laugh, Dad's tears, the sound of your voice from the night we got the call. I told you I needed air and grabbed my keys. You asked if I wanted you to come. I said no. I remember the look on your face and wish I had let it stop me. Instead I drove like the road owed me an escape.

I ended up in a parking lot on the far side of town, hands shaking on the steering wheel. There was a friend there—someone who had been kind after the funeral, who kept saying, "You can talk to me anytime." I let myself lean on that offer more than I should have. We didn't cross physical lines. I need you to know that plainly. But I handed thoughts and fears and pieces of my story to someone who had not made vows with me. I let them see parts of my heart that still should have been turned toward you.

At the moment, it felt like oxygen. Like somebody had cracked a window in a smoke-filled room. The guilt didn't hit until I pulled back into our driveway and saw the light on in the kitchen and your shadow at the table.

When I walked inside, you were waiting. You asked where I'd been. I told you. You asked why I hadn't called. I said, "I didn't think it mattered." The second the words left my mouth, I wanted to grab them back. I watched something in your face dim, like someone had turned down the brightness on the man I loved.

We started fighting for real after that. Not about dishes or laundry—those were just the words we used. Underneath, we were fighting about trust. You asked questions that weren't cruel; they were honest. "Why didn't you come to me?" "What did you tell them that you couldn't tell me?" I answered with anger because anger felt safer than admitting I was afraid you'd leave if you saw how broken I was.

The worst nights weren't the ones when we yelled. They were the ones when we didn't speak at all. You'd sit on the edge of the bed with your head in your hands. I'd lie on my side, back to you, staring at the dresser, feeling every inch of mattress between us like a canyon. I could feel your hurt without touching you, and still I didn't move. Fear had both of my hands pinned to my sides.

I told myself I was protecting my heart by pulling away first. I thought if I loosened my grip on us, it would hurt less when life ripped you from me the way it had ripped Jeff. I didn't realize that letting go early was its own kind of grief.

Through all of it, you stayed.

You stayed when you had every right to slam the door and not come back. You stayed when I wouldn't meet your eyes. You stayed when I answered your worry with coldness. You still checked the doors at night. You still made sure there was cocoa in the cabinet. You still reached for my hand sometimes in the dark, even when I pretended to be asleep.

Then came the night at the kitchen table when everything turned a different direction.

I was sitting there after dinner, staring at nothing. The house was quiet in that heavy way it gets when people are trying not to step wrong. You came in and sat across from me. You didn't ask what was wrong. You just watched me for a long time, fingers laced so tight your knuckles were white.

When you finally spoke, your voice shook. You said, "I'm not afraid you'll walk out of this house. I'm afraid you're already gone and I'm the only one who can see it."

It broke something in me to see you cry for us instead of just with me about losing Jeff. For the first time in months, I saw the man who had held me up through every awful phone call and long night, not just the person I was mad at for not fixing the unfixable. I realized I wasn't the only one grieving. I was asking you to watch me disappear and pretend it wasn't happening.

We talked that night until the heater had kicked on and off so many times I lost count. I told you the truth I'd been afraid to say: that I felt guilty for being alive when Jeff wasn't, that I was angry at God and scared of Him at the same time, that I was terrified you would die and leave me too. You told me you were scared of saying the wrong thing and making it worse, scared I'd decide you weren't enough, scared that the girl you married was gone and wouldn't come back.

We did not fix everything in one conversation. But the crack stopped widening. We both turned toward it together instead of standing on opposite sides, kicking at it from different angles.

Months later, when your chest became the battlefield and the doctors said "pulmonary embolism" in calm voices that did not match the panic in mine, that old crack came roaring back in my mind. I remember watching them wheel you toward those big double doors. I remember thinking, I almost threw this away because I was afraid of losing it.

In that waiting room chair, with my hands shaking and my prayers sounding more like begging than faith, I made a promise I never said out loud. If God let me keep you, I would stop trying to protect myself by pushing you away. I would not be the first one to turn my back on us again. If life took you someday, it would not be because I loosened my grip out of fear.

I can't say I kept that promise perfectly. You know I didn't. But from that season on, every time the ground shook—through the fire, through money scares, through layers of bad news—I found myself reaching for you faster instead of hiding. That change began here, in this crack, in this almost-broken place.

I am sorry for every way I made you doubt your worth and your place. You were enough. You always were. The brokenness was not in your love; it was in my ability to trust that love wouldn't be ripped away. Thank you for staying when I was too afraid to.

If you are reading this, I hope you can see this chapter of our story not as the beginning of our end, but as proof that love can bend without breaking. We were not the ones holding everything together. God was. He still is.

Your wife,

Lauren

Caleb's voice softened on the last lines until the words seemed to sit more in the space between them than in the air. He folded the letter slowly, thumb resting for a moment on the crease where her name lay hidden.

Connor stared at the paper, jaw tight. The room felt smaller, like the walls had leaned in to listen too.

"So that was... it," he said finally. "The almost-break."

Caleb nodded once. "Yeah," he said. "That was it."

"She talked to somebody else," Connor said, the words careful. "Not... that way, but... still."

"Still," Caleb agreed. He didn't rush to defend her, and he didn't tear her down. "She gave pieces of her heart to someone who hadn't promised to carry them. That hurt."

"Were you mad?" Connor asked. "Like... really mad."

"I was," Caleb said. "I felt left out. Replaced. Scared. I wondered what was wrong with me. But I also knew she was drowning. Some of the anger belonged to what happened to Jeff, not just to me."

Connor frowned at the table. "Seems like she should've known better."

"She should have," Caleb said quietly. "And so should I, in the places I failed her. That's the thing about cracks. They don't usually come from one side only."

He tapped the edge of the envelope. "This letter is her saying, 'I know I hurt you. I see what I did. I'm not pretending it didn't happen.' That means something."

Connor thought about that. About all the apologies in his own life that had come late or never at all. "Did you ever think about leaving?" he asked.

"No," Caleb said, and there was no hesitation in it. "I thought about how broken we were. I wondered if we'd ever feel normal again. I wondered if I was enough. But walking away?" He shook his head. "I promised God and your mom that I'd stay. My feelings didn't get to cancel that."

He let out a breath. "Doesn't mean it was easy. It just means I chose the promise over the hurt."

Connor's gaze drifted to the cedar box. The line of read letters on the little shelf had grown uneven, their edges softened by new hands. Down near the bottom, he could see the corner of the unmarked envelope—no title, just thick paper, and silence.

"That one still freaks me out," he admitted.

"Me too," Caleb said, honesty plain. He reached out and closed the lid with a gentle motion. The soft sound of wood meeting wood felt more like a bookmark than a door slamming. "We're not ready for that one yet. And that's okay."

Connor's shoulders eased a little. "Okay," he echoed.

For a moment they just sat there, listening to the rain hush itself against the glass.

"Can I ask you something?" Connor said.

"Always."

"Do you think me and you will ever have a crack like that?" he asked. "The kind that almost breaks everything."

Caleb considered the question instead of waving it away. "We already have cracks," he said. "The day you moved in and didn't know if you could trust me. The times I said the wrong thing and hurt you without meaning to. The nights you felt alone even in this house. Those are lines in the foundation too."

He gave a small, honest smile. "But we're talking about them. We're reading these together. We're staying at the table. That's how you keep the crack from splitting all the way through."

Connor looked at his hands. "I don't want to run when it gets hard," he said.

Caleb's throat tightened. "Then we're already ahead of where we used to be," he said. "We're learning from our cracks instead of hiding them."

He pushed his chair back. "Come on," he added, voice softer. "We've done enough heavy lifting for one day. How about cocoa?"

"You always think cocoa is the answer," Connor muttered, but there was the faintest curve at the corner of his mouth.

"Not the answer," Caleb said. "Just good company while we look for it."

They moved through the small kitchen in a quiet rhythm—Connor reaching for the mugs, Caleb filling the kettle. The heater hummed. The rain softened even more, a faint whisper now instead of a steady drum.

When the kettle whistled, Caleb poured and stirred. They took their mugs back to the table, this time sitting side by side with the cedar box a little off to the left, close but not between them.

Connor wrapped his hands around the warm ceramic and stared into the swirl on top. "So this was the first big crack," he said.

"The first one we knew by name," Caleb replied. "And the first one we survived on purpose."

He took a sip, then looked over. "We're not perfect, you and me. We'll have our own rough years. But we can decide now that cracking isn't the same as breaking. And we can trust that God's holding the edges tighter than we are."

Connor let the words sink in. They didn't erase the ache, but they made the ache feel less like an ending and more like part of something still being built.

"We're not broken all the way," he said quietly.

"No," Caleb agreed. "We're not."

The rain outside faded to a mist. Inside, the house felt like it had let out a breath of its own. The cedar box sat quiet on the table, no longer just a box of what they'd lost, but proof of everything that had somehow held.

For the first time since they'd found it, Connor didn't see it as something waiting to crush him.

He saw it as something they were learning to carry together.

CHAPTER FOURTEEN

Our First Collapse

By midafternoon, the light coming through the kitchen window had shifted from winter gray to something softer. The rain that had soaked everything the week before was gone, leaving the yard damp and patchy with early green. A few stubborn clumps of daffodils had pushed up near the fence, their yellow heads bowed like they weren't quite ready to commit to blooming.

Connor sat at the table with his chair tipped back on two legs, toes hooked under the rung to keep his balance. The cedar box rested where it always did now, just off-center between him and Caleb. On the little shelf behind them, the growing line of opened envelopes leaned against one another, edges softened by new hands.

The house felt different than it had that first snowy week. The air wasn't as heavy. It still hurt—Lauren's absence still hung in the quiet—but grief had shifted from a suffocating blanket to more of a weight they had learned to carry together. The heater clicked on less often. Sometimes, on good days, they cracked the kitchen window for a few minutes and let in the smell of wet dirt and distant grass.

Today the window was closed, but the world outside looked like it was thinking about waking up.

"You sure you're up for another one?" Caleb asked, wrapping both hands around his mug of cocoa. Steam no longer billowed from it, but the cup still held warmth.

Connor let the front legs of his chair drop back to the floor. "Yeah," he said. "I was thinking about it all night."

"About which part?" Caleb's tone stayed easy, but his eyes stayed attentive. He didn't ask that kind of question lightly anymore.

"About y'all almost breaking," Connor said. "And then not. It's... I don't know. It feels important to know that it wasn't always good, but you stayed anyway."

Caleb nodded slowly. "It is important," he agreed. "This next one...it's not about us fighting with each other. It's about us fighting something else together."

Connor glanced at the shelf of letters, reading the titles he could see from where he sat. When We First Met. The Camping Letter. The Wedding That Almost Wasn't. Cosby. Cherokee. The Quiet Return. The Crack in the Foundation.

"There one about when you all went broke?" he asked, half-testing, half-curious. "You said there was a time like that."

"There is," Caleb said. "And yeah, she wrote about it." He set his mug down and turned the cedar box toward himself. "If we're following the way she ordered them, that should be the next one."

The hinges whispered as he lifted the lid. The faint smell of cedar and old paper rose up between them, familiar now, a scent Connor was beginning to associate with both ache and comfort. Inside, the remaining envelopes sat in their neat rows, Lauren's handwriting looping across each front.

Caleb's fingers skimmed along the sealed edges until he found the one he was looking for. The ink had bled just a little at one corner, as if a drop of water had landed there and dried. Across the front, in her careful script:

Our First Collapse

Caleb let out a breath through his nose, halfway between a sigh and a quiet laugh. "She didn't really pull punches with her titles, did she?"

Connor huffed. "At least you know what you're getting into," he said. "No surprises."

Caleb turned the envelope over in his hands, then looked up. "Same deal as before," he said. "You're allowed to ask me to stop anytime. Or to skip sections. Or to come back to it later."

Connor shook his head. "If she trusted you to read it," he said, "and you trusted me to be here, I want to hear all of it. Even the bad stuff."

Something in Caleb's expression flickered—pride, sorrow, gratitude all tangled together. "Okay," he said. "All of it, then."

He slid a finger under the flap and opened the envelope with the same care he always used, as if the paper itself were fragile and not just what it carried. He unfolded the letter, smoothing creases that had been pressed by Lauren's hands years before, and began to read.

Caleb, my love,

By the time you read this, I hope the word "broke" doesn't sting quite the way it did when we first walked through it. I hope we're past sitting at the table with bills spread out like battlefield maps and that the sound of a phone ringing doesn't make either of us flinch the way it used to. But I don't ever want us—or whoever is reading this with you—to forget what we learned in that season. Not about money. About us.

You remember it in numbers; I remember it in sounds.

I remember the rustle of envelopes we didn't want to open. The hollow thump of past-due notices hitting the kitchen table. The way the phone rang with that particular tone that meant "unknown number," and how my stomach would drop before the second ring because we both knew it was another person asking for money we didn't have.

I also remember the sound of you coming in late, tired down to the bone from whatever overtime you could scrape together. The way your keys hit the hook by the door a little heavier each week. The way your shoes sounded on the hallway floor—slow, careful, like you were trying not to make any more noise than necessary in a life that already felt too loud.

We weren't careless. That's the part that used to sting the most. We didn't throw money away on foolish things. We were just young and trying to build a life, and the ground under us kept shifting.

It started with that first layoff at the plant. One "restructuring," they called it, like moving numbers around on a page somehow hurt less than telling people they no longer had a paycheck. They cut your hours first. Then they cut your position. Watching you carry that cardboard box to the car that day felt like seeing our future shrink in real time.

You did what you always do: you went looking for work. Any work. You took what came, even when it wasn't steady, even when it didn't match the skills you'd spent years building. Office gigs that lasted three months. Temp jobs that ended with a phone call on a Friday: "We won't be needing you Monday." Each ending felt like a little collapse of its own.

I picked up extra hours where I could. We learned how to stretch one grocery run farther than it should have been able to go. We ate a lot of noodles and whatever meat was on sale. We joked about being "creative with hamburger," because if we didn't laugh about it, I think we might have cried every single night.

For a while, we managed. It was tight, but we stayed afloat. Then came the car repairs, and the medical bills, and the interest rates written in tiny numbers that grew into monsters when they showed up on the statements. One unexpected prescription here, one emergency room co-pay there, and suddenly we were juggling instead of budgeting.

We told ourselves it was temporary. "Once things settle," we said. "Once the next job sticks." We used words like "bridge," to describe the credit cards. "Just to get us through this month. Just until tax time. Just until…"

Bridges are meant to be crossed, not lived on. We learned that the hard way.

The worst of it wasn't the numbers on the page. It was the shame that came with them. The sense that every envelope with a red stamp on it wasn't just a bill; it was a verdict. I remember one afternoon at the grocery store, standing in line with a cart full of the absolute cheapest version of everything I could find. Generic cereal. Store-brand pasta. Meat with a reduced sticker. I remember praying under my breath that our card wouldn't decline. The beeps of the scanner sounded too loud. When it finally approved, I could have cried with relief right there at the register.

You hated that I felt that way. Not because you were angry at me, but because you felt like you'd failed us. I saw it in the way you studied the job ads long after your eyes were too tired to read. In the way you kept track of every dime in a little notebook, as if writing it down might somehow make it stretch farther. In the way you apologized for things you had no control over.

We started fighting then, not because we stopped loving each other, but because we didn't know where to put all that fear. I'd bring up a bill and your shoulders would go tight. You'd talk about applying for a job two towns over and I'd hear it as you wanting to leave, even when that's not what you meant. We argued over ten-dollar decisions because the big ones felt too impossible to touch.

Do you remember the night the power almost got cut off? I do. There was a notice hanging on the door when we came home—thin paper, big words. I felt something in my chest cave in. Before I could even fully read it, you took it out of my hand and pressed it flat on the table. "We'll fix it," you said. "Somehow."

We found a way that time. You sold something you loved to cover it. I cried in the shower afterwards so you wouldn't see. Not because I thought you resented it. Because I knew you didn't, and that almost made it worse.

The break didn't come from one big failure. It came from a hundred little cuts. The day the bank letter arrived. The way the lady at the counter looked over her glasses when we asked for an extension. The quiet in the car after our first meeting with the lawyer, when the word "bankruptcy" stopped being something other people went through and became the road in front of us.

I remember sitting in that office under fluorescent lights that made everything look harsher. The walls were lined with certificates and framed photos that tried to make the space feel less clinical, but all I saw was the stack of forms on the desk between us. I kept thinking, This is the paperwork for our failure. You sat beside me, hands folded so tightly in your lap that your knuckles went white.

The lawyer talked in measured tones about "fresh starts" and "relief" and "restructuring." It all sounded like words you use when you're trying to dress up something ugly. I nodded when he spoke, answered when he asked questions, but inside I felt like I was shrinking. I thought about every promise we'd made at that little wedding chapel, about how we'd told each other we'd build a life together. It felt like the foundation we'd poured had cracked straight through.

On the drive home, you were quiet. I stared out the passenger window at houses with neat lawns and kids' bikes in the yards and wondered if any of them had sat under those same fluorescent lights. Shame has a way of convincing you that you're the only one who's ever been there.

When we pulled into the driveway, I didn't get out right away. I kept my hand on the door handle, frozen. You turned off the ignition and just let the keys rest in your palm. We sat in the still car, listening to the tick of the cooling engine.

Finally, you said, "We're going to walk into that house together. We're going to sign whatever we have to sign. We're going to start over. But I need you to hear me, Lauren. This is not you failing. This is not us failing. This is life being hard, and us doing what we have to do to keep going."

I wanted to believe you. Part of me did. Another part of me kept picturing the word "bankrupt" stamped like a label across our foreheads. I worried about what people at church would say if they found out. About what our families would think. About whether you would look at me differently once it was official, like I was damaged goods.

You must have seen some of that on my face, because you reached across the console and took my hand. "We still have us," you said. "We still have God. The rest is just paper."

I didn't say anything clever back. I just squeezed your hand hard enough that you probably felt it all the way up your arm. For the first time in months, instead of pulling away from you, I found myself leaning in. Maybe because I was too tired to stand alone anymore. Maybe because I'd finally realized you weren't going anywhere.

The weeks that followed were a blur of paperwork, long days, and even longer nights. We signed forms that felt like confessions. We answered questions that made me want to disappear under the table. We sat through meetings where people spoke in money-language that didn't feel like it belonged to real human lives. But through all of it, you kept reaching for my hand—sometimes across a desk, sometimes across a parking lot, sometimes across the table at home while we stared at numbers that didn't add up.

The day the court approved everything, it didn't feel like freedom. Not at first. It felt like standing in the wreckage of something we had built with so much hope. I cried in the car afterward, not because I regretted doing it, but because I didn't know how to start over. You let me cry. You didn't try to talk me out of it. You just held my hand against your chest like you were anchoring me so I wouldn't drift off somewhere you couldn't follow.

That night, we ate the last box of macaroni in the cabinet. You sprinkled the cheese in careful little circles like you were decorating a birthday cake, and I remember laughing for the first time in what felt like months. Not a big laugh—just a tiny one. But it was real. And it was because of you.

That was the moment the collapse stopped being the end. It became the beginning of something steadier.

We didn't snap back to normal overnight. We rebuilt slowly—paycheck by paycheck, prayer by prayer, tiny decision by tiny decision. We learned to celebrate small victories: a bill paid on time, a week without overdraft fees, a grocery trip where we bought a name-brand cereal just because we could.

It wasn't the money that came back first. It was the peace. And it came back in pieces.

Like the day you came home grinning because the temp agency had called you back for a second interview. The night we sat on the couch and made a list of things we were grateful for, and somehow the list ended up longer than either of us expected. The Sunday morning we sat in church and the sermon wasn't about finances, but the Scripture felt like it had been written for us, anyway.

"God is our refuge and strength, a very present help in trouble." I wrote that verse on a sticky note and kept it in my purse until it wore soft around the edges.

The real turning point, though—the one I still think about when things feel shaky—came on a day that should have been ordinary.

We were sitting at the kitchen table, the same table where we'd cried and argued and prayed, paying the first round of bills after the bankruptcy. There weren't many envelopes left, but there were still more than we wanted. You slid the last one across to me—a water bill that felt like such a small thing compared to the ones we'd faced before.

"You want to do the honors?" you asked.

I wrote the check. My hands didn't shake. When I put it in the envelope, you kissed the top of my head and said, "Look at us. Still here."

Still here. That became our quiet anthem for a long time.

This season—our collapse—wasn't about money. It was about learning the difference between being broken and being humbled. Between losing things and losing each other. Between shame and surrender. We didn't fail, Caleb. We survived. And we survived because when the bottom fell out, you held on tighter instead of letting go.

If you are reading this, I hope we've walked through many more storms since then. Not because I want them—but because I know storms come whether we want them or not. I just pray we weathered them the same way: together, hands clasped tight, trusting that God was holding the pieces we couldn't fix.

Your wife,

Lauren

Caleb lowered the pages slowly, letting the last lines settle into the quiet kitchen. The spring light outside had shifted again—still cool, still soft, but brighter now, like it was pressing gently through the window instead of waiting behind the clouds.

Connor stared at the letter as if trying to read the words from where he sat.

"So you... went bankrupt," he said softly. Not judgment. Just absorbing.

"We did," Caleb answered. "And we survived it."

Connor swallowed, his fingers tracing the rim of his mug. "I didn't know money got that bad for you."

"We didn't talk about it much," Caleb admitted. "Not to many people. Folks get funny about money. Either they whisper or they judge. Neither helped us back then."

"But y'all fought," Connor said. "A lot."

"We did," Caleb said, honestly warm and steady. "We didn't know how to talk about fear yet. We didn't know how to name what we were feeling. So the fear did all the talking."

Connor nodded slowly. "I get that," he murmured. "Sometimes fear sounds like anger."

"It does," Caleb said. "And shame sounds like silence."

They sat with that for a moment, a quiet understanding settling between them.

Connor finally asked, "Were you scared? Like... that she'd leave?"

Caleb looked at the shelf where the opened letters leaned in their uneven line. "No," he said softly. "Not scared she'd leave. Scared I'd fail her. Scared I couldn't give her what she deserved. Scared she'd look at our life and think she chose wrong."

"Did she?" Connor's eyes lifted.

Caleb smiled gently. "She chose me every day. Even on the bad ones."

Connor breathed out slowly through his nose, as if trying to steady something inside himself. "It's weird," he said. "I don't like hearing about y'all hurting. But... it makes me feel less broken. Like... I'm not the only one who's ever had hard years."

Caleb reached over and rested his hand on Connor's arm. "You're not alone in that. Not a single day."

Connor nodded, eyes a little bright. "Good," he whispered.

Caleb squeezed once, then pulled his hand back, so the moment didn't feel too heavy. "You want to put this one on the shelf?"

Connor hesitated, then shook his head. "Can I... can I put it there? Like you let me do with the first one?"

"Of course."

Connor stood, carefully taking the folded letter from Caleb's hand as though it were something sacred. He walked to the small shelf where the others rested and slid Our First Collapse beside The Crack in the Foundation. For a second he kept his hand on it, palm warm against the paper.

Then he stepped back and looked toward the cedar box.

That thick, unmarked envelope still waited at the bottom—the only one without Lauren's handwriting, the only one without a title, the only one heavy enough to bow the velvet slightly beneath it.

"Still not today," Caleb said quietly.

Connor nodded. "Yeah. Not today."

The rain from earlier in the week had left faint streaks on the window, but the sky outside was clear now. Pale blue, thin clouds drifting the way early spring likes to do—uncertain, but hopeful.

"You hungry?" Caleb asked, pushing back from the table.

"For what?" Connor asked.

"Anything that's not noodles." Caleb grinned.

Connor snorted. "Mom would've hated that part," he said. "All the noodles."

"She made the best of it," Caleb said. "We both did."

They moved around the kitchen together, falling into an easy rhythm—opening cabinets, checking the freezer, debating whether thawing something counted as cooking or cheating. It felt normal in a way that still surprised them sometimes.

As Connor reached into the fridge, he paused. "Dad?"

"Yeah?"

"You think... you think me and you will be okay even when we hit our own collapse someday?"

Caleb didn't answer right away. He walked over, leaned a hip against the counter, and let the truth settle in his tone.

"We already have," he said. "When you moved in. When you didn't trust me yet. When you thought I'd give up on you. When you were scared to get close. That was our first collapse."

Connor blinked, throat working. "But we didn't break."

"No," Caleb said softly. "We didn't. And we won't. Because every time life gives us a crack or a collapse or a storm, we face it together. That's what family is."

The boy nodded, wiping his nose with the back of his wrist like he hoped Caleb didn't see.

Caleb did see. And he smiled.

"Come on," he said, reaching for the skillet. "Let's make something good."

As the stove warmed and the scent of cooking filled the kitchen, the house felt less like a place waiting to remember pain and more like a place learning how to hold hope again.

On the shelf, the letters stood steady. In the box, the unmarked envelope waited. And at the table, two people who once didn't know how to breathe through grief now stood side by side, building something steady out of the cracks.

Still here.

Still together.

Still held.

CHAPTER FIFTEEN

When the Air Changed

By late spring, the light slanted across the living room floor in quiet bands of gold, giving the room a peaceful glow that made breathing feel a little easier. The air smelled faintly of fresh-cut grass from somewhere down the street. The windows were cracked just enough to let in a breeze, and Connor nudged his foot against the side of the cedar box like he wasn't sure whether he wanted to open it or shove it away.

Caleb watched him from the other end of the couch, one arm stretched along the back, posture easy but eyes careful. "We can take a break," he said. "It doesn't have to be every day."

Connor shook his head. "It's not too much. Just... different."

He tapped the lid. "Feels heavier lately."

"That's because you're carrying more of it with me," Caleb said quietly.

Connor didn't reply, but his shoulders eased in a way that meant he had heard it. He slid the box closer and lifted the lid. The warm scent of cedar breathed out, mixing with the breeze drifting through the window. Inside, the letters they'd read sat neatly on the small shelf he'd cleared for them—no two arranged exactly the same way anymore, their edges softening. Today they simply looked used, like stories that had been lived in again.

Connor ran a fingertip across the remaining envelopes inside the box. "What's next?" he asked.

Caleb leaned in, squinting slightly at the labels. "Fourteen's done. So next would be..." His hand hovered before he touched it gently.

"When the Air Changed."

Connor blinked. "Is that about... weather?"

Caleb smiled faintly. "Not the kind you can see."

The boy hesitated. "Do you want to read it, or...?"

He swallowed. "I could try."

Caleb's eyebrows lifted in mild surprise, but not disapproval. "If you want to," he said softly. "She wrote them for us. Not just me."

Connor nodded, more to himself than anyone, and carefully removed the envelope. He handled it like it might crack if he breathed wrong. "She wrote my name weird," he said quietly, tracing the curls in Lauren's looping script on the front. "Like she smiled while she did it."

"She did," Caleb murmured. "She always smiled when she wrote to people she loved."

Connor didn't answer, but he opened the envelope with a softness that made Caleb's breath catch. He unfolded the first page, cleared his throat once, then began to read.

Caleb, my love,

There are days I still wake up and feel the air shift in my memory, the way it did that year when everything I feared met everything I almost lost. I've never fully told you what it felt like from my side. I only ever said, "It scared me," and hoped you could hear the rest between the words. If you are reading this, then time has softened the edges enough that I can finally tell the truth without shaking.

This is the story of the days when your lungs tried to leave me. When I realized grief had taught me all the wrong lessons, and love was trying to teach me the right ones.

Connor paused, eyes flicking toward Caleb. "This is the embolism thing, isn't it?"

Caleb nodded once. "Yeah. This is when everything almost stopped."

Connor drew a slow breath and looked back at the page.

You remember the week it started. You said you felt tired in a way you couldn't explain, like you were walking up a hill even when you were standing still. You brushed it off. You always did. You said work had been busy, that maybe you weren't sleeping enough, that lots of people felt heavy in their bones when the weather changed.

I remember watching you breathe one night, lying there in the dark. Your chest didn't rise the way it usually did. It stuttered. Paused. I touched your shoulder, and you woke instantly, like you'd been standing on the edge of something in your sleep.

The next morning you looked gray around the mouth. I told you to go to the ER. You said you would after work. I told you I meant now. You still said after work.

Connor snorted softly. "Sounds like you."

Caleb lifted a hand in a sheepish half-shrug. "I wasn't very smart then."

"You're not very smart now when it comes to doctors," Connor corrected.

Caleb laughed under his breath. "Fair enough."

Connor kept reading.

Then you collapsed in the hallway on your way to get your jacket. One second you were standing. The next you were grabbing the doorframe like the world had tilted. I don't remember crossing the room. I just remember your face—eyes wide, skin going pale, lips forming my name without sound.

I called 911. My voice didn't shake until after I hung up.

I kneeled beside you and you tried to act like you were fine, even as you struggled to pull in air. Your hand found mine, and you squeezed like you were apologizing for scaring me.

I wasn't scared.

I was terrified.

Connor's voice wavered, but he blinked fast and kept going.

By the time the paramedics arrived, your breathing sounded too fast and too thin. They asked you questions. You answered some. The rest you didn't. I could see them exchange a look I'll never forget—quick, sharp, worried.

"Possible PE," one said under his breath. I didn't know the letters yet. I learned them fast.

Connor looked up. "PE... that's pulmonary embolism, right?"

"Right," Caleb said softly.

"Does it hurt?" Connor asked.

Caleb hesitated. "It feels like someone is sitting on your chest with their whole body. Like you can't get enough air even though you're trying."

Connor swallowed and looked back at the page.

At the hospital, everything moved too fast and too slow at the same time. They took you back behind those double doors and told me to wait. I remember pressing my palms together so hard my fingers went numb. People walked by. Machines beeped somewhere behind the wall. A television in the waiting room played a cooking show, and I kept thinking how ridiculous it was that someone, somewhere, was chopping onions while my world balanced on a knife-edge.

When the doctor finally came to me, he spoke quietly but clearly: blood clots in both lungs.

Connor froze mid-sentence. "Both?"

Caleb nodded. "Both."

"That's... that's bad, right?"

"It usually is."

Connor didn't say anything for a long moment. Then he cleared his throat and picked up again, slower.

They let me see you once they had you stabilized enough to talk. You looked tired—so tired your eyes barely focused on me. But when they did, when you found me, something in the room shifted. The air changed. I felt it. Like time itself leaned in to listen.

You reached for my hand and whispered, "I'm sorry."

I didn't let go. I told you if you apologized again, I'd climb on the bed and shake you. You almost smiled.

Connor paused and gave Caleb a sideways look. "She would've actually done it, wouldn't she?"

"Oh, she absolutely would've climbed right up there," Caleb said.

They kept you for days. Each morning the doctor used words like "stable" and "improving," but none of them reached the part of me that still heard the echo of that first paramedic saying "possible PE." I stayed in the chair beside your bed, legs tucked under me, hands wrapped around the railing like if I let go you might drift away.

You tried to be brave for me. You asked about home, about work, about whether the neighbors had mowed yet. But when you slept—when the monitors beeped steadily beside you—I watched your chest rise and fall in shallow waves, and I prayed the way people pray when they aren't sure their hearts can take another loss.

I told God I wasn't ready to lose you. I told Him He'd given me too much grief already, and if He took you too, I didn't know what my soul would look like afterward. I begged Him—not with perfect words, not with good theology, just with the raw fear of a woman who had seen death steal too many chairs from her table.

When you opened your eyes on the third morning and said my name like it was the first thing you remembered, the air changed again. I knew then that even if life wasn't done shaking us, God had not let go of the edges.

Connor exhaled shakily and lowered the page into his lap.

He didn't say anything.

Caleb didn't rush him.

Outside, a light wind brushed the curtain hem. A single ray of sunlight broke through and landed across Connor's knee like a quiet hand.

The boy finally looked up. "I didn't know it was like that," he whispered.

Caleb nodded. "You were years away from being born. And your mom... she carried that fear a long time."

Connor closed his eyes briefly, pressing the page to his chest without meaning to.

"I wanna finish it," he said.

His voice was small, but steady.

"Give me the next page."

Caleb handed it to him gently.

Connor lifted it, breathed once, and began again.

The days after you came home were some of the quietest we ever lived through. Not empty—just gentle in a way that made everything feel breakable and precious at the same time. You walked slower. You breathed carefully. You laughed only when you had to, because even joy made your chest pull in ways that scared me.

I hovered. I know I did. I watched your color. I counted your breaths at night without meaning to. When you stood up too fast, my heart jumped. When you coughed, my whole body tensed. I wish I could say I trusted God perfectly in that season. I didn't. I trusted Him enough to keep praying, but not enough to stop fearing.

But something else was happening too: we had been walking in opposite directions for a long time before that hospital stay. Grief had turned me inward, and worry had turned you quiet. We had been drifting without admitting it. Then the clots snapped the world in half, and suddenly everything unnecessary fell away. You needed me. I needed you. And there was no room left for old arguments or walls.

One night, about a week after you came home, you couldn't sleep. You sat on the edge of the bed staring at the window like the dark was speaking a language you almost understood. I had been awake for an hour already, counting your breaths again. When I finally whispered your name, you didn't startle. You just looked back at me with eyes that held something I hadn't seen in months—fear, yes, but also something softer.

"I thought I wasn't coming back," you said.

Connor froze mid-sentence again. "Did you?" he asked, glancing at Caleb.

Caleb didn't look away. "I did," he said quietly. "In the ambulance, I remember thinking, 'This is it. This is where it ends.'"

Connor's brow tightened. "She must've been out of her mind."

"She was scared," Caleb said. "And strong. Both can exist at the same time."

Connor nodded once and kept reading.

When you said those words — "I thought I wasn't coming back"—something inside me cracked, but not in the breaking way. More like a shell falling away. I realized I had spent so much of my life bracing for loss that I had forgotten how to hold joy without squeezing it too tight. I had been preparing myself to lose you from the moment I married you, convinced the world took things without warning and that loving you too much might tempt fate.

But there, in that dark room, I saw the truth: love is not fragile. Fear is.

You leaned your head against my shoulder that night. You hadn't done that in weeks—not really. I felt your breath warm against my skin. I felt your weight settle like trust returning one inch at a time. And I knew the air had changed for good. Not because the danger was gone, but because something holy had settled between us, reminding me that God was still stitching us together in ways I couldn't see.

I told you that night that we were going to breathe differently from then on. Not perfectly. Not without fear. But with our hands open instead of our hearts locked in separate rooms. You held my hand and said, "I don't want to waste anything." And for the first time since the day Jeff died, hope didn't feel like something I had to chase—it felt like something that was already standing in the doorway waiting for me.

We weren't healed in that moment. But we were turned toward healing, and that mattered more. Because when life shook the ground again—and it always does—our feet were standing closer together instead of on opposite sides of the fault line.

Sometimes I think Heaven really did stand still for us that season. Not in the dramatic sense, not with thunder or miracles you could see with your eyes. More in the quiet way: like time paused long enough for our hearts to find each other again after months of wandering.

That's what this letter is, in case you ever doubt it again: the reminder that God didn't just pull you through the clots. He pulled us through the distance between us.

Your wife,

Lauren

Connor's voice softened on the last lines until it was barely more than breath. He let the page fall into his lap slowly, as though putting it down too fast might undo something tender.

Caleb didn't speak. He let the quiet settle around them. Outside, the breeze shifted again, carrying the faintest hint of honeysuckle from the neighbor's fence. Spring had finally arrived, not in a sudden burst, but in soft edges—warmer air, lighter evenings, the quiet return of birdsong.

Connor finally whispered, "She thought she might lose you."

"She almost did," Caleb said. "It was close. Too close."

"And that made you two... different?"

Caleb considered, then nodded. "We stopped assuming we had more time. We stopped letting fear make decisions for us. We started choosing each other on purpose again."

Connor traced a line on the arm of the couch. "I don't like thinking about you dying. Even back then."

"You shouldn't like it," Caleb said gently. "But life has shadows. We don't pretend they're not there—we just learn not to live in them."

Connor nodded, though the crease between his eyebrows stayed. His eyes drifted toward the shelf of read letters—the uneven row, the softened edges, the stories that felt more like shared breath than paper now.

"You think she was right?" he asked. "About God holding the edges?"

Caleb's voice was quiet. "I think He held more than the edges. I think He held us in the middle too."

The boy's gaze shifted to the cedar box. Down at the bottom, nearly hidden, the corner of the unmarked envelope peeked out like a quiet reminder.

"We're not ready for that one," Connor said.

"No," Caleb agreed softly. "But we're getting closer."

They sat for another moment, listening to the house breathe. The breeze moved the curtains again, slow and warm, carrying the scent of new leaves and distant magnolias. The light outside settled toward evening, and the shadows stretched but didn't feel heavy.

"Dad?" Connor murmured.

"Yeah?"

"I'm glad you stayed alive."

Caleb swallowed hard. "Me too, buddy."

"And I'm glad she wrote it down," Connor added, touching the letter with his fingertips. "Feels like she's still talking."

"She is," Caleb said. "And we're listening together."

Connor nodded, then leaned back against the couch—not quite touching Caleb, but close enough that the space between them felt intentional, not distant.

Spring had opened the windows, literally and not. And for the first time in a long time, the surrounding air didn't feel like something waiting to break.

It felt like something gently beginning again.

Chapter Sixteen

Fire in the Attic

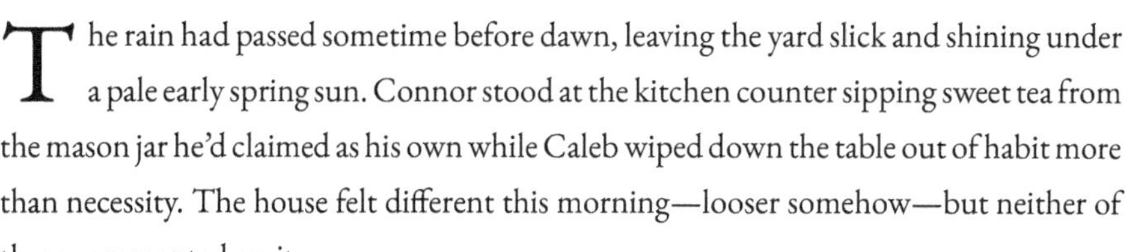

The rain had passed sometime before dawn, leaving the yard slick and shining under a pale early spring sun. Connor stood at the kitchen counter sipping sweet tea from the mason jar he'd claimed as his own while Caleb wiped down the table out of habit more than necessity. The house felt different this morning—looser somehow—but neither of them commented on it.

The cedar box waited on the table, quiet, patient.

Connor set his jar down. "We doing another one today?"

His voice wasn't guarded or pressed. Just steady. Caleb turned, studying the boy's expression. "If you're up for it."

Connor shrugged. "Yeah. I think I am."

They didn't sit immediately. They moved around each other in the small kitchen, gathering warmth in the form of a fresh pitcher of sweet tea and a couple of leftover biscuits. The heater clicked on, adding a low hum beneath the clatter of plates. Outside, the trees held early buds—spring trying its best even if the air wasn't fully convinced yet.

Finally they sat. Caleb eased the cedar box toward them, the scent of warm wood rising softly between them.

"This one…" Caleb murmured, letting his hand drift above the envelopes, "is another hard chapter. But it's one we survived."

"The fire?" Connor asked.

Caleb nodded once.

Connor pulled in a breath. "Okay," he said. "Let's do it."

Caleb lifted the lid. The letters they'd already finished rested on the small shelf behind the box—each one marked differently by fingerprints and time. He reached deeper, fingers gliding past sealed envelopes until he found the one written on thicker paper, the ink slightly faded.

Across the front, in Lauren's familiar curve:

Fire in the Attic

Caleb offered it to Connor. The boy hesitated a beat, then opened the flap. He slid the pages out and paused, reading the first line to himself.

"You want me to take this one?" Connor asked, voice steady but cautious.

Caleb blinked, surprised but grateful. "If you want to."

Connor nodded, swallowed, and began.

Caleb,

I don't know how to tell this story without my hands shaking a little. Some memories soften over time. Some never do. This one still wakes me up at night sometimes—not because of the fire itself, but because of what we almost lost without even realizing how close it came.

It was late 2016, and the whole region smelled like wildfire smoke. The wind kept shifting, carrying the scent from the Smokies all the way into Kingsport. So when we pulled into the driveway that night and the air tasted like smoke, we didn't think anything of it. Everybody's yard smelled like that.

We went inside, tired, ready to settle in. You tried to turn on the TV, and it wouldn't come on. You frowned but didn't say much, and we ended up deciding—like always—that a short visit to your parents' house would do us both good. So we left. No sirens, no alarms. Just a quiet evening with the wrong smoke in the air.

When we got back home later, the house felt… off. Some lights worked; others didn't. That's when I told you, "Go check my office and make sure I have power for work in the morning."

You walked down the hall. I remember the sound of your footsteps stopping. You flipped the switch. Nothing. Then you stepped inside, and you felt the heat rising through the drywall.

You called my name, and something in your voice told me not to move. You grabbed the flashlight and shined it upward—and that was when you saw it: the burn mark spreading across the ceiling like a bruise the house didn't know how to hide.

Connor paused, looking at Caleb with wide eyes. Caleb gave a small nod, letting him continue.

The house had been airtight enough that no smoke leaked down from the attic into the rooms where we lived. And outside, the wildfire smoke masked everything. That's why we never smelled danger. God spared us by nothing more than timing and mercy.

You told me to get outside and call 911. You said it steady, but your eyes were scared in a way I had never seen. I stepped out into the cold night air, phone shaking in my hand. When I looked back at you, you were already running—not away, but back into the house.

At first I couldn't understand. Then I realized who you were going after.

Sebastian.

My solid-black baby, the cat we'd brought home back when we were still living in Bristol. The one who slept against my legs every night and trailed me from room to room like a shadow with a heartbeat. You ran into a burning house for him without hesitating. I think that was the moment I understood what kind of man I had married—not just in vows, but in instinct.

When you came back out, you were coughing, and Sebastian was curled in your jacket, trembling but alive. I still believe that was the first mercy of the night.

Connor lowered the page. "You really did that?"

Caleb rubbed the back of his neck. "I wasn't leaving her cat inside."

Connor shook his head, impressed. "That's... kind of awesome."

Caleb huffed a soft laugh. "In hindsight, maybe not smart. But I'd do it again."

Connor smoothed the page and kept reading.

When the fire department arrived, the attic looked like a war zone—melted wires, beams charred black, insulation burned through like tissue. The chief told us later: "If you'd gone to bed tonight, neither of you would've made it out." Six hours, he said. Maybe less.

I didn't know how to breathe when he said that.

They made us stand back as they pulled open the attic access and soaked everything until the water poured through the ceiling. The living room, the hallway, the office—everything below the attic was drenched. That was the last moment our house looked like our house.

We were not allowed back inside after that.

Water had destroyed what fire didn't. The whole inside would have to be gutted—walls torn open, wiring replaced, rooms rebuilt from the studs out. The fire had burned the attic. The water had taken the rest.

We stood in the driveway in the dark, the engines pulling away one by one, their lights disappearing down the road. You wrapped Sebastian tighter in your jacket. I remember you resting a hand on his head like you needed to be sure he was still yours, still here.

We followed the firefighters' instructions and left everything behind—clothes, photos, the bed we'd slept in the night before. We drove to your parents' house in Gray with nothing but the clothes on our backs and a terrified black cat in your jacket. I remember sitting in the passenger seat, staring straight ahead, my whole body shaking without feeling cold. Shock is a strange kind of silence, Caleb. It fills all the places words should go.

Your parents opened the door before we even made it up the steps. They didn't ask questions. They didn't scold us for not knowing the wiring was bad. They didn't say "It could've been worse," even though it could have. They just let us in. They made room for us on the couch, the bed, the dinner table. They held space for our fear without trying to rush it away.

I didn't know then that we'd be living with them for more than a year—fourteen months, give or take. I didn't know how many times I'd stand in the unfinished shell of our home, staring at open studs and exposed wiring, wondering if we'd ever feel safe sleeping under that roof again. I didn't know how frustrated we'd become with the contractor who didn't seem to care if the work ever got done, or how many nights we'd lie awake in your parents' extra room wondering if our life was on pause or if this was just another chapter to survive.

I only knew one thing: we hadn't died. God had closed a door at just the right time, in just the right way, and we walked out of a house that could have burned through the floorboards while we slept. I didn't feel grateful at first—I just felt shaken. But gratitude came later, slow but steady, like something rebuilding itself from the inside out.

Your mom cooked for us like we'd always lived there. Your dad made jokes when he caught us staring at the ceiling as if checking for smoke. And slowly, the fear settled into something quieter. I started calling their place "home" without meaning to. They made room for me in ways that weren't loud but were steady. I never forgot it.

Meanwhile, our home in Kingsport became a construction zone. Walls came down. Wiring was pulled. The attic was rebuilt from charred beams into clean lumber. Slowly—so slowly—I began seeing our life return in pieces. Not the same as before, but redeemed. Renewed. Safe.

And though we didn't know it yet, that rebuild would matter more than anything. The inspections that followed, the updated wiring, the safety codes brought up to standard—that fire prepared our home for two little boys we hadn't met. Our house became the place Noah would run through laughing, the place Connor would sleep safely for the first time in his life. Fire tried to take everything, and God turned it into the reason two children would someday have a home with us.

But that came later. For now, the year after the fire was quiet in its own way. A season of waiting. A season of learning to breathe again in a house that wasn't ours and trust that someday we'd return to one that would feel like ours again.

I still remember the night we moved back in—February 2018. The walls smelled new. The floors looked different. The house was the same shape, but not the same place. I think part of me was still afraid to sleep there, but you held my hand until I drifted off. And for the first time since the fire, I slept without waking up every hour to listen for danger.

If you are reading this now, I hope you remember not just what we lost, but what survived. We survived. Our home survived. And something in me began to heal the night I watched you run into that house just to bring out a trembling black cat who trusted us more than he understood the danger.

Even mercy has footprints, Caleb. I still see yours running through that smoke.

Your wife,

Lauren

Connor set the last page down slowly, as if the words were still settling in the air. The kitchen felt warmer, fuller—not because of the heater, but because the weight of the story had shifted something in both of them.

"Fourteen months," he murmured. "That's... a long time not to be home."

"It was," Caleb said. "But we were safe. And we were together. That mattered more than anything."

Connor glanced at him. "You really ran in for a cat."

Caleb scratched his jaw, sheepish. "He was her baby. And... he was ours too."

A small smile tugged at Connor's mouth. "Still kinda heroic."

Caleb shrugged. "Just stubborn, maybe."

They sat quietly. Outside, the sun had risen higher, catching on the damp branches and turning them to thin lines of silver. Inside, the sweet tea in Connor's jar had warmed a little, the ice melting into soft clinks.

"So," Connor said, tapping the cedar lid lightly, "because of the fire... everything changed."

"Everything," Caleb agreed. "The house became safe enough for fostering. Safe enough for Noah. Safe enough for you."

Connor nodded, his expression unreadable for a moment. "I guess... I guess good things can start in really scary places."

Caleb felt his throat tighten. "Yeah," he said softly. "They really can."

They didn't reach for another letter. The cedar box sat between them, closed but not heavy, like it understood they'd done enough for one morning. Spring sunlight warmed the table. The house didn't feel haunted by loss—it felt steadied by the stories it still held.

Connor lifted his jar again. "When it gets warm enough," he said casually, "we should grill. Just us."

Caleb smiled. "I'd like that."

They rose in a quiet rhythm—collecting plates, wiping crumbs, rinsing the sweet tea glasses. When the table was clear, Connor reached out and brushed his fingertips over the cedar lid—not to open it, not to rush anything, just to acknowledge it.

"We'll read another one," he said. "But later."

"Later," Caleb agreed.

They stepped out onto the porch. Cool air rolled over them—clean, damp, nothing like smoke. Somewhere in the yard, the earth released the scent of new beginnings, soft and dark and promising.

Caleb glanced at the sky, then at Connor. For the first time in months, spring didn't feel like a season happening without them.

It felt like something opening. Something they were stepping into together.

CHAPTER SEVENTEEN

Home Again

———— ♥ ————

The rain had passed sometime before dawn, leaving the yard slick and shining under a pale early spring sun. Connor stood at the kitchen counter sipping sweet tea from the mason jar he'd claimed as his own while Caleb wiped down the table out of habit more than necessity. The house felt different this morning—looser somehow—but neither of them commented on it.

The cedar box waited on the table, quiet, patient.

Connor set his jar down. "We doing another one today?"

His voice wasn't guarded or pressed. Just steady. Caleb turned, studying the boy's expression. "If you're up for it."

Connor shrugged. "Yeah. I think I am."

They didn't sit immediately. They moved around each other in the small kitchen, gathering warmth in the form of a fresh pitcher of sweet tea and a couple of leftover biscuits. The heater clicked on, adding a low hum beneath the clatter of plates. Outside, the trees held early buds—spring trying its best even if the air wasn't fully convinced yet.

Finally they sat. Caleb eased the cedar box toward them, the scent of warm wood rising softly between them.

"This one…" Caleb murmured, letting his hand drift above the envelopes, "is another hard chapter. But it's one we survived."

"The fire?" Connor asked.

Caleb nodded once.

Connor pulled in a breath. "Okay," he said. "Let's do it."

Caleb lifted the lid. The letters they'd already finished rested on the small shelf behind the box—each one marked differently by fingerprints and time. He reached deeper, fingers gliding past sealed envelopes until he found the one written on thicker paper, the ink slightly faded.

Across the front, in Lauren's familiar curve:

Fire in the Attic

Caleb offered it to Connor. The boy hesitated a beat, then opened the flap. He slid the pages out and paused, reading the first line to himself.

"You want me to take this one?" Connor asked, voice steady but cautious.

Caleb blinked, surprised but grateful. "If you want to."

Connor nodded, swallowed, and began.

Caleb,

I don't know how to tell this story without my hands shaking a little. Some memories soften over time. Some never do. This one still wakes me up at night sometimes—not because of the fire itself, but because of what we almost lost without even realizing how close it came.

It was late 2016, and the whole region smelled like wildfire smoke. The wind kept shifting, carrying the scent from the Smokies all the way into Kingsport. So when we pulled into the driveway that night and the air tasted like smoke, we didn't think anything of it. Everybody's yard smelled like that.

We went inside, tired, ready to settle in. You tried to turn on the TV, and it wouldn't come on. You frowned but didn't say much, and we ended up deciding—like always—that a short visit to your parents' house would do us both good. So we left. No sirens, no alarms. Just a quiet evening with the wrong smoke in the air.

When we got back home later, the house felt... off. Some lights worked; others didn't. That's when I told you, "Go check my office and make sure I have power for work in the morning."

You walked down the hall. I remember the sound of your footsteps stopping. You flipped the switch. Nothing. Then you stepped inside, and you felt the heat rising through the drywall.

You called my name, and something in your voice told me not to move. You grabbed the flashlight and shined it upward—and that was when you saw it: the burn mark spreading across the ceiling like a bruise the house didn't know how to hide.

Connor paused, looking at Caleb with wide eyes. Caleb gave a small nod, letting him continue.

The house had been airtight enough that no smoke leaked down from the attic into the rooms where we lived. And outside, the wildfire smoke masked everything. That's why we never smelled danger. God spared us by nothing more than timing and mercy.

You told me to get outside and call 911. You said it steady, but your eyes were scared in a way I had never seen. I stepped out into the cold night air, phone shaking in my hand. When I looked back at you, you were already running—not away, but back into the house.

At first I couldn't understand. Then I realized who you were going after.

Sebastian.

My solid-black baby, the cat we'd brought home back when we were still living in Bristol. The one who slept against my legs every night and trailed me from room to room like a shadow with a heartbeat. You ran into a burning house for him without hesitating. I think that was the moment I understood what kind of man I had married—not just in vows, but in instinct.

When you came back out, you were coughing, and Sebastian was curled in your jacket, trembling but alive. I still believe that was the first mercy of the night.

Connor lowered the page. "You really did that?"

Caleb rubbed the back of his neck. "I wasn't leaving her cat inside."

Connor shook his head, impressed. "That's... kind of awesome."

Caleb huffed a soft laugh. "In hindsight, maybe not smart. But I'd do it again."

Connor smoothed the page and kept reading.

When the fire department arrived, the attic looked like a war zone—melted wires, beams charred black, insulation burned through like tissue. The chief told us later: "If you'd gone to bed tonight, neither of you would've made it out." Six hours, he said. Maybe less.

I didn't know how to breathe when he said that.

They made us stand back as they pulled open the attic access and soaked everything until the water poured through the ceiling. The living room, the hallway, the office—everything below the attic was drenched. That was the last moment our house looked like our house.

We were not allowed back inside after that.

Water had destroyed what fire didn't. The whole inside would have to be gutted—walls torn open, wiring replaced, rooms rebuilt from the studs out. The fire had burned the attic. The water had taken the rest.

We stood in the driveway in the dark, the engines pulling away one by one, their lights disappearing down the road. You wrapped Sebastian tighter in your jacket. I remember you resting a hand on his head like you needed to be sure he was still yours, still here.

We followed the firefighters' instructions and left everything behind—clothes, photos, the bed we'd slept in the night before. We drove to your parents' house in Gray with nothing but the clothes on our backs and a terrified black cat in your jacket. I remember sitting in the passenger seat, staring straight ahead, my whole body shaking without feeling cold. Shock is a strange kind of silence, Caleb. It fills all the places words should go.

Your parents opened the door before we even made it up the steps. They didn't ask questions. They didn't scold us for not knowing the wiring was bad. They didn't say "It could've been worse," even though it could have. They just let us in. They made room for us on the couch, the bed, the dinner table. They held space for our fear without trying to rush it away.

I didn't know then that we'd be living with them for more than a year—fourteen months, give or take. I didn't know how many times I'd stand in the unfinished shell of our home, staring at open studs and exposed wiring, wondering if we'd ever feel safe sleeping under that roof again. I didn't know how frustrated we'd become with the contractor who didn't seem to care if the work ever got done, or how many nights we'd lie awake in your parents' extra room wondering if our life was on pause or if this was just another chapter to survive.

I only knew one thing: we hadn't died. God had closed a door at just the right time, in just the right way, and we walked out of a house that could have burned through the floorboards while we slept. I didn't feel grateful at first—I just felt shaken. But gratitude came later, slow but steady, like something rebuilding itself from the inside out.

Your mom cooked for us like we'd always lived there. Your dad made jokes when he caught us staring at the ceiling as if checking for smoke. And slowly, the fear settled into something quieter. I started calling their place "home" without meaning to. They made room for me in ways that weren't loud but were steady. I never forgot it.

Meanwhile, our home in Kingsport became a construction zone. Walls came down. Wiring was pulled. The attic was rebuilt from charred beams into clean lumber. Slowly—so slowly—I began seeing our life return in pieces. Not the same as before, but redeemed. Renewed. Safe.

And though we didn't know it yet, that rebuild would matter more than anything. The inspections that followed, the updated wiring, the safety codes brought up to standard—that fire prepared our home for two little boys we hadn't met. Our house became the place Noah would run through laughing, the place Connor would sleep safely for the first time in his life. Fire tried to take everything, and God turned it into the reason two children would someday have a home with us.

But that came later. For now, the year after the fire was quiet, in its own way. A season of waiting. A season of learning to breathe again in a house that wasn't ours and trust that someday we'd return to one that would feel like ours again.

I still remember the night we moved back in—February 2018. The walls smelled new. The floors looked different. The house was the same shape, but not the same place. I think part of me was still afraid to sleep there, but you held my hand until I drifted off. And for the first time since the fire, I slept without waking up every hour to listen for danger.

If you are reading this now, I hope you remember not just what we lost, but what survived. We survived. Our home survived. And something in me began to heal the night I watched you run into that house just to bring out a trembling black cat who trusted us more than he understood the danger.

Even mercy has footprints, Caleb. I still see yours running through that smoke.

Your wife,

Lauren

Connor set the last page down slowly, as if the words were still settling in the air. The kitchen felt warmer, fuller—not because of the heater, but because the weight of the story had shifted something in both of them.

"Fourteen months," he murmured. "That's... a long time not to be home."

"It was," Caleb said. "But we were safe. And we were together. That mattered more than anything."

Connor glanced at him. "You really ran in for a cat."

Caleb scratched his jaw, sheepish. "He was her baby. And... he was ours too."

A small smile tugged at Connor's mouth. "Still kinda heroic."

Caleb shrugged. "Just stubborn, maybe."

They sat quietly. Outside, the sun had risen higher, catching on the damp branches and turning them to thin lines of silver. Inside, the sweet tea in Connor's jar had warmed a little, the ice melting into soft clinks.

"So," Connor said, tapping the cedar lid lightly, "because of the fire... everything changed."

"Everything," Caleb agreed. "The house became safe enough for fostering. Safe enough for Noah. Safe enough for you."

Connor nodded, his expression unreadable for a moment. "I guess... I guess good things can start in really scary places."

Caleb felt his throat tighten. "Yeah," he said softly. "They really can."

They didn't reach for another letter. The cedar box sat between them, closed but not heavy, like it understood they'd done enough for one morning. Spring sunlight warmed the table. The house didn't feel haunted by loss—it felt steadied by the stories it still held.

Connor lifted his jar again. "When it gets warm enough," he said casually, "we should grill. Just us."

Caleb smiled. "I'd like that."

They rose in a quiet rhythm—collecting plates, wiping crumbs, rinsing the sweet tea glasses. When the table was clear, Connor reached out and brushed his fingertips over the cedar lid—not to open it, not to rush anything, just to acknowledge it.

"We'll read another one," he said. "But later."

"Later," Caleb agreed.

They stepped out onto the porch. Cool air rolled over them—clean, damp, nothing like smoke. Somewhere in the yard, the earth released the scent of new beginnings, soft and dark and promising.

Caleb glanced at the sky, then at Connor. For the first time in months, spring didn't feel like a season happening without them.

Connor went to bed knowing the question hadn't left—but for the first time, he wasn't carrying it alone.

CHAPTER EIGHTEEN

♥

The morning light drifted through the kitchen in soft, early spring bands, the kind that made everything look a little gentler than it felt. Caleb set two plates of eggs and biscuits on the table while Connor poured sweet tea into mason jars—his idea, and one he'd stuck with long enough that Caleb didn't bother getting out the regular glasses anymore.

They ate quietly at first, not because anything was wrong, but because some mornings had their own kind of hush. Outside, the yard still looked half asleep, dew clinging to the grass, a cool breeze nudging the wind chimes just once in a while.

The cedar box sat at the far end of the table. Not waiting. Not looming. Just there—part of the room now, the way a piece of furniture becomes familiar simply because two people decide to make space for it.

Connor buttered his biscuit, paused halfway through, and glanced at the box.

"We haven't read one in a couple days," he said.

Caleb nodded. "We haven't."

"Is today... a good day for it?"

The question didn't sound nervous. Just thoughtful. Older than it used to sound.

Caleb took a sip of sweet tea. "Could be," he said. "Depends which one you feel ready for."

Connor's fork stilled. His gaze lingered on the box a long moment before he pushed his plate away, wiped his hands on a napkin, and spoke quietly.

"I want the one about Noah."

Caleb didn't look surprised, but something softened in his expression—something tender, careful. "All right," he said. "We can do that."

They cleared their plates, moving around each other with an ease that came from shared rhythms—one rinsing dishes, the other stacking them, the hum of the dishwasher filling the background. When they returned to the table, Connor was the one who pulled the cedar box closer.

He opened the lid slowly, not out of hesitation but out of respect. The familiar scent rose—cedar, paper, a faint whisper of time. The read letters rested on the small shelf behind the box. Below them, the unopened envelopes sat in neat, quiet rows.

Connor reached in without waiting for Caleb to guide him. His fingers skimmed the names until he stopped on one with slightly thicker paper, Lauren's handwriting curved steady across the front:

Noah

He didn't hand it over. Not yet. He held it in his palm a moment, as if measuring the weight of a story he knew mattered—not just for the past, but for him too.

Finally, he slid it to Caleb. "You can read it," he said. "I just... want to hear it."

Caleb nodded, lifted the envelope, and unfolded the pages with the gentleness he always used with her letters.

He began.

Caleb,

Some stories take root immediately. Some grow slowly. And some arrive like a little boy bursting through every door you didn't even realize you'd shut. This is the story of the child who made you a father long before either of us knew how to carry that word.

His name was Noah, but I think you knew before I did that he was yours from the moment he first looked at you.

It started months before he ever came home. The agency called us and said they wanted us to meet a four-year-old boy who needed a long-term placement. They didn't tell him who we were. They didn't tell him what the visits meant. They just asked if we'd sit with him, play with him, see how he responded.

I remember you were nervous—more than you wanted to admit. You kept smoothing your shirt, checking your hair in the car mirror like you were meeting someone important.

And you were.

More important than either of us understood.

When we walked in, he was sitting on the floor with a bin of Legos and a couple of toy cars. The caseworker said, "This is Noah," and he barely looked up—until you kneeled down beside him.

He didn't know your name, didn't know your story, didn't know we were being considered to be his foster parents. But he glanced at you once, really looked at you, and something in him settled. He scooted a little closer. You picked up a blue Lego brick and asked what he was building.

He said, "A tower." And without thinking, you said, "Can I help?"

He nodded, just like that, and the two of you sat there—your big hands next to his little ones—building crooked towers and laughing like you'd been doing it for years.

Connor swallowed hard, his eyes fixed on the table. Caleb kept reading, voice steady.

We met him again the next week. And the next. Each time, he ran to you faster. Each time, he talked more. He showed you his favorite toy truck. He told you what he liked for breakfast. He sat in your lap without asking permission, like he'd already decided where he belonged.

He didn't know why we were there. He didn't know the word "placement." He didn't know that each visit was another layer of God stitching our family together. He just knew you felt safe.

The fourth visit is the one I'll never forget.

We played with him just like always—Legos, cars, silly noises that made him cackle until he fell against your shoulder. Then the caseworker came in and sat down with us. She looked at Noah and said, "Buddy, remember Caleb and Lauren?" He nodded, swinging his legs.

Then she said, "How would you feel about going to live with them?"

Noah froze for half a second—just long enough to inhale—and then he launched forward, arms around your neck, shouting "YES!" so loud it startled everyone in the room. He didn't even look at me at first. He buried his face in your shoulder and held on like he'd been waiting his whole life to hear those words.

You wrapped your arms around him and said, "We'd love that." You looked at me over his shoulder, eyes shining, and I nodded because I couldn't speak.

He chose us before he knew we were choosing him too.

Connor blinked hard, the corner of his eye catching a shimmer of light. "He really did that?" he asked softly.

"He did," Caleb murmured. "He jumped straight into my arms."

Connor nodded once, as if letting that truth settle somewhere private.

Caleb returned to the letter.

After the visit, you kept telling me, "We've got to hurry the contractors. Our boy is waiting." And you meant it. You called them. You pushed them. You explained that a four-year-old child needed a safe home to come to.

And finally—finally—the house passed inspection.

Then came the day we went to pick him up from his foster home. I remember knocking on the door, my heart in my throat. Noah ran to us the moment he saw you. He didn't pack slowly. He didn't cling to the house or to the people there.

He grabbed his little jacket, his bicycle helmet, and ran straight to the car. Straight to you.

He climbed into the car seat like he'd been waiting his whole life for someone to buckle him in.

He didn't even say goodbye.

Part of me hurt for the family he was leaving. But another part saw something holy in the way he leaped into our arms without fear. He recognized home before he had words for it.

Caleb paused as Connor let out a small breath—quiet, but full.

Outside, a breeze spun the wind chimes once, just enough to stir the room.

Connor lifted his chin. "Keep reading," he whispered.

Caleb nodded and turned the page.

When we got home, he wanted to ride his bicycle, so we drove to the church down the road where the parking lot was smooth and wide. He pedaled in circles, laughing as if joy was something that lived in his lungs.

Then he coasted to a stop right in front of you, lifted his chin, and asked, "Can I call you Daddy?"

You went still—completely still—like your whole heart had leaned forward at once. You kneeled down, looked him in the eyes, and said, "Yes. You can."

His smile—I still see it. It was the kind that could split open the heaviest grief. He wrapped his arms around your neck, and you held him the way a man holds something he knows is sacred.

That night, he wanted spaghetti. You asked if he wanted Parmesan, and when you turned your back for half a second, he dumped the entire container onto his plate. He looked so proud of himself that neither of us could stop laughing.

The next morning, he padded into the kitchen in his little pajamas, climbed into a chair, and said, "Mommy?" for the first time.

I cried over burned toast that morning. The good kind of crying.

Caleb's voice softened as he reached the end of the page.

Connor stared at the table, jaw working, trying to decide what to do with the feelings piling up in his chest.

Caleb waited. No pressure. No rush.

Outside, the early spring sun slowly climbed higher.

Caleb waited for Connor to move first. The boy didn't speak right away. His fingers tapped lightly against the mason jar, the soft clinks almost like he was steadying his thoughts one by one.

Finally, Connor drew in a slow breath. "I didn't know he... chose you like that."

Caleb nodded gently. "It all happened fast. But it felt... right. Like something God arranged when we weren't even looking."

Connor's brows pulled together. "So... was that when you knew you wanted to adopt? Before me?"

There was no jealousy in his tone—only curiosity, the kind that came from wanting to understand where he fit in the story.

Caleb didn't rush. "We didn't know the word 'adopt' belonged to Noah yet," he said. "The plan was long-term foster care. Maybe permanency someday. But what I *did* know was that he was meant to be ours for as long as we could keep him safe."

Connor nodded, absorbing that.

Caleb went on, gently, "When he asked to call me Daddy—it wasn't because he knew what families were supposed to look like. It was because something in him felt safe enough to try. And when he called your mom 'Mommy' the next morning... I think that healed something in her she didn't even know was hurt."

Connor's throat bobbed once. "I'm glad he had that."

"So am I," Caleb said softly.

Connor pressed his palm flat against the table as if grounding himself. "Does it... hurt to talk about him?"

"It did," Caleb admitted. "For a long time. But now it feels more like remembering sunlight. Some memory hurts still have warmth in them."

Connor gave a small nod. "I get that."

He reached toward the letter again, not to read it but to feel it—just lightly, with the tips of his fingers. "I didn't know how loved he was," he murmured. "I mean... I knew. But I didn't *know*."

Caleb's voice gentled. "Love doesn't run out, Connor."

Connor looked up.

Caleb continued, "When Noah came, we didn't love him instead of someone else. And when you came, we didn't love you instead of him. Love isn't a bottle that empties. It grows. Makes room."

Connor swallowed again. A tiny breath shivered out of him.

"Then why didn't he stay?" he asked quietly. "If he loved you like that?"

The question didn't sting—it simply settled like a truth Caleb had already made peace with long ago.

"Because sometimes life is bigger than wanting," Caleb said. "His story bent in a different direction. Not because he didn't love us. Not because we didn't love him. Just... because things don't always get to stay in the shape they start in."

Connor nodded, shoulders tight.

Caleb reached across the table and rested his hand lightly on Connor's forearm. "You came to us when the house was already rebuilt. When the rooms were safe. When the timing had shifted. You came at the exact moment God meant you to."

Connor drew in a breath that trembled only once. "So we both were supposed to be here," he said.

"Yes," Caleb whispered. "In different ways. Both true. Both important."

The room went quiet again—not heavy this time, but full.

After a moment, Connor slid the letter back into its envelope. "He sounds like he was fun," he said softly.

"He was," Caleb murmured. "He was wild and sweet and stubborn and loud and gentle all at once. And he loved big. Just like you do."

Connor tried to hide his smile, but it tugged at the corner of his mouth, anyway.

Caleb closed the cedar lid—not shutting the moment, only settling it. "We don't have to read another one today," he said.

"I know." Connor stood, stretching his arms a little. "But... thanks for reading this one."

"Thank you for choosing it."

They cleaned up together, the motions easy, familiar. The dishwasher hummed. The morning light shifted from pale to warm as the sun climbed.

After the kitchen was set back in order, Connor nodded toward the back door. "You wanna go outside for a bit?" he asked. "Feels nice out."

Caleb smiled. "Yeah. It does."

They stepped onto the porch. The early spring air carried the smell of damp earth and new grass—the kind of morning that made the world feel rebuildable.

Connor leaned against the railing. "Do you think... Noah remembers you?"

Caleb didn't hesitate. "Yes," he said. "And I think he remembers the feeling of home."

Connor nodded, satisfied in a way he didn't try to explain.

They stood there a while longer, letting the breeze move around them, letting the past settle into something softer.

Inside, the cedar box waited on the table.

Not pressing.

Not demanding.

Just holding the stories of the family that shaped them both.

And for the first time since they'd begun reading, Connor didn't look at it with fear or distance.

He looked at it with belonging.

The Dream and the Boy

By late-summer evening, the heat had settled over the backyard like it wasn't quite ready to let go. Sunlight slanted across the yard in long strips, catching on the edge of the fence and the first few leaves that had decided to trade green for gold. The kitchen window stood open, letting in a breeze that smelled like cut grass and the faint smoke from somebody's grill a few houses over.

Connor sat at the table with a root beer sweating in front of him, beads of condensation sliding onto the coaster he definitely hadn't used on purpose. Caleb moved around the kitchen with a lazy kind of efficiency, scraping the last of the dinner dishes, rinsing plates, stacking them in the sink to soak. The ceiling fan hummed overhead, stirring the warm air without quite cooling it.

The cedar box waited on the far end of the table. It didn't loom anymore. It just existed with them, part of the room's landscape, like the salt shaker or the old calendar still turned to last month.

"You know," Connor said suddenly, tracing a fingertip through the circle his bottle had left on the wood, "it's weird."

Caleb glanced over his shoulder. "What is?"

"We've gone from cocoa to sweet tea to root beer," Connor said. "Feels like the drinks are changing with the weather."

Caleb huffed a quiet laugh. "Keeps us from getting bored."

"Yeah." Connor's gaze slid toward the cedar box. "Letters too, I guess."

Caleb dried his hands on a dish towel, then came over and sat across from him. The late sun threw a soft line of light across his forearms. "You thinking about another one?"

Connor didn't flinch at the question anymore. He looked at the box, then back at his dad. "Yeah. But..." He hesitated, searching for the words. "Can we just assume I'm ready if I say I am? No more 'are you sure' every time?"

A smile warmed the corners of Caleb's mouth. "Deal," he said. "If you say you're ready, I'll believe you."

Connor nodded once, as if the agreement settled something deeper than just tonight. He reached for the box and pulled it closer. The lid lifted with a soft rasp, and the scent of cedar and paper rose between them, familiar now but not any less tender.

Inside, the remaining envelopes sat in their rows, the cream and white and soft blue of their paper catching the evening light. Behind the box, on the little shelf, the letters they'd already read stood in a line, edges a little softened from being handled, titles like small chapter headings for their life.

Connor didn't go straight for any one spot. He let his fingers hover across the tops of the envelopes, feeling for something he couldn't have named out loud. Then his hand stilled near the middle. He pinched one envelope carefully by the sides and drew it out.

Lauren's handwriting curved across the front, steady and familiar.

The Dream and the Boy

Connor's chest did a strange, quiet flip. "Is this... me?" he asked.

Caleb's eyes softened. "Yeah," he said. "This is the story of how you came home."

Connor ran his thumb along the edge of the flap. "Okay," he said. "Then I want to read at least part of it."

"Go for it," Caleb said. "If you want to hand it off at any point, you can."

Connor nodded. He opened the envelope slowly, like the paper itself might be listening, then unfolded the pages. The ink had faded just a touch, but the lines were still clear. He swallowed once, then began to read.

Caleb,

Some stories don't start with paperwork or meetings. They start with a promise and a whisper from God that we don't recognize until we're standing in the middle of it.

This one began on a Sunday.

We were driving back from Chattanooga, the highway stretching ahead of us in long gray ribbons, the mountains hazy in the distance. We'd just left the hospital after visiting Noah. My heart felt like someone had wrung it out and hung it up to dry, hopeful and aching all at once.

We still believed he was coming home.

On that drive, I remember you staring straight ahead, both hands on the wheel, knuckles white. I remember you saying you hated leaving him there, even for a few days, and how you told him before we left that we weren't going to bring any other kids into our home until he was back where he belonged. You meant it. I could hear it in your voice. You weren't just making a promise to him. You were making one to yourself.

We had every intention of keeping it.

Then my phone rang.

It was the agency.

I answered, and the worker on the other end sounded tired and hopeful and careful all at the same time. She asked if I was driving; I told her no, that you were. She said, "We have a nine-year-old boy who needs a placement."

I felt you tense beside me before I even repeated it out loud.

She went on. "He's been in a pre-adoptive home, but the foster parents have decided they're not going to adopt him after all. He has some issues, and they don't feel like they can handle them. We're trying to find somewhere safe for him to go."

I turned to look at you. Your jaw tightened. Your eyes stayed on the road. I knew what you were thinking before you said it.

You said, "Tell them no."

So I did. I relayed your answer, voice steady even though something in me flickered. Not because I didn't agree with you—we had promised Noah. But because my heart knew too well what it felt like to be the child someone decided they couldn't keep.

The worker understood. She said she'd keep looking.

We rode in silence for a few miles after that. The hum of the tires on the road filled up the car. I watched the skin between your eyebrows crease the way it does when you're arguing with yourself.

Then, a few minutes later, you said, "Call her back."

I asked why. You kept your eyes on the road and said, "I at least need to know who he is."

So I called. I asked for more information. The worker told us what she could tell without breaking confidences. That he was scared and smart. That he had been through more than most adults. That he needed someone patient who wouldn't give up on him when his past showed up in his behavior.

You listened to every word. You didn't rush. When she finished, you said, "Tell her we'll think about it."

We drove home with those words sitting between us like an extra passenger—Noah in the hospital, a nine-year-old boy in a house that didn't want him anymore, and us somewhere in the middle, trying to be faithful to all the promises at once.

That night, we went to bed tired.

I fell asleep first. You lay there beside me, staring at the ceiling like you were waiting for God to answer a question you hadn't quite found the words to ask out loud.

When you finally slept, you dreamed.

You told me about it the next morning.

You woke me up gently, hand on my shoulder, eyes already wet. I remember thinking something bad had happened—another phone call, another loss. Instead you sat on the edge of the bed and said, "I had a dream."

You said it slowly, like you were still half in it.

You told me you had seen a boy standing in our house. Not just any house—ours. The light from the kitchen window was behind him the way it is in the late afternoon. He was small for nine, shoulders pulled in like he was trying to take up less space. His eyes... you said his eyes were old and scared and hopeful all at the same time.

In the dream, you walked toward him. You didn't say anything. You didn't know if you were allowed to touch him. So you did the thing you always do when you're not sure—you opened your arms and waited.

You said he stepped forward.

You said you felt him lean into you, all at once, like someone finally falling into sleep after fighting it for too long.

When you woke up, your chest hurt from how hard your heart was pounding. That's what you told me. You said, "Lauren, it wasn't just a dream. It felt like God was telling me that boy is supposed to be here."

I asked if you were sure.

You said, "I promised Noah we wouldn't bring anyone else in until he came home. But I think... I think God knew this boy was coming before I made that promise. And maybe—maybe it's not breaking it. Maybe it's making room for something bigger than I understand yet."

You weren't careless with that thought. I could see the weight of it in the way you held your head in your hands. You were torn between two loves you hadn't asked to have at the same time.

Then you lifted your head and said, "Call them. Tell them we'll take him."

So I did.

I didn't know what would happen after I made that call. I only knew that once the words were spoken, the house felt different—like something unseen had shifted its weight and settled in.

The agency moved faster than I expected. Things moved faster than I expected. By midmorning, they called back and said they would bring him that afternoon, as soon as he got out of school. They told us he didn't know yet. That they would explain it to him first. That it might be a lot for him to process.

You stood in the kitchen with your arms crossed while I talked, nodding at things the voice on the other end couldn't see. When I hung up, you exhaled slowly and said, "Okay." Not scared. Not excited. Just steady.

The waiting was the hardest part.

The hours stretched. I cleaned things that were already clean. You walked through the house once, checking doors and windows the way you always do when something important is coming. Neither of us said much. We didn't need to.

When the car finally pulled into the driveway, I felt my heart climb into my throat. You stepped onto the porch first. I stayed just behind you, close enough to feel your shoulder brush mine.

They opened the back door.

He stepped out slowly, backpack hanging off one shoulder. He looked smaller than I expected, thinner, like he'd learned how to fold himself inward. His eyes moved fast, cataloging everything—the yard, the house, the porch, you.

And then he looked straight at you.

Not close. Not similar. The same boy.

I watched your face change in an instant. Shock. Recognition. Awe. Your mouth fell open just a little, like your body reacted before your mind caught up.

You didn't say anything at first. You couldn't. I don't think your heart had caught up yet.

The worker said his name and explained what was happening—that he was going to stay with us now, that this was his home. He nodded, not really looking at her, eyes never leaving you.

You finally found your voice. You kneeled down, just like you had in the dream, slow and careful, keeping your hands open where he could see them.

You said, "Hey. I'm Caleb."

He stared at you for a long second. Then he took a step closer.

Not all the way. Just enough.

I saw the moment something inside him decided to risk it.

When he crossed the threshold into our house, I felt it—like a door inside me had opened too.

The first evening passed quietly. He didn't talk much. He followed you everywhere, close enough to know you were there, far enough not to ask for anything yet. When you showed him his room, he stood in the doorway and didn't go in until you asked if he wanted you to sit with him for a while.

You sat on the second bed—the one we'd kept, the one we never could quite let go of—and waited. He sat on his own bed, hands folded tight in his lap, eyes flicking to you every few seconds.

That night, you stayed in the room. You didn't make a speech about it. You just stayed.

In the morning, he hovered in the doorway while you made breakfast. He watched how you moved, how you spoke, how you smiled without asking anything of him. He copied you without realizing it—how you held your fork, how you leaned against the counter, how you breathed when things were quiet.

At some point that afternoon, when you thought I wasn't listening, I heard him ask you in a small, careful voice, "Are you really my dad?"

You didn't hesitate. You didn't qualify it. You didn't promise things you couldn't control.

You said, "I'm here. And I'm staying."

That was enough.

I don't know if you understand how holy that moment was. How much of his future balanced on those words. How much of mine did too.

Later, after he fell asleep, you finally told me. You sat beside me on the couch and said, "Nothing about him was different. He was the boy from my dream."

I stared at you, stunned. Then I laughed and cried at the same time because suddenly everything made sense. The call. The timing. The ache that wouldn't leave us alone.

God had already decided. He just waited for us to catch up.

If you're reading this now, I want you to remember something. You didn't fail Noah by opening your heart to another child. You honored the promise by being the kind of man who keeps his heart open even when it's already breaking.

The dream wasn't an accident. And the boy wasn't either.

Love doesn't divide when it grows. It multiplies.

That day, when he walked into our house and you recognized him before you ever knew his name, I knew this family was bigger than our fear.

And I knew God was still writing.

Your wife,

Lauren

Caleb folded the letter slowly, his fingers lingering on the crease as if the paper itself needed a moment to rest.

Connor hadn't moved. He stared at the table, eyes glossy, breathing steady but deliberate.

"So," he said finally, voice quiet. "You dreamed me before I ever showed up."

Caleb nodded. "Yeah."

Connor swallowed. "You still said no first."

"I did," Caleb said. "I was scared. I didn't want to break a promise."

"But you changed your mind."

"I listened," Caleb said. "There's a difference."

Connor let that settle. Outside, a breeze stirred the leaves, carrying the faint sound of someone mowing a yard down the street. Summer loosening its grip.

"I'm glad you listened," Connor said.

Caleb reached across the table. Connor met him halfway.

"So am I," Caleb said.

They closed the cedar box together, tucking the story back into its place until it was needed again.

The light outside had shifted, leaning toward evening. Somewhere between summer and fall, a family had been formed long before it knew its own shape.

And tonight, sitting at the table with empty bottles and quiet hands, it finally felt real.

CHAPTER TWENTY

Brothers

The air had that early-fall feel to it—still warm in the afternoons, but cooler once the sun slipped behind the trees. Caleb had the back door cracked open while he rinsed out two plates, letting in the sound of wind moving through leaves that hadn't decided yet whether to let go.

Connor sat at the kitchen table with his phone facedown beside him, not scrolling, not fidgeting. Just present. He'd gotten older in the weeks since they started reading—older in that quiet way grief does when it's finally being spoken to.

Caleb didn't ask if he was ready. He didn't offer to wait. He'd learned that those words made Connor feel like the choice was a test.

Instead, Caleb set the plates in the drying rack and slid into the chair across from him.

"This one," Caleb said softly, "is the one I've been nervous about for you."

Connor's eyes stayed on the table for a beat, then lifted. "Because it's about Noah and me."

Caleb nodded once.

Connor reached for the cedar box without ceremony and nudged it closer, like moving a book they'd both been reading for weeks. "Then read it," he said. "I don't want to keep guessing what happened."

Caleb lifted the lid. The inside smelled like cedar and something faintly sweet—paper that had been kept safe. The letters they'd already opened were not inside anymore. They were on the small shelf behind them, arranged carefully in order, each envelope closed back up and set aside like a chapter marker.

Caleb found the next one and stopped, thumb resting over Lauren's handwriting.

Brothers

He opened it and unfolded the pages. The paper made that soft sound that always felt louder than it should.

Connor didn't look away.

Caleb began.

Caleb, my love,

I have tried to write this letter three times. Each time I stopped halfway through because I could hear my own fear in the words. Not fear of telling the truth—fear of the truth being misunderstood.

So I'm going to say the most important thing first, before anything else has a chance to twist it:

We did not love Noah more than Connor.

We did not love Connor less than Noah.

But love does not feel the same when it lands on two different kinds of hurt.

And this letter is about the season when we learned that the hard way.

When Noah came home to us in February of 2018, he came like a little comet—bright, loud, all movement and laughter and questions. He was four years old. He had been through things he couldn't name. But in those first weeks, he acted like the world was simple: if you wanted a hug, you climbed into it. If you were hungry, you asked. If you were happy, you shouted it.

He didn't walk into our house carefully. He ran.

I still remember the first time he asked if he could call you "Daddy." The way you looked like you were trying not to cry and failing, anyway. And the next morning when he called me "Mommy," and I did cry—right there in the kitchen, holding a spoon, because I didn't know how to carry that kind of joy without letting it spill.

Noah loved out loud.

And then, once he felt safe, his past started pushing its way back into the room.

It didn't arrive like a single moment. It came in pieces: nightmares, sudden panic, that strange way his body would go rigid as if it was bracing for something that wasn't happening anymore. He started telling you things while he played—little fragments of memory spoken like they were facts about Legos or cartoons. And I watched your face change, Caleb. I watched you stand up from the floor after he wandered off, and the color had left you.

You told me later, quietly, "He remembers."

And after that, the air in our house changed.

We kept loving him, but we started loving him while afraid.

We held him through night terrors. We soothed him through storms that didn't match the present. We said "You're safe" so many times it became part of our breathing. Sometimes he believed us. Sometimes he looked right through us like he was somewhere else entirely.

He was too young to carry what came back.

And we were too human to fix it.

When the first hospitalization happened, it felt like someone had taken the floor out from under our family. Not because we didn't expect struggle—because we did—but because no amount of preparation tells your heart what it feels like to watch a four-year-old walk into a locked unit with stuffed animals in his arms.

Those months were their own kind of grief.

We drove to Chattanooga again and again. We sat in waiting rooms. We watched him through the glass. We promised him he was coming back home. We meant it. We built our days around that promise.

And you made him a promise too, Caleb.

You told him you wouldn't bring any other children into our home until he came back.

I heard you say it. I watched Noah's face soften when you said it.

You were not making a casual statement. You were giving him something solid to stand on.

So when we got the call about a nine-year-old boy, it hit that promise like a hammer.

It was a Sunday. We were driving back from Chattanooga, the road stretching ahead like it always did. I answered the phone because it was the agency and because, in those days, every call felt like it might be about Noah.

It wasn't.

They told me they had a nine-year-old boy who needed placement. They said he had been in a home where he was supposed to be adopted and it was falling apart because the foster parents "weren't willing to move forward." They said he had "some issues." They always hide whole worlds inside that word.

Before I could even finish repeating it to you, you said, "No."

Not cruel. Not impatient. Just immediate. You were thinking of Noah's face when you promised.

So I told them no.

And then a few minutes later, you told me to call back and get information.

That part matters, so I'm writing it plain.

You didn't say yes.

You didn't say maybe.

You said, "Get information."

Because even then—tired, heart-sore, committed to one little boy—you still had room in you to wonder if God was asking something hard.

We told them we would think about it.

That night, after we went to bed, God answered the part we couldn't.

You dreamed of him.

You didn't tell me right away. You sat with it like you always did, listening before speaking. But when you finally looked at me the next morning, I could see it in your eyes—the steadiness that only comes when you've already decided.

"Call them," you said. "Tell them yes."

And I did.

They brought Connor to our house that afternoon after school. They told him in the hallway at his school that he was moving. Just like that. No ceremony. No time to process. And then they drove him to us, carrying his life in a bag like it was an overnight trip.

When he walked into our home, you went still.

I didn't understand at first.

Then later—after he'd been shown his room, after he'd sat on the couch like a guest who didn't know if he was allowed to breathe—you told me the truth in a whisper.

"That's him," you said. "That's the boy from my dream."

I remember staring at you, startled.

And then I believed you.

Because your face wasn't the face of a man making a story to feel better.

It was the face of a man recognizing God's handwriting.

Connor did not come into our home like Noah.

He did not run.

He did not claim us with words.

He watched.

He measured.

He moved through the rooms like he was learning where the exits were.

Noah wanted closeness like a reflex. Connor treated closeness like a risk.

So we did what we thought was right. We gave Connor space. We let him come to us on his terms. We didn't force hugs. We didn't demand "I love you." We tried to show him we were steady without crowding him.

But here is the part that hurts to admit:

We were so focused on not overwhelming Connor that we didn't realize how lonely it can feel to be the child who never gets pulled into somebody's lap.

Noah was still in the hospital when Connor arrived.

That is important too.

Connor met our home first, before he met his "brother." He met our routines. He met our kindness. He met the empty space where Noah was supposed to be.

And then—months later, in July of 2019—Noah came back home.

He came back beaming.

He came back older in ways a four-year-old shouldn't be older.

He came back like he had been holding his breath for months and finally got to exhale.

Connor was excited. Truly. I saw it. He stood in the doorway when Noah came in, watching him like he was watching a miracle—this boy we had talked about, visited, waited for. Connor smiled a little when Noah ran straight to you. Connor even laughed when Noah started talking a mile a minute, telling us what he liked and what he didn't and what he wanted for dinner like he owned the place.

For a little while, it felt like the kind of happy we'd been begging for.

But happiness has shadows when trauma is nearby.

Noah's love was loud. Noah's affection was obvious. Noah climbed into your arms like it was the most natural thing in the world.

Connor watched.

And the thought started growing in him, even if he never said it out loud at first:

They love him more.

It wasn't true. But trauma does not care about truth. Trauma cares about what it looks like from the inside.

And from Connor's inside, it looked like Noah got the version of you and me that laughed more, touched more, held more. Noah got kisses on the head without asking. Noah got comfort the second he needed it because his need was obvious.

Connor's need was quiet.

And quiet needs are easy to miss even when you're trying your best not to.

That's where the jealousy started.

Not because Connor was bad.

Because Connor was terrified.

And fear will always try to protect itself by turning into anger.

Caleb's voice slowed there, almost unconsciously, like his body remembered the weight of it. The kitchen had gone still enough that the cicadas outside sounded sharper, like someone had turned the volume up on the world.

Connor didn't blink much. His jaw was tight, but he wasn't shutting down. He was staying.

Caleb lifted his eyes briefly, just to check that Connor was still with him.

Connor nodded once—small, almost invisible.

Caleb went back to the page.

This is the part where things began to tilt, Caleb.

Not all at once. Not with shouting or slammed doors. Just with small, sharp moments that didn't heal cleanly.

Connor started getting short with Noah. Not openly cruel. Just edged. Correcting him. Snapping when Noah touched his things. Rolling his eyes when Noah climbed into your lap.

At first, we explained it away. "He's adjusting." "He's older." "He needs time."

And he did.

But time does not always soften fear. Sometimes it teaches fear new ways to hide.

Noah, for his part, didn't understand any of it. He didn't know why Connor suddenly didn't want to play. He didn't know why the laughter stopped when he entered the room. He didn't know why the brother he had imagined in his head felt farther away than the people he'd lost before.

And then the nights got worse.

Noah's memories didn't stay buried the way everyone hoped they would. Safety unlocked them. Love gave them permission to surface. And once they did, he couldn't control them.

There were nights you held him while his body shook, while his words came out wrong and broken and full of apology that didn't belong to a child. "I'm sorry, Daddy," he would say, over and over, for things he didn't know how to explain.

Connor heard it.

He heard the crying through the walls. He heard the whispers. He heard the way your voice changed when Noah needed you—lower, urgent, focused.

He heard love.

And because he didn't yet know how to trust love that didn't demand him, he mistook it for proof that he was second.

That is the truth I need you to hear gently, Caleb.

Connor didn't want Noah gone.

Connor wanted to be chosen the same way.

But instead of saying that—because he didn't yet know how—he turned that ache outward.

He became sharper.

Meaner.

Not all the time. Just enough to wound.

And I know this part is hard for you to read, because you carry it heavier than you should.

When Noah's second hospitalization came, it wasn't because Connor failed him.

It wasn't because you failed either of them.

It was because Noah's body and mind could not carry the weight of what had returned to him—and because the system did what the system does.

They said it would be better for Connor to be an only child.

They said Noah needed a "different environment."

They said words that sounded clinical and reasonable and ignored the fact that love does not come with interchangeable parts.

When they told us Noah would not be returning this time, it felt like being cut open quietly.

Connor didn't understand it at first.

He thought Noah was coming back like before.

And when he finally understood that Noah wasn't, he did something that broke my heart in a different way.

He came to you one night after bedtime. He stood in the doorway twisting his hands and said, "I think it's my fault."

You told him no.

You told him again.

You told him in every way you knew how.

But fear doesn't let go easily once it's learned a shape.

Much later—years later—Connor would tell us the truth in words he finally had.

"I was jealous," he said. "I wish I'd been nicer to him."

That sentence has lived in my chest ever since.

Not because it was wrong.

But because it was said by a boy who had learned to blame himself for losses that were never his to carry.

Caleb, I need you to hear this clearly, because I know how you replay those years in your mind.

We did not choose wrong.

We did not love wrong.

We were asked to love two hurting children whose wounds required opposite approaches—and we did the best we could with the information and strength we had.

Noah needed constant closeness.

Connor needed permission to approach.

Both deserved safety.

Both deserved permanence.

And the fact that the system couldn't hold that complexity does not mean our love failed.

It means love was bigger than the container they tried to put it in.

If you are reading this with Connor beside you, I hope you can tell him this for me:

Nothing he felt made him bad.

Nothing he needed made him weak.

Nothing he did erased the love we had for Noah.

Some losses come not because of what we did wrong—but because the world does not know how to keep what is fragile.

We were a family that learned how to hold broken things gently.

Even when they were taken from our arms.

And Caleb—this matters too—

You stayed.

You stayed with Connor when he was ashamed of feelings he didn't understand.

You stayed with me when I cried for a child I couldn't tuck in anymore.

You stayed with Noah in every way that mattered, even after he was gone.

Love doesn't end when proximity does.

It echoes.

And those echoes shaped the man Connor is becoming.

I believe that with everything in me.

Your wife,

Lauren

Caleb folded the letter slowly, like he needed the motion to keep his hands steady. The kitchen light hummed above them. Outside, the night had gone quiet enough that even the cicadas had paused, like the world was holding its breath.

Connor didn't wipe his face right away. He stared at the table, then finally looked up.

"I really did feel that," he said. "Like... like I was watching something I didn't know how to ask for."

Caleb nodded. "I know."

"I didn't want him gone," Connor added quickly. "I just—" He stopped, swallowed. "I didn't know how to be... loud like him."

Caleb reached across the table, not pulling Connor in, just resting his hand where Connor could choose it.

"You didn't need to be," he said. "You never did."

Connor let his fingers curl around Caleb's hand this time, tentative but real.

They sat like that for a long moment—no box between them, no words pressing for space.

Outside, a leaf finally let go of its branch and drifted down, the sound too soft to hear but somehow felt.

The crack had been named.

And naming it didn't break them.

It held.

CHAPTER TWENTY-ONE

The Breaking Point

The windows were closed, but the house still felt drafty, as if grief had learned how to slip through seams no one else could see.

Connor sat cross-legged on the living room floor, sorting Lego pieces into uneven piles that didn't seem to follow any real system. He wasn't building anything. Just moving pieces from one place to another, hands busy while his thoughts stayed somewhere else.

Caleb watched him from the couch for a moment before standing. He didn't say anything yet. He walked into the kitchen, poured two glasses of sweet tea, and brought them back. He set one down within Connor's reach without comment.

Connor nodded once, a thank you without looking up.

The cedar box sat on the dining table this time, not brought over yet. Caleb had left it there on purpose, giving Connor space to decide when—and if—they were ready.

After a while, Connor spoke without looking up.

"This is the one where Noah doesn't come back, isn't it?"

Caleb didn't rush to answer. He sat on the edge of the chair across from him.

"Yeah," he said quietly. "It is."

Connor's fingers stilled around a red brick. "I don't remember everything," he said. "Just... pieces."

"That's okay," Caleb said. "You don't have to."

Connor finally looked up. His eyes were steady but young. "I want to know what she said about it."

Caleb nodded. He stood, crossed the room, and carried the cedar box over. He set it on the table between them and opened the lid.

The envelopes inside were fewer now. The shelf behind them held the letters already read—kept there not as relics, but as markers of ground already crossed.

Caleb reached for the envelope Lauren had titled carefully, almost sparingly.

The Breaking Point

He didn't hand it to Connor this time. He opened it himself.

Caleb,

I have rewritten this letter more times than I can count. Not because I don't know what happened—but because I still don't know how to hold it without bleeding.

This is the chapter where loving wasn't enough to keep someone.

Noah was already hurting before Connor ever came to us. You remember that better than anyone. The safety we gave him let the memories loose. Once they came, they didn't go quietly. They tore through his sleep, his body, his sense of now and then.

By the time Connor arrived, Noah was already in the hospital. I know that matters. I know timelines matter when pain starts asking for reasons.

Connor didn't replace Noah.

Connor arrived while we were still holding space for him.

You and I believed—truly believed—that Noah would come back. We told him so. We promised we wouldn't bring another child into our home until he did. And when the agency called that Sunday, coming back from Chattanooga, we said no.

You said no immediately.

I heard it in your voice before I repeated it. Firm. Protective. Certain.

It was only after we asked questions—after we learned there was a nine-year-old boy who was supposed to be adopted, but wasn't going to be—that you told me to call them back. To listen. To think.

You went to sleep still unsure.

And then God spoke to you in the only language you've ever fully trusted.

A dream.

You told me the next morning with your face still pale from it. "I know this sounds strange," you said, "but I think I just met our son."

When Connor walked through the door that afternoon, I watched your mouth fall open. I watched recognition cross your face before you ever told me why.

I believed you when you said God had gone ahead of us.

But even then, I still believed Noah was coming home.

And when he did—months later—I thought we were finally breathing again.

For a moment, it was beautiful.

Noah was older. Bigger. Still affectionate. Still open in a way Connor wasn't yet. Connor watched him closely. He didn't say much, but I saw the questions forming.

Why does he get to climb into laps?

Why does he say what he needs out loud?

Why does it seem like his pain gets answered faster than mine?

Connor didn't know how to ask those things. So instead, he became smaller. Quieter. Sharper around the edges.

And Noah—sweet, fragile Noah—felt it.

Not as rejection. Just as confusion.

The balance we were trying to keep was heavier than it looked.

Caleb paused, breath shallow. Connor had gone still again, Lego piece forgotten in his hand.

"She knows," Connor said quietly.

"Yes," Caleb replied. "She did."

Connor swallowed. "I didn't hate him."

"I know."

"I just... didn't know how to be like that," Connor said. "How to need people."

Caleb leaned forward. "You didn't need to be like him. You needed to be you."

Connor nodded, eyes back on the floor.

Caleb turned the page.

The second hospitalization came faster than either of us expected.

The calls were calmer this time. Clinical. Measured. Like they were trying to make it easier.

It didn't.

Noah didn't understand why he was back there. He didn't understand why the rules had changed. He kept asking when he could come home.

And Caleb—this is the part I need you to stop carrying alone.

The decision that followed wasn't about what happened inside our walls.

It wasn't because Connor failed him.

It wasn't because we loved one of them more.

The agency decided Noah would not return because they believed Connor needed to be an only child.

They didn't say it like that at first.

They used words like "stability," and "environment," and "best interest."

But when it came down to it, they chose simplicity over complexity.

They chose systems over people.

They chose a rule that didn't know our children.

And once that decision was made, the door closed fast.

Visits were limited.

Then stopped.

We weren't given a goodbye.

We weren't given time.

One day, we were his parents.

The next, we were not allowed to see him.

Caleb's voice broke on the last line. He stopped.

Connor didn't speak.

Caleb folded the page carefully, like the paper might tear if he didn't respect it.

"That's enough for tonight," he said gently. "We can finish later."

Connor shook his head once. Not angry. Just certain.

"No," he said. "I want to hear the rest."

Caleb met his eyes. "Okay."

Connor didn't understand at first.

He kept asking when Noah was coming back.

When he realized the answer had changed, he turned it inward.

"I think it's my fault," he said to you one night.

I heard it from the hallway.

I heard your answer too.

Over and over.

No.

No.

No.

But guilt is stubborn when it finally finds language.

Connor carried it quietly.

You carried it loudly.

And I carried it like a wound that never quite closed.

Caleb lowered the page.

Connor's voice was barely there. "I remember that."

"I know."

"I remember thinking if I'd been nicer..."

Caleb reached out, resting his hand on the floor near Connor's knee—not touching, just there.

"That wasn't your burden," he said. "It never was."

Connor nodded, tears gathering but not falling.

Caleb set the letter back inside the envelope.

"We'll finish it next," he said softly. "There's more."

Connor leaned back, staring at the ceiling. "I don't like this part."

"I don't either."

"But I'm glad she told it."

Caleb closed the cedar box gently.

Outside, the wind moved through the trees, steady and indifferent. Inside, father, and son sat with the weight of something that had been broken not by lack of love—but by forces love couldn't out-argue.

And they stayed.

Caleb didn't move right away after he closed the box.

He stayed where he was, hand still resting on the floor beside Connor's knee, close enough to be felt but not forced. Connor's breathing was shallow—quiet, controlled, like he was holding the tears back with willpower and pride.

The sweet tea on the table had gone lukewarm. The ice in the glasses had melted into pale rings.

Caleb glanced toward the shelf where the read letters sat. They looked ordinary lined up like that—paper and ink and thin envelopes—until you remembered each one carried a whole life inside it.

He lifted the cedar lid again, not because they needed another letter, but because he needed to finish this one for Connor. This chapter didn't deserve to end halfway. It deserved to be told all the way through—so the pain didn't get the last word.

Connor shifted, finally, and sat up straighter. He didn't pick up the Legos again. He let them sit where they were, scattered like pieces of a story that still needed assembling.

"Go on," he said.

Caleb nodded, opened the envelope again, and unfolded the remaining pages.

I want to tell you what it felt like when they took him—not because you don't remember, but because sometimes memory turns into a blur when it hurts too much.

The day the agency told us we couldn't see him, I stood in the kitchen with the phone pressed to my ear and I couldn't speak. I could only listen to that voice on the other end saying calm words like they were discussing scheduling and paperwork, not a little boy who called us Mommy and Daddy.

I remember hanging up and staring at the wall. Not crying. Not yet. Just staring. Because my mind couldn't make it real.

Then I walked into the living room and you were there, and I watched your face change the moment you saw mine.

You didn't ask "What did they say?" right away.

You already knew.

Your mouth opened like you were going to say something strong and righteous and determined. And then you didn't.

You sat down hard and put your elbows on your knees and looked at the floor like you were trying to keep yourself from falling through it.

I wanted to yell. At the agency. At God. At the whole world.

Instead, I just sat beside you and tried to breathe.

We had survived the fire.

We had survived money problems.

We had survived years of waiting.

But this was different.

Because this wasn't a hardship that could be fixed.

This was a child being taken.

Caleb swallowed, throat tight.

Connor's eyes stayed on the pages. He wasn't reading them, but he was absorbing them. Every word landed. Caleb could see it in the way Connor's shoulders held tension like armor.

Caleb kept reading.

You tried to fight it.

You made calls. You left messages. You asked for meetings. You asked what we had done wrong. You asked what Noah had done wrong.

No one could give an answer that matched the weight of the loss.

They kept saying "best interest," but none of it sounded like the best interest of a child who had finally stopped asking where home was.

And then the hardest part arrived:

The silence.

No updates.

No visits.

No goodbye.

Just a child somewhere else, and two parents who still loved him, and no place for that love to go.

I started doing something that embarrassed me at first.

I started setting an extra plate in my head.

I'd be cooking, and I'd think, Noah likes cheese, don't forget.

I'd be folding laundry, and I'd reach for a little shirt that wasn't there.

I'd hear a bicycle chain outside and my heart would jump like it was him in the driveway.

Grief plays tricks like that, Caleb. It makes you see ghosts in ordinary sounds.

You and I didn't grieve the same way.

You carried it like a mission, like if you could find the right person and say the right thing and file the right appeal, you could bring him back.

I carried it like a hollow place, like my body had made room for him and couldn't figure out how to shrink again.

And Connor—our quiet boy—carried it like guilt.

He didn't say much.

But I watched him.

I watched him sit at the end of the couch staring at the TV without watching it.

I watched him hover near your chair and then retreat like he wasn't sure he was allowed to need you while you were hurting.

I watched him clean his room too perfectly, like being "good" might stop loss from happening again.

There is a kind of grief that teaches children to disappear.

And Caleb, you and I have spent years trying to undo that lesson in him.

Connor's throat moved as he swallowed. He didn't wipe his face, but his eyes were wet now.

Caleb continued.

There were nights you lay awake and I could feel it even when you didn't move.

There were mornings you left for work and your shoulders looked heavier than the day before.

There were afternoons when Connor would ask, "Are we ever going to see him again?" and your face would go blank for a half-second before you answered.

We learned how to speak carefully in our own house.

As if the wrong word might make the loss permanent.

It was already permanent, and we just didn't know how to accept that without feeling like we were betraying him.

This is what I want you to remember most from that season:

We kept loving him.

Even when loving him hurt.

Even when loving him had nowhere to land.

We loved him into empty air, and somehow that love did not die.

It stayed in us.

It made us different.

It made us more tender.

It made us more furious at a system that treats children like paperwork.

And it made us more determined to be the kind of parents who don't disappear when a child is hard to love.

Because Noah taught us that love isn't proven by keeping someone.

Love is proven by how you hold them while they're leaving.

Caleb blinked hard, fighting the sting behind his eyes, and turned to the next page.

I know you still ask yourself: Why did God let this happen?

I asked that too.

I asked it in whispers at night.

I asked it in anger in the shower.

I asked it while folding tiny clothes I couldn't throw away.

I don't have a clean answer.

But I believe this:

God did not abandon Noah just because the agency did.

God did not leave that little boy alone in the dark places of his mind.

And God did not waste the love we gave him.

I don't say that to make it sound easier.

Nothing about this was easy.

I say it because I need you to know that even when the world took him out of our arms, Heaven did not.

If the day ever comes when Noah finds his way back to the truth—that he was loved, that he belonged here, that he had two people who fought and prayed and ached for him—then this season will not have been for nothing.

But even if he never comes back to our door...

the love we gave him still counts.

And Connor needs to know that too.

Caleb's voice softened as he read the next lines, as if he was laying the words down instead of throwing them into the room.

Connor will blame himself unless you keep telling him the truth.

He will carry guilt like it's his birthright unless you show him it isn't.

He will think love is a competition unless you show him love is a home with room for more than one child.

I know you are tired, Caleb.

I know you are angry.

But please keep doing what you've been doing.

Keep staying.

Keep choosing him.

Keep choosing me.

Noah's loss could have cracked us open in ways that never healed.

But instead, it carved out a deeper place for compassion.

It taught us how to be gentle with fear.

It taught us how to keep the light on for someone who might never walk back through the door.

And it taught Connor something too, even if he didn't know it at the time:

People can leave and love can still remain.

That lesson is going to save him someday.

It might already be saving him now, with you.

So yes, this was our breaking point.

But the thing about breaking points is that they show you what you're made of.
And Caleb...
we were made of staying.
Your wife,
Lauren

Caleb finished and didn't immediately fold the letter.

He let the last words settle.

Connor stared at the table, jaw trembling just slightly. When he spoke, his voice was rough.

"I remember feeling like I ruined it," he said. "Like if I'd just... been different... maybe they wouldn't have decided that."

Caleb shook his head, slow and certain. "They made that call because it was easier for them," he said. "Not because you were jealous. Not because you were scared. Not because you were a kid with trauma trying to survive."

Connor swallowed. "But I was mean to him."

"You were mean sometimes," Caleb said, honest but gentle. "And you were also ten and terrified and confused. Those two things can be true. And you've already done what grown people struggle to do—you admitted it. You learned from it."

Connor's eyes squeezed shut for a second, and one tear finally spilled. He wiped it fast like he was embarrassed by it.

Caleb didn't comment on the tear. He just kept his hand where it was.

"You know what I still do?" Caleb said quietly.

Connor looked up, suspicious. "What?"

"I still think about him when I see a kid riding a bike near a church," Caleb said. "I still hear him in my head when I open the fridge and see spaghetti leftovers." He paused, breath catching. "And I still pray he knows we didn't stop loving him."

Connor's face shifted—something opening in it.

"Do you think he remembers us?" he asked.

Caleb didn't lie. He didn't force hope into a shape it couldn't hold.

"I think parts of him do," Caleb said. "And I think the parts that don't—God can carry for him until he's old enough to hold it."

Connor nodded slowly, the way someone nods when they're not sure but they want to believe.

Caleb folded the letter and slid it back into the envelope. He didn't put it on the shelf yet. He held it a moment longer, like he wasn't ready to let it become "past."

Finally, he stood and placed it with the others. Another line added to the shelf. Another weight set down gently.

Connor's eyes drifted to the cedar box again, to the remaining letters inside, and—down low—the corner of the thick, unmarked envelope waiting under everything.

He looked away quickly.

Caleb closed the lid.

They sat in the quiet for a long time. Not empty quiet. Working quiet.

Then Connor reached for his glass of sweet tea and took a drink.

His voice came out smaller, but steadier.

"So... the next one," he said carefully. "That's about me, isn't it?"

Caleb's throat tightened. "Yeah."

Connor stared at the table. "That one's... about me."

Caleb nodded. "It is."

Connor hesitated, then asked the question that mattered.

"Do you think she wrote it so I'd know I wasn't... second?"

Caleb reached out, this time letting his hand rest on Connor's shoulder—light, asking permission.

"I think she wrote it because she knew you'd wonder," he said. "And she wanted you to have an answer that wasn't fear."

Connor nodded once. Then, quietly, like he was testing the words:

"I'm glad you stayed."

Caleb closed his eyes for a moment. When he opened them, his voice was steady.

"I'm glad I did too."

Outside, the wind shifted. Leaves scraped softly along the porch steps. The season was moving forward, one day at a time, whether they were ready or not.

Inside, father, and son stayed at the table.

Caleb closed the box without choosing a letter, the quiet afterward louder than anything he might have read.

Becoming Connor's Dad

The house had settled into one of those quiet afternoons where the air felt suspended, as if it was waiting for something to move first. Sunlight filtered through the window above the kitchen sink, not bright, not dim—just enough to soften the edges of the room. The season had shifted again. Summer was thinning out, easing toward fall, and the heat no longer pressed against the glass the way it had weeks before.

Caleb stood at the counter rinsing two mugs, listening to the water run longer than necessary. Behind him, Connor sat at the table, one knee pulled up under his chair, his attention split between the cedar box and the open window.

Neither of them spoke for a while.

They didn't need to.

Eventually, Caleb turned off the faucet and dried his hands on the towel draped over his shoulder. He didn't reach for the box yet. He took his time crossing the room, then sat down across from Connor instead of beside him.

Connor noticed.

"You okay?" he asked, not looking up.

Caleb nodded. "Yeah. Just... thinking."

Connor let that sit. He had learned when to press and when to leave space, even if it still felt strange to be the one doing the waiting.

After a moment, Connor rested his forearms on the table. "This one's about... when it was just me, right?" he asked carefully.

Caleb met his eyes. "It's about when we became a family," he said. "Not all at once. Not cleanly. But for real."

Connor breathed out slowly, like he'd been holding that question for longer than he'd realized.

"Okay," he said.

Caleb reached for the cedar box then, drawing it closer. The wood felt warmer now than it had the first weeks after Lauren's death—handled enough times that it no longer felt fragile, just familiar.

He lifted the lid.

The remaining envelopes lay inside, fewer now. The ones they'd already read were no longer part of the ritual inside the box; they rested elsewhere, set aside with intention. The unmarked envelope remained where it always had, heavier than the rest without saying why.

Caleb didn't look at it.

He chose the next letter instead, the one with Lauren's handwriting slightly slanted, the ink pressed just a bit harder at the beginning of each word.

Connor read the front before Caleb said anything.

"So this is the one," Connor said quietly.

Caleb nodded. "Yeah."

He unfolded the pages and held them steady, then began to read.

My Caleb,

I used to think becoming a family would be loud. Big moments. Clear lines. Papers signed, doors opened, everything changing all at once.

I was wrong.

It happened in pieces. In fear. In waiting rooms. In quiet mornings when we weren't sure what came next.

It happened when Connor came into our lives and didn't know yet whether he could stay.

And when we didn't know if we were allowed to hope.

I want to tell you what that season felt like from the inside, because I don't think I ever said it out loud the right way.

When Connor arrived, I saw something in him immediately—not trust, not relief, but awareness. The kind that comes from surviving. He watched everything. Every movement, every tone change, every silence. He didn't lean into us the way Noah did. He didn't ask for comfort. He waited to see if it was safe to want it.

I remember thinking how brave that kind of waiting must be.

You loved him the same way you love everyone—steadily, openly—but you were careful not to crowd him. You let him choose when to sit near you. When to talk. When to pull away.

I loved you for that.

But I also watched him notice things he didn't have words for yet.

He saw how Noah climbed into your lap without asking. How Noah cried openly when memories came back to him. How you held him through the nights when the past wouldn't stay quiet.

Connor didn't know then that Noah needed that kind of holding because he was drowning in things too big for his body to carry.

All Connor could see was that Noah took up space where he didn't yet know how.

And slowly—so quietly we almost missed it—jealousy crept in.

Not because he wanted more love.

But because he was afraid there wasn't enough.

Caleb paused.

Connor's jaw had tightened, his gaze fixed on the tabletop.

"That's... accurate," Connor said after a moment. Not defensive. Just honest.

Caleb nodded and kept reading.

You and I knew Noah's hurt had surfaced long before Connor came. We had already walked through hospital hallways. Already sat in rooms that smelled like disinfectant and fear. Already learned how to hold a child who said "I'm sorry, Daddy" for things that were never his fault.

Connor didn't know that history yet.

All he knew was that Noah was loud with his pain and open with his need, and that we responded because that's what parents do when a child is hurting.

We tried to balance it. We tried to explain without burdening him. We tried to give him space without letting him feel forgotten.

But fear doesn't always listen to logic.

And love doesn't always look the same when you're learning how to receive it.

I saw Connor grow quieter in that season. More careful. More watchful. I saw moments when his frustration slipped out sideways—small cruelties that didn't match his heart but came from a place of confusion.

And I saw the guilt that followed.

He loved Noah.

He just didn't know how to share us yet.

Caleb stopped again.

Connor swallowed. "I didn't hate him," he said quickly. "I really didn't."

"I know," Caleb said. "Your mom knew too."

Connor nodded, eyes burning but dry.

Caleb continued.

When Noah was hospitalized again, I don't think Connor understood why the house felt so different. Relief and fear tangled together in a way that made him feel ashamed for breathing easier.

And when the decision was made that Noah wouldn't come back—not because he wasn't loved, but because the system decided Connor needed to be an only child—I watched Connor carry a weight that wasn't his to hold.

He wondered if it was his fault.

He wondered if love could be taken away just because it got complicated.

I wish I could have told him then what I know now.

That love doesn't disappear because it hurts.

That being honest about jealousy is not the same as being cruel.

That wanting to be enough doesn't make you selfish.

Caleb's voice softened, but he didn't stop.

Becoming Connor's parents didn't happen on the day paperwork was signed.

It happened every time we chose to stay when fear whispered that attachment was dangerous.

Every time Connor tested whether we meant it.

Every time you answered patience with patience.

We were becoming a family even when we didn't have permission to believe it yet.

Caleb folded the pages slowly and set them on the table.

The kitchen was quiet again.

Connor leaned back in his chair, staring at the ceiling for a moment before speaking.

"She really saw that," he said.

"Yes," Caleb said. "She always did."

Connor nodded, once.

"I didn't know how to explain it back then," he said. "I just knew I felt... less important."

Caleb stood and crossed the room, resting a hand on Connor's shoulder. "You never were," he said. "But I understand why it felt that way."

Connor let out a breath he'd been holding for years.

"I wish I'd done some things different," he said.

"So do I," Caleb said gently. "That doesn't mean we failed. It means we were learning."

They stayed there like that for a moment, grounded in the quiet, before Connor straightened.

"Okay," he said. "I can do the next part when you're ready."

Caleb nodded. "Then we'll keep going."

The cedar box remained on the table, steady between them.

Not fragile.

Not finished.

Just waiting.

The quiet lingered after Connor's words, not heavy, just full—like a room after someone finally says the thing that's been waiting to be said.

Caleb didn't rush to fill it.

He returned to his chair, not across from Connor this time, but beside him, close enough that their shoulders nearly touched. Outside, a breeze moved through the trees, the sound of leaves brushing against one another faint but steady. Summer was loosening its grip. Fall was learning the shape of the days.

Caleb reached for the folded pages again, smoothing them once, then turning to the next sheet.

He began reading.

There was a stretch of time when everything felt uncertain—where love existed, but stability did not.

We lived in that in between longer than I expected.

Connor didn't know yet whether he belonged permanently. The system made sure of that. Reviews, delays, paperwork that felt more about money than about children. Adoption was discussed, then postponed, then quietly stalled.

I watched him carry that uncertainty like a second backpack—one he never took off, even when he slept.

He didn't ask us if we were keeping him.

He waited to see if we would.

That kind of waiting changes a child.

It makes you careful with joy.

It makes you ration hope.

Connor shifted slightly in his seat. Caleb noticed, but kept his voice steady.

There were moments—small ones—that felt enormous to me.

   The first time Connor asked where to put his shoes instead of leaving them by the door.

   The first time he checked to see if you were watching when he laughed.

   The first time he argued back.

   Each one told me the same thing: he was testing whether this place could hold him.

   You passed those tests without even knowing they were tests.

   You stayed calm when he pulled away.

   You didn't punish him for protecting himself.

   You let him come to you at his own speed.

Caleb paused, a faint smile tugging at his mouth.

   Connor noticed. "What?" he asked.

   "Nothing," Caleb said softly. "Just... remembering."

   He went on.

I think there's a moment in every family where love shifts from effort to instinct.

   For us, it didn't happen all at once.

It happened the night Connor woke from a nightmare and came to the hallway without knocking.

He didn't cry. He didn't ask for comfort.

He just stood there, waiting to see if the door would open.

You opened it without hesitation.

You didn't ask what was wrong.

You just said, "Hey. You're okay. Come here."

And he did.

He climbed into bed like he'd always belonged there.

Connor swallowed hard.

"I remember that," he said quietly. "I almost went back to my room."

"I know," Caleb said. "You stood there a long time."

Connor shook his head. "I was scared you'd be annoyed."

Caleb met his eyes. "Never," he said. And meant it.

He returned to the letter.

That night, something settled.

Not everything. But something important.

From then on, Connor didn't ask whether he was allowed to stay.

He started asking where he fit.

And that's when I knew—no matter how long the paperwork took, no matter what the system decided—we were already a family.

Adoption would be the seal, not the beginning.

The words landed gently, like they knew where they belonged.

Caleb turned the page.

I want Connor to know this, even if he doesn't read these words himself.

He was never loved less.

He was loved differently, because he needed something different.

Love doesn't run out.

It learns new shapes.

And every version of it mattered.

Caleb folded the letter again, slower this time, as if he were giving the words time to settle back into the paper.

The kitchen felt warmer now. Not from the heater—just from the shared air between them.

Connor leaned back, rubbing his hands together. "So... you were already my dad," he said. "Before anyone said it out loud."

Caleb nodded. "Long before."

Connor was quiet for a moment, then let out a breath that sounded lighter than the ones before it.

"I didn't know she noticed all that," he said.

"She noticed everything," Caleb replied. "Especially the things we didn't say."

Connor nodded. "I wish she were here to tell me."

Caleb felt the familiar ache, but it didn't hollow him out the way it once had. "She did," he said gently, tapping the folded pages. "She just chose a different way."

Connor reached out and touched the letter, not opening it again, just resting his fingers there.

"I'm glad we're doing this," he said. "Even the hard ones."

"Me too," Caleb said.

They sat there until the shadows lengthened, the afternoon sliding closer to evening. Somewhere down the street, a screen door slapped shut, then the neighborhood went quiet again.

Eventually, Caleb gathered the pages and set them aside with the others they'd already read—not with ceremony, just with care.

The cedar box stayed on the table, its lid still open, like it trusted them not to rush.

Connor stood first. "I'm gonna get a drink," he said. "You want anything?"

"Sweet tea's fine," Caleb said.

Connor nodded and headed to the fridge.

Caleb stayed where he was, one hand resting on the table, the other brushing the edge of the box.

For the first time in a long while, the story of how they became a family didn't feel like something unfinished.

It felt lived.

It felt held.

And it felt strong enough to keep going.

Connor returned with two glasses of sweet tea, setting one beside Caleb before dropping back into his chair. Ice clinked softly against the glass, a small, ordinary sound that felt grounding after everything the letter had stirred loose.

He took a long drink, then another, like he was resetting himself.

"Can I ask you something?" he said.

Caleb nodded. "Always."

Connor stared into the tea for a moment, watching the ice slowly turn. "When it took so long... the adoption. Did you ever worry it wouldn't happen?"

Caleb didn't answer right away—not because he didn't know, but because the truth deserved care.

"Yes," he said finally. "I worried about it a lot."

Connor's jaw tightened. "Did that ever make you... pull back?"

Caleb turned fully toward him now. "No," he said. "It made me lean in harder."

Connor looked up, surprised.

"The waiting didn't change how I felt about you," Caleb went on. "It changed how much I paid attention. I noticed every laugh. Every slammed door. Every time you pretended not to care about something that mattered. I knew if the system took too long—or made the wrong call—I wanted you to leave knowing exactly how loved you were."

Connor let that sit with him. His shoulders loosened just a little.

"I didn't know that," he said.

Caleb smiled softly. "A lot of parenting is invisible until you look back."

They sat in silence for a few seconds, the kind that didn't demand filling.

Connor broke it first. "I remember the day it finally went through," he said. "I didn't believe it at first."

Caleb chuckled under his breath. "You read that letter three times."

"I thought maybe I misunderstood," Connor admitted. "Or that someone would call and say there'd been a mistake."

Caleb reached over and rested his hand on Connor's forearm. Not tight. Just there. "There wasn't."

Connor swallowed. "That was the first day I slept all the way through the night."

Caleb closed his eyes briefly at that. "Your mom cried," he said. "Not the quiet kind either."

Connor smiled faintly. "I remember. She hugged me so hard I thought she might knock me over."

"She'd been waiting for that day almost as long as you had," Caleb said.

Connor nodded, then leaned back in his chair, stretching his legs out under the table. "So... this chapter," he said slowly. "It's not really about paperwork."

"No," Caleb agreed. "It's about belonging."

Connor tapped the table once with his fingertip. "That's what it felt like. Like she was saying... the title came later, but the family came first."

"That's exactly it," Caleb said.

He gathered the folded pages again, this time placing them gently on the small shelf behind the box, alongside the others. They didn't look uniform anymore—some slightly bent, some creased more than others—but they felt right together.

Connor watched him do it. "We've read a lot already."

"We have," Caleb said.

"And there's still a lot left," Connor added, glancing at the box.

"Yes," Caleb said, honest but calm. "There is."

Connor exhaled, not sharply—just thoughtfully. "I don't feel as scared about the rest as I thought I would."

Caleb studied him. "Why do you think that is?"

Connor shrugged. "Because... even the hard parts don't end where I thought they would."

Caleb smiled. "That's something your mom understood really well."

The light in the kitchen had shifted again, longer now, stretching shadows across the floor. Outside, someone laughed—brief, distant, ordinary.

Connor stood and carried his empty glass to the sink. "I think I'm done for today," he said. Not overwhelmed. Just finished.

"That's good listening," Caleb said. "Knowing when to stop."

Connor rinsed the glass and set it in the rack. "Tomorrow maybe?"

"Whenever you're ready," Caleb said.

Connor paused at the doorway, then looked back. "Hey, Dad?"

"Yeah?"

"Thanks for not giving up... even when it took forever."

Caleb's chest tightened, but his voice stayed steady. "There was never a version of this where I did."

Connor nodded once, satisfied, and headed down the hall.

Caleb remained at the table a moment longer, eyes resting on the cedar box. It no longer felt like something fragile or dangerous.

It felt like a record of promises kept.

He closed the lid gently, not because the story was finished—but because it was safe to rest there for now.

Outside, the day kept moving forward.

And so did they.

CHAPTER TWENTY-THREE

The Slow Fade

The first real cold of the season came quietly.

Not snow yet—just the kind of chill that slipped in through the cracks at night and lingered into the morning. Caleb noticed it when he stepped into the kitchen barefoot and felt the tile bite back. He crossed the room and turned the thermostat up a notch before Connor came in, then stopped himself.

Connor would've noticed, anyway.

Connor stood at the counter pouring sweet tea into two glasses, his sleeves pushed up, movements careful and unhurried. The cedar box sat where it always did now—on the kitchen table, close enough to touch without being in the way.

No one mentioned it at first.

They drank in silence, the kind that didn't ache anymore. Outside, leaves clung stubbornly to the trees, browned at the edges but not ready to let go.

Connor broke the quiet. "This one's different, isn't it?"

Caleb didn't ask how he knew. He just nodded. "Yeah. It is."

Connor carried his glass to the table and sat. He didn't reach for the box. He just rested his forearms on the wood, grounding himself.

"Is it bad?" he asked—not frightened, just honest.

Caleb considered the question. "It's not sudden," he said. "That's what makes it hard."

Connor nodded slowly. "Okay."

Caleb lifted the lid.

The letters they'd already read were no longer there. They rested behind him now, set aside where they belonged.

Inside the box, fewer envelopes waited.

Caleb reached for one marked in Lauren's steady handwriting:

The Slow Fade

Connor exhaled through his nose. "You're reading?"

"Yeah," Caleb said. "This one's for me first."

Connor leaned back in his chair, listening without bracing.

Caleb unfolded the pages.

My Caleb,

I don't know when you'll read this. I hope it's not too soon. I hope it's at a time when my name doesn't still knock the wind out of you. But I also know how you love to understand things—to trace them back to where they began. So this letter is about beginnings. Quiet ones. The kind you don't notice until they've already changed you.

I think that's how my body started saying goodbye.

Not loudly. Not all at once.

Just... slowly.

At first it was infections. Little ones. Things doctors shrugged at and treated like nuisances. Sinus infections that lingered too long. Chest infections that took more antibiotics than they should have. I told myself it was stress. Or the weather. Or the years catching up.

You noticed before I did.

You always seemed to.

Caleb paused, breath steady, and kept reading.

You'd say things like, "You've been sick a lot lately," and I'd brush it off. I didn't want to worry you. And if I'm honest, I didn't want to worry myself. Saying it out loud made it real.

Then came the shortness of breath.

Just a little at first. Enough to make me pause longer than I meant to after standing. Enough to make me choose the recliner sooner than I used to. Enough to make me feel old in ways I didn't recognize.

I never told you how scared that made me.

I'd sit and count my breaths. In and out. In and out. Telling myself not to panic because panic only steals air faster.

Connor shifted slightly in his chair, but didn't interrupt.

When they finally said COPD, I remember thinking they had the wrong chart.

I had never smoked. I'd never lived with smokers. I'd done everything "right." I asked the pulmonologist twice if he was sure.

He was.

I watched your face while he explained it. You nodded. Asked questions. Took notes. You always go into protector mode when something threatens the people you love.

I went quiet.

I didn't want to ask the questions I was afraid of the answers to.

Caleb swallowed and continued.

Diabetes followed not long after. Another diagnosis. Another pill bottle. Another adjustment. I joked about it because that's what I do when I don't want to cry.

What I didn't tell you was how heavy it felt—how it started to feel like my body was slowly slipping out of my control, piece by piece.

The kidney numbers came later. Quietly. A lab result here. A follow-up appointment there. Words like "monitor" and "progression" and "eventually."

Eventually is a dangerous word.

Caleb's hand tightened on the page, but his voice stayed even.

I didn't tell you right away how bad the fear got.

Not because I didn't trust you—but because I trusted you too much. I knew if I let you see how scared I was, you'd carry it for me. And I didn't want to add that weight to everything else you already held.

You were working. Parenting. Loving. Staying.

So I prayed instead.

Sometimes real prayers. Sometimes just whispered ones in the dark: Please don't let this take me before Connor is ready. Please don't let Caleb be alone. Please don't let my body become the thing that defines our story.

Caleb stopped for a moment.

Connor looked up at him. "You okay?"

Caleb nodded. "Yeah. Just... give me a second."

Connor waited. No pressure.

Caleb went on.

The truth is, I was more afraid of leaving than I was of dying.

I knew where I was going.

I didn't know how you'd live without me.

I watched you sleep some nights and tried to memorize the way your face softened when you rested. I watched Connor move through the house—quiet, careful, still learning how to trust that floors wouldn't fall out from under him.

I thought: I don't get to be the reason he learns loss again.

And yet...

I could feel my strength changing.

Not disappearing—but changing.

I tired faster. I needed help with things I'd never needed help with before. I hated that part. Not out of pride—but because I knew you'd notice.

You always do.

Caleb lowered the page slightly, breath slow.

You never said, "You're getting worse."

You said things like, "Let me carry that."

And sometimes I let you.

Sometimes I didn't.

I'm sorry for the times I pushed you away when you were only trying to stand closer.

The slow fade didn't look like illness to the outside world.

It looked like life.

Doctor appointments squeezed between school schedules. Medication bottles lined up next to vitamins. Nights where we laughed at the same old shows and pretended nothing had shifted.

But inside, I knew.

My body was teaching me how to let go in inches.

Caleb folded the page and reached for the next.

Connor sat very still now.

The kitchen felt warmer than it had earlier, though the thermostat hadn't changed. The heater hummed softly, a background sound that made the space feel held.

Caleb finished the page and let it rest on the table.

Connor spoke quietly. "She knew for a while, didn't she?"

"Yes," Caleb said. "Longer than she let on."

Connor nodded. "That sounds like her."

Caleb smiled faintly. "Yeah. It does."

Connor glanced at the cedar box but didn't touch it. "This isn't everything, is it?"

"No," Caleb said gently. "This is just where it starts."

Connor leaned back, exhaling. "Okay."

They sat there together, not rushed, not bracing—just present.

Outside, a leaf finally let go and drifted past the window.

Not falling fast.

Just... ready.

Caleb folded the letter carefully and placed it on the shelf behind him with the others.

The box stayed open.

Not waiting.

Just allowing.

Caleb didn't close the box right away.

He stayed seated, hands resting flat on the table, as if the wood itself might anchor him. The heater clicked off again, leaving the kitchen quieter than before. Outside, the afternoon light had shifted, thinning as clouds moved in—gray but not heavy.

Connor noticed before Caleb said anything.

"She didn't tell you everything at first," Connor said, not accusing. Just observing.

"No," Caleb replied. "She told me enough to keep me from panicking. She kept the rest to herself."

Connor frowned slightly. "That doesn't seem fair."

Caleb smiled, small and sad. "She thought it was kindness."

Connor nodded. "Yeah. That tracks."

Caleb reached for the remaining pages.

There are things I didn't say out loud right away.

Not because I didn't trust you—but because saying them felt like giving them permission to come true.

The arteriovenous fistula scared me more than anything else.

The idea of my body being altered in a way I couldn't undo. The idea of machines doing work my body was failing to do. The idea of being tethered to something that reminded me, every time, that I was no longer whole in the way I once was.

I didn't want to be the woman you had to take care of.

I wanted to be the woman who stood beside you.

So I cried in the bathroom instead.

I learned how to hide fear behind routine. How to smile through appointments. How to talk about "next steps" like they were far away and theoretical, instead of something inching closer with every lab result.

Some days I felt almost normal. Those were the days I treasured quietly. The days I helped with dinner without having to sit down first. The days I forgot my inhaler in the other room and didn't panic.

Other days, I could feel my body reminding me—gently at first, then more firmly—that it was changing the rules without my permission.

Caleb's voice didn't waver, but his hand tightened slightly on the edge of the page.

You started watching me differently.

Not like I was fragile.

Like I was precious.

You offered help without hovering. You learned which days I needed quiet and which days I needed distraction. You never once made me feel like I was a burden, even on the days I felt like one.

If I didn't say it enough: thank you.

You gave me dignity when I was afraid of losing it.

Connor shifted in his chair, crossing one ankle over the other. His face was thoughtful now, eyes tracking the words as if he could see them without holding the paper.

I worried about Connor more than I worried about myself.

I watched him carefully, wondering how much he sensed. Children like him read rooms the way other people read books. He noticed the pauses. The quieter days. The way you sometimes checked on me before you checked on anything else.

I prayed for him differently than I prayed for myself.

I asked God to give him roots that would hold even if the ground shook again.

I asked God to let him feel loved enough that fear wouldn't define him.

And I asked—more than once—that if my body failed me, my love would not.

Caleb stopped again, breath catching just slightly.

Connor didn't look away.

The slow fade wasn't dramatic.

It didn't announce itself.

It showed up in the way I had to rest between tasks. In the way I planned my days more carefully. In the way I started thinking about the future in shorter sentences.

I didn't tell you every time I felt it.

But I don't think I needed to.

You were already walking closer.

Holding my hand longer.

Listening harder.

The fade was slow—but it wasn't lonely.

Caleb folded the final page and set it down.

For a long moment, neither of them spoke.

Then Connor said, quietly, "She was trying to protect all of us."

"Yes," Caleb said. "Even when it cost her."

Connor leaned forward, resting his elbows on the table. "I don't think she should've had to do that alone."

Caleb nodded. "I wish she hadn't."

Connor's brow furrowed. "Did you ever get mad at her? For not telling you everything?"

Caleb considered the question carefully. "I don't think 'mad' is the right word. I felt... sad. That she thought she had to be strong by herself."

Connor absorbed that. "I do that sometimes."

Caleb met his eyes. "I know."

They shared a look—one that didn't need explaining.

Connor glanced at the shelf where the letters rested. "So this part... is like the warning?"

Caleb shook his head gently. "It's the truth before the storm. It's her saying, 'This didn't come out of nowhere.'"

Connor nodded slowly. "That helps."

Caleb gathered the pages and placed them with the others on the shelf. He didn't line them up perfectly this time. He just set them down where they belonged.

The box stayed open a moment longer.

Connor reached out—not to the letters, but to the edge of the table. "Can we stop here?"

"Yes," Caleb said immediately.

Connor exhaled, relieved. "Not because it's too much. Just... because I want to sit with it."

"That's a good instinct," Caleb said.

They stayed there a while longer, the kitchen dimming as the day slid toward evening. Somewhere down the street, a car door shut. Life continuing, ordinary and insistent.

Finally, Caleb closed the lid of the cedar box.

Not sealing anything away.

Just giving it rest.

Outside, the air cooled another degree.

Inside, the house held steady.

And though the fade had begun long ago, love—quiet, stubborn, and faithful—had already learned how to stay.

Caleb leaned back in his chair, one hand braced against the edge of the table, the other resting loosely in his lap. The kitchen light hummed faintly overhead. Evening had settled in without ceremony, the way it often did now—no sharp edges, just a gradual dimming.

Connor sat quietly, gaze fixed on nothing in particular.

After a while, he spoke. "I think I noticed it before I knew what it was."

Caleb turned slightly toward him. "Noticed what?"

Connor shrugged, then tried again. "That things were... shifting. With her."

Caleb didn't rush him.

"She didn't stop being herself," Connor continued. "That's what's weird. She still laughed. Still teased me. Still got onto me when I left my shoes in the middle of the floor." He paused. "But sometimes she'd just sit. Like she was listening to something nobody else could hear."

Caleb nodded slowly. "I saw that too."

Connor glanced at him. "You did?"

"All the time," Caleb said. "She'd be in the room with us, but part of her was already... paying attention to something farther out."

Connor frowned, trying to find the right shape for the thought. "Like when someone's getting ready to leave a place, even if they're not packing yet."

"Yes," Caleb said softly. "Exactly like that."

Connor absorbed that, fingers tracing the grain of the table. "I didn't know if I was allowed to ask her about it."

Caleb's chest tightened at the honesty. "You were," he said. "But it's okay that you didn't."

Connor nodded. "I think I was afraid if I named it, it would become real."

Caleb leaned forward slightly. "That's a very human fear."

They sat with that a moment.

Connor broke the quiet again. "I remember her getting tired faster. Not sleepy—just... worn. Like her energy ran out before her kindness did."

Caleb smiled faintly. "That's a good way to put it."

"She still showed up," Connor said. "Even when she didn't feel good. Even when she probably shouldn't have."

"Yes," Caleb said. "She believed love was something you practiced, not something you saved for better days."

Connor swallowed. "Do you think she knew how much that mattered?"

Caleb didn't hesitate. "I think she hoped."

Connor's jaw worked as he considered that. "I wish I'd said more."

Caleb reached across the table then, resting his hand lightly over Connor's. "You said plenty," he said. "Some of it just wasn't in words."

Connor didn't pull away.

"She knew," Caleb added. "I promise you that."

Connor exhaled slowly, shoulders easing. "Okay."

The house creaked softly as it always did when the temperature dropped another degree. Somewhere in the walls, heat moved.

Connor glanced toward the shelf where the letters rested. "So this is when it started," he said. Not a question.

"Yes," Caleb said. "But not when it ended."

Connor nodded. "That helps too."

Caleb stood and moved toward the window, looking out at the darkened yard. The last leaves clung stubbornly to the branches, silhouettes against the fading sky.

"She didn't want this chapter to scare you," Caleb said without turning around. "She wanted it to make sense."

Connor considered that. "It does."

Caleb turned back. "You sure?"

Connor met his eyes. "Yeah. It explains why she was both here and... already letting go at the same time."

Caleb felt something loosen in his chest at that.

"That's a brave thing to understand," he said.

Connor shrugged, but there was a steadiness in him now that hadn't been there before. "She taught me."

Caleb returned to the table and closed the cedar box—not carefully this time, just naturally, like something familiar being set aside for the night.

"We don't have to read another one yet," he said.

Connor nodded. "I know."

He stood, stretching his arms overhead. "But I think... when we do, I won't be as confused."

Caleb smiled. "That was the point."

Connor hesitated, then stepped forward and wrapped his arms around Caleb's middle. Not tight. Not desperate. Just sure.

Caleb rested his chin lightly against Connor's hair.

Outside, the season continued its quiet turning.

Inside, the story held—no longer fading, but unfolding exactly as it needed to.

Chapter Twenty-Four

The Weight of a Fistula

A thin crust of frost had turned the yard silver overnight.

By midmorning it was mostly gone, melted off the grass and the mailbox post, but the air still had that sharp, clean bite that made every breath feel like it had edges. Caleb stood at the sink rinsing two mugs, watching Connor through the window reflection more than he watched the water.

Connor was at the table, hoodie on, knees pulled up in the chair in a way that would've earned a comment from Lauren—*Feet on the floor, mister*—except she wasn't here to say it, and Caleb didn't want to replace her voice with his own.

Not for that.

The cedar box sat closed between them. Not center stage, not shoved away. Just there—like a third presence in the kitchen that never spoke but always listened.

Connor traced the grain of the tabletop with one finger. "Is this the one you said was... scary?"

Caleb dried his hands on a dish towel. "It's the one your mom was scared of," he corrected gently.

Connor nodded, eyes dropping to the box. "Dialysis stuff."

"Yeah," Caleb said. "The dialysis access. The arteriovenous fistula."

Connor's mouth tightened. He didn't look squeamish so much as braced. "I still don't really know what that means."

Caleb took a moment. "It's a surgery they do in your arm," he said carefully, keeping it plain. "It makes a stronger blood-flow spot for dialysis. Like… a doorway."

Connor swallowed. "So her arm had to—"

"Change," Caleb finished softly. "Yeah."

Connor stared at the box like it might move. "And she was afraid of that more than… everything else?"

Caleb felt the weight of it land again. "She was afraid of suffering," he said. "Not dying. There's a difference."

Connor's eyes lifted a fraction. "Did she tell you that?"

"In her way," Caleb said.

He sat down across from Connor, not reaching for the box yet. He slid a plate between them—two biscuits he'd warmed up, split and buttered. Not a meal, just something steady.

Connor took one bite out of habit.

Caleb rested his palm on the cedar lid. The wood was cool.

"All right?" he asked.

Connor didn't give him the usual "yeah" out of reflex. He thought for a second, then nodded once. "Yeah. Go ahead."

Caleb opened the box.

The remaining envelopes sat in their neat rows. Behind him, the finished letters stayed together where they belonged—set aside and quiet.

He found the one Lauren had labeled with the kind of blunt honesty she rarely used in everyday life.

The Weight of a Fistula

Caleb slid it out slowly and held it a second longer than he needed to, thumb resting on the ink as if he could feel her hand through it.

He opened the envelope.

The paper inside was thicker than some of the earlier letters. The kind she used when she knew the words might have to carry more.

Caleb read the first line silently, then out loud.

My Caleb,

If you're reading this, it means I'm not there to wave my hand and say, "Don't worry about it," and then change the subject like I always did.

So I'm going to do the thing I avoided in real time.

I'm going to tell you the truth about the fistula.

People talk about dialysis like it's just a treatment. Like it's an appointment you learn to live with. Like it's only hard in a practical way.

But for me, it wasn't practical first.

It was personal.

Caleb's voice stayed steady, but Connor watched him more closely now.

The fear didn't start the day the doctor said the word.

It started the first time I saw someone's arm up close—how the skin rose and shifted, how the vein looked like it was trying to escape. I remember thinking, I don't want my body to look like that. I don't want to feel like that. I didn't want to be tethered to a machine and told it was just part of life now.

I felt guilty for thinking that.

Because I know life is a gift, and I know people endure hard things every day, and I know I am not special in my suffering.

But fear doesn't listen to theology when it gets loud.

It listens to imagination.

Connor's jaw flexed once. He didn't interrupt.

When my kidney numbers started slipping, I told myself I could outwork it.

Drink more water. Rest more. Be better.

Like my body would reward me for trying hard enough.

But the truth is, you can do everything right and still end up standing in a doctor's office hearing the word "progression."

You remember how calm the doctor's voice was.

That's the part that made me angry.

Like he was telling us the weather.

Caleb breathed in through his nose and continued.

Then he said it: "You'll need to start thinking about access."

Access.

Like my arm was going to become a place people entered.

I nodded like I understood. I asked one question. I pretended I was fine.

And then, later—when you were in the other room—my hands started shaking and I couldn't stop them.

That's when I realized it wasn't just fear of a procedure.

It was fear of becoming someone I didn't recognize.

I didn't want you to look at me and see illness first.

I didn't want Connor to look at me and think, Here we go again, another thing that changes everything.

Caleb's throat tightened slightly on Connor's name. Connor stared at the table, listening.

I tried to hide it from you.

Not because you aren't safe. You're the safest place I've ever had.

But because your love makes me want to be brave, and I was tired of being brave.

I wanted one corner of my life where I could be small and not have anyone ask me to stand back up.

So I cried in the places you wouldn't see.

In the bathroom with the fan running.

In the car with the radio up.

In the laundry room with a towel pressed to my mouth so I wouldn't make a sound.

Caleb paused for half a second, eyes dropping to the page. He kept going.

I know you noticed anyway.

You'd ask, "Are you okay?"

And I'd say, "I'm fine," because it was easier than explaining the kind of fear that doesn't have a clean shape.

Here is the clean shape:

I was terrified of pain.

Not the normal pain. Not a headache or a pulled muscle. I mean the kind of pain that takes away dignity. The kind that makes you feel like your body belongs to strangers in gloves.

I was terrified of being trapped.

Of appointments three times a week.

Of needles.

Of fatigue so deep it changes your voice.

Of needing help to do things that used to be mine.

Connor's shoulders rose and fell with one slow breath.

I wasn't afraid of Heaven.

I was afraid of the hallway that leads to it.

I was afraid of the long waiting that comes before goodbye—where you are trying not to cry and I am trying not to beg.

I was afraid of you watching me suffer and having no way to take it from me.

Caleb's voice softened without breaking. Connor's eyes were wet, but he didn't wipe them.

And then there was the fistula itself.

The idea of my arm being changed on purpose.

I know how that sounds.

But my body has always been the place I lived my life—hugging my boys, cooking dinners, folding laundry, holding your hand in the dark.

I didn't want it to become a symbol before it became a memory.

I didn't want strangers to see it and know what was happening before I was ready to say it.

I didn't want to be looked at with pity.

Caleb turned the page.

One afternoon I sat in the parking lot after an appointment and I did something I hadn't done in a long time.

I prayed without trying to sound strong.

I didn't say the right words.

I didn't say polished words.

I said, "Lord, I'm scared."

That was it.

Just the truth.

And I felt—quietly, not dramatically—like God wasn't disappointed in me for being afraid.

Like He was simply there.

Holding the edges of me the way you always tried to.

Connor's chin dipped, as if that sentence landed somewhere tender.

I went home and tried to act normal.

You were making dinner, and the house smelled like something safe.

You asked me how it went and I said, "Same old," and you nodded like you believed me.

But later, when we were in bed and you reached for my hand, I realized something.

I was more afraid of losing control than I was of losing time.

And control is the thing God never promised me.

Only presence.

Caleb read on, slower now.

So here is the truth I want to give you, not as a burden but as a gift:

If there were moments when I seemed stubborn, it wasn't because I didn't want to live.

It was because I didn't want to live afraid.

And I didn't know how to do one without the other.

If I ever snapped at you, if I ever went quiet, if I ever pulled my arm away when you tried to touch it, it wasn't because I didn't love you.

It was because panic was louder than my manners.

I am sorry for that.

And I am grateful that you loved me anyway.

Caleb reached the bottom of the page and looked up for a heartbeat.

Connor's voice came out small. "Did you know all that?"

Caleb's answer was honest. "Not all of it."

Connor nodded like he'd expected that.

Caleb continued.

There is something else I need to say.

You were never asking me to be a hero.

I turned your love into a performance in my own head—like I had to be brave enough to deserve it.

That wasn't you.

That was me.

You would've held me through every appointment if I had let you.

You would've sat in every waiting room and made jokes that weren't funny just to make me smile.

You would've prayed quiet prayers beside me and never once made me feel like faith required perfection.

I want you to know that I saw that.

Even when I was scared, I saw it.

Connor's gaze moved to Caleb's hands, then back to Caleb's face. Like he was learning a new piece of his dad in real time.

And I want you to know something about Connor too.

He was watching.

Not in a way that made me feel pressured—just in the way a child watches when they love someone and don't have language for what they're seeing.

If he pulled away sometimes, it wasn't because he didn't care.

It was because caring cost him something he had run out of before he ever came to us.

So if you ever needed a reason to be gentle with him, there it is.

Caleb's voice caught slightly, then smoothed.

I don't know what the future held when I was living it.

But I know this: I loved you with my whole self—fear and all.

And if the fistula became part of my story, it was never meant to be the only part.

It was just one heavy thing in a life filled with light.

If you are reading this now, and you are tempted to remember me only in hospitals and numbers and alarms, please don't.

Remember me in the kitchen. In the car singing. In the yard when the sun hit the grass just right. Remember me leaning into you on the couch, laughing at something dumb.

Remember that I was more than what my body did.

And so are you.

And so is our son.

God did not love me less because I was afraid.

He loved me through it.

So did you.

That is what I want to leave you with.

Not fear.

Love.

Your wife,

Lauren

Caleb finished the last word and let the silence settle.

It wasn't a dramatic silence. It was the kind that rearranged things inside you without asking permission.

Connor looked at the letter like it might speak again if he stared long enough.

Then he said, "She was scared of being... seen like that."

Caleb nodded. "Yeah."

Connor swallowed. "I get that."

Caleb's eyes lifted. "You do?"

Connor's shoulders rose in a small shrug, but his voice was steady. "When people look at you like you're a problem... you don't want anything new that gives them a reason."

Caleb didn't correct it. He didn't soften it. He just let Connor's truth stand.

"That's why she wrote it this way," Caleb said quietly. "She didn't want to be reduced."

Connor stared at the table again. "Did she ever... talk to you about Heaven when she was scared?"

Caleb thought. "Not like a speech," he said. "More like... she'd say one sentence. And it would carry more than it should."

Connor nodded. "That's her."

Caleb folded the letter carefully and held it a second before setting it aside.

Connor didn't move.

His voice came out thin. "Can we... not do another one tonight?"

Caleb shook his head gently. "We're done."

Connor let out a breath he'd been holding and nodded once, grateful.

Caleb placed the letter on the shelf with the others, not fussing with alignment. Just returning it to its place.

He closed the cedar lid.

The frost outside had melted, but the day still held its bite.

Inside, the kitchen felt warmer—not because anything had gotten easier, but because they'd named something true without it swallowing them.

Connor stood and reached for his mug. "Do you think," he asked quietly, "she knew we'd be reading these?"

Caleb's mouth tightened with love and ache. "Yeah," he said. "I think she knew."

Connor nodded, eyes down. "Okay."

Caleb rose too. "Let's eat something real," he said softly. "Soup? Chili? Whatever you want."

Connor hesitated, then gave a small, almost embarrassed nod. "Chili sounds good."

Caleb felt a flicker of gratitude for ordinary food and ordinary evenings.

He reached for the pot, and Connor reached for bowls, and in the small movements of living, the letter's weight didn't vanish —

but it became carriable.

Later that night, Caleb stood in the hallway outside Connor's room, listening.

Not because he was worried—just because that had become a habit he didn't seem able to break. The house made its usual settling sounds, soft pops, and creaks that once would have meant nothing and now carried stories with them.

Connor was awake. Caleb could hear the faint rustle of sheets, the low click of the bedside lamp.

He knocked lightly.

"Yeah?" Connor called.

Caleb pushed the door open. "Just checking in."

Connor sat cross-legged on the bed, hoodie pulled up around his neck, phone face-down beside him. He didn't look startled or guarded. Just thoughtful.

"Can't sleep?" Caleb asked.

Connor shrugged. "Not tired yet."

Caleb leaned against the doorframe. "You want company, or you want space?"

Connor considered it. "Company's okay."

Caleb crossed the room and sat on the edge of the bed, careful not to crowd him. They sat shoulder to shoulder without touching.

After a moment, Connor said, "I keep thinking about that hallway she talked about."

Caleb nodded. "The one before the good part."

"Yeah," Connor said. "I didn't know grown-ups were scared of stuff like that too."

Caleb smiled faintly. "We just get better at hiding it."

Connor frowned. "Why?"

Caleb thought for a second. "Because we think being strong means being quiet about fear."

Connor picked at a loose thread on his blanket. "That doesn't seem right."

"It isn't," Caleb said. "But it's common."

Connor went still. "Do you think she was scared like that when… the end got closer?"

Caleb didn't dodge it. "I think she was scared sometimes," he said. "And I think other times she was calm in a way I didn't understand until later."

Connor's voice came soft. "Did she talk to God about it?"

"Yes," Caleb said. "In her own way."

Connor glanced up. "Did He answer?"

Caleb hesitated—not from uncertainty, but from respect for the question. "I think He did," he said. "Not by taking the fear away. But by staying with her inside it."

Connor nodded slowly, absorbing that. "That sounds like her prayers."

Caleb smiled. "It does."

Connor leaned back on his hands. "I don't think I'm scared of the letters anymore."

Caleb tilted his head. "No?"

Connor shook his head. "I mean... they're heavy. But they're not trying to hurt me."

Caleb felt something settle in his chest. "They never were."

Connor's gaze drifted to the wall. "I think I used to believe sickness meant God was leaving."

Caleb's voice stayed gentle. "And now?"

Connor thought. "Now it kind of feels like... God was already there. Before anyone else noticed."

Caleb swallowed. "That's a hard truth to learn. And a good one."

Connor's shoulders relaxed a fraction. "She didn't sound angry at Him."

"No," Caleb said. "She sounded honest."

Connor smiled faintly. "She was good at that."

They sat in silence again—not awkward, not strained.

After a while, Connor said, "Tomorrow... do we read another one?"

Caleb nodded. "If you want."

Connor hesitated. "Not right away."

"That's okay," Caleb said. "There's no clock."

Connor let out a slow breath. "I like that."

Caleb stood and rested a hand briefly on Connor's shoulder—not gripping, just grounding. "Try to sleep."

Connor nodded. "Night, Dad."

"Night," Caleb said.

He turned off the light and closed the door halfway, leaving the hall lamp on like Lauren used to.

Back in the kitchen, Caleb passed the table where the cedar box sat closed, steady, no longer looming.

And when Caleb finally went to bed, the fear didn't follow him.

Only the quiet understanding that love had already done more than fear ever could.

CHAPTER TWENTY-FIVE

What Her Body Was Telling Her

The first cold snap had come in quiet, like it was trying not to wake anybody.

A thin film of frost clung to the grass outside the kitchen window, and the world had that clean, brittle look it gets when the air decides it's done being gentle. Somewhere in the neighborhood a leaf blower whined for a minute and stopped. The house itself felt sealed up against the season—windows latched, curtains pulled just enough to keep the draft off Connor's chair.

Connor sat at the table with his hoodie on, sleeves swallowed over his hands. He wasn't shivering. He just liked being wrapped up lately, like warmth was something you could hold onto if you layered enough fabric between you and everything else.

Caleb didn't bring the cedar box out right away.

He moved around the kitchen first—quiet, purposeful motions that didn't need an audience. He rinsed a couple of plates from breakfast. He set a pan on the stove like he might cook and then decided not to. He checked the mail on the counter and tossed the junk into the trash without looking at it.

Connor watched him without saying much, eyes following the small routines like he was learning the shape of a man's grief by watching what he did with his hands.

Finally, Caleb came to the table and sat.

Not across from Connor—beside him.

That was new enough that Connor noticed it.

"You doing okay?" Connor asked, like it was casual, like he hadn't been practicing the question in his throat.

Caleb leaned back in the chair, exhaled through his nose. "Some days I'm fine until I'm not," he said. "Today's... in the middle."

Connor nodded once. He turned his gaze to the empty spot on the table where the box would go.

Caleb followed his eyes and didn't pretend he hadn't seen it.

"You don't have to pick a hard one," Caleb said. He kept his tone steady—no warning, no permission, just truth. "We can read something lighter. Something that lets you breathe."

Connor gave a short, humorless laugh. "That's kind of the problem," he said.

Caleb's face tightened the smallest amount.

Connor rubbed his thumb across the seam of his sleeve. "I keep thinking... if I read enough, I'll know what's coming. Like it won't blindside me anymore."

Caleb let that sit. Not because he didn't have words—but because he knew the feeling. He'd spent his whole life trying to get ahead of pain with preparation, only to learn pain doesn't care how ready you are.

"Alright," Caleb said finally. "Then we don't pick the easy one. We pick the true one."

Connor's shoulders rose and fell in a single breath. "Okay."

Caleb reached under the table and pulled the cedar box up from the chair beside him, setting it down gently. The wood made a soft, solid sound against the tabletop—an ordinary noise for an object that carried so much weight.

He didn't describe it. Didn't narrate it. He just opened it.

Inside, the remaining envelopes lay like quiet promises, Lauren's handwriting familiar and steady in the dim winter light. Caleb's fingers hovered, then moved with purpose.

He stopped on one that felt thicker than the rest—more pages, more time.

Across the front, in her neat curve:

The Day I Couldn't Breathe

Connor's gaze pinned to the title. His jaw tightened, and he didn't look away.

Caleb slid the letter free and held it between them. "This is the day we realized how serious it was getting," he said softly.

Connor swallowed, eyes still locked on the title. "Okay."

"Do you want me to read?" Caleb asked.

Connor stared at the envelope. "Yeah," he said. Then, after a beat, "Don't... soften it."

Caleb's throat worked. "I won't."

He opened the envelope and unfolded the pages. The paper had that worn feel letters get when they've been handled once or twice before being tucked away—creased carefully, smoothed down, remembered.

Caleb took a breath and began.

Caleb,

There are some days that split your life into Before and After, even if you don't know it while you're living it.

I keep coming back to this one because it was the day I heard fear in your voice the way you usually tried to hide it. You've always been steady when something goes wrong. Even when you're scared, you become practical. You become motion. You become solutions.

That day, you became prayer.

I had been coughing for a while by then. We both knew that. We talked about it like it was annoying, like it was seasonal, like it was something we could manage with doctor visits and medicine and your gentle reminders that I needed to rest.

I told you I was fine more times than I meant it.

But that morning, something felt different. It wasn't pain. It wasn't even a sharp warning. It was just the strange sensation of my chest not doing what it had always done without asking.

Breathing is supposed to be automatic, Caleb. You don't think about it until it refuses to obey.

I woke up, and the room felt too thick. The air felt heavy, like someone had put a blanket over my face in the night. I sat up and tried to breathe deeper, and my body answered with shallow little sips instead—like I was trying to drink through a straw.

I sat there on the edge of the bed and told myself it would pass.

I didn't want to scare you. I didn't want to scare Connor. I didn't want to become the reason the whole day changed shape.

So I got up anyway.

I moved slower than usual. I didn't say much. You watched me the way you do when you're taking in more than you're willing to admit. You asked if I wanted something warm and I shook my head. My stomach felt like it was trying to float.

You asked if I was okay, and I said yes.

I wish I could go back and replace that yes with honesty.

Because then the coughing started.

Not the ordinary kind. Not the "give me a minute" kind. This was the kind that takes over your whole body and makes you bend forward like your ribs are trying to protect your lungs from themselves.

I remember your chair scraping back so fast it startled Connor. I remember you crossing the room in two steps. I remember your hand on my back, firm and warm, like your touch could force my body to behave.

You asked me to look at you. I couldn't. I was trying too hard to pull in air.

You said my name the way you do when you need me to hear you.

And then I saw your face.

You were afraid.

It wasn't dramatic. It wasn't panic. It was that quiet fear that sits behind a man's eyes when he realizes something is out of his control. The kind you used to get when Connor was too quiet and you knew something was wrong.

You told Connor to get his shoes.

Connor hesitated. He asked what was happening. You said, "We're going to get Mom checked. Right now."

You tried to sound calm.

I heard the crack anyway.

I don't remember everything after that in order. I remember pieces, like snapshots: your hand steadying my elbow as we walked; the cold air outside making my lungs fight harder; Connor's face in the passenger seat looking straight ahead like he was trying not to fall apart.

I remember you driving with one hand and holding mine with the other when you could.

I remember the emergency room doors and the smell of disinfectant and the way the lights always feel too bright in places where people are hurting.

They put that little clip on my finger and the numbers on the screen made your face go pale. You asked what the numbers meant. You asked if it was dangerous. You asked if I could die.

I heard you say those words, Caleb.

I heard you say them out loud.

I had been thinking them quietly for a while.

I watched Connor standing near the wall, trying to look older than he was, trying to look like a boy who knew hospitals and wasn't scared of them.

But I saw his hands.

They were shaking.

The nurse moved faster after that. They put oxygen on me. The first deep breath I got felt like someone had handed me my own body back. I cried, not because it hurt, but because I hadn't realized how close I was to losing something as basic as air.

They asked questions. They asked about my history. They asked about infections and breathing and fatigue and the way my body had been changing.

You answered most of them because you always remember details when I'm too tired to.

You spoke for me, but you didn't speak over me. You kept looking at my face, checking my eyes, asking silently, "Are you still with me?"

Connor sat in a chair that was too big for him and tried to disappear into it. He didn't cry. He didn't make a scene. He just watched and learned in that quiet way that breaks my heart.

At one point, when the staff stepped out, Connor asked you, "Is she going to die?"

You didn't say, "No."

You said, "I don't know. But we're here, and they're helping her, and God is with us."

I want you to know something about that moment.

Even if Connor never says it out loud, he heard you.

He heard that you didn't lie.

He heard that you didn't leave room for hopelessness either.

That is fatherhood, Caleb. That is love.

They admitted me after that. The hours blurred. The machines beeped. People came and went. You slept wrong in a chair and still woke up every time I coughed. You kept checking the monitor like it could answer questions you weren't brave enough to speak.

I lay there thinking about all the ordinary things I still wanted: folding laundry, fussing at you for leaving your shoes where I'd trip, sitting at the table while Connor pretended he wasn't listening to our stories.

It surprised me how badly I wanted to keep living inside the small things.

Because the truth is, Caleb... I wasn't afraid of Heaven.

I was afraid of leaving you with too much.

I was afraid of leaving Connor with another empty space.

I was afraid of you having to be the one to explain to him that love doesn't always get to stay in the form you want it to.

That night in the hospital, when Connor finally fell asleep with his head against your arm in the waiting area, you bowed your head.

You didn't make a show of it.

You just closed your eyes and breathed like you were borrowing air too.

I could see your lips moving.

I couldn't hear what you said, but I knew the shape of it.

Please. Please. Please.

I think God listens especially closely to prayers that don't have good grammar.

I don't know if this was the day everything began to end.

But I know it was the day we stopped pretending time was unlimited.

It was the day I saw Connor look at you like, "Don't let her go," and I saw you look back like, "I won't—if I can help it."

It was the day my breath became something we all paid attention to.

And it was the day I realized, with a clarity that hurt, that love doesn't just happen in weddings and anniversaries and laughter in the kitchen.

Love happens in emergency rooms.

Love happens in chairs you can't sleep in.

Love happens when a boy who's been through too much watches his dad keep showing up anyway.

If you are reading this now, I want you to remember: we were scared, yes.

But we were also together.

And God held us in that place the way He holds all frightened hearts — not always by stopping the storm, but by keeping the edges from tearing all the way through.

Your wife,

Lauren

Caleb's voice thinned toward the end, not from weakness, but from careful control. Like a man trying to carry something fragile without dropping it.

When he finished, he didn't immediately fold the pages.

Connor stared at the tabletop, eyes fixed on a knot in the wood as if he could anchor himself there.

Caleb didn't rush him.

A minute passed. Maybe two.

Connor's breath came shallow, then steadier, then shallow again.

"You really told me you didn't know," Connor said finally, voice low.

Caleb nodded. "Because I didn't," he said. "And because you deserved the truth."

Connor's mouth tightened. "I hated that day."

"I did too," Caleb said.

Connor rubbed his sleeve across his face hard, like he was erasing a feeling. "I remember sitting there and everybody walking past like they had places to be," he said. "And I thought... how can they just keep moving? My whole world was—" He stopped, swallowed. "It was like the floor felt different."

Caleb's eyes burned. He kept his voice steady, anyway. "That's what fear does," he said. "It makes everything feel unstable."

Connor looked up then, and it startled Caleb how much he saw of Lauren in his eyes—not just sadness, but the sharp intelligence underneath it.

"She said she didn't want to leave me with another empty space," Connor said.

Caleb didn't answer too fast. He knew this wasn't a question. It was a wound naming itself.

"She loved you," Caleb said quietly. "In a way that wasn't confused. In a way that didn't hesitate. In a way that chose you."

Connor's throat bobbed. "I didn't even know how to let people love me then."

Caleb's hand moved—slow, deliberate—until it rested on the table near Connor's sleeve. Not grabbing. Not demanding. Just present.

"She knew," Caleb said. "She saw it. And she loved you anyway."

Connor stared at Caleb's hand like it was an object he had to decide whether to touch.

Then he slid his own hand forward, just enough that his knuckles brushed Caleb's fingers.

It wasn't dramatic.

It was everything.

Caleb blinked hard and looked away for a second, because he wasn't going to make Connor feel like he'd done something that required comfort.

But it did.

Connor drew in a breath and let it out slow. "So this is when you realized time wasn't unlimited."

"Yes," Caleb said. "We started paying attention in a different way. Like we didn't want to miss anything."

Connor stared at the letter. "And then we still had... normal days."

Caleb nodded. "We did," he said. "Normal days that didn't feel normal once we knew what we could lose."

Connor went still. "Is that what the next one is?" he asked. "The normal week?"

Caleb folded the pages carefully and slid them back into the envelope. "Yeah," he said. "The last normal week."

Connor's jaw tightened again. "That's cruel," he whispered. "How it's normal until it isn't."

Caleb's voice softened. "That's why it matters," he said. "Because you can miss it if you're not looking. You can walk past the most important things because they're wearing ordinary clothes."

Connor didn't respond to that right away.

He sat with it like he was turning it over in his hands.

Then he said, almost casually, "When she said you prayed... did you?"

Caleb's eyes lowered. "Yes," he said. "Not because I was strong. Because I was scared."

Connor's voice cracked, just a little. "What did you say?"

Caleb swallowed. "Mostly 'please,'" he admitted. "Over and over. Like I didn't know any other word that fit."

Connor stared at him for a long moment. Then he nodded, like that was the first thing that had sounded honest enough to hold.

Caleb tucked the envelope beside the others they'd already opened and closed the cedar lid gently.

Neither of them stood up right away.

Outside, the late-day light faded another shade, turning the yard steel-colored.

Connor's voice came small. "I don't like hospitals."

"I know," Caleb said.

Connor swallowed. "But I'm glad she wrote it."

Caleb's throat tightened again. "Me too."

Connor shifted in his chair, and for a second he looked younger than he usually allowed himself to be. "Do you think she was scared that day?" he asked. "Like... really scared?"

Caleb thought about the oxygen line, the bright ER lights, Lauren's eyes trying to stay calm for their son.

"Yes," he said. "I think she was. But I also think she was brave."

Connor frowned slightly. "Brave people still get scared."

Caleb gave a small nod, grateful for Connor's truth. "They do," he said. "Bravery isn't the absence of fear. It's love deciding to stay present, anyway."

Connor looked down at his sleeve. "That sounds exhausting."

Caleb exhaled softly. "It can be," he said. "But you do it too."

Connor glanced up, startled. "No I don't."

"You do," Caleb said. "Every time you stay in the room when you want to run. Every time you tell me something real. Every time you pick the hard letter."

Connor's mouth twitched like he didn't want to accept that compliment. "Whatever," he muttered, but his voice didn't have bite in it.

Caleb stood and moved to the counter, not to escape the moment, but to give Connor room to breathe.

"You hungry?" Caleb asked.

Connor hesitated. "Yeah," he admitted. "Kind of."

Caleb nodded once, already reaching for the skillet. "Alright," he said. "Then we eat. Because that's what we do in this house. We read hard things, and then we eat something warm, and we keep living."

Connor watched him for a moment, then stood and came over without being asked. He grabbed two plates from the cabinet and set them on the counter.

Caleb glanced at him. "Thanks."

Connor shrugged. "Don't make it a thing."

Caleb smiled faintly. "Wouldn't dream of it."

They moved in that quiet rhythm again—the kind that didn't require a lot of talking. Caleb cooked. Connor set out plates. They didn't fix anything. They didn't solve grief.

But they stayed.

When the food was ready, they sat back down at the table. The cedar box remained closed, nearby but not between them.

Connor picked at his plate for a moment, then said, almost casually, "So... the next letter is about the last normal week."

Caleb paused with his fork halfway up, then set it down. "Yeah," he said gently. "The next letter is about that week."

Connor nodded, chewing slowly. "Okay."

He looked at the box again, but this time his gaze didn't look like a boy bracing for impact.

It looked like a boy learning how to stand in a storm without losing his footing.

Caleb watched him and felt something familiar and painful and holy all at once—the steady, stubborn truth that love could still hold.

They ate in quiet, the kind of quiet that wasn't empty—just full of things they didn't need to say out loud yet.

Outside, the last light slipped away.

Inside, they stayed.

CHAPTER TWENTY-SIX

The Last Normal Week

♥

The first thing Connor noticed was the calendar.

It was still pinned to the side of the cabinet, the same one Lauren had bought because it had room to write in the margins. The paper curled slightly at the corners from months of steam and fingers brushing past it, but the ink hadn't faded. Appointments. Reminders. Small notes written like promises to herself.

Connor stood there longer than he meant to, hoodie pulled up around his neck, reading the last week she had filled in. Not skimming—studying. Like if he looked closely enough, the week might explain itself.

Caleb noticed but didn't comment.

He was at the stove, not cooking so much as moving—adjusting a burner that didn't need it, wiping the counter twice in the same spot. A pot of beans warmed low. Cornbread sat on a plate under a folded dish towel. The kitchen smelled like something steady, something meant to pass for normal.

"She wrote in here like she was planning," Connor said finally.

Caleb turned the burner down a notch, then rested his hand on the edge of the counter. "She always did," he said. "Especially when she didn't feel good."

Connor nodded once. "So this is... that week."

"Yes."

They sat at the table with their bowls. Connor broke his cornbread in half, then quarters, then pushed it back together like it might change shape if he handled it carefully enough. Caleb watched without staring, the way you watch a candle when you're not sure if it's going to last.

Outside, the sky hung low and gray—not dramatic, just tired. Bare branches scratched thin lines against the window. Somewhere down the road, a car door shut. Life continuing.

Caleb brought the cedar box over and set it on the table—not between them like a barrier, just near enough to belong. He didn't explain it. Connor didn't ask.

"I can read," Caleb said. "Or you can. Or we can switch."

Connor kept his eyes on the table. "You start," he said. "If it gets heavy, I might... tag in."

Caleb nodded. He opened the box.

The remaining envelopes rested inside, fewer now. Lauren's handwriting was familiar enough to feel like a voice in the room. Caleb's fingers paused, then moved with intent.

He lifted one free.

Across the front, in her careful curve:

The Last Normal Week

Connor's jaw tightened, but he didn't look away.

Caleb slid the letter from the envelope and unfolded the pages. The paper made a soft, dry sound—familiar, deliberate.

He took a breath and began.

Caleb, my love,

I don't know why I called it that, except that I needed a name that didn't sound like an ending.

If you're reading this, then you already know how it turns out. I wish I could tell you that I knew too—that I saw the line where everything tipped and marked it clearly. But I didn't. I only knew I was tired in a way sleep didn't fix, and I wanted one more week that felt like we were still inside our lives.

I wasn't getting better that week.

I need you to know that, because I don't want you wondering later if you missed something obvious. I was conserving. Rationing energy. Choosing where to spend what little I had left without saying out loud that it was limited.

Monday started with me already worn down. Not sick-sick. Just... thin. Like my body was stretched too tight over itself.

You were in the bathroom shaving. I sat on the edge of the bed and listened to the water running, thinking how strange it is that something can sound peaceful and dangerous at the same time. I counted my breaths without meaning to. In. Out. In. Out.

You asked if I was okay.

I said yes.

Not because it was true—but because I wasn't ready to name what I felt. Saying it out loud felt like admitting I might not be able to carry everything the way I used to.

Caleb's voice stayed even. Connor leaned forward slightly, elbows on the table.

When you left for work, the house went quiet in that way it does when everyone is holding something in. I moved slower than usual. I didn't try to do much. I sat in my chair and let the morning pass instead of fighting it.

That chair became my world long before I admitted it to myself.

Connor's fingers tightened around his spoon.

Connor came through the living room at some point. He didn't say much. He rarely did unless he had to. But he glanced at me more than once, like he was checking something he didn't have words for.

I asked if he was hungry.

He shrugged.

So I fixed him something small and set it where he could reach it. He ate a little. That was enough.

Caleb swallowed and continued.

Tuesday was the day you asked me to call the doctor again.

You didn't push. You never did. You said it gently, like you were handing me an option instead of a warning.

I said I would if I wasn't better the next day.

Tomorrow always felt safer than today.

Connor shifted in his chair, then went still again.

I spent most of that day sitting. Watching light move across the floor. Listening to the house breathe around me. I remember thinking how strange it was that life could keep happening at the same pace even when my body felt like it was slowing down on purpose.

I rested because I had to. Not because I was recovering.

Caleb's voice softened on the last line, but didn't break.

Wednesday, I tried to do one thing that made me feel like myself.

I made a grocery list.

Not because we were out of everything, but because writing it down made me feel useful. Milk. Bread. Cheese. Sweet tea.

I remember smiling at that—how I always wrote it even though you already knew we'd need it.

I sat back down after that. The chair held me. I let it.

Connor's eyes dropped to the table.

You came home tired that night. You kissed my forehead and asked again if I was okay.

I said I was worn down.

You frowned and said, "I know. I just don't like how worn down sounds."

You made cocoa anyway, because you always tried to offer warmth when you couldn't fix the problem.

Connor walked through the room and hesitated when he saw the mugs. You asked if he wanted one. He said no. Then maybe later.

I remember thinking how much courage it took for him to stay nearby instead of disappearing.

Caleb paused briefly, then kept reading.

Thursday, I woke up with my chest tight and my body heavy.

Not dramatic. Just enough that I noticed.

I told myself it was anxiety. I told myself I was making it worse by paying attention to it. I told myself I had been through worse things.

I sat in my chair with a blanket over my legs and let the morning show play without absorbing it. I measured time in segments instead of hours.

Connor's breathing slowed, deliberate.

You called me from work.

You said my name the way you only do when you're worried.

I wanted to tell you the truth then. I wanted to say I was scared.

But fear makes you stubborn. It makes you quiet.

So I said I was fine.

And you believed me because you wanted to.

Caleb lowered the page slightly, then lifted it again.

Friday, Connor asked me if I was sick.

I said a little.

He told me I should lay down.

So I did.

I let him see me rest instead of pretending I could still carry the house by myself.

You came home and saw me there. You didn't comment. You just looked at Connor, then back at me, like you were asking the same question in two directions.

We didn't say it out loud—but we were all paying attention.

Caleb folded the page and reached for the next.

Connor didn't speak. He didn't need to.

The kitchen felt smaller somehow. Not closing in—just focused.

Caleb kept reading.

Saturday was the day I tried to look normal—not because I felt better, but because I wanted to recognize myself.

I got dressed. I fixed my hair. I didn't stay up long.

I was tired in a way that felt structural.

We sat together. We talked about nothing important. Connor ate a little more than he had all week.

I held onto that.

Caleb stopped there.

He didn't turn the page yet.

Connor stared at the calendar again, like he could see the days Lauren was describing.

"She wasn't getting better," Connor said quietly.

"No," Caleb said. "She wasn't."

Connor nodded once. "She was staying."

"Yes."

Caleb looked down at the letter in his hands.

"There's more," he said gently. "We can stop here if you want."

Connor shook his head, just once. "No. Keep going."

Caleb took a breath.

And turned the page.

Sunday was quiet—not peaceful, just muted. Like the world had turned the volume down without asking us.

You asked me again to go to the doctor. You didn't raise your voice. You didn't argue. You just asked, the way you do when you're hoping love will do what fear can't.

I said tomorrow.

I said it gently. Almost kindly.

You didn't push.

You looked at me the way you do when you know something matters but you're afraid to force it. Like your hands were already on the edge of whatever was coming, even if you couldn't see it yet.

Connor swallowed. His eyes stayed on the page, not Caleb.

I remember thinking that morning how strange it was that the house still felt like ours.

The couch held the same shape. The kitchen smelled the same. The calendar still had plans written in it.

I remember thinking: If this is the last ordinary week, then ordinary is braver than we give it credit for.

Caleb's voice slowed, careful.

I wasn't pretending I was better.

I was pretending I had time.

There's a difference.

I stayed close to the living room that day. Not because I was afraid to move—but because I didn't want to waste the energy I had left pretending I didn't need to sit.

Connor stayed nearby too. Not hovering. Just... present.

He didn't say much. He didn't need to.

He listened.

Connor's fingers curled slightly into the edge of the table.

That week wasn't normal because I felt good.

It was normal because we were still loving each other in small, unremarkable ways.

You checking on me.

Connor staying close without asking questions.

Me pretending that tomorrow was still a promise instead of a hope.

Caleb paused for a breath, then continued.

I need you to hear this clearly: I wasn't giving up.

I was tired.

And there is a difference.

I wanted to stay.

I just didn't know how to say out loud that staying was starting to cost me more than I had.

Caleb's voice wavered for the first time. He steadied it.

If you ever look back on that week and wonder why I didn't say more—why I didn't insist, why I didn't push myself harder—please don't let guilt live there.

I was doing the best I could with a body that had already started drawing its own boundaries.

I was choosing rest over denial.

I was choosing love over panic.

I was choosing to stay present instead of brave.

Connor blinked hard but didn't look away.

That was the last normal week.

Not because everything after was chaos.

But because that was the last time we all still believed tomorrow would show up exactly the way we expected.

I want you to remember it gently.

Not as the week before everything broke.

But as the week where love stayed steady even as the ground underneath us began to shift.

Caleb reached the final lines.

If you are reading this now, then I want you to know something simple and true:

I loved you in that week.

I loved Connor in that week.

I loved our quiet house and our small routines and the way you kept trying to carry more than you should.

I was not already gone.

I was here.

And I was loving you with everything I had left.

Your wife,

Lauren

Caleb folded the pages carefully.

He didn't rush. He didn't stall.

Connor sat very still.

After a long moment, he said, "She wasn't getting better."

"No," Caleb said softly. "She was managing."

Connor nodded once. "So when she said tomorrow..."

"She meant she hoped," Caleb said. "Not that she knew."

Connor pressed his lips together. "That makes sense."

The kitchen felt heavier, but not crushing—like something had finally settled into its proper place.

"She saw me," Connor said quietly. "That whole time."

Caleb looked at him. "Yes. She did."

Connor nodded again, slower this time. "I thought I was invisible back then."

"You weren't," Caleb said. "You were quiet. That's different."

Connor let that sit.

Outside, the light had thinned even more. Not dark yet—just dim, like the day was easing itself out.

"I don't like that she kept saying tomorrow," Connor said.

"I don't either," Caleb replied. "But I understand why she did."

Connor frowned. "Why?"

Caleb took a breath. "Because if you say tomorrow, you're still choosing life. Even if it scares you."

Connor stared at the table. "She was trying to stay."

"Yes," Caleb said. "She was."

The heater clicked on, a low hum filling the quiet.

Connor rubbed his hands together, then rested them flat on the table. "So what do we do now?"

Caleb answered without hesitation. "We keep going. One letter at a time."

Connor nodded. "Okay."

Caleb slid the letter back into its envelope and set it aside. He didn't mention the unmarked one. He didn't need to.

Connor stood and carried his bowl to the sink. He rinsed it without being asked, the sound of water steady and grounding.

Caleb watched him, feeling the weight of the letter settle—not as fear, but as understanding.

"It's almost been a year," Connor said quietly from the counter.

"Yes," Caleb said. "It has."

Connor swallowed. "I don't know how I'm supposed to feel about that."

"You don't have to know," Caleb said. "You just have to be honest when something shows up."

Connor nodded, eyes on the window. "She said she saw me trying."

"She did," Caleb said.

Connor breathed out slowly. "Okay."

Caleb came to stand beside him—not touching, just close.

Outside, the gray sky lightened at the edges, not into blue, but into something gentler.

"Your mom loved you," Caleb said quietly. "Even when you didn't know how to believe it yet."

Connor nodded once, quick and tight. "I know."

But the way he said it—soft, cracked—told Caleb something important had shifted.

He was starting to carry the truth, not just hear it.

In a story built out of letters, that mattered.

And for the first time since they'd started reading them, the box on the table didn't feel like a warning.

It felt like a bridge.

CHAPTER TWENTY-SEVEN

An Ordinary Day

The morning didn't arrive all at once.

It seeped in around the edges of the house—thin winter light pressing against the curtains, the heater clicking on and off like it was thinking about giving up. Outside, the yard was gray and stiff, the ground hardened by cold that hadn't decided whether it would snow or just punish everything quietly.

Caleb stood at the sink, hands braced on the counter, staring out the window without really seeing it.

January had a way of doing that—flattening the world until everything important felt like it had already happened somewhere else.

Connor came down the hall slow, socks sliding against the floor. He didn't speak at first. He just went to the table and sat in the chair he always chose now, angled slightly toward the living room instead of the kitchen.

The recliner sat empty.

That still surprised Caleb sometimes—the way his eyes kept checking it like she might just be late getting up.

Connor pulled his hoodie tighter around himself and stared at the tabletop. "It's colder today," he said.

"Yeah," Caleb answered. "It is."

They let that be enough.

Caleb poured cocoa into two mugs, the steam curling up and disappearing before it warmed anything. He set one in front of Connor, then sat across from him—not beside him this time, but close enough that the space didn't feel like distance.

The cedar box sat on the sideboard where they'd left it the night before.

Neither of them looked at it right away.

Connor wrapped his hands around the mug and frowned. "I keep thinking... today should feel different," he said.

Caleb didn't ask what he meant. He already knew.

"It does," Caleb said quietly. "Just not in a way that announces itself."

Connor nodded once. His eyes flicked toward the box, then away again. "Is there one... for today?"

Caleb swallowed. "There's still one we haven't read yet," he said.

Connor looked up. "Do you know what it's about?"

Caleb shook his head. "No."

That answer seemed to matter more than any explanation.

Connor stared down into his mug, watching the surface ripple. "I think I want that," he said quietly. "Not knowing. Just for a minute."

Caleb stood and carried the box to the table. The wood made that familiar, soft sound when he set it down—solid, real, unavoidable.

He opened it.

The envelopes lay in their careful order, Lauren's handwriting steady and unmistakable. Caleb didn't hesitate this time. His fingers went straight to one that had always felt unassuming, like it wasn't trying to prepare anyone for anything.

Across the front, in her neat curve:

A Regular Day

Connor let out a breath he hadn't realized he was holding.

Caleb slid the envelope free. "She wrote this months before," he said. "Back when days still stacked up like they always had."

Connor nodded. "Okay."

Caleb opened it.

Caleb,

I almost didn't write this one—not because it was hard, but because it felt too ordinary to matter.

But I've learned something about ordinary days: they're only invisible when you're standing inside them.

This morning started the same way most of them do. You were already awake when I opened my eyes, lying quietly the way you do when you don't want to wake me. I could tell by the way you were breathing—you always get careful when you think someone you love needs rest.

You asked if I slept okay. I said yes, even though my body still felt heavy, like it hadn't quite caught up with morning yet. Some days are like that. You don't feel sick. You don't feel well. You just feel... slower.

You kissed my forehead before you got out of bed, and I remember thinking how steady you felt. Like whatever happened during the day, that moment could anchor me.

Connor was already up. I could hear him moving around, opening and closing cabinets like he was looking for something without knowing what it was. He didn't say much when I came into the kitchen. He hasn't, lately. But he stayed.

That mattered.

I made breakfast the easy way—nothing fancy, nothing that asked too much of me. You didn't tease me about it. You just ate and smiled like it was exactly what you wanted.

We talked about nothing important. Work. A show Connor half-watches. Whether the weather might turn again.

Normal things.

After you left, the house settled into that quiet it gets when everyone's gone but the day hasn't really started yet. I sat in the living room for a while and watched the light move across the floor. It surprised me how comforting that felt, just watching time do what it always does.

I folded laundry slowly. I rested when I needed to. I told myself it was okay to move at the pace my body was setting instead of the one I wished it still could.

Connor came out of his room once and asked if I was okay. Just once. Like he was checking a box his heart told him mattered.

I told him I was.

It wasn't a lie. It also wasn't the whole truth. But sometimes the truth lives in layers, and you hand people what they can carry.

That afternoon, I thought about how much I love this life. Not the big milestones—those are easy to point to—but the small rhythm of it. The way you always double-check the doors at night. The way Connor pretends he isn't listening when we talk, even though I know he is.

I don't know why this day felt worth writing down. Nothing remarkable happened. Nobody cried. No one celebrated.

But we were together.

And sometimes, that's the whole miracle.

Your wife,

Lauren

Caleb's voice didn't break when he finished, and that surprised him.

He folded the letter carefully and set it on the table between them.

Connor stared at it for a long moment. "She didn't know," he said.

"No," Caleb said. "She didn't."

Connor nodded slowly, like something painful had finally clicked into place. "That almost makes it worse."

Caleb didn't disagree.

But he also knew it was the point.

Outside, the winter light climbed, pale and indifferent.

Inside, the day waited—quiet, ordinary, and already carrying more weight than either of them had expected it to.

Caleb didn't put the letter away right away.

He left it where it was, between them, like a third presence at the table. Not intruding. Not asking anything. Just existing.

Connor kept his eyes on it for a while, then finally looked up. "She thought it was just... a day."

"Yes," Caleb said. "That's why she wrote it."

Connor frowned slightly, like he was trying to line something up inside himself. "She didn't write it because she was scared."

"No," Caleb said. "She wrote it because she was alive."

That landed.

Connor leaned back in his chair and crossed his arms, the motion small, and protective. "I don't remember that day."

Caleb nodded. "That doesn't mean it didn't matter."

Connor exhaled through his nose. "I remember days like that, though. Where nothing happened. And then later I couldn't tell them apart."

"That's how normal works," Caleb said gently. "It hides."

They sat in the quiet again, the heater clicking on and off like it was negotiating with the cold. Outside, a thin wind moved through the bare trees, branches tapping once against the side of the house before settling.

Connor broke the silence. "I keep thinking I should remember more."

Caleb tilted his head. "Why?"

Connor shrugged, but his voice didn't. "Because if I remembered more, maybe it wouldn't feel like it just... stopped."

Caleb felt that ache settle in his chest—the familiar one, the one that came when he realized how much Connor had carried without knowing what to call it.

"It didn't stop," Caleb said. "It changed."

Connor looked unconvinced. "It feels like it stopped."

"I know," Caleb said. "That's how it feels when something steady disappears. Your brain looks for a cliff because that makes sense. But most of the time, it's more like fog. You don't notice how far you've walked until you turn around."

Connor considered that. "So she was still... here."

"Yes."

"Even when she was tired."

"Yes."

"Even when she said she was fine."

Caleb hesitated for half a breath. Then: "Yes."

Connor stared at the table. "That makes me angry."

Caleb didn't correct him. "At who?"

Connor's jaw tightened. "At time," he said. "At the fact that it didn't warn us."

Caleb nodded slowly. "Time rarely does."

Connor's fingers traced the edge of the table, following the grain like it might lead somewhere. "She wrote about me staying," he said. "I didn't know I was doing that."

"You didn't have to," Caleb said. "You were."

Connor's voice dropped. "I thought I was just... in the way."

Caleb's chest tightened. He leaned forward slightly, not crowding, but close enough that Connor could feel the truth before it reached his ears. "You were never in the way," he said. "You were part of it."

Connor swallowed. "She noticed things I didn't think anyone saw."

"She was very good at that," Caleb said. "Especially with you."

Connor nodded once, quick and sharp, like if he moved too slowly something might crack. "I wish she'd told me."

Caleb didn't rush the answer. "She did," he said finally. "Just not with words."

Connor frowned. "How do you know?"

"Because she trusted you to stay," Caleb said. "Not to fix anything. Just to be present. That's not something you ask of someone you think is invisible."

Connor leaned back again, this time letting his head rest against the chair. He stared at the ceiling, blinking fast.

The house made a small settling sound—wood adjusting to the cold, a pipe ticking once in complaint.

"I don't like that she thought she had to be okay," Connor said.

Caleb closed his eyes for a moment. "Neither do I."

Connor's voice wavered, just barely. "She didn't want to scare us."

"I know."

"But she was scared," Connor said.

"Yes."

Connor turned his head and looked at Caleb directly now. "Were you?"

Caleb didn't pretend. "Every day."

Connor absorbed that. "You didn't act like it."

Caleb gave a small, tired smile. "That was the part I got wrong."

Connor was quiet again for a stretch. Then: "I think I was scared too."

Caleb nodded. "You were."

Connor frowned. "I didn't know what of."

"That's okay," Caleb said. "Fear doesn't always come with instructions."

Connor let out a humorless huff. "That figures."

They sat there, the letter still between them, the cocoa long since gone cold.

After a while, Connor spoke again. "If she didn't know—if she really thought there were more days like that—does that mean we didn't miss anything?"

Caleb considered the question carefully. "No," he said. "It means you didn't fail."

Connor's shoulders loosened just a little. "It still feels like we should've done more."

Caleb leaned back, choosing his words with care. "You lived the days you had with the information you had at the time," he said. "That's all any of us ever do."

Connor stared at the letter again. "She called it a miracle."

"Yes."

Connor frowned. "It doesn't feel like one."

Caleb nodded. "Miracles don't always feel miraculous from the inside."

Connor let that sit.

Outside, the light had shifted again, fading toward afternoon. The gray had thinned slightly, the sky not brighter but lighter, like it was trying to remember another color.

Connor finally reached out and slid the letter closer to himself. He didn't open it again. He just rested his palm on it, flat and careful.

"She loved us," he said.

Caleb nodded. "Very much."

Connor's voice dropped. "Even when she was tired."

"Yes."

"Even when she was scared."

"Yes."

Connor's throat worked. "Even when she thought it was just a normal day."

Caleb felt the truth of that settle deep. "Especially then."

Connor's eyes burned, but he didn't look away. "I think... I think I've been waiting for something big to make sense of it all."

Caleb tilted his head. "What kind of something?"

"I don't know," Connor said. "A sign. A reason. Something that explains why it had to be her."

Caleb was quiet for a long moment. Then he said, "Sometimes the only thing that makes sense is love."

Connor gave a short, broken laugh. "That's not very helpful."

"I know," Caleb said. "But it's honest."

Connor wiped at his face quickly, like the motion embarrassed him. "I don't want to forget her," he said.

"You won't," Caleb said immediately.

Connor shook his head. "I mean... the real her. Not just the sick parts. Not just the end."

Caleb gestured to the letter. "That's why she wrote things like this."

Connor nodded. "She didn't want to be reduced."

"No," Caleb said. "She wanted to be remembered living."

Connor sat with that, his hand still on the paper.

After a while, he asked, "Can we keep it out?"

Caleb understood. "For today?"

Connor nodded. "Just today."

Caleb closed the cedar box and slid it back to the sideboard, then returned to the table. He didn't touch the letter. He left it where Connor had placed it.

They stayed there together, not talking much, the afternoon slowly giving way to early winter evening.

Later, Connor stood and stretched, the movement stiff but deliberate. "I'm gonna do homework," he said. "Or... at least sit in my room with it."

Caleb smiled faintly. "That counts."

Connor paused, then added, "Thanks for reading it."

Caleb met his eyes. "Thanks for listening."

Connor nodded and headed down the hall.

Caleb remained at the table, staring at the letter a while longer.

A regular day.

He thought about how many of them they'd had. How many had passed without ceremony. How many he'd assumed would keep coming.

Carefully, he folded the letter again and placed it back in its envelope.

Not because it was finished, but because it had been honored.

Outside, the cold deepened.

Inside, something steadied.

And though the day had ended like so many others—quiet, unremarkable, unfinished—Caleb understood now why she had written it.

Because sometimes the most important thing you can leave behind is proof that you were here.

Living.

Loving.

Staying.

The Day After Everything Changed

The house had learned how to hold its breath.

That was the first thing Caleb noticed as winter settled in for its last hard stretch. Not the cold itself—he was used to that—but the way the rooms no longer startled when he moved through them. No sharp echoes. No sudden silences. Just a steady, practiced stillness, like the walls had accepted what they were guarding.

Nearly a year had passed.

Not a clean year. Not one that wrapped itself neatly around anniversaries or milestones. Just a year measured in grocery lists, doctor appointments, school assignments, and mornings that asked to be lived whether he felt ready or not.

Outside, winter still held the ground firmly. Frost coated the grass each morning, refusing to lift even by afternoon, and the air carried that sharp, metallic cold that settles in when January has no intention of letting go. The trees stood bare and rigid, branches dark against the sky—not waiting, not hopeful, just enduring.

Caleb stood at the sink, rinsing a mug he didn't remember using. The water ran longer than it needed to. He let it. Some habits didn't need correcting.

Behind him, Connor sat at the kitchen table, one knee pulled up into his chair, hoodie sleeves covering his hands. He wasn't cold. He just preferred the weight of fabric now, like warmth was something you had to anchor on purpose.

Connor's attention drifted to the quiet itself.

The house sounded different now—no background noise competing for space, no television murmuring from another room. Just a faint mechanical whir from the kitchen and the steady tick of the clock marking time whether they acknowledged it or not.

He shifted his weight, uneasy. "It feels like everything keeps going," he said. "Like the world didn't notice."

Caleb nodded once. "It rarely does."

Connor exhaled through his nose. "That doesn't seem fair."

"No," Caleb said quietly. "It isn't."

That was the part that still caught him sometimes—not the dying, but the *not knowing*. The way life had continued right up until it didn't. The way she'd written reminders for a week she never got to finish.

They moved back to the table with their bowls. Connor ate without much interest, nudging his food around like it was something he needed to negotiate with. Caleb watched him without staring, the way you learn to watch when looking too closely feels like pressure.

Outside, the sky sat low and gray, not threatening, just tired. A crow landed on the fence, shook itself, and flew off again like it had someplace else to be.

Connor broke the quiet. "It doesn't feel like a year."

Caleb considered that. "No," he said. "It doesn't."

"It feels longer," Connor added. Then, after a beat, "And shorter. Both."

Caleb nodded. "Yeah."

That had surprised him too—the way time had stretched and collapsed at the same time. How some memories still sat right at the surface, sharp as glass, while others had drifted far enough away that he had to reach for them.

Connor leaned back in his chair, gaze fixed on the ceiling. "People keep asking if I'm doing better."

Caleb kept his voice even. "What do you tell them?"

Connor shrugged. "Depends who it is."

Caleb understood that answer more than Connor probably realized.

"They don't mean it wrong," Connor went on. "I just don't know what they think 'better' looks like."

Caleb set his spoon down. "I don't either."

Connor glanced at him then, searching. "Are you?"

The question landed softly—but it landed.

Caleb didn't rush to fill the space. He had learned that answering too quickly often meant answering dishonestly.

"I think I'm... steadier," he said finally. "That's different than better."

Connor absorbed that. "Yeah. That makes sense."

They sat for a moment, the quiet settling around them without tension. This was new too—the way silence no longer demanded fixing. The way it could exist without swallowing the room.

Connor spoke again, quieter. "Sometimes I forget she's gone."

Caleb felt the familiar pull in his chest. "Me too."

"And then I remember," Connor said. "And it's not like being surprised. It's like... remembering how gravity works."

Caleb looked at him, struck by the accuracy of it. "That's exactly what it's like."

Connor's mouth twitched, not quite a smile. "I thought something was wrong with me."

"There isn't," Caleb said. "Your brain is just learning a new world."

Connor nodded, eyes down. "I don't like it."

"I know."

The house creaked softly as the temperature shifted, a familiar sound that no longer startled either of them. Somewhere down the street, a car door closed. Life moving forward, indifferent and relentless.

Connor pushed his bowl away. "Do you ever feel like... if you're not sad enough, it means you're forgetting her?"

Caleb's breath caught—not because the question was new, but because it still hurt to answer.

"No," he said gently. "It means you're carrying her differently."

Connor frowned. "How do you know?"

Caleb thought about mornings that didn't knock the air out of him anymore. About laughter that no longer felt like betrayal. About the way love had shifted shape without disappearing.

"Because forgetting feels empty," he said. "This doesn't."

Connor considered that. "It still hurts."

"Yes," Caleb said. "But hurt isn't the same as loss."

Connor nodded slowly, like that distinction mattered.

He glanced around the kitchen—the worn table, the familiar counters, the places she used to lean without thinking. "The house feels different."

"It does," Caleb agreed.

"Not bad," Connor added quickly. "Just... quieter."

Caleb swallowed. "It learned how to be."

Connor looked at him then, really looked. "You did too."

The words landed heavier than Connor probably intended. Caleb felt them settle somewhere deep, not as praise, but as recognition.

"I had help," he said.

Connor didn't deflect that. He just nodded.

They stood together a few minutes later, rinsing dishes side by side. Connor worked carefully, methodical, like he'd decided that doing things right mattered more than doing them fast. Caleb watched him from the corner of his eye, struck again by how much growing up could happen in silence.

When they finished, Connor didn't retreat to his room like he used to. He stayed, leaning against the counter, arms crossed.

Connor stared out the window. "It's getting close," he said.

Caleb nodded. "Yeah."

Connor hesitated. "I don't know what I'm supposed to feel when it does."

"You don't have to know," Caleb said. "You can just notice what shows up."

Connor breathed out slowly. "Okay."

They stood there together, not touching, not distant—just present in the same space, holding something neither of them could put down.

Outside, the sky remained flat and winter gray, unmoved by their timing, uninterested in anniversaries.

Inside, the house stayed still.

Not frozen.

Just holding.

Later that night, the house creaked the way it always did when the temperature dropped.

Not a loud sound—just the quiet settling of wood and pipes, the kind of noise you stop noticing unless you're already awake. Caleb lay on his back staring at the ceiling, hands folded loosely over his stomach, listening to Connor move around in the next room. The sounds were familiar now: the soft thud of drawers, the rustle of blankets, the faint click when Connor turned his lamp off and then—after a minute—back on again.

Caleb didn't call out.

He'd learned the difference between needing help and needing time.

Eventually the light stayed off.

The house grew still again.

Sleep came in fragments. Not the deep, unthinking kind he used to know, but the shallow drifting that let memories slip in around the edges. He dreamed of ordinary things—Lauren standing at the sink, Lauren asking where he'd put her glasses, Lauren laughing at something that wasn't especially funny.

He woke before morning, chest tight with the quiet realization that for a moment he hadn't remembered she was gone.

The forgetting never lasted long.

But it always hurt when it ended.

Morning arrived gray and undecided.

Caleb moved through his routine slowly, deliberately. Cocoa for Connor. Cocoa for himself. Toast left a little too long in the toaster because his mind wandered. He scraped it anyway. Some imperfections didn't need correcting.

Connor came into the kitchen rubbing sleep from his eyes, hair sticking up in the back. He paused when he saw the mug waiting for him.

"You didn't have to," he said.

Caleb shrugged. "I wanted to."

Connor took it and wrapped both hands around the ceramic, standing there like the warmth mattered more than the drink. He didn't sit right away. He stared out the window, watching his breath fog the glass when he leaned close.

"Does it ever feel weird," he asked, "that the world didn't stop?"

Caleb considered that. "Sometimes it feels wrong," he said. "But mostly it just feels... confusing."

Connor nodded. "Like everything kept going without checking if we were ready."

"Yeah."

They ate quietly. Not heavy silence. Just the kind that didn't need filling.

After breakfast, Connor lingered instead of disappearing into his room. He hovered near the doorway like he was waiting for something to happen or be said.

Caleb noticed. He always did.

"You got plans today?" Caleb asked.

Connor shrugged. "Homework. Maybe."

Caleb nodded. "I've got some stuff to do around the house."

Connor hesitated. "Can I... help?"

The word still surprised Caleb when Connor offered it voluntarily. He kept his voice casual. "Sure."

They worked side by side through the late morning—small, unremarkable tasks. Connor held the ladder while Caleb changed a lightbulb. Caleb steadied a cabinet door while Connor tightened the hinge. They didn't talk much. The work itself did something talking couldn't.

At one point, Connor stopped and stared at the hallway.

"She used to sit there," he said suddenly.

Caleb followed his gaze to the small bench by the door. "Yeah," he said. "She liked that spot."

"She said it helped her catch her breath before going out," Connor added.

Caleb swallowed. "I remember."

Connor's brow furrowed. "I didn't know that meant... what it meant."

"No," Caleb said gently. "Most of us didn't."

Connor went quiet again, like he was filing the memory somewhere new.

By afternoon, the light had shifted. Not brighter—just thinner. The kind of day where winter loosens its grip without fully letting go.

Connor sat on the couch with his laptop open, homework half-finished. Caleb moved through the living room picking up small things that had gathered in corners—mail, an empty cup, a folded blanket Lauren used to keep there.

Connor watched him.

"You don't have to clean everything," Connor said.

Caleb paused. "I know."

"But you do it, anyway."

Caleb smiled faintly. "Some days I need to move things so they don't move me."

Connor absorbed that. "That makes sense."

A few minutes passed.

"Dad?" Connor said.

"Yeah?"

"Do you ever feel like you're... failing her?"

The question landed hard, sharp enough to catch.

Caleb lowered himself into the chair across from Connor, careful with his words. "In what way?"

Connor stared at the screen, not really seeing it. "Like... you're still here. Living. Laughing sometimes. And she's not."

Caleb felt the old guilt stir—the one that whispered survival was a betrayal.

"Yes," he said honestly. "I've felt that."

Connor nodded. "Me too."

Caleb leaned forward. "But here's what I've learned." He waited until Connor looked up. "Loving her didn't end when she died. It just stopped needing her body to keep going."

Connor frowned. "That feels unfair."

"It is," Caleb said. "But it's also the only way love survives."

Connor thought about that, chewing on the inside of his cheek. "So... it's okay if I have good days?"

"Yes," Caleb said firmly. "It's okay if you have great ones."

Connor's eyes searched his face. "Even if she doesn't get them?"

Caleb didn't answer right away. He looked down at his hands, then back at Connor. "She is," he said quietly.

Connor frowned, confused. "She is what?"

"Having good days," Caleb said. "Better ones than we can imagine. No pain. No lungs that fight her. No body that keeps letting her down."

Connor swallowed.

"She's whole," Caleb went on. "And if Heaven is even half of what I believe it is, then she's not missing anything we're doing down here. She's cheering us on."

Connor stared at him. "You really believe that."

Caleb nodded. "I do. And I think she'd want you to live every good day you're given without feeling guilty about it."

Connor let that sit for a moment, then whispered, "Okay."

Connor let out a breath he'd been holding. "Okay."

That evening, they ate dinner in the living room, plates balanced on their knees. Something mindless played on the TV—voices filling the space without demanding attention.

Halfway through the meal, Connor paused.

"Do you remember the way she used to say my name?" he asked.

Caleb smiled before he could stop himself. "Yeah."

"Like she was testing it," Connor said. "Like she wanted to make sure it fit."

Caleb laughed softly. "She was."

Connor smiled too, then the smile faltered. "I didn't always answer."

Caleb met his eyes. "She knew you heard."

Connor swallowed. "I wish I'd answered more."

Caleb reached out and squeezed his shoulder—brief, grounding. "She didn't measure love by response time."

Connor nodded, eyes shining but steady.

Later, after dishes and showers and the slow winding down of the day, Connor lingered in the hallway again.

"Can I... sit with you for a minute?" he asked.

Caleb nodded immediately. "Yeah."

They sat on the edge of Caleb's bed, not touching at first. The room felt different without Lauren's presence—emptier, but not hollow. Just changed.

Connor stared at the floor. "I'm scared," he admitted.

Caleb didn't ask of what. "I know."

"I don't want to forget her," Connor said.

"You won't," Caleb said.

"But what if I do?" Connor pressed. "What if it fades?"

Caleb thought about all the ways love had already changed shape and stayed. "Then it won't be gone," he said. "It'll just live somewhere quieter."

Connor nodded slowly. "Like the house."

"Yes," Caleb said. "Like the house."

Connor leaned against him then—not collapsing, not desperate. Just resting his head on Caleb's shoulder like it made sense to be there.

Caleb closed his eyes and let himself hold the moment without trying to name it.

After a while, Connor straightened. "I think... I think I'm okay tonight."

Caleb nodded. "I'm glad."

Connor hesitated at the door. "Dad?"

"Yeah?"

"Thank you for staying."

The words hit deeper than Connor could know.

"I'm not going anywhere," Caleb said.

Connor nodded once and went to his room.

Caleb stayed seated a long time after the door closed.

Outside, the night pressed gently against the windows. Somewhere, water moved through pipes. The house breathed.

Nearly a year later, grief no longer shouted.

It spoke in quieter ways now—in moments that asked to be noticed, in silences that didn't need filling, in love that had learned how to stay without demanding anything back.

Caleb turned off the light and lay down.

Tomorrow would come whether he was ready or not.

But tonight, he let himself rest inside what remained.

And that, he realized, was still living.

Chapter Twenty-Nine

Still Holding

---❤---

The house did not feel empty.

That was the lie Caleb had to correct first.

Empty implied something missing in a way you could fix—like a chair pulled out or a shelf waiting to be filled. This house wasn't empty. It was occupied by absence. By the weight of someone who had been here long enough that the rooms still remembered how to hold her.

Late winter leaned against the windows without asking to come in. The sun showed up more often now, but it didn't stay long, like it was still unsure whether it was welcome. Patches of frost clung to the yard in the mornings, retreating by afternoon. The season couldn't decide what it was yet.

Neither could they.

Caleb stood in the living room, one hand resting on the back of Lauren's recliner.

He hadn't meant to stop there. He'd been moving through the house with purpose—laundry, trash, the small tasks that made a day look functional from the outside. But his hand had landed on the fabric without instruction, and now he was still.

The chair hadn't moved.

Not because it was sacred. Not because it was forbidden.

Because it still felt... right.

Connor was on the couch, legs folded under him, hood up even though the heat was on. A game controller rested loose in his hands, untouched. The screen glowed in front of him, frozen on a paused image that had been waiting a long time.

Caleb noticed that first—the waiting.

"You gonna play?" he asked, keeping his voice casual.

Connor shrugged. "Maybe."

Caleb nodded and didn't push. They had learned not to interrogate pauses.

The afternoon light shifted, thin and pale, stretching across the floor. Dust moved through it slowly, like it wasn't in a hurry to land anywhere.

Nearly a year.

Not the kind of year people mean when they say it out loud. Not a year of progress or healing or milestones. A year of learning how to stand in a world that had quietly rearranged itself when no one was looking.

Caleb moved again, this time to the kitchen doorway. He leaned against the frame and watched his son without letting Connor feel watched.

Connor had grown in the last year. Not taller exactly—though maybe a little—but heavier in a way that didn't show up on a scale. His expressions had changed. Less quick. More measured. Like he now knew how fast something could be taken away.

"You remember how loud this place used to be?" Connor asked suddenly.

Caleb smiled faintly. "Yeah."

"Not yelling," Connor added. "Just... noise. Mom talking. You walking around. The TV on even when nobody was watching."

Caleb exhaled. "She hated quiet."

Connor nodded. "She said it made her think too much."

"She wasn't wrong."

The silence that followed wasn't the kind she'd complained about. It was gentler. Settled. The kind that came from two people choosing to stay in the same room without trying to fix each other.

Connor lowered the controller to the cushion beside him. "Sometimes it feels like if I move too fast, I'll mess something up."

Caleb turned his head slightly. "Like what?"

Connor searched for words. "Like... whatever this is. Like there's a way we're supposed to exist now, and I don't know the rules yet."

Caleb felt that one land deep.

"I don't either," he said. "But I don't think there's a wrong way, as long as we're honest."

Connor's mouth tightened. "I don't always know what honest looks like."

"That's okay," Caleb said. "Most adults don't either."

Connor let out a short breath that might have been a laugh if it hadn't sounded so tired. "Figures."

The furnace clicked on in the background, a low mechanical hum that filled the space without demanding attention. Caleb realized how often he now noticed sounds—small, ordinary ones. Things that proved the world was still functioning.

"You ever think about how weird it is," Connor said, "that people out there are just... living?"

Caleb followed his gaze to the window. The street beyond it was quiet but not still. Somewhere a car passed. Somewhere a neighbor's door opened and closed.

"All the time," Caleb said.

Connor's voice dropped. "It makes me angry sometimes."

"That doesn't make you a bad person."

"I know," Connor said. "It just... feels unfair."

Caleb nodded. "It is."

They sat with that. No lesson attached. No silver lining offered.

After a while, Connor spoke again. "I don't really miss the hospital part."

Caleb's chest tightened. "No?"

"I miss before," Connor said. "And after. But not that middle part where everybody kept explaining things like they made sense."

Caleb understood. The way professionals talked around pain like it was a problem to be solved instead of something to be survived.

"She hated that too," Caleb said.

Connor glanced up. "Yeah?"

"She used to say, 'I don't need a plan. I need someone to sit with me.'"

Connor swallowed. "She was good at that."

"She was."

The light faded another notch. Shadows grew longer, softer. The house adjusted the way it always did, settling into evening.

Connor pulled his sleeves down over his hands again. "Dad?"

"Yeah."

"If this is what a year looks like... does it ever get easier?"

Caleb didn't answer right away. He'd learned that some questions deserved time.

"I think it gets different," he said finally. "And sometimes different feels easier. And sometimes it doesn't."

Connor absorbed that, gaze fixed on the floor. "Okay."

Caleb stepped fully into the room then and sat in the chair across from him—not Lauren's chair. Never that one. He rested his elbows on his knees.

"We don't have to be good at this," Caleb said. "We just have to keep showing up."

Connor nodded once. "I can do that."

Caleb believed him.

Outside, the last of the light slipped away, leaving the windows dark enough to reflect the room back at itself.

Inside, the house held steady.

Not empty.

Just learning.

Later, after dinner dishes sat rinsed and drying in the rack, Connor drifted back toward the living room without saying where he was going.

Caleb noticed because Connor usually announced things now. Small departures. Bathroom. Bedroom. Outside. Silence used to swallow him whole if no one tracked it.

Tonight, Connor just moved.

Caleb waited a few seconds—long enough not to crowd, not long enough to disappear—and followed.

Connor stood in front of the bookshelf.

Not the whole thing. Just one section. The lower shelf where things had slowly collected over the years: old paperbacks, a few DVDs no one watched anymore, a small wooden box Lauren had bought at a craft fair because she liked the way it smelled.

Connor crouched, resting his elbows on his knees, eyes fixed on the spines like he was reading a language he used to know.

"I was looking for something," he said quietly.

Caleb leaned against the wall. "What?"

Connor shook his head. "I don't know. That's the problem."

Caleb didn't correct him. Grief did that—sent you searching for unnamed things, convinced you'd recognize them if you found them.

Connor reached out and touched the wooden box, then pulled his hand back like the contact surprised him.

"She kept stuff," he said.

Caleb smiled faintly. "She did. You too."

Connor snorted. "I don't keep stuff. I forget stuff."

"That's still a kind of keeping," Caleb said.

Connor tilted his head, considering it. Then he opened the box.

Inside were small things. Not important in the way museums mean it. A folded note. A couple of old ticket stubs. A bracelet missing one bead. A photo Caleb hadn't seen in years—Lauren and Connor on the couch, Connor leaning into her side like he hadn't yet learned how not to.

Connor picked up the photo first.

He stared at it longer than Caleb expected.

"She looks... normal," Connor said finally.

Caleb nodded. "She was."

Connor's voice tightened. "I keep thinking she's supposed to look sick in pictures."

Caleb crouched down beside him. "She wasn't sick all the time," he said gently. "And even when she was, she didn't want that to be the only thing people saw."

Connor swallowed. "I don't remember her like this."

Caleb studied the photo. Lauren's arm was around Connor's shoulders, loose but certain. Her smile wasn't big. It was content.

"You were younger," Caleb said. "And things were different then."

Connor's thumb traced the edge of the picture. "I wish I remembered more."

Caleb felt that familiar ache—the one that came from knowing memory wasn't something you could summon on command.

"You remember what you needed to," he said. "Your brain kept you safe."

Connor frowned. "From what?"

Caleb hesitated. "From breaking too early."

Connor absorbed that in silence.

He set the photo back in the box and closed the lid, slower this time.

"I don't like that she's becoming... a story," Connor said.

Caleb's chest tightened. "What do you mean?"

"Like—people talk about her like she's finished," Connor said. "Like she's something that already happened."

Caleb nodded slowly. "Yeah. I know."

"But she's not," Connor said, frustration creeping into his voice. "She's not done. She's just—" He broke off, jaw tight.

"Not here," Caleb finished softly.

Connor pressed his lips together. His eyes shone, but he didn't cry. Not yet.

They stayed there for a moment, both crouched, both still.

Then Connor said, almost angrily, "I hate when people say she's in a better place."

Caleb didn't flinch. "Me too."

Connor's head snapped up. "Really?"

"Yes," Caleb said. "Because it skips the part where she should still be here."

Connor exhaled hard. "Exactly."

Caleb reached out, not touching Connor yet—just close enough to be felt. "We can let Heaven be real without pretending this doesn't hurt," he said. "Both can exist."

Connor nodded slowly. "I don't think people know how to hold both."

"Most people don't," Caleb said. "They rush to comfort because they're scared of sitting in the ache."

Connor stared at the floor. "I'm not scared of it."

Caleb believed him.

They stood after a while, joints protesting quietly, and moved back toward the couch. Connor didn't turn the game back on. He just sat, arms crossed, gaze unfocused.

Caleb sat too.

The clock ticked on the wall, marking time without commentary. Outside, a neighbor's porch light flicked on. Somewhere, a dog barked once and stopped.

Connor broke the silence. "Do you ever feel like you're doing grief wrong?"

Caleb let out a breath that might have been a laugh if it didn't hurt so much. "All the time."

Connor frowned. "Like—some days I'm okay. And then I feel guilty for that."

Caleb nodded. "That doesn't go away," he said. "But it gets quieter."

Connor studied him. "Why?"

"Because you start realizing being okay isn't a betrayal," Caleb said. "It's survival."

Connor considered that. "She'd want that."

"Yes," Caleb said. "She would."

Connor leaned back against the couch, eyes on the ceiling. "I think sometimes I pretend I don't need her."

Caleb turned toward him. "You don't have to do that here."

Connor swallowed. "I know. I just... don't want to fall apart."

Caleb's voice softened. "Falling apart isn't failing."

Connor didn't answer right away.

Then, quietly, "I miss her voice."

Caleb felt that land like a physical thing.

"Me too," he said.

Connor's breath hitched. "I can't remember exactly how she said my name."

Caleb closed his eyes for a second. He could hear it. The cadence. The warmth tucked into the syllables.

"She said it like it mattered," Caleb said. "Like she was glad you existed."

Connor nodded, tears finally breaking free. He didn't wipe them away. He just let them fall.

Caleb didn't rush him. He didn't shush or fix or explain.

After a moment, Connor leaned sideways, shoulder brushing Caleb's arm. Not asking. Just arriving.

Caleb shifted, careful and slow, until their shoulders touched fully. He rested his hand on the couch between them—not gripping, not hovering. Present.

They sat like that as the room darkened.

Eventually, Connor spoke again, voice rough. "I don't want to forget her."

"You won't," Caleb said. "She's part of how you see the world now."

Connor sniffed. "Even the bad parts?"

"Especially those," Caleb said. "They make you honest."

Connor nodded. "I don't feel broken," he said after a moment. "Just... changed."

Caleb felt something settle in his chest. "That means you're healing," he said. "Even if it doesn't feel like it."

Connor glanced at him. "You sure?"

Caleb met his eyes. "I am."

They stayed there until the house fully surrendered to night. No grand realization. No closure.

Just two people sharing the quiet without being swallowed by it.

Eventually, Connor stood and stretched. "I'm gonna head to my room."

"Okay," Caleb said.

Caleb remained on the couch, listening to the house settle around him.

Not empty.

Still holding.

And somehow—still alive.

Later that night, the house finally went quiet.

Not the kind of quiet that follows exhaustion—but the deeper one that comes when there's nothing left to distract from what's waiting underneath.

Caleb stood in the hallway for a long time without moving. The lights were off. The clock in the living room ticked steadily, the sound sharp in the dark, like something counting whether he wanted it to or not.

Connor's door was closed now.

That, too, was still new enough to notice.

Caleb walked into the living room and sat down in the chair across from the empty recliner.

He didn't sit *in* it. He never did.

The recliner stayed angled slightly toward the television, the way she'd left it, like she might come back and claim it if he didn't move it too much. He told himself it was practical—moving it would require effort, rearranging, decision-making.

The truth was simpler.

As long as it stayed where it was, she hadn't fully left the room.

Caleb leaned forward, elbows on his knees, hands clasped together. He stared at the floor, at a spot in the rug where the fibers were worn thin from years of pacing and stopping and starting again.

This was the part no one warned you about.

Not the grief—that came with casseroles and cards and quiet nods from people who meant well.

This was what came after.

The staying.

The getting up again.

The part where the world expected you to keep living, even though the person you had built your life around was no longer there to witness it.

Caleb exhaled slowly.

For months, survival had felt like purpose. Wake up. Take care of Connor. Keep the house running. Put one foot in front of the other. Survival had rules. It gave him something to do with his hands.

But now?

Now survival was just... expected.

And that terrified him more than the nights he'd thought he wouldn't make it through at all.

He rubbed a hand over his face and let it drop back to his knee.

"I don't know how to do this part," he said aloud.

The words sounded strange in the room, like they didn't quite belong anywhere. He hadn't meant to speak. He hadn't meant to pray, either.

But the house had learned how to listen.

Caleb swallowed.

"I knew how to be your husband," he said quietly. "I knew how to fight for you. I knew how to stay when things were hard."

His voice tightened, but he didn't stop.

"I don't know how to be the man who comes *after* you."

That was the truth he hadn't said yet—not to Connor, not to anyone.

He was afraid of a future where loving her became something that lived entirely in the past tense.

Afraid of waking up one day and realizing the ache had dulled—not because he'd healed, but because time had done what it always did and kept moving without permission.

Afraid of forgetting things he didn't even know how to name.

Caleb leaned back and stared at the ceiling, at the faint shadow where the fan blades cut through the dark.

"You always knew what came next," he whispered. "You planned. You adjusted. You made room."

A humorless breath left him.

"I'm not built like that."

The clock kept ticking.

Caleb closed his eyes.

For the first time since she'd died, the fear wasn't about losing her.

It was about living long enough to have a life she wasn't part of.

That was the part that felt like betrayal.

He sat there until the feeling passed—not disappeared, just loosened enough to breathe through.

When he finally stood, his legs felt stiff, like they'd forgotten how to move without urgency.

He walked to the window and pulled the curtain back a few inches.

Outside, the yard lay quiet under the dim glow of the streetlight. No movement. No answers. Just space.

Caleb rested his forehead against the glass.

"I'm still here," he said softly. Not as a declaration. Not as strength.

Just fact.

And somewhere in that truth—thin, unsteady, unfinished—was the beginning of whatever came next.

He let the curtain fall back into place and turned off the lamp.

The house did not respond.

It did not need to.

It had already learned how to hold him.

CHAPTER THIRTY

The First Letter That Didn't Break Us

The house no longer felt like it was holding its breath.

That was the difference Caleb noticed first—not that the grief was gone, but that it had stopped tightening every room it entered. The walls still remembered her. So did the floors, the doorframes, the worn place on the couch where her weight used to settle. But the air itself had softened. It moved again.

Late winter light slipped through the kitchen window, pale and thin, the kind that didn't promise warmth but hinted at it. Outside, the trees were still bare, but their branches no longer looked brittle. Just patient.

Connor sat at the table with a mug between his hands, hoodie sleeves pulled down over his knuckles. He wasn't cold. He just liked the way heat stayed put when you wrapped it carefully.

Caleb rinsed a spoon at the sink, slower than necessary. He'd learned that mornings didn't need to be efficient anymore. They just needed to happen.

Neither of them spoke for a while.

It wasn't an empty silence. It was the kind that had learned how to live with them.

Connor broke it first. "I don't feel like I'm bracing today."

Caleb turned slightly. "No?"

Connor shook his head. "Usually when we read one, I feel like I have to get ready. Like... something's about to hit."

Caleb nodded. He knew that feeling well. "And today?"

Connor considered it. "Today just feels... quieter."

Caleb dried his hands and came to sit at the table, setting the cedar box down gently—not between them, not hidden. Just present.

"That's okay," Caleb said. "We don't have to read anything if you don't want to."

Connor looked at the box, then back at his mug. "I do," he said. "I just don't want it to wreck the whole day."

Caleb studied him for a moment, then nodded. "I think she wrote at least one for days like that."

Connor's eyes lifted. "You do?"

"Yeah," Caleb said softly. "I think she knew not every letter needed to shatter us."

Connor exhaled, the tension easing just a little from his shoulders. "Okay."

Caleb lifted the lid.

Inside, fewer envelopes waited now. The stack behind them—letters already read—rested on the small shelf nearby, no longer needing to be cataloged or acknowledged. They'd earned their place.

Caleb reached for an envelope that felt lighter than the others. Not thinner—just less heavy somehow. Across the front, in Lauren's familiar handwriting, was a simple title.

For When You're Still Standing.

Connor blinked. "That sounds... different."

Caleb smiled faintly. "It does."

"You reading?" Connor asked.

Caleb hesitated, then shook his head. "I think this one's yours to start."

Connor's fingers tightened around his mug. "You sure?"

"I'm here," Caleb said. "But yeah. I think she was talking to you."

Connor nodded slowly, then reached out and took the envelope. He didn't rush. He held it for a second, like he was adjusting to the weight of it.

When he opened it, the paper made that soft, dry sound that letters always did—careful, deliberate.

He cleared his throat once and began.

My Connor,

If you're reading this, it means something important has already happened.

It means you made it through the part where everything hurts all the time.

Not because it stopped hurting—just because you learned how to keep breathing anyway.

Connor paused, eyes moving back over the sentence.

Caleb didn't interrupt.

I want you to know something before you read any further: this letter is not here to make you cry.

If you do, that's okay. But that's not its job.

This one is here because I know what it's like to survive something and still not know what to do with yourself afterward.

Connor swallowed and kept going.

People will say things like "You're so strong" or "You're doing so well" and you'll nod because it's easier than explaining the truth.

The truth is, surviving doesn't always feel like winning.

Sometimes it just feels like standing in the aftermath, wondering who you're allowed to be now.

Caleb felt his chest tighten—not sharply, not painfully. Just enough to remind him he was listening to something real.

I watched you closely after hard things happened.

Not because I was worried you'd fall apart—though sometimes I was.

But because I could see you changing in ways other people missed.

Connor's voice wavered, then steadied.

You learned how to read rooms.

You learned how to listen for danger.

You learned how to keep parts of yourself quiet so other people wouldn't leave.

Caleb closed his eyes briefly.

Those skills kept you alive.

But they are not the same thing as living.

Connor stopped reading.

His fingers curled into the paper, then relaxed again.

Caleb spoke gently. "You want me to take over?"

Connor shook his head. "No. I'm okay."

He drew a breath and continued.

I need you to hear this clearly: the things you learned to survive are not the same things you'll need to stay whole.

You don't have to keep scanning the horizon.

You don't have to stay braced.

You don't have to be on guard with the people who love you.

Connor's eyes burned, but he didn't wipe them.

I saw you learning how to stay.

Not all at once. Not easily.

Just in moments.

The way you lingered in the kitchen a little longer.

The way you started asking questions again.

The way you didn't disappear when things got quiet.

Caleb felt something loosen in his chest.

That matters more than you know.

It means your heart didn't shut down—it adapted.

And adaptation is not the same thing as damage.

Connor's voice cracked on the last word. He stopped again.

Caleb waited.

After a moment, Connor spoke—not reading. "She really saw me."

"Yes," Caleb said. "She always did."

Connor nodded once and went back to the page.

If this is one of the first letters you read when things feel steadier, I want you to know something else.

You are not betraying your grief by having a good day.

You are not forgetting anyone by laughing.

You are not moving on—you are moving forward.

Caleb opened his mouth, then closed it again. The words didn't need commentary.

Grief doesn't disappear when you survive it.

It just stops demanding all of you.

And when that happens, you get to choose who you become next.

Connor's breath came slow and deliberate now.

You don't owe your pain your entire future.

You owe yourself a life.

Connor lowered the page slightly.

The kitchen felt warmer, though nothing had changed.

He looked at Caleb. "This one doesn't feel like a warning."

Caleb shook his head. "No. It feels like permission."

Connor nodded, absorbing that.

He glanced back down and read the final lines on the page.

If you're still standing when you read this, I'm proud of you.

Not because you were brave.

But because you stayed.

And staying—after everything you've been through—is its own kind of miracle.

Connor folded the page carefully and set it on the table.

He didn't cry.

He didn't smile either.

He just sat there, breathing.

Caleb let the moment exist without reaching for it.

After a while, Connor said quietly, "I don't feel broken."

Caleb's throat tightened. "No," he said. "You aren't."

Connor nodded once, like he was committing that to memory.

The box stayed open.

Not because it needed to be.

But because, for the first time, neither of them felt the urge to close it yet.

The kitchen light had shifted by the time Connor came back in.

Not much—just enough that the room looked less like late afternoon and more like it was deciding whether it wanted to be evening. The gray outside had thinned and turned the color of watered-down steel. Somewhere down the road, a dog barked once and quit, like even it didn't have the energy to argue with the season.

Caleb was still at the table, but the cedar box wasn't there. He'd moved it back to its spot—close, but not center. Like he was trying to remember the difference between *inviting* grief and *living inside it.*

Connor set his empty glass in the sink without a clatter. He didn't look at Caleb right away. That was a tell. It meant something had followed him out of the room, something he'd been carrying down the hall like a secret.

Caleb didn't ask the usual "you okay?" question.

He'd learned that question could feel like pressure if it was asked too quickly.

Instead, he said, "You want more tea?"

Connor shook his head. "No."

Caleb nodded like that was all the answer needed. He reached for the dish towel and wiped a clean spot on the table just to give his hands something to do. His fingers paused on the grain, catching on a shallow scratch—one of those old marks that had been there since before sickness and letters, since before the world had rearranged itself around what they lost.

Connor finally sat. Not across from him. Beside him again.

That was still new.

For a moment neither spoke, and the quiet felt like it had weight but not teeth.

Connor broke it first. "People think the year mark is... like a finish line."

Caleb's chest tightened. "Yeah."

Connor huffed a laugh that wasn't humor. "Like you cross it and you're magically a different person."

Caleb leaned back in his chair, careful. "You don't feel different."

Connor shook his head. "I feel... tired of everybody expecting me to be 'better' because time happened."

Caleb's gaze stayed on the window. The yard looked unfamiliar in the way familiar places do when someone's missing from them. "Time happens whether we want it to or not," he said. "That doesn't mean it heals on schedule."

Connor stared at the table, then said, "Sometimes I wish people would just say her name."

Caleb turned his head. "They don't?"

Connor shrugged. "Not much. They talk around it. Like if they don't say it, it's less real."

Caleb swallowed. "Lauren," he said quietly, like the word itself was a small flame.

Connor's eyes blinked hard, but he didn't look away.

Caleb went on, low and steady. "Lauren isn't a curse word. She isn't a problem. She's your mom."

Connor's mouth pressed together. He nodded once.

Then, softer: "I hate how quiet it gets when I bring her up."

Caleb didn't rush. He let the sentence have its space.

"I hate it too," he said. "It makes it feel like... we're the only ones still holding her."

Connor's voice was almost a whisper. "Aren't we?"

Caleb felt that one hit somewhere deeper than the ribs.

He didn't answer right away, not because he didn't have an answer, but because he had several, and he wanted the truest one.

Finally: "We're the ones who knew her in the ways other people didn't. So yeah—some of what we're holding, it's ours."

Connor stared at the table. "That feels unfair."

Caleb nodded. "It is."

Connor's fingers worried the cuff of his sleeve. "Do you ever... get mad?"

Caleb exhaled through his nose. "At God?"

Connor didn't say yes, but he didn't say no either. His silence was an answer.

Caleb sat with it. He didn't flinch from it.

"I've been angry," he admitted. "Not the kind where I throw things. The kind where I'm washing dishes and suddenly I can't breathe because I'm thinking, *why her?*"

Connor's head tipped slightly, listening.

Caleb continued, voice calm but honest. "And then I'm also... grateful. Because she loved us. Because we got her. Because she was ours."

Connor's eyes shone, but he kept them steady. "Both can be true."

Caleb looked at him—really looked. "Yes," he said. "Both are true."

Connor swallowed. "I don't know how to do that. Hold both."

Caleb's hand moved, slow, and rested on the table near Connor's sleeve. Not grabbing. Not demanding. Just there.

"You're already doing it," Caleb said.

Connor scoffed softly. "No I'm not."

"You are," Caleb insisted gently. "You get up. You do school. You laugh sometimes. You hate it sometimes. You miss her. You don't talk. Then you talk. That's both."

Connor stared at his hands. "It doesn't feel like I'm doing anything."

Caleb's voice softened. "Surviving doesn't always feel like progress. Sometimes it just feels like... carrying."

Connor's jaw tightened. "I don't want to carry her like she's weight."

Caleb's chest ached at the care inside that sentence. "You're not carrying her like weight," he said. "You're carrying her like... a name you refuse to drop."

Connor's eyes flicked to Caleb's face. "That's different."

"It is," Caleb said. "And it matters."

The house creaked softly as the temperature dropped. The heater kicked on with a faint click, a background sound that made the kitchen feel held.

Connor drew a breath. "Do you ever think about that day..."

Caleb didn't ask which one. He knew.

Connor's voice roughened. "Not the day she died. The day after. When the house still smelled like her and it was like... nobody told the rooms she was gone."

Caleb's throat tightened. "Yeah."

Connor swallowed. "I keep thinking I should remember it clearer."

Caleb shook his head once. "Your brain did what it had to do. It kept you alive."

Connor's fingers twisted in his sleeve. "Sometimes I feel guilty if I have a normal day."

Caleb turned fully toward him. "Connor."

Connor looked at him, startled by his tone.

Caleb kept it gentle, but firm. "A normal day isn't betrayal."

Connor stared, as if he didn't trust the permission.

Caleb went on. "Lauren loved normal. She fought for it. If you have a day where you laugh or you forget for a second—she wouldn't call that betrayal. She'd call it proof that love did what it was supposed to."

Connor's eyes narrowed slightly, like he was trying to decide if he believed that.

Caleb added, quieter: "And if you don't believe me, that's okay. But I need you to hear it, anyway."

Connor's throat bobbed. "Okay."

They sat like that a moment, side by side, the kitchen dimming around them.

Then Connor said, almost casually, like he was trying to keep his voice from breaking: "Do you still talk to her?"

Caleb's breath caught.

Not because the question was wrong.

Because it was right.

He stared at the sink for a second, at the mug he'd rinsed too long earlier, and the answer came up through him like something he couldn't stop.

"Yeah," he said. "I do."

Connor's eyes widened just a fraction. "Like... out loud?"

Caleb nodded slowly. "Sometimes. Mostly when it's quiet. Mostly when I'm doing something small. Dishes. Taking out the trash. Folding a shirt and realizing it's one she'd tease me about."

Connor's voice came thin. "What do you say?"

Caleb's lips pressed together. He let the truth come out plain. "I tell her what you're doing. I tell her when you make me proud. I tell her when I'm scared for you. I tell her I miss her."

Connor stared at the table, and a tear slipped down his cheek like it had been waiting.

He didn't wipe it fast.

Caleb didn't make it a thing.

Connor's voice cracked. "Does it help?"

Caleb nodded. "It doesn't fix it. But it... keeps me from feeling like the love stopped just because she did."

Connor's breath shuddered once. "I don't know how to do that."

Caleb's hand shifted closer. "You don't have to do it my way," he said. "But if you ever want to… you can. She's not offended by silence. She knew you."

Connor gave a small, miserable laugh. "Yeah. She did."

Caleb swallowed. "She knew your quiet was love too."

Connor blinked hard. "I wish I had been louder."

Caleb's chest tightened. "You were learning. She knew that. And she loved you in the learning."

Connor's shoulders hunched slightly, like he was trying to fold himself smaller. "I hate that I didn't understand until after."

Caleb's voice stayed gentle. "That's how most things are. We don't understand the sacred until it's already behind us."

Connor stared at Caleb then. "Do you think God… did that on purpose?"

Caleb didn't answer fast. He respected the question too much.

"I don't think God wanted her gone," he said slowly. "I don't think He enjoys breaking people. But I do think… He was with her. And with us. Even when it felt like He wasn't."

Connor's eyes stayed fixed on his. "How do you know?"

Caleb's throat worked. "Because we're still here," he said. "Because something kept holding us when we couldn't hold ourselves."

Connor looked down, considering. "That's not a very good answer."

Caleb gave a small, tired smile. "No. It's not."

Connor's mouth twitched. "But it's the only one we got."

Caleb nodded. "Yeah."

The light outside dimmed further, and the kitchen became its own little island of warmth.

Connor's voice softened. "Do you ever think… she would be mad at us for reading the letters?"

Caleb shook his head. "No."

Connor frowned. "How do you know?"

Caleb looked toward the cabinet where the calendar still hung, the ink loops still present like fingerprints. "Because she wrote them," he said. "Because she wanted us to have something when she couldn't be here. She wasn't leaving us empty."

Connor swallowed. "It still feels empty."

Caleb nodded. "Sometimes it does."

Connor leaned back, staring at the ceiling. "I hate that I'm getting used to it."

Caleb's voice stayed steady. "Getting used to it isn't forgetting her. It's learning how to breathe with the scar."

Connor went still at that.

Caleb watched him, careful. "That's what this year has been," he added. "Not healing like it didn't happen. Healing like... learning how to live with what did."

Connor's gaze drifted back down. "So what now?"

Caleb didn't pretend he had a clean roadmap. "Now we keep going," he said. "Not because we're trying to force closure. But because love doesn't stop. It just changes shape."

Connor's eyes narrowed slightly. "That sounds like something she would say."

Caleb smiled faintly. "Yeah. It does."

Connor hesitated, then said, "Can we... go look at the box?"

Caleb didn't move too fast. He didn't want to spook the moment. "Yeah," he said. "We can."

He stood and crossed to where the cedar box sat, hands steady. He carried it back to the table and set it down between them—not like a wall, but like a shared altar.

Connor didn't touch it right away.

He rested his forearms on the table and stared at the lid, breathing slow.

Caleb waited.

Finally, Connor lifted his hand and placed his palm flat on the wood.

Just that.

Just contact.

Caleb's throat tightened, but he didn't speak.

Connor's voice came out rough. "I don't want to read tonight."

Caleb nodded. "Okay."

Connor's eyes stayed on the box. "I just wanted to... remember it's there."

Caleb felt tears press behind his eyes and held them back with care. "It's there," he said. "And so is she. In every word."

Connor blinked hard. "I hate that this is what we have."

Caleb's voice softened. "Me too."

Connor drew a shaky breath. "But I'm glad it's something."

Caleb nodded once. "Yeah. Me too."

They sat with the box between them, not opening it, not running from it. Just letting it exist in the room like a truth that didn't have to be solved to be honored.

Outside, the first hints of spring waited behind winter's last stubborn breath.

Inside, two people held what they could.

For the first time, the future didn't frighten him—but it hadn't asked permission yet, either.

CHAPTER THIRTY-ONE

Nearly a Year, and Still Hovering

—— ♥ ——

The first thing Caleb noticed was the sound.

Not silence—silence had teeth. This was different. This was the low, lived in quiet of a house that had learned which noises mattered and which ones didn't anymore.

The furnace hummed. Pipes clicked once in protest and settled. Somewhere in the walls, the house shifted its weight like an old animal getting comfortable.

Connor was still asleep.

Caleb knew that without checking the clock, without listening for movement. He could feel it in the way the morning held itself—unrushed, undecided. The kind of morning that didn't demand anything yet.

He stood at the kitchen window with a mug cooling in his hands, watching the backyard wake slowly. The grass was hard with frost, every blade glassed over like it had been dipped in quiet. The yard looked bleached and stiff under a sky that couldn't decide whether to be dark or just tired. Winter wasn't easing up. It was still settled in, still claiming everything it touched, like it had time to spare.

That felt familiar.

Nearly a year, and still—hovering.

He hadn't marked the date on the calendar this time, even though he knew it was coming. He hadn't circled it or braced for it. He'd learned the hard way that grief didn't respect preparation. It showed up when it wanted, wearing whatever day it pleased.

Behind him, the house breathed.

Caleb took a sip of cocoa that had gone lukewarm and didn't bother reheating it. Some things didn't need fixing.

Connor padded into the kitchen a few minutes later, hair sticking up, hoodie already on like armor. He moved quietly, but not carefully. That was new too. He wasn't tiptoeing around grief anymore. He lived with it now.

"Mornin'," Caleb said.

Connor nodded and opened the cabinet without looking. He grabbed a mug, filled it, leaned against the counter while the microwave hummed.

Neither of them mentioned the date.

That was intentional.

Connor broke the quiet first. "School called yesterday."

Caleb glanced over. "Good or bad?"

"Neutral," Connor said. "Which somehow feels worse."

Caleb huffed a quiet breath. "What'd they want?"

"Checking in," Connor said. He stared into his mug like it might answer for him. "You know. 'Support.'"

Caleb nodded. He did know. The calls always came dressed as concern but carried expectation underneath—progress, resilience, improvement.

"And?" Caleb asked.

Connor shrugged. "I told them I was fine."

Caleb didn't correct him.

Connor added, quieter, "I'm not lying. I just... don't know what 'fine' means anymore."

Caleb set his mug down. "That's fair."

Connor glanced at him. "You ever notice how people stop asking real questions once they think enough time has passed?"

Caleb felt that one settle in his chest. "Yeah."

"They think grief has an expiration date," Connor went on. "Like milk."

Caleb smiled faintly despite himself. "Ours definitely doesn't."

Connor snorted once, then went still. "Do you think it ever changes? Like... really changes?"

Caleb leaned back in his chair. "It already has."

Connor frowned. "Doesn't feel like it."

"It won't," Caleb said. "Not from the inside."

Connor considered that. "So how do you know?"

Caleb didn't answer immediately. He watched the steam rise from Connor's mug, curl, vanish.

"Because it used to feel like drowning," he said finally. "And now it feels like... carrying something heavy while you keep walking."

Connor's brow furrowed. "That doesn't sound better."

Caleb met his eyes. "It's different. That's all."

Connor stared down again. "I don't want to get used to her being gone."

Caleb's voice stayed steady. "You won't."

Connor looked up sharply. "You said—"

"I said grief changes," Caleb interrupted gently. "Not love."

Connor's jaw worked like he was holding something back. "Good."

Caleb let the word sit between them like a promise.

Later, Caleb found himself in the hallway outside the bedroom without remembering how he'd gotten there.

That happened sometimes.

The door was open. It always was now.

The room looked the same in all the ways that mattered and different in the ones that didn't. The bed was made, not because it needed to be, but because routine was easier than decision. The dresser held fewer things now, but the shape of her absence still occupied space.

Caleb stood there longer than he meant to.

He didn't touch anything. He didn't need to. The room remembered her without his help.

Footsteps sounded behind him.

Connor leaned against the doorframe, arms crossed. He didn't comment on where Caleb was standing.

"You okay?" Connor asked—not casual, not forced. Real.

Caleb nodded once. "Yeah. Just... checking in."

Connor watched him, then stepped inside, stopping near the bed. He didn't sit.

"I had a dream about her last night," Connor said.

Caleb's chest tightened. "What kind?"

Connor shrugged. "Normal. She was just... there. Fussing at you for something dumb."

Caleb smiled softly. "That tracks."

Connor hesitated. "She didn't say goodbye."

Caleb swallowed. "She usually doesn't."

Connor nodded, relieved. "Good."

They stood there together, two people sharing a space that held more than it should have.

Connor broke the quiet. "Do you think she knows?"

Caleb didn't ask what he meant.

"I think she knows we're trying," Caleb said.

Connor's shoulders relaxed just a fraction.

That afternoon, they went to the grocery store.

It wasn't symbolic. It wasn't intentional. They just needed food.

The fluorescent lights buzzed softly overhead, and the store smelled like bread and cleaning solution. People moved around them with carts and lists and conversations that didn't pause for grief.

Connor walked beside Caleb, hands in his pockets.

"She used to hate this place," Connor said suddenly.

Caleb glanced over. "She hated the parking lot."

Connor nodded. "Said it was designed by someone who hated humanity."

Caleb laughed quietly. "She wasn't wrong."

They stood in the cereal aisle longer than necessary, staring at boxes.

Connor picked one up, frowned. "She always bought the boring kind."

"High fiber," Caleb said. "For 'long-term health.'"

Connor smirked. "She never ate it."

"Nope."

Connor put the box in the cart, anyway.

Caleb didn't comment.

At the checkout, Connor reached for his wallet automatically, then stopped himself. He flushed.

"Sorry," he muttered.

Caleb shook his head. "You're learning."

Connor nodded, eyes fixed forward.

Outside, the air felt softer. Not warm—just kinder.

Connor exhaled. "I didn't think I'd ever be able to do normal stuff again."

Caleb loaded bags into the truck. "Normal doesn't disappear," he said. "It just changes meaning."

Connor leaned against the door. "You always say that."

Caleb smiled faintly. "Because it keeps being true."

That night, the house settled early.

Connor retreated to his room with homework and headphones. Caleb moved through the kitchen, putting things away slowly, deliberately. He paused with his hand on the counter, feeling the cool surface ground him.

The cedar box stayed where it was.

Unopened.

Not avoided. Just... resting.

Caleb stood there a long moment, then turned off the light.

In the darkened kitchen, the quiet felt full—not empty.

And for the first time in a while, that didn't scare him.

Caleb woke sometime after midnight to the sound of Connor moving.

Not loud. Not frantic. Just the soft creak of a floorboard that had learned the exact weight of a growing boy.

Caleb stayed still.

He'd learned that too—when to intervene, when to let a moment unfold on its own.

The footsteps paused outside his door, then continued down the hall toward the kitchen. A cabinet opened. Closed. The refrigerator hummed, then quieted again.

After a minute, Caleb swung his legs out of bed and followed.

Connor sat at the kitchen table with a glass of water in front of him, fingers wrapped around it like he needed the chill to anchor him.

He didn't startle when Caleb entered.

"I couldn't sleep," Connor said.

Caleb nodded. "Me neither."

That wasn't entirely true, but it felt close enough to honest.

Caleb poured himself water and sat across from Connor. The house was dim, lit only by the stove clock and a sliver of moonlight through the window. Shadows gathered in the corners but didn't feel threatening. Just present.

Connor stared at the tabletop. "Do you ever worry that we're... forgetting her wrong?"

Caleb tilted his head slightly. "What do you mean?"

Connor hesitated, choosing his words like they were sharp. "Like... people say you remember the good stuff. But what if remembering only the good stuff isn't real? What if it turns her into something she wasn't?"

Caleb felt the weight of that settle slowly.

"She was human," he said. "Remembering her as human isn't forgetting. It's honoring."

Connor frowned. "But what if I forget her voice?"

Caleb didn't rush the answer.

"You won't," he said finally. "It might get quieter sometimes. But it won't disappear."

Connor's fingers tightened around the glass. "It already feels quieter."

Caleb leaned forward slightly. "That doesn't mean it's gone," he said. "It means your life is getting louder again."

Connor's eyes lifted. "Is that... allowed?"

Caleb's throat tightened. "Yes."

Connor swallowed. "Sometimes I feel bad when I laugh."

Caleb nodded. "Me too."

They sat with that confession between them, heavy but shared.

Connor spoke again. "I don't want her to think I moved on."

Caleb's voice stayed steady. "She wouldn't think that."

"How do you know?"

Caleb didn't answer with logic. He answered with memory.

"Because she loved you," he said. "Not the version of you frozen in grief. The version of you who keeps living."

Connor stared at him, eyes wet but unblinking. "That sounds like something she'd say."

Caleb smiled faintly. "She did."

The next morning came slow and pale, the kind of day that didn't make promises.

Connor slept late. Caleb let him.

He moved through the house quietly, brewing cocoa, opening curtains just enough to let light in without forcing the day to announce itself.

When Connor finally emerged, he looked more like himself than he had in days—still tired, still guarded, but present.

"Morning," Connor said.

"Morning," Caleb replied.

Connor grabbed a mug and sat at the table. He stared into it for a moment, then said, "I think I want to do something today."

Caleb waited.

"I don't know what," Connor added quickly. "Just... something."

Caleb nodded. "Okay."

They ate without much conversation, the quiet comfortable this time. Outside, the sky had thinned to a pale blue, tentative but real.

After breakfast, Connor stood near the doorway like he was deciding whether to step forward or retreat.

"Can we go somewhere?" he asked.

Caleb didn't ask where.

"Sure," he said.

They drove without music at first, the road familiar enough that it didn't require directions.

Eventually, Connor spoke. "Can we go by the park?"

Caleb's hands tightened on the wheel for half a second. "Yeah," he said. "We can."

The park was quiet, late winter keeping most people indoors. The swings moved slightly in the breeze, chains clinking softly. The field stretched wide and empty, grass dull but waiting.

Connor walked ahead, hands shoved deep into his pockets.

"She used to sit right there," Connor said, nodding toward a bench near the trees.

Caleb followed his gaze. "I remember."

Connor sat on the edge of the bench, staring out at nothing in particular. "I didn't like coming here at first."

Caleb stood beside him. "I know."

"It felt like pretending," Connor said. "Like if I enjoyed it, I was lying."

Caleb shook his head gently. "Grief lies to us. Tells us joy is betrayal."

Connor kicked at the dirt. "It's convincing."

"Yeah," Caleb said. "It is."

They stood there a while, letting the memory breathe without forcing it into meaning.

Connor broke the silence. "Do you think she's proud of us?"

Caleb didn't answer quickly. He didn't need to.

"Yes," he said. "I do."

Connor's shoulders slumped slightly, like he'd been holding that question up for a long time.

That evening, back home, Connor lingered in the living room instead of retreating to his room.

Caleb noticed, pretended not to.

Connor flipped channels without really watching, the glow of the screen painting his face in shifting colors.

"Dad?" Connor said.

"Yeah?"

"Are you scared of the future?"

Caleb considered that. "Sometimes."

Connor nodded. "Me too."

Caleb added, "But I'm not scared of it being empty."

Connor looked at him. "What do you mean?"

"I mean," Caleb said, choosing his words carefully, "that love doesn't stop working just because the shape changes."

Connor absorbed that quietly.

After a while, he reached for the blanket folded on the couch and pulled it over his legs.

Caleb didn't comment.

They sat together, not touching, not distant. Just existing in the same space, the way they'd learned to do.

Later, as the house settled into night again, Caleb stood in the hallway outside Connor's room.

The door was half open. Connor lay on his bed, staring at the ceiling.

"Hey," Caleb said softly.

Connor turned his head. "Yeah?"

"You okay?"

Connor nodded. "I think so."

Caleb hesitated, then asked, "Do you want the light off?"

Connor considered. "Not yet."

Caleb left it on.

As he turned to walk away, Connor spoke again. "Dad?"

Caleb stopped.

"Thanks for staying," Connor said. "Like... really staying."

Caleb felt something tighten and ease at the same time. "Always," he said.

Back in the kitchen, Caleb stood alone for a moment.

The house didn't feel like it was holding its breath anymore.

It felt like it was breathing again—carefully, unevenly, but alive.

Nearly a year later, grief still lived here. It always would.

But so did love.

And that—Caleb realized—was enough to keep going.

Sometime later that night, Caleb stood alone on the back porch.

He hadn't planned to come out here. The door had just been closer than the couch, and the quiet had felt easier to carry in the open air.

The porch light cast a weak yellow circle over the boards, leaving the yard beyond it mostly shadow. The air had a bite to it—not cruel, just honest. Winter loosening, but not gone.

Caleb leaned against the railing and let his hands rest there, palms flat, grounding himself in something solid.

Nearly a year.

He still couldn't say it without his chest tightening.

There were moments—whole stretches of days—where he functioned well enough that he almost believed he'd learned how to live inside the absence. Then there were nights like this, when the quiet didn't feel peaceful. It felt observant. Like the world was waiting to see what he'd do next.

He thought about the man he had been before everything broke open.

Not younger. Not happier. Just... less aware.

Grief had stripped something away, but it had also sharpened everything left behind. Sounds carried farther. Memories landed harder. Love felt heavier—but truer.

Inside, the house settled with a familiar creak. Pipes ticking. Wood adjusting. The ordinary noises of a place that had learned loss and kept standing, anyway.

Caleb exhaled slowly.

He wasn't afraid of forgetting her anymore.

That fear had burned itself out months ago, replaced by something quieter and harder to name—the fear of carrying her memory alone.

Connor helped with that.

Caleb smiled faintly at the thought.

His son was changing. Not all at once. Not in obvious ways. But there was a steadiness growing there, a willingness to stay present even when staying hurt.

That mattered.

Caleb rested his forehead briefly against the cool wood of the railing.

"I'm trying," he said aloud.

The words weren't dramatic. They weren't meant to be heard.

They were just true.

Inside, a floorboard creaked—Connor moving in his room, maybe turning over, maybe just stretching. A reminder that Caleb wasn't carrying this house, or this grief, by himself.

That realization settled deeper than relief.

It felt like permission.

Caleb straightened and took one last look at the darkened yard, then went back inside, closing the door gently behind him.

The house didn't protest.

It accepted him.

And for the first time that day, Caleb felt certain of one thing:

Whatever came next, they would meet it together.

CHAPTER THIRTY-TWO

The Chair in the Living Room

The cold had a different sound when it wasn't snowing.

Not the hush that came with white yards and muffled roads—this was the sharper kind, the kind that let the wind scrape branches against each other and made the gutters tick with leftover ice. Outside the kitchen window, the streetlight turned the damp air a pale gold. Somewhere down the road, a truck passed, and the tires whispered on wet asphalt, then the sound thinned until it was gone.

Caleb stood at the counter with a pot on the stove, stirring slow like the motion itself could settle something in him. Chili—real chili, not just something warmed up—because the house felt like it needed a smell that belonged to living. The beans had been simmering long enough to soften. The spices had finally opened up. When he lifted the lid, steam rolled toward his face and fogged his glasses for a second.

Behind him, Connor sat at the kitchen table with his feet tucked under the chair, hoodie sleeves pulled down over his hands. A glass of sweet tea sweated against the wood. He kept shifting the ice with the straw, not really drinking, just keeping his hands busy.

Caleb didn't say, "You okay?"

He'd learned that question could become a trap if you asked it too often—like you were trying to force an answer into a shape it didn't fit.

Instead, he set two bowls on the table, then a stack of crackers. He didn't add a lecture about eating. He just made room for it.

Connor glanced up. "Smells good."

Caleb nodded once. "Figured we needed something warm."

Connor's eyes dropped back to the table. "Yeah."

The cedar box wasn't out yet.

It stayed where it had been living lately—nearby, within reach, never hidden and never shoved in the center of everything like a dare. Caleb had stopped pretending it was a thing they could put away with enough willpower. The box didn't behave like an object. It behaved like a door.

The house was quiet in that way it got when the heater cycled off and the world outside had already chosen night. Caleb could hear the faint drip of the kitchen faucet—one drop every so often, stubborn as a habit he hadn't fixed yet. He made a mental note to tighten it tomorrow and knew he wouldn't.

Connor cleared his throat like he was about to say something and then didn't.

Caleb served the chili and sat down across from him, hands resting on the table for a moment before he picked up his spoon.

They ate a few bites in silence. Not tense. Not empty. Just the kind of quiet that lived in their house now without needing permission.

Connor finally spoke. "I keep thinking... if we'd known."

Caleb didn't ask what he meant. He knew.

Connor's voice stayed low. "If we'd known it was going to be that day. Would we have done anything different?"

Caleb looked down into his bowl. The chili was thick, dark red, steady. Ordinary.

"I don't know," he said truthfully. "Part of me wants to say yes. Because that makes me feel like I could've controlled something." He lifted his eyes. "But I also know... your mom didn't live like she had one foot out the door. She lived like she was staying."

Connor's jaw tightened. "That's what messes with me. She wasn't—" He stopped, swallowed. "She wasn't preparing us."

Caleb nodded slowly. "No. Not in the way we think of preparing."

Connor pushed a cracker through the chili and ate it without tasting it. "So what were the letters for then?"

Caleb breathed in, then out. "I think… the letters were how she held what she couldn't say out loud without scaring us. She didn't want the house to become a hospital, Connor." His voice softened. "She didn't want you to wake up every day and feel like you were watching a countdown."

Connor didn't respond right away. He stared at the surface of his sweet tea like he could read answers in the ripples.

Caleb added, quieter, "And she didn't want you thinking you had to carry it."

Connor's shoulders rose in a small shrug that wasn't really a shrug. "I carried it anyway."

Caleb didn't argue. He didn't correct. He just nodded once because his son was right.

Connor stabbed another cracker, then stopped mid-motion. "This one," he said, eyes still down, "is it going to be about… her being sick again?"

Caleb didn't answer like he knew. He answered like a man who had lived it.

"I don't know what she wrote," he said quietly. "But… she picked titles that told the truth."

Connor's lips pressed together. "I just don't want it to sound like she's getting better."

Caleb's throat tightened. "It won't," he said, and this time it wasn't a promise about the letter. It was a promise about how they would read it.

Connor looked up, eyes sharp with something that was half fear and half insistence. "Because in the last year… she didn't."

Caleb held his gaze. "I know," he said simply. "We're not going to pretend otherwise."

Connor stared at him for a long moment, then nodded once. "Okay."

Caleb stood and carried the cedar box to the table. The wood made that familiar soft sound when he set it down—solid, real. Not cruel. Just true.

He opened the lid.

The envelopes inside were fewer now. Lauren's handwriting still curved across the fronts, steady and unmistakable. Connor leaned forward slightly, not touching anything, just looking—like reading with his eyes first made it safer.

Caleb's fingers hovered, then stopped on one near the middle. The paper was thicker than some of the others. A small stack.

Across the front, in her neat curve:

The Chair in the Living Room

Connor exhaled, a quiet sound that didn't quite become a word. "That's... the recliner."

Caleb swallowed. "Yeah."

Connor's gaze stayed fixed on the title. "She wrote a letter about that chair."

Caleb slid the envelope out, careful. "She wrote a letter about what that chair meant," he corrected softly.

Connor blinked hard, but he didn't look away. "You read it," he said. "I'll listen."

Caleb nodded once, opened the envelope, and unfolded the pages.

My Caleb,

If you're reading this, then the chair is still there.

I know you, and I know the way you hold onto things when they feel like part of a person. You'll keep it longer than you need to. You'll tell yourself it's practical—because you always need a practical reason for anything that hurts.

But I want you to hear me say this first:

It was never just a chair.

It was the place my life narrowed down into, little by little, until everything I could still do lived inside one room.

I didn't think it would happen that way.

People imagine sickness like a cliff—like you're fine and then you're not. Like there's one moment where everything changes and you can point to it and say, "That's when it started."

But for me, it was a slow folding.

A chair pulled closer to the TV because I needed to sit more often.

A blanket because my skin stayed cold.

A small table beside me because I got tired of asking you to hand me things.

Then, one day, without meaning to, I stopped getting up unless I had to.

I told myself it was temporary. I told myself I was just "resting." I told myself I would bounce back when the weather changed, when the infection passed, when my lungs calmed down, when my numbers looked better.

I told myself a lot of things.

Some of them were hope.

Some of them were denial dressed up like optimism.

I need you to know that, Caleb—because you are going to be tempted, after I'm gone, to rewrite those months into something gentler than they were.

Don't.

Not because I want you to suffer.

But because I want you to remember me honestly, and I want you to forgive both of us for the ways we tried to make it feel normal.

There were days I sat in that chair and watched you move through the house like you were carrying the whole structure of it on your shoulders.

Work.

Bills.

Meals.

Laundry.

Medication schedules.

Trash.

Appointments.

Phone calls.

You did it without complaining the way people imagine complaining looks. You didn't slam doors or throw fits. You just got quieter. More focused. Like if you stayed in motion, the fear couldn't catch you.

I saw you, Caleb.

Even when you thought I was too tired to notice anything.

I noticed the way you'd pause in the doorway of the living room and look at me like you were taking a picture with your eyes.

I noticed the way you'd ask, "Need anything?" and make your voice sound casual, like you weren't bracing for the answer.

I noticed how you'd sit on the edge of the couch sometimes and talk to me about the boys or about nothing at all—just to keep me tethered to the day.

And I noticed the way you tried to protect Connor from seeing too much.

You didn't always succeed, sweetheart. But you tried.

Connor —

If he's hearing this too, tell him I'm smiling right now because I know he'll pretend he isn't listening, even if he's the one reading it.

That boy has a way of feeling everything with the volume turned down on the outside.

He would come into the living room and hover like he didn't know what to do with his love.

Sometimes he'd sit on the other end of the couch, not touching me, not looking at me, just existing in the same room like he was learning the rules of being safe.

Sometimes he'd ask if I needed anything, and his voice would come out flat, like kindness was a language he was still learning how to speak without an accent.

And sometimes he would just stand there and watch the TV over my shoulder, pretending he wasn't watching me too.

I want you to tell him something for me:

I never once mistook his quiet for indifference.

I knew what it cost him to stay in the room.

I knew what it meant when he didn't run.

Caleb, I also need you to hear the hard part.

There were days I hated that chair.

Not because it hurt my back—though it did—but because it made me feel like I was shrinking.

It made me feel like my world was getting smaller while yours got heavier.

I would sit there and listen to you in the kitchen, making dinner, and I would feel guilty in a way that didn't have logic to it.

Guilty because you were doing it.

Guilty because you were tired and still doing it.

Guilty because Connor would warm something up or carry a bag of trash out or pick up his own mess, and it would hit me that he was learning responsibility from my weakness.

I know he had been helping with little things since he was thirteen, and I was proud of him for it.

But pride and guilt can sit in the same place.

I would watch him do a chore and think, This isn't how it's supposed to be.

Then you would come in and kiss my forehead and say, "Don't you start that," like you could hear my thoughts.

Sometimes I did start it anyway.

I would apologize for being tired. For being slow. For needing help.

You would tell me I wasn't a burden.

I believed you, but not always all the way.

Because the hardest part of being loved is believing you don't have to earn it.

That chair taught me that.

It taught me how to receive.

How to let you bring me a glass of ice water without saying I could get it myself.

How to let you fix my blanket without acting like I didn't need it.

How to let Connor do something kind without turning it into a speech that made him retreat.

How to let myself be small sometimes without believing it made me less.

Caleb, there's one more thing I have to say here, and I want you to hear it without flinching:

I didn't wear makeup in those months because I couldn't.

You know that. My skin wouldn't tolerate it. My eyes wouldn't tolerate it. Even if I'd wanted to paint myself into looking "better," my body would've said no.

So if you ever look back and wish I'd tried harder to look like myself, please don't.

I was still myself.

Even bare-faced. Even in that chair. Even when my hair was a mess and my hands shook and my breath sounded like work.

I was still the woman who loved you.

Still the woman who teased you.

Still the woman who watched our son like he was a miracle we got to keep.

Still the woman who would've gotten up and done everything if I'd had the strength.

But I didn't.

And that is not a moral failure.

It is just the truth.

I didn't know I was going to die, Caleb.

I need you to hold onto that.

I knew I was declining. I knew my body wasn't turning back. I knew the last year was the roughest, and the last few months were the hardest, and there were days I felt like I lived inside that chair more than I lived inside my own skin.

But I did not sit there thinking, This is my last season.

I sat there thinking, Please let me feel a little better tomorrow.

I sat there thinking, If I can just get through winter, maybe spring will be easier.

I sat there thinking, I don't want to scare them.

I sat there thinking, I still have time.

That's why I wrote reminders on calendars.

That's why I asked you about dinner.

That's why I watched TV and laughed at things that weren't that funny.

Because I was still here.

I want you to remember that I was still here.

And I want you to remember this too:

Even in that chair, even in the slow fade, love stayed loud.

Not loud like a performance.

Loud like a heartbeat.

Loud like the way you kept showing up.

Loud like the way Connor stayed in the room.

Loud like the way God kept meeting me in ordinary minutes—sometimes just in the warmth of your hand on my shoulder, sometimes in a quiet peace that didn't make sense, sometimes in a breath that came easier than it had the day before.

If you are reading this and you're angry at that chair, I understand.

If you are reading this and you miss the version of me who moved faster, I understand.

But don't let the chair become the villain in our story.

It was just where I sat when my strength ran out.

The villain is always the same, Caleb:

The lie that love stops being love when it becomes care.

Don't believe that lie.

You never did when I was there.

Don't start believing it now.

Your wife,

Lauren

Caleb's voice went thin on the last line—not breaking, just careful, like he was carrying something glass and didn't trust his hands.

He set the pages down in front of him without folding them yet.

Connor didn't move.

He sat very still, eyes fixed on the table, like if he lifted his face too fast the grief might spill out in a way he couldn't catch.

A long moment passed.

Then Connor cleared his throat, and his voice came out rough. "She... she knew I stayed."

Caleb nodded slowly. "Yeah," he said. "She did."

Connor blinked hard, once. Twice. "I didn't even know what I was doing half the time," he muttered.

"You were staying," Caleb said gently. "That's what you were doing."

Connor's jaw worked like he was biting down on something sharp. "And you—" He stopped. Tried again. "You did everything."

Caleb shook his head once. "Not everything," he said. "But a lot."

Connor finally looked up. His eyes were wet, but his expression wasn't fragile. It was something harder than that—something honest.

"It makes me mad," Connor said quietly. "Not at you. Not at her. Just... mad."

Caleb understood. "Yeah," he said. "Me too."

Connor stared at the letter again. "I don't like thinking about her feeling guilty."

Caleb's throat tightened. "I know."

Connor swallowed. "Because she wasn't a burden."

Caleb's answer came steady. "No. She wasn't."

Connor's gaze dropped back to his sleeves. His fingers worried the hem like he was trying to unthread a feeling without letting it snap.

Caleb didn't rush him.

The heater clicked on in the other room, then settled into a soft, steady push of warm air through the vents. Outside, wind lifted the last wet leaves and skittered them across the road.

Connor finally spoke again, quieter. "So what now?"

Caleb looked at the pages—still open, still there.

He thought about the chair in the living room, and the way grief could turn furniture into landmarks.

He thought about his son, sitting across from him, learning how to name love without being ashamed of it.

"We sit with it," Caleb said. "For a minute."

Connor nodded once, barely. "Okay."

Caleb reached for the pages and began folding them carefully—slow, respectful—like he was tucking something precious back into its place.

And when he slid the letter into the envelope again, he didn't feel like he was putting her away.

He felt like he was holding the part of her that still knew how to speak.

CHAPTER THIRTY-THREE

The Day Before

The date sat on the calendar like a bruise you couldn't cover.

January 14.

It wasn't circled. Caleb didn't need ink to remember it. The week had been moving toward it in small, ordinary steps—trash day, a grocery run, Connor's schoolwork, a bill due—like life was trying to pretend it didn't know what was coming.

But Caleb knew.

Connor knew too, even when he didn't say it.

The morning of the thirteenth came in gray and damp, the kind of cold that didn't sparkle or crackle—it just seeped into the seams of the house and made everything feel heavier. Caleb stood at the kitchen sink with the water running, washing a bowl that was already clean. He watched the soap slide off the ceramic and disappear down the drain and thought, stupidly, about how many things disappeared without asking permission.

Behind him, Connor moved through the kitchen without a sound.

He had stopped wearing his hoodie all the time lately, not because he didn't want it, but because the house had been warm enough, and because Caleb had started turning the heat up sooner than he used to. He'd caught himself doing it—one small mercy he could still offer.

Connor poured sweet tea into a glass, then set the pitcher back in the fridge. The door thumped closed with a quiet finality that felt louder than it should have.

Caleb shut off the water and dried his hands. He turned, leaned back against the counter, and watched his son for a second longer than a casual glance.

Connor didn't look up. He stared at the table like it had something written on it.

Caleb tried a neutral voice. "You hungry?"

Connor shrugged. "Not really."

Caleb nodded. He didn't push. Pushing was how you turned an ordinary morning into a fight neither of them had energy for.

He moved to the stove and started a pot of soup anyway, because one of them needed to eat and the smell of something warm made the kitchen feel less like a waiting room.

Connor sat at the table and pulled his phone closer, then didn't unlock it. Just rested his hands on it like it was a paperweight.

Caleb could feel the thing between them—unsaid, unmissable—like a storm line on the horizon.

Finally, Connor said it without looking up.

"Tomorrow."

Caleb didn't pretend he didn't understand. He just nodded once. "Yeah."

Connor's jaw tightened. "Everybody keeps acting like tomorrow is just... a day."

Caleb's throat worked. "It is," he said. "And it isn't."

Connor gave a short exhale that wasn't quite a laugh. "That's a stupid answer."

Caleb's mouth twitched. "Probably."

Connor glanced up then, eyes sharp and tired. "Are we doing something?"

The question sounded casual, but it wasn't. It was Connor trying not to ask the real question—what are we supposed to do with a day that feels like it can swallow you?

Caleb leaned on the counter, thinking. "We can," he said. "We don't have to. But we can."

Connor's gaze dropped again. "Like... the cemetery?"

Caleb felt his chest tighten at the word. He nodded anyway. "If you want."

Connor stared at his hands. "I don't know if I want," he admitted. "I just... I don't know what else to do."

Caleb understood that too well. "We can go," he said softly. "And we can leave whenever you want. No speeches. No trying to make it feel better. Just... show up."

Connor's shoulders rose and fell slowly. "Okay."

Caleb let the quiet return. He didn't fill it with advice. He'd learned Connor didn't need advice in moments like this—he needed someone willing to stand in the same weather.

The soup began to simmer, the small bubbles breaking the surface like tiny breaths.

Caleb set out two bowls. Connor ate a few bites without tasting it, then stopped and stared past the table, eyes fixed on the living room doorway.

Caleb followed his gaze.

The recliner sat where it had always sat. The chair in the living room.

He had kept it.

Not because it was useful. Not because he wanted to sit in it. Mostly because moving it felt like an admission that time could rearrange her shape in their house.

Connor's eyes stayed on it a second longer than they needed to, then he looked away.

Caleb pretended he didn't notice. Some things were better approached sideways.

By afternoon, the sky had gone a flat, washed-out white. The kind of winter day that never fully turned into day.

Caleb drove to the grocery store because they were out of milk and because leaving the house kept his thoughts from stacking into something dangerous.

Connor came with him without being asked.

They rode in silence, the heater pushing warm air into the cab, the windshield wipers squeaking every few seconds on a light mist.

At a red light, Connor said quietly, "Do you think she'd be mad we don't know what to do?"

Caleb's hands tightened on the wheel, then eased. "No," he said. "She'd understand."

Connor's voice stayed low. "What if she expected something?"

Caleb glanced over, then back to the road. "Your mom didn't love in conditions," he said. "She loved in presence. If we show up tomorrow—even if we don't say much—that's enough."

Connor stared out the window. "I don't want to cry in front of people."

Caleb nodded. "Then we won't."

Connor's eyes cut to him. "You can control that?"

Caleb's mouth tightened into something honest. "No," he admitted. "But we can choose where we are. We can choose not to make it a public performance."

Connor looked away again, shoulders easing slightly. "Okay."

At the store, they walked the aisles like they were doing something normal. Caleb put things in the cart—milk, bread, canned beans, crackers—small necessities that felt absurd beside what tomorrow meant.

Connor trailed behind, hands in his pockets.

In the aisle with the greeting cards, Connor stopped.

Caleb realized it too late to steer them around it. Rows of Valentine's Day cards already out. Bright red hearts. Glitter. Promises. *Forever.*

Connor stared at them, face blank. Then his throat bobbed.

Caleb stepped closer, not touching him, just near.

Connor's voice came out rough. "We're not even to the anniversary yet and they're already selling... that."

Caleb nodded, feeling something hot behind his eyes. "Yeah."

Connor swallowed hard. "It's like the world doesn't care."

Caleb's voice stayed steady. "The world keeps moving," he said. "It's not cruelty. It's just... what it does."

Connor's jaw clenched. "Feels like cruelty."

Caleb didn't argue. "I know."

Connor turned away from the cards and walked faster toward the front of the store. Caleb followed with the cart, letting his son set the pace.

At checkout, the cashier chatted about the weather like weather was the biggest thing happening in anyone's life. Caleb answered politely. Connor didn't speak.

When they got back in the truck, Connor exhaled like he'd been holding his breath the whole time.

Caleb started the engine. "We don't have to go back there again," he said quietly. "Not that aisle."

Connor nodded. "Okay."

They drove home under a sky that looked like it couldn't decide whether to snow or rain. The tires hummed on the road. The wipers kept time.

When they pulled into the driveway, Connor didn't get out right away.

He stared at the house. The porch. The windows. The familiar shape that still felt unfamiliar sometimes, like grief had changed the dimensions.

Caleb didn't rush him.

Connor finally said, "I hate that I still think she's going to be in there."

Caleb's chest tightened. "Me too."

Connor's voice cracked. "It's stupid."

"It's not," Caleb said. "It's love doing what it always did. Reaching for her."

Connor stared forward, blinking hard. "Tomorrow's going to suck."

Caleb nodded. "Yeah," he said quietly. "It is."

Connor looked over then, eyes red around the edges. "You're not going to tell me it'll be okay?"

Caleb held his gaze. "It will be survivable," he said. "That's what I can promise."

Connor's face softened just a fraction, like the honesty gave him something solid to stand on.

"Okay," Connor whispered.

They went inside.

That night, Caleb found Connor in the living room.

Not on the couch. On the floor, back against the recliner, knees drawn up. He had a blanket over his legs and the TV on low, but he wasn't watching. His eyes were unfocused, like his mind was somewhere else entirely.

Caleb paused in the doorway, heart clenching at the sight.

Connor didn't look up. "I'm not doing anything," he said quickly, as if he'd been caught.

Caleb walked in slowly. "I know," he said. "You don't have to justify sitting."

Connor's jaw tightened. "I just—" He stopped. His voice came out small. "I didn't want to be in my room."

Caleb nodded. "That makes sense."

He didn't sit in the recliner. He couldn't. Not tonight.

Instead, he lowered himself onto the carpet a few feet away, back against the couch. Close enough to share the room, far enough not to crowd.

They sat with the TV murmuring in the background, a show neither of them cared about. The house creaked softly as the temperature dropped.

After a while, Connor spoke. "Do you remember what you were doing this time last year?"

Caleb's stomach tightened. "Yeah," he said. "Too well."

Connor swallowed. "I keep replaying it," he admitted. "Not the whole day. Just... pieces."

Caleb didn't ask which pieces. He knew they were different for each of them, and that Connor would offer what he could when he could.

Connor's voice came out strained. "I keep thinking I should've known."

Caleb sat up a little. "Connor—"

Connor cut him off, not angry, just desperate. "I know," he said quickly. "I know you're going to say nobody knew. I know that's true. But my brain doesn't care what's true. It just keeps... doing it."

Caleb nodded slowly. "I know," he said. "Mine does too."

Connor stared at the carpet. "How do you turn it off?"

Caleb's throat tightened. "You don't," he admitted. "Not all at once. You just... learn how to live with the noise."

Connor's voice went thin. "I don't want to live with it."

Caleb felt something break open in him, careful and painful. He didn't reach for Connor. He didn't force comfort. He just said the honest thing.

"I don't either," he whispered. "But we are."

Connor blinked hard and looked away, jaw trembling for a second before he locked it down.

Caleb stared at the TV without seeing it. He thought about tomorrow. About the cemetery. About the bell near Lauren's resting place. About the cold air on his face.

He thought about what he could do to make tomorrow less cruel.

Maybe nothing.

Maybe just be there.

Connor finally spoke again, almost too quiet to hear. "I don't want to go to the cemetery and feel nothing."

Caleb turned his head slightly. "You won't," he said. "You'll feel something."

Connor swallowed. "What if I don't cry? What if I just... stand there."

Caleb's voice stayed steady. "Then you stand there," he said. "That's still love."

Connor's shoulders rose and fell, slow. "Okay."

The TV flickered with some bright commercial. Caleb reached for the remote and muted it.

The silence was immediate.

Connor's eyes stayed on the recliner. The chair.

After a minute, he said, "Do you think she knew we'd be like this?"

Caleb's breath caught. "I think she knew we'd hurt," he said carefully. "And I think she believed we'd keep loving each other through it."

Connor's mouth tightened. "That sounds like something you'd say."

Caleb's lips pressed into a faint, sad smile. "Yeah," he admitted. "Because it's something she taught me."

Connor went still. The blanket slipped a little down his legs. He pulled it back up without looking at it.

"Dad," he said, voice thin.

Caleb's heart clenched. "Yeah?"

Connor's eyes finally lifted. "Tomorrow... if I lose it... don't talk to me like I'm a little kid."

Caleb nodded once, immediately. "I won't."

Connor's jaw worked. "And if you lose it," he added, almost reluctantly, "I'm not going to freak out."

Caleb felt his eyes sting. "Okay," he whispered.

Connor stared at him for a long moment, then nodded like a decision had been made inside him.

They sat there until the house settled deeper into night.

Caleb didn't tell Connor to go to bed. Connor didn't ask to stay up. They just existed in the living room like it was the only place that could hold them.

And when Caleb finally stood, he didn't look at the recliner with anger.

He looked at it with the same exhausted respect he'd learned to give every ordinary object that had become sacred by association.

"Ready to turn in?" Caleb asked softly.

Connor nodded. "Yeah."

Caleb walked him down the hall and left the lamp on like Lauren used to.

And when Connor's door clicked shut, Caleb stood in the hallway for a second, hand resting on the wall, breathing through the tightness in his chest.

Tomorrow.

The date he couldn't circle.

The day that would come whether he was ready or not.

He went back to the kitchen, turned off the light, and stood in the dark for a moment, letting the quiet press against him.

Then he whispered, not loud enough for anyone else to hear, "Help us."

Not a polished prayer.

Just the truth.

CHAPTER THIRTY-FOUR

January 14

♥

The morning arrived the way it always did now—quiet, deliberate, almost careful.

No storm. No thunder. No sense that the sky knew what it was holding.

Just January.

Cold that settled into the bones instead of biting. Light that never fully committed to being light. A grayness that didn't threaten anything outright, just lingered like it had nowhere better to go.

Caleb woke before the alarm.

He had learned that about himself this past year—his body no longer trusted sleep to keep him safe on certain days. It stirred early, alert in a way that felt less like readiness and more like vigilance.

January 14.

He didn't need to look at the clock to know it.

The house was still. Not empty—never empty—but quiet in the way of something familiar that had learned how to hold sorrow without cracking under it. The floorboards didn't complain when he shifted his weight. The walls didn't echo. Even the air felt practiced, like it had done this before and would do it again.

Nearly a year.

Not a clean year. Not one measured in neat milestones or tidy progress. Just a year of getting up, going to work, making meals, paying bills, sitting beside his son in silences that said more than conversation ever could.

A year of learning how grief didn't fade—it changed shape.

Caleb sat up and planted his feet on the floor. Cold crept through his socks. He stayed there longer than necessary, hands braced on his thighs, breathing like he was preparing to lift something heavy.

Down the hall, Connor's door was closed.

Caleb didn't check the time. He didn't need to. Connor had been waking early too lately—not rushing into the day, just... awake. Like something inside him kept watch now.

In the kitchen, Caleb moved quietly, not out of fear of waking anyone, but out of instinct. Reverence, almost. He filled the kettle. Set out two mugs. Cocoa, not coffee.

Some things hadn't changed.

The stove clock glowed a faint blue. He didn't turn on the overhead light. The dimness felt appropriate—like brightness would be rude.

The kettle began to whisper.

Caleb leaned against the counter and watched steam gather. He tried not to think about how many mornings Lauren had stood in this same spot—waiting, listening, already smiling before Connor came into the room.

Today the kitchen felt like it was holding its breath.

A soft sound behind him.

Connor stood in the doorway, hoodie already on, hair rumpled, eyes tired in a way sleep never fixed. He didn't say good morning. Caleb didn't ask for it.

"Cocoa's almost ready," Caleb said quietly.

Connor nodded and took a seat at the table, sleeves pulled over his hands like warmth was something you had to anchor on purpose.

Caleb poured the cocoa and slid a mug toward him. The smell filled the room—rich, familiar, almost cruel in how ordinary it was.

Connor wrapped both hands around the mug but didn't drink.

Caleb sat beside him instead of across from him. Not touching. Just close enough to be felt.

They stayed that way for a long minute.

Then Connor said it—flat, unguarded, like he'd been holding it since waking.

"I hate this day."

Caleb nodded. "Me too."

Connor stared into the mug. "People keep texting. Saying they're thinking about us. Praying."

Caleb's jaw tightened. "You don't have to answer."

"I know," Connor said. "It's just... it doesn't help."

"No," Caleb agreed. "It usually doesn't."

Silence settled again, thick but not hostile.

Connor finally took a sip, hands shaking once before steadying. "Are we going?"

Caleb didn't ask where. "Yeah," he said. "If you want to."

Connor nodded. "I don't want to."

Caleb exhaled slowly. "I know."

"But I think we should," Connor added.

Caleb nodded again. "Okay."

They didn't rush.

They finished their cocoa. Caleb rinsed the mugs. Connor grabbed his coat without being asked. No one made it bigger than it already was.

The drive to Blountville felt longer than it should have, even though Caleb could have driven it blindfolded. Winter fields stretched pale and flat. Trees stood bare but patient, like they knew something the ground hadn't learned yet.

Connor sat rigid in the passenger seat, eyes fixed straight ahead.

"Do you think she knows?" he asked suddenly.

Caleb didn't answer right away. "I don't know," he said finally. "But I don't think love forgets."

Connor nodded—not fully satisfied, but willing to accept it.

The cemetery appeared too quickly.

Caleb parked and turned off the engine.

Neither of them moved.

Connor stared through the windshield. "I don't want to cry."

"You don't have to," Caleb said.

"But I probably will."

"That's okay too."

They stepped out into the cold.

The air was sharp, clean, honest. Gravel crunched beneath their boots, then softened to grass. Rows of names and dates passed quietly, other people's grief arranged in orderly lines.

Lauren's headstone came into view.

Connor stopped short.

Caleb stopped with him.

Her name sat carved into stone—unchanged, unyielding. It still startled him how something so permanent could represent someone so alive in his memory.

Caleb reached into his coat pocket.

Two small envelopes rested in his palm.

Connor noticed immediately. "What's that?"

Caleb swallowed. "Your mom wrote these," he said. "They were in the cedar box. Separate."

Connor frowned. "For today?"

Caleb nodded.

"She didn't know," Connor said quickly. Not accusing. Just stating truth.

"I know," Caleb said. "But she knew someday."

Connor hesitated, then reached out and took the envelope with his name on it.

They stood there holding paper like it weighed more than stone.

"I don't want to read it," Connor whispered.

"Me neither," Caleb admitted.

"But I want to hear her," Connor said.

Caleb nodded. "Me too."

He unfolded his letter carefully, shielding it from the wind, and took a breath that felt like stepping off a ledge.

And began.

My Caleb,

If you're reading this, then you're standing in a moment I hoped you wouldn't have to carry alone.

I don't know what day it is for you. I don't know what the sky looks like or how cold the air feels on your hands. I don't know if Connor is taller now, or if he still shrugs before he speaks.

But I know you.

I know how you hold yourself together by doing the next right thing. I know how you stay busy when being still hurts too much. I know how you carry love like a responsibility.

So I'm writing to remind you of something you forget when grief gets loud.

You did not fail me.

Not when my body grew weaker. Not when my breath shortened. Not when you didn't know what to fix because there was nothing left to fix.

You loved me.

You loved me in the quiet. In the waiting. In the days that didn't look heroic. In the nights you pretended you weren't scared so I wouldn't be.

You loved me when I couldn't give much back.

That mattered more than you know.

I never needed you to save me. I needed you to stay.

And you did.

Please don't turn this day into a verdict on yourself. Don't replay it like there was a right sentence you missed or a moment you should've caught.

You were never meant to be perfect.

You were meant to be mine.

Stay close to Connor.

He's braver than he lets on, but he still needs you more than he'll say. Let him see you hurt. Let him see you heal slowly. Teach him that strength doesn't mean silence.

And Caleb—don't make my memory heavy.

Let it breathe.

Laugh when you laugh. Eat when you're hungry. Rest when you're tired.

Love again—whatever that looks like.

I don't want to be the reason you shrink your life.

I want to be part of the reason you keep living it.

I am proud of you.

I always have been.

Your wife,

Lauren

Caleb's voice broke at the end.

Not loudly. Not all at once.

Just enough.

The wind tugged at the edges of the paper. He folded the letter carefully, like he was afraid rushing might tear something that couldn't be replaced.

Connor hadn't moved.

He stared at the ground, jaw tight, eyes fixed on the frozen grass like it was holding him upright.

"She knew," Connor said finally, voice thin.

Caleb nodded. "Yeah."

Connor swallowed. "She really knew."

Caleb reached for the second envelope, hands steady in a way that surprised him.

"You want me to read yours?" he asked gently.

Connor hesitated, then nodded. "Yeah."

Caleb unfolded the paper.

My Connor,

I don't know how old you are when you're reading this.

But I know you've always been watching.

I saw you in doorways. In hallways. Standing just close enough to hear, pretending you weren't listening.

I saw you bring me things and act like it didn't cost you anything.

You were never invisible.

You were never in the way.

You were never a burden.

Not to me. Not to your dad. Not to God.

You don't have to earn love by being quiet.

You don't have to disappear to be good.

Let your dad be your dad.

Let him see you.

If you're angry, tell God. He can take it.

If you're sad, don't apologize.

Love stays, Connor.

Mine does too.

Always.

Mom (Lauren)

Connor's breath hitched once.

Then he stepped forward and leaned into Caleb, forehead pressed hard against his shoulder like his body had finally stopped arguing.

Caleb wrapped his arms around him without thinking.

Connor cried—not neatly, not quietly.

Caleb let himself cry too.

They stood there longer than either of them knew how to measure.

When Connor finally pulled back, he wiped his face with his sleeve and shook his head like he was trying to clear water from his ears.

"She saw me," he said hoarsely.

Caleb nodded. "She did."

"I don't know what to do with that."

"You don't have to do anything," Caleb said. "Just let it be true."

They walked back to the truck slowly.

As they passed the small church nearby, the bell began to ring—low, steady, unhurried.

Connor paused. "Do you think that's for her?"

Caleb listened. "I think it's for anyone still learning how to live."

Connor nodded.

At home, they set the envelopes side by side on the table.

Caleb heated soup. Connor got bowls.

They moved together in quiet rhythm, like the house had remembered how.

Outside, the gray day held.

Inside, the air felt different.

Not lighter.

Just... possible.

They were still here.

And love—quiet, stubborn, faithful—had not let go.

That night, the house felt different again.

Not hollow like it had been in the beginning. Not sharp the way it had felt in the weeks after. Just tired—like something that had finally been named and was now allowed to rest.

Connor sat on the floor of the living room, back against the couch, the letters folded and unfolded again in his hands. He didn't read them. He didn't need to. Just knowing they were there felt like enough for the moment.

Caleb stood in the doorway for a long time before stepping in.

"You okay if I sit?" he asked.

Connor nodded without looking up.

Caleb lowered himself onto the carpet a few feet away, close enough to share the room, far enough not to crowd. He leaned back against the recliner—careful, like he was asking permission from the space itself.

They didn't speak at first.

The television was off. The lamps were low. Outside, the wind moved through the trees with a sound that felt like breathing.

Connor broke the silence. "I thought today was going to destroy me."

Caleb nodded. "Me too."

"But it didn't," Connor said. Then, quieter, "It still hurt. Just... different."

Caleb let that settle. "Yeah."

Connor traced the edge of the envelope with his thumb. "It's weird. I always thought an anniversary would feel like reopening something."

"And?" Caleb asked gently.

Connor shrugged. "It felt more like... standing inside it. Like it was already open, and we just stopped pretending it wasn't."

Caleb swallowed. "That's a good way to put it."

Connor leaned his head back against the couch. "I don't feel better."

"I wouldn't expect you to," Caleb said.

"But I don't feel worse either," Connor added. "I just feel... here."

Caleb closed his eyes for a second. "That might be enough for tonight."

Connor nodded.

After a while, he asked, "Do you still hear her?"

Caleb opened his eyes. "Sometimes."

"Like her voice?"

"Not exactly," Caleb said. "More like... the way she'd be about something. I'll be standing somewhere and suddenly I know what she'd say. Or what face she'd make."

Connor huffed quietly. "She had that face."

Caleb smiled despite himself. "Yeah. She did."

Connor was quiet for a moment. Then, "I'm scared it'll fade."

Caleb felt that land deep. "Me too."

"What if one day I can't remember her voice?" Connor asked. "Like really remember it."

Caleb thought carefully before answering. "I think some parts fade," he said. "But others settle in deeper. They change shape, but they don't disappear."

Connor looked at him. "Like what?"

"Like how you stand," Caleb said. "Like the way you pause before you talk. Like the way you notice things most people don't."

Connor frowned slightly. "That's her?"

Caleb nodded. "That's her."

Connor looked back down at the letters. His voice wobbled just a little. "She really loved us."

Caleb's throat tightened. "Yeah. She did."

Connor pressed his lips together, breathing through something heavy. "I didn't think I deserved that."

Caleb shifted closer, just an inch. "You always did."

Connor shook his head. "I was hard. I was quiet. I didn't know how to be what she needed."

Caleb answered immediately, voice firm but gentle. "You were exactly who she needed. You didn't need to perform. You just needed to be you."

Connor stared at the carpet, eyes glossy. "She didn't leave because of us, right?"

Caleb's heart clenched. "No. Never. Not even a little."

Connor nodded, once, like he was filing that away somewhere important.

The clock on the wall ticked. Slow. Steady.

Caleb finally said, "I'm glad we read them today."

Connor nodded. "Me too."

"Even though it hurt?"

"Yeah," Connor said. "Because it hurt *together*."

Caleb exhaled. That mattered more than Connor probably realized.

They sat there until the house settled deeper into night.

When Connor finally stood, he didn't rush away. He paused, then leaned down and hugged Caleb again—shorter this time, steadier.

"Thanks for not trying to fix it," Connor said.

Caleb held him just long enough. "Anytime."

Later, when the lights were off and the house had gone quiet, Caleb lay awake listening to the familiar sounds—the heater clicking on, the walls shifting, the soft weight of another day finished.

January 14 had come.

And gone.

It hadn't taken everything.

It had taken enough.

Caleb stared into the dark and let himself believe something small and fragile and true:

They would carry her forward.

Not as an ache they avoided.

But as a love they learned how to live inside.

And for tonight —

That was enough.

CHAPTER THIRTY-FIVE

Still Here

The house did not feel empty anymore.

That was the first thing Caleb noticed.

Not full. Not healed. Just... inhabited in a new way. Like grief had finally stopped pacing and chosen a place to sit.

Morning light crept through the living room windows, thin and pale, catching dust in the air that moved when no one touched it. The clock on the wall ticked steadily, unapologetic in its insistence that time still worked.

Caleb sat at the kitchen table with his hands wrapped around a mug that had gone cold. He hadn't noticed when he stopped drinking it. He'd been watching Connor instead.

Connor sat across from him, shoulders slightly hunched, one foot hooked around the rung of the chair like he needed something to anchor him. His hair was still damp from the shower. He hadn't put his hoodie on yet.

That felt like progress, even if Caleb didn't know why.

Neither of them spoke for a while. Silence no longer felt like something they had to survive. It had become a language of its own.

Finally, Connor said, "It doesn't hurt the same today."

Caleb didn't answer too fast. He let the words sit between them, turning them over in his mind.

"No," he said carefully. "It doesn't."

Connor nodded, eyes on the table. "It's still there. Just... quieter."

Caleb exhaled. "That's been my experience too."

Connor looked up then, searching Caleb's face like he was checking for honesty. "Is that okay?"

Caleb met his gaze. "Yeah," he said. "I think it means we're learning how to carry it."

Connor absorbed that. He picked at the edge of a napkin, tearing it slowly into neat strips.

"I don't feel guilty today," he said after a moment. "And that almost makes me feel guilty."

Caleb felt something ache in his chest—not sharp, just deep. "I know that feeling."

Connor's mouth tightened. "I thought I was supposed to feel worse. Like if I didn't, it meant I was forgetting her."

Caleb shook his head gently. "Your mom didn't want to be remembered through pain."

Connor frowned slightly. "How do you know?"

Caleb smiled, small and sad. "Because she hated when either of us hurt."

Connor let out a quiet breath. "That sounds right."

They sat with that.

Outside, a car passed. Somewhere down the street, a dog barked once and stopped. Life continued, unbothered by anniversaries or memory.

Connor broke the quiet again. "What happens now?"

Caleb blinked. "What do you mean?"

"I mean—" Connor gestured vaguely. "The big thing happened. The date. The letters. The crying. So... what now?"

Caleb considered that. "Now we wake up tomorrow," he said. "And the day after that. And we figure out what living looks like without pretending we're not missing someone."

Connor stared at him. "That sounds exhausting."

Caleb smiled a little. "It can be."

Connor leaned back in his chair. "But not impossible?"

"No," Caleb said. "Not impossible."

Connor nodded, then stood. He walked into the living room and stopped in front of the recliner.

The chair.

It still sat where it always had, angled just slightly toward the television. Caleb had dusted around it but never moved it. Not out of reverence exactly—more like caution. As if touching it might rearrange something he wasn't ready to disturb.

Connor studied it for a long moment.

"She spent a lot of time there," he said.

Caleb joined him, standing a few feet away. "She did."

"She didn't like it," Connor added. "But she pretended she did so we wouldn't worry."

Caleb nodded. "She thought shielding us meant hiding herself."

Connor turned. "She wasn't a burden."

Caleb's throat tightened. "No."

Connor swallowed. "I wish she knew that."

Caleb stepped closer, placing a hand on the back of the chair—not sitting, just touching. "I think she did. I just don't think she could believe it all the time."

Connor stared at the chair again. Then, unexpectedly, he reached out and rested his hand beside Caleb's.

They didn't say anything.

The moment passed without ceremony, without revelation—but something shifted, anyway.

Later that afternoon, they went outside.

Not anywhere special. Just the backyard.

The grass was patchy and dull, winter still clinging stubbornly to the edges. The air smelled like damp earth and the promise of something warmer.

Connor sat on the back steps while Caleb leaned against the railing. The sun was weak but present, like it was doing its best.

"Do you ever think about who you were before?" Connor asked.

Caleb tilted his head. "Before what?"

Connor didn't need to clarify. "Before all of it."

Caleb thought. "Sometimes," he said. "Mostly I think about who I am now."

Connor nodded. "Me too."

They watched a pair of birds hop along the fence, arguing quietly over something invisible.

"I don't feel like the same person," Connor said.

Caleb smiled faintly. "You aren't."

Connor frowned. "Is that bad?"

"No," Caleb said. "It's just... true."

Connor kicked at the concrete with the toe of his shoe. "I feel older."

Caleb chuckled softly. "That tracks."

Connor glanced at him. "You don't think that's sad?"

Caleb considered. "I think it's sad that you had to grow that way. But growing itself isn't sad."

Connor nodded slowly. "Okay."

They sat in companionable silence.

After a while, Connor said, "Do you think she can see us?"

Caleb didn't rush his answer. "I don't know how it works," he said honestly. "But I believe love doesn't stop paying attention."

Connor smiled faintly at that.

"She'd like that," he said.

Caleb smiled too. "Yeah. She would."

The sun dipped lower. The day moved on without asking permission.

Connor stood and stretched. "I'm going to start my homework."

Caleb nodded. "I'll make dinner in a bit."

Connor paused at the door, then turned back. "Hey, Dad?"

Caleb met his eyes. "Yeah?"

Connor hesitated, then said, "Thank you. For staying."

Caleb's chest tightened. "Always."

Connor nodded once and went inside.

Caleb stayed outside a little longer, listening to the quiet.

For the first time in a long while, it didn't feel like something he had to endure.

It felt like something he could live with.

And that felt like enough—for now.

Caleb didn't go inside right away.

He stayed on the back steps with his forearms on his knees, letting the damp winter air sit against his face. The sun was already dropping, the light thinning into that washed-out gold that didn't warm you so much as remind you warmth still existed somewhere. The yard looked tired—patches of grass flattened, a few leaves pinned to the fence like they'd given up trying to travel.

From inside, he could hear Connor moving. Not loud, not restless. Just... there. Cabinet closing. A chair shifting. A drawer opening and shutting again like Connor was looking for something and then deciding he wasn't ready to find it.

Caleb listened for a minute longer than he needed to, then finally stood and went in.

The kitchen smelled faintly like cocoa and dish soap. Connor had already put his mug in the sink, but he hadn't rinsed it. He'd left it there like a small flag, proof he had been hungry and human and in the same room without bolting.

Connor stood at the counter with his phone in his hand, screen dark. He wasn't scrolling. Just holding it like it was an object with weight.

When he noticed Caleb, he set it down.

"Sorry," Connor said, like he'd done something wrong.

Caleb shook his head. "For what?"

Connor shrugged and gestured vaguely toward the house. "For being... quiet."

Caleb almost laughed—not because it was funny, but because it was so Connor to apologize for surviving the only way he knew how.

"You don't have to apologize for quiet," Caleb said. "Quiet's been doing a lot of work around here."

Connor's mouth twitched, not quite a smile. He leaned back against the counter, sleeves pushed up now, hands visible. That still felt new sometimes—Connor existing without armor on every inch of him.

Caleb nodded toward the living room. "You want to eat something later?"

Connor hesitated. "Yeah," he said, then added quickly, "If you're hungry."

"I'm hungry," Caleb said. "So that works."

Connor nodded once, like that settled it.

Caleb moved around the kitchen and pulled out what they had—beans, rice, corn-bread mix, something simple that wouldn't ask too much of either of them. He set a pot on the stove and poured in water. The burner clicked when it caught. He didn't turn on music. He didn't fill the room with noise just to prove they could.

Connor stayed at the counter for a minute, watching without being obvious about it.

Then he said, "Do you think... we're supposed to do something now?"

Caleb didn't pretend not to understand.

Connor's eyes stayed down. "I mean, after... yesterday. After all that. It feels like there should be instructions. Like there's a next step, and we missed it."

Caleb stirred the pot even though it didn't need stirring yet. He chose his words carefully, not because Connor was fragile, but because the truth deserved a steady hand.

"I don't think there are instructions," Caleb said. "I think there's just... living. And some days living is quiet. Some days it's loud. Some days you do the same thing three times because your brain can't tell what you already did."

Connor gave a short breath that could've been a laugh if it wasn't so tired. "That's comforting."

Caleb glanced at him. "I didn't say it was pretty. I said it was true."

Connor nodded and looked toward the living room doorway, the angle where the chair would be if you stared long enough.

Caleb felt the pull too, like an invisible thread that always led back to the same handful of objects.

Connor's voice came softer. "I keep thinking... we can't just keep everything exactly the same."

Caleb turned the heat down and leaned on the counter. "No," he agreed quietly. "We can't."

Connor swallowed. "But changing it feels like... erasing."

Caleb shook his head. "Changing it isn't erasing. It's just admitting time is still happening."

Connor stared at the floor for a long moment like he didn't like that truth but couldn't argue with it either.

"What if we do it wrong?" Connor asked.

Caleb answered without hesitation. "Then we do it wrong," he said. "And we keep loving each other, anyway."

Connor's eyes flicked up, sharp and uncertain, like he was checking whether Caleb believed his own words.

Caleb held his gaze. "We don't have to get it perfect," he added. "We just have to keep showing up."

Connor's shoulders dropped a fraction, like he'd been holding them up by sheer will.

"Okay," he said. "That's... okay."

Caleb nodded once and turned back to the stove. He watched the pot until it began to move, little signs of life breaking the surface. He reached for the cornbread mix and set it on the counter.

Connor stepped forward. "Do you need help?"

Caleb looked at him. "Do you want to help?"

Connor hesitated, then nodded. "Yeah."

Caleb handed him the bowl and the spoon without making a big deal out of it. Connor poured the mix in, then paused, reading the back like it was a test he didn't want to fail. Caleb slid the milk closer.

Connor stirred slowly, careful not to splash. His movements were deliberate, like he was trying to earn steadiness through repetition.

Caleb watched him and felt the strangest thing: not relief, exactly, but something like gratitude. Connor was in the room. Connor was doing a normal thing. Connor was letting his hands be useful.

They didn't talk for a while. The kitchen filled with small sounds—the spoon scraping the bowl, the stove clicking, the quiet rush of air through the vent. It wasn't silence that swallowed. It was silence that held.

Connor finally said, "I thought it was going to feel worse today."

Caleb slid the cornbread pan onto the counter. "Because you didn't?"

Connor shrugged. "Because it wasn't... as sharp." His jaw tightened. "And then I started thinking something was wrong with me."

Caleb took a slow breath. "Nothing's wrong with you."

Connor's eyes stayed on the batter. "It feels like if I'm not hurting the same way, it means I'm moving on."

Caleb leaned back against the counter. "You are moving," he said. "But that's not betrayal."

Connor's mouth pulled tight. "It feels like it."

Caleb didn't try to argue him out of his feelings. He just spoke into the place beneath them.

"Listen," Caleb said softly. "Your mom didn't love you so you'd stay stuck. She loved you so you could live."

Connor blinked hard, stirring slower.

Caleb continued, voice steady. "Missing her will always be part of you. But missing her doesn't have to be the only part."

Connor swallowed. "How do you know?"

Caleb's throat tightened. "Because every time she saw either of us hurting, she tried to pull us back toward life. Food. Warmth. Routine. Laughing at something dumb. She didn't fix pain by pretending it wasn't there—she just wouldn't let it be the whole room."

Connor stopped stirring. His fingers tightened around the spoon. "I don't remember her laughing much at the end."

Caleb felt that land in him—heavy and true and unfair.

"I remember it," Caleb said quietly. "Not all the time. But enough. She'd laugh and then pay for it later. Like it cost her something she was willing to spend."

Connor's eyes went glassy. He blinked fast, then looked down again. "I hate that."

Caleb nodded. "Me too."

The batter had thickened. Connor poured it into the pan carefully, then set the bowl in the sink without being asked. He rinsed it, slow, like motion itself was a kind of prayer.

Caleb turned the oven on and slid the pan inside. The door closed with a soft thump.

Connor leaned back against the counter again, arms crossed. "So what do we... do about the chair?"

Caleb didn't look toward the living room. He didn't have to.

He said, "We don't have to do anything today."

Connor's jaw worked. "But we could."

Caleb nodded once. "Yeah. We could."

Connor stared at the doorway. "What if we move it just a little?"

Caleb felt a tightness in his chest—not panic, not grief exactly. More like the way you feel before you touch a bruise you've been protecting.

"A little," Caleb repeated.

Connor nodded. "Not throwing it out. Not... pretending she didn't sit there. Just... moving it so it's not... the center of the room."

Caleb considered that. He could hear Lauren in his head, not as a ghost, not as a miracle—just as memory. He could hear her saying, Don't make my absence the loudest thing in the house.

Caleb exhaled. "Okay," he said.

Connor looked surprised. "Okay?"

Caleb nodded. "Okay."

They walked into the living room together. The light had shifted, making the corners softer. The chair sat there like it always had—familiar, stubborn, holy in the way ordinary things become holy when love has leaned on them.

Connor stood beside it, hands hovering like he wasn't sure how to touch it without waking something.

Caleb stepped in and placed his palms on the back.

"You ready?" he asked.

Connor swallowed. "Yeah."

They moved it—only a few inches. Not a relocation. Not a statement. Just a gentle shift, like adjusting a picture frame that's been crooked for months because nobody wanted to admit it was crooked.

The chair ended up angled a little more toward the window than toward the television.

Connor let out a breath he'd been holding. "That's... weird."

Caleb nodded. "Yeah."

Connor's eyes stayed on it. "But not bad."

Caleb swallowed, feeling a sting behind his eyes. "No," he said. "Not bad."

Connor stepped back and looked around the room like he was seeing it for the first time in a long time.

"I thought that would hurt more," Connor admitted.

Caleb's voice came gentle. "It might later," he said. "Or it might not. Either way, you're not doing it alone."

Connor nodded once, then stepped forward and—carefully, like he was handling something fragile—picked up the throw blanket draped over the chair. He folded it. Not perfectly. Just folded.

Then he laid it back down, neat.

Caleb's throat tightened at the smallness of it, the tenderness. Connor wasn't erasing anything. He was tending.

They went back to the kitchen without saying much.

The beans were simmering now. The cornbread began to smell like home.

Connor took two bowls from the cabinet and set them on the counter. Caleb didn't comment on the fact that Connor had chosen the bowls Lauren used to pick because they were "the right size." Some things didn't need to be named to matter.

They ate at the table, quiet and steady.

Halfway through the meal, Connor said, "Do you think... we'll ever laugh like we used to?"

Caleb didn't answer fast. He watched his son's face—the guarded hope, the fear of disappointment.

"I think we'll laugh again," Caleb said. "Not the same way. But real."

Connor's eyes dropped. "I miss that."

Caleb nodded. "Me too."

Connor hesitated, then said, "When people talk about her... I don't want them to only talk about the sick version of her."

Caleb's chest tightened. "Me either."

Connor looked up. "I want to remember her in the kitchen. Rolling her eyes at you. Making fun of how you stir stuff like it's a science experiment."

Caleb let out a breath that was almost a laugh. "It is a science experiment," he said.

Connor's mouth twitched. "No. It's you being you."

Caleb's eyes burned. He blinked and looked down at his bowl. "Then we'll do that," he said quietly. "We'll remember her alive."

Connor nodded. "Okay."

They finished eating. Connor stood and took his bowl to the sink, rinsed it, set it in the rack. He didn't disappear after. He stayed in the kitchen, leaning against the counter like he belonged there.

Caleb watched him and felt that quiet, stubborn thing again—love, not dramatic, not miraculous, just persistent.

Connor's voice came out low. "Dad?"

Caleb looked at him. "Yeah?"

Connor swallowed. "I'm still scared sometimes."

Caleb nodded. "Me too."

Connor's jaw tightened. "But I don't want to live scared."

Caleb's chest ached. "Then we won't," he said. "Not forever."

Connor stared at him like he was trying to decide whether to trust that promise.

Caleb added, softer, "We'll be careful. We'll be honest. And we'll keep choosing each other."

Connor's eyes shone. He looked away fast, but he didn't leave.

"Okay," he whispered.

Caleb stepped closer—not to grab him, not to force anything. Just close.

Connor leaned in first, like his body already knew where safety lived.

Caleb wrapped an arm around him.

Connor didn't cry. Not like yesterday. Not like a storm.

Just a few quiet breaths against Caleb's shoulder, like something unclenched inside him.

Caleb held him anyway, because you don't wait for tears to justify being held.

When Connor finally pulled back, he rubbed his face once and muttered, "This is weird."

Caleb's mouth twitched. "Yeah," he said. "It is."

Connor looked at him, almost embarrassed. "But... thanks."

Caleb nodded. "Always."

Connor stood there another second, then said, "I'm going to go start my homework."

Caleb nodded. "I'll clean up."

Connor started down the hall, then paused and turned back.

"Dad?"

"Yeah?"

Connor hesitated, then said, "I'm glad we moved it."

Caleb's throat tightened. "Me too."

Connor nodded once and went on.

Caleb stayed in the kitchen, listening to his son's footsteps fade, and let himself breathe.

Not because everything was okay.

But because, for the first time in a long time, the house felt like it was moving with them instead of against them.

And that—small as it was—felt like something worth keeping.

Sometime in the early hours of morning, Caleb woke again.

Not from a dream. Not from panic.

Just awake.

The house was quiet in the particular way that only came after midnight, when even the walls seemed to rest. He lay there listening—to the faint tick of the clock down the hall, to the soft rush of air through the vents, to the sound of his own breathing finally steady enough not to feel like work.

He turned his head and looked at the other side of the bed.

The space still startled him sometimes. Not because it was empty—but because it had learned how to be.

Caleb sat up slowly and swung his legs over the side. The floor was cool beneath his feet. He didn't bother with slippers.

He padded down the hallway, careful not to wake Connor, and stopped in the doorway of the living room.

The chair was still there.

It always would be.

But tonight, it didn't feel like a wound.

It felt like a marker. Proof of a life that had existed fully enough to leave an imprint.

Caleb crossed the room and sat on the couch instead, elbows resting on his knees, hands loosely clasped.

He thought about the first weeks after she died—how the nights had stretched endlessly, how silence had pressed in on him until it felt like another loss piled on top of the first.

Tonight, the silence felt different.

It wasn't empty.

It was listening.

Caleb leaned back and closed his eyes.

"I don't know how to do this perfectly," he whispered, voice barely sound. "But I'm trying."

The words weren't directed anywhere specific. He didn't need them to be.

He sat there until the sky outside the window lightened just a shade, until the dark softened into something gentler.

Then, from down the hall, a door creaked.

Connor stood there, rubbing sleep from his eyes, hair sticking up at odd angles.

"You're up," Connor said quietly.

Caleb smiled faintly. "So are you."

Connor wandered into the room and dropped onto the opposite end of the couch, pulling his knees up.

They sat like that for a moment—both awake, neither surprised by it.

"I couldn't sleep," Connor said.

"Me neither."

Connor glanced at the chair, then away. "It doesn't hurt as much tonight."

Caleb nodded. "I noticed that too."

Connor frowned slightly. "Is that bad?"

Caleb shook his head. "No. It just means we carried enough today."

Connor considered that, then nodded.

After a moment, he said, "I don't feel like I'm betraying her anymore."

Caleb's breath caught—not sharply, but deeply. "I'm glad."

Connor shrugged. "I think she'd want us to keep doing... this." He gestured vaguely between them.

Caleb followed the motion. "I think so too."

They sat together until the sky shifted again, dawn edging closer.

Eventually, Connor leaned sideways and rested his head against Caleb's shoulder.

Caleb didn't move.

He let the weight be there.

It wasn't heavy.

It was grounding.

"You know," Connor said softly, "I don't think I'm scared of the future anymore."

Caleb glanced down. "Really?"

Connor nodded. "I don't know what it looks like. But I know I'm not facing it alone."

Caleb swallowed. "You never will."

Connor's voice wavered just a little. "Promise?"

Caleb answered without hesitation. "Promise."

They stayed there until the morning light finally filled the room, until the house woke with them instead of against them.

When they stood, it wasn't abrupt. Just natural.

Connor stretched. "I'm hungry."

Caleb smiled. "That's progress."

They moved toward the kitchen together.

Outside, the day waited.

Not perfect.

Not painless.

But open.

And that was enough.

Epilogue

The house lights dimmed slowly, not all at once. No sharp drop. Just a gradual softening, like the room itself was being asked to lean in.

The murmur of voices faded. The air shifted. The theater became what it had always been at its best—a place where people agreed, quietly, to pay attention together.

Caleb felt Connor's hand still resting against his leg. Not gripping. Just there. A reminder. A tether.

Someone—Caleb wasn't even sure who—stepped to the microphone first and spoke a few words. Nothing polished. Nothing long. A welcome. A thank you. An acknowledgment that they were gathered not for a performance, but for remembrance.

Caleb barely heard it.

His attention stayed fixed on the envelope in his hand.

The unmarked one.

It looked smaller than he remembered. Or maybe he was bigger now in ways he hadn't planned to be. He had tried to open it once before, months ago, and stopped. Not because he couldn't read the words—but because he couldn't yet hear them. Grief had stretched him. Love had reshaped him. Time had forced him to stand in rooms he never would have chosen and learn how to breathe, anyway.

Connor leaned closer and whispered, "Whenever you're ready."

Caleb nodded.

He stood.

The sound of it—the scrape of his shoes against the floor, the slight shift of the seat—felt amplified in the quiet. He stepped into the aisle, then toward the stage, the lights warming his face as he approached.

This was different than rehearsal.

Different than opening night.

Different than anything he'd ever done on this stage before.

He stopped at the microphone and looked out.

Faces stared back—soft, open, expectant. Not hungry for entertainment. Just present. Friends. Family. People who had brought casseroles, sent texts, sat in silence, prayed when they didn't know what else to do.

Caleb swallowed.

Connor sat in the front row on Lauren's side, eyes never leaving him.

That mattered more than anything.

Caleb adjusted the microphone once, then let his hands fall to his sides. He didn't grip the stand. He didn't need the support.

"Thank you," he said, his voice steady enough to surprise him. "For being here. For... staying."

He paused, breathing through the familiar tightness in his chest.

"This place," he continued, gesturing lightly around him, "was never just a theater to us. It was... a second living room. A place where time slowed down for a couple of hours and the rest of the world didn't get to interrupt."

A few soft smiles flickered through the crowd.

"My wife loved this room," Caleb said. "Not because of the stage lights. But because of what happened before and after them. The waiting. The hush. The moment right before applause, when everyone is holding their breath together."

He glanced down briefly, then back up.

"She always sat front row. On this side." He nodded toward Connor. "She said that way she could see everything—the show, the crowd, and me—without missing any of it."

A quiet ripple moved through the audience. Recognition. Memory.

Caleb reached into his jacket and drew out the envelope.

"This letter," he said softly, "has been waiting a long time."

The room went still.

"She didn't know when she wrote it," Caleb went on. "She wasn't preparing to leave. She was just... being herself. Thoughtful. Intentional. Loving in ways that reached farther than she could see."

He glanced toward Connor again. Connor nodded once, barely perceptible, but solid.

Caleb broke the seal.

The sound of it—a soft tear of paper—felt louder than it should have.

He unfolded the letter slowly.

The paper shook once in his hands, then stilled.

He read.

My love,

If you are reading this, then you are standing somewhere you never wanted to stand.

I know you.

You're trying to keep your breathing even. You're worried about doing this "right." You're wondering whether reading my words will make everything heavier instead of lighter.

So let me begin by taking something from you.

You don't owe me anything.

Not bravery.

Not suffering.

Not a life paused at the exact shape it had when I was still in it.

You stayed. That was never in question.

You stayed when the days blurred and the nights stretched too long. You stayed when my body stopped cooperating and the house grew quiet in ways that scared us both.

You stayed without applause, without witnesses, without certainty.

That was love.

Nothing more was required.

If you are tempted to measure what came after me—how much it hurts, how often you think of me, how carefully you hold your memories—don't.

Love is not proven by weight.

It doesn't ask to be carried forever in the same way.

It changes shape because we do.

I need you to hear this without turning it into an assignment: I am not fragile.

You do not make me smaller by speaking my name.

You do not lose me by laughing.

You do not betray me by moving forward into days I will never touch.

I am already where I belong.

And you are exactly where you are allowed to be.

Take care of Connor.

He has always felt deeply, even when he didn't have the language for it. He learned early how to stay quiet so other people wouldn't worry. He learned responsibility before he learned ease.

Please don't mistake his steadiness for distance.

Let him grow without guarding me.

Let him live without performing strength.

He does not need to hold me anymore.

Neither do you.

If you are reading this somewhere with lights and seats and people watching, I want you to look up.

Let yourself be seen.

I loved watching you stand where you belonged—even when you didn't realize you were already there.

Love doesn't end when life does.

It just learns how to live in a wider room.

Yours,

Lauren

Caleb didn't realize he had stopped breathing until his lungs burned.

The room was silent.

Not awkward.

Not stunned.

Reverent.

Caleb lowered the page slowly.

It wasn't that the letter was hard to read—it was that it asked him to keep living.

He didn't rush the moment. He let it exist.

Then, from the front row, Connor stood.

It wasn't planned. It wasn't announced. He just stood.

Caleb felt it before he saw it—the shift in the room, the way attention widened instead of narrowed.

Connor stepped into the aisle and walked toward the stage.

Caleb didn't move. He didn't stop him. He didn't wave him back.

He knew better.

Connor climbed the steps and stood beside him, shorter, younger, but steady.

He took the microphone gently, like it was something fragile.

"I don't really like talking," Connor said, voice low but clear. "So I won't do it long."

A few soft breaths of laughter moved through the room.

He swallowed once.

"My mom used to sit right there," he said, pointing to the front-row seat. "On the side. Every time."

His voice wavered, then steadied.

"She thought she was watching Dad," Connor continued. "But I think she was watching all of us. Making sure we were okay."

He looked down, then back up.

"I used to think love was loud. Like something you had to prove." He shook his head slightly. "Turns out it's quieter than that."

Connor turned and looked at Caleb.

"She taught us how to stay," he said. "Even when it hurts."

He handed the microphone back.

Caleb wrapped an arm around Connor without hesitation.

Connor leaned into him.

Not hiding.

Not collapsing.

Just present.

The room stayed quiet.

No applause yet.

This wasn't that kind of moment.

Together, they stepped aside as two volunteers approached the covered bench.

The cloth was pulled back slowly.

Lauren's name was etched cleanly into the wood. No dates dominating it. No finality. Just her name and a simple line beneath it:

Love stays.

Caleb felt Connor's breath hitch.

They moved down from the stage and stood beside the bench.

Caleb rested his hand on it. Solid. Real.

"This bench," he said quietly, "isn't here because she's gone."

He looked out at the crowd.

"It's here because she was here."

A few heads nodded. A few tears fell.

"And because this place mattered to her," Caleb added. "Because it mattered to us."

He glanced down at Connor. "And because sometimes you need a place to sit and remember you're not alone."

Connor pressed his hand flat against the bench too.

Then—finally—someone began to clap.

Not loud.

Not explosive.

Just enough.

The sound grew, gentle and steady, until the theater filled with it.

Caleb didn't bow.

He didn't wave.

He just stood there with his son, letting the moment pass through them instead of over them.

Later—much later—the crowd thinned.

People hugged. People whispered. People sat on the bench for a moment, like they were testing whether it would hold them.

Caleb and Connor stayed until the lights came up fully.

They returned to the front row one last time.

Connor sat in Lauren's seat.

Caleb didn't stop him.

They sat in silence, the kind that no longer demanded fixing.

Connor finally said, "I'm glad we read it."

Caleb nodded. "Me too."

Connor looked at the stage, then at the empty room. "It doesn't feel like the end."

Caleb smiled faintly. "It isn't."

They stood and walked out together.

Outside, the summer night wrapped around them—warm, alive, ongoing.

As they reached the car, Connor said quietly, "Dad?"

Caleb looked at him.

"We're going to be okay," Connor said. Not as a question. As a statement.

Caleb felt something settle in his chest.

"Yeah," he said. "We are."

They drove home with the windows down, the sound of cicadas following them into the dark.

And somewhere between the theater and the house, between the letter and the living, grief loosened its grip just enough to let love breathe.

Acknowledgements

— ♥ —

This book exists because of love, and because of those who stood quietly beside me when words were hard to find.

First, my deepest gratitude is for Jennifer. Everything in these pages traces back to the life we shared, the love we built, and the memory that continues to guide me. This book is not a replacement for her voice, but it was written in response to it.

To our son, thank you for your patience, your courage, and your willingness to walk this road with me. You have taught me more about strength, honesty, and grace than I ever expected to learn, and I am endlessly proud of the person you are becoming.

I am grateful to my family and close friends who offered steady presence rather than answers, and who understood that sometimes showing up mattered more than saying the right thing. Your support carried me through moments when the work felt impossible.

I am also thankful for the Lamplight Theatre community, whose creativity, patience, and quiet kindness gave me a place to breathe and belong during a season when both were hard to find. The stage, the work, and the people there reminded me that stories still matter — and that life continues, even in grief.

Thank you to the readers who chose to spend time with this story. I hope you felt seen somewhere in these pages, and that the words met you with the same care with which they were written.

Finally, I give thanks to God — for presence in the silence, for strength when there were no words left, and for the grace that carried me through loss into love that did not end.

About the author

Ricky Kiser is a writer from Tennessee. *The Letters We Couldn't Read* is a novel shaped by lived experience, exploring love, loss, faith, and the enduring presence of memory.

His work often centers on grief, family, and the quiet ways people learn to keep living after profound loss. In addition to writing, he works in the mental health field, where he continues to believe in the power of listening and story.

He lives in Tennessee with his son.

Stay Connected

Thank you for reading The Letters We Couldn't Read.

If you'd like to stay connected or learn more about my work, you're welcome to visit the link or scan the QR code:

https://summitandshorepublishing.com

There, you can find updates on future writing projects and occasional reflections shared with readers.

I'm grateful you spent time with this story.

— Ricky Kiser

9 798993 327440